Usher's Passing

Robert R. McCammon

USHER'S PASSING

Holt, Rinehart and Winston | New York

Published by Holt, Rinehart and Winston,
383 Madison Avenue, New York, New York 10017.
Published simultaneously in Canada by Holt, Rinehart
and Winston of Canada, Limited.

Library of Congress Cataloging in Publication Data
McCammon, Robert R.
  Usher's passing.
  I. Title.
PS3563.C3345U8   1984   813'.54   84-568

ISBN: 0-03-061833-9
First Edition
Designer: Victoria Hartman
Printed in the United States of America
10 9 8 7 6 5 4 3 2 1

ISBN 0-03-061833-9

To Michael Larsen and Elizabeth Pomada

I dread the events of the future.
                    —*Roderick Usher*

The Devil's passing.
                    —*Old Welsh expression for calamity*

Usher's Passing

Prologue

I

Thunder echoed like an iron bell above the sprawl of New York City. In the heavy air, lightning crackled and thrust at the earth, striking the high Gothic steeple of James Renwick's new Grace Church on East Tenth Street, then sizzling to death a half-blind drayhorse on the squatters' flatlands north of Fourteenth. The horse's owner bleated in terror and leaped for his life as his cart overturned, sinking its load of potatoes into eight inches of mud.

It was the twenty-second of March, 1847, and the *New York Tribune*'s weather scholar had predicted a night of "dire storms, fit for neither man nor beast." His prediction, for once, was entirely accurate. Sparks exploded into the sky on Market Street, where the cast-iron stovepipe chimney of a hardware store had been lightning-struck. The clapboard building burned fiercely while a crowd gawked and grinned in its merry heat. Steam-spouting fire engines were delayed, wooden wheels and horses' hooves mired in Bowery ooze. Packs of dogs, rats, and pigs scuttled through the alleys, where gangs like the Dover Boys, the Plug Uglies, and the Moan Stickers shadowed their victims along the constricted, cobblestoned streets. Policemen stayed alive by standing like statues under gas lamps.

A young city, New York was already bursting her seams. It was a riotous spectacle, as full of danger in the hoodlum's blackjack as of opportunity in a spilled purse of gold coins. The confusion of streets led from dockyard to theater, ballroom to bawdyhouse, Murder Bend to City Hall, with equal impartiality, though some avenues of progress were impassable due to swamps of debris and garbage.

Thunder rang out again, and the troubled sky split open in a torrent. It soaked dandies and damsels strolling out the doors of Delmonico's, slammed against the lofty windows on Colonnade Row, and leaked down black with soot through the roofs of squatters' shanties. The rain dampened fires, broke up fights, sped indecent propositions or murderous attacks, and cleared the streets in a sluggish tide of filth that rolled for the river. At least for the moment, the nightly farrago of humanity was interrupted.

Two chestnut Barbary horses, their heads bowed against the downpour, pulled a black landau coach along Broadway Avenue, heading south toward the harbor. The Irish coachman huddled within a soggy brown coat, water streaming from the brim of his low-slung hat, and cursed the decision he'd made early that afternoon to trot his team around to the De Peyser Hotel on Canal Street. If he hadn't picked up that passenger, he thought gloomily, he might now be home warming his feet in front of a fire with a mug of stout at his side. At least he had a gold eagle in his pocket—but what good would a gold eagle be when he was dead with the wet shivers? He flicked a halfhearted whipstrike at the flank of one of his horses, though he knew they would move no faster. Hell's bells! he thought. What was the passenger lookin' for?

The gentleman had boarded in front of the De Peyser, laid a gold eagle on the driver's palm, and told the driver to make all possible haste to the *Tribune* office. Instructed to wait, he'd held the horses until the black-garbed gentleman had reappeared fifteen minutes later with a new destination. It was a long trek into the country, up near Fordham in the shadow of the Long Island hills, while purple-veined storm clouds began to gather and thunder throbbed in the distance. At a rather dismal-looking little cottage, a rotund middle-aged woman with gray hair and large, frightened eyes admitted the gentleman—very reluctantly, it had seemed to the coachman. After another half hour in which a downpour of chilly rain had promised the driver an acquaintance with hot salve and oil of wintergreen, the gentleman in black came out with yet another series of directions: back to New York, as quickly as possible, to a number of tawdry taverns in the most unsavory section of the city. South into the Triangle at night! the coachman thought grimly. The gentleman either wanted a cheap trollop or a brush with death.

As they moved deeper into the lawless southern streets, the coachman was relieved to see that the heavy rain was keeping most of the thugs under wraps. Saints be praised! he thought—and at that instant two young boys in rags came running out of an alleyway toward the coach. One of them, the driver saw with horror, held a brick intended to smash the spokes of a wheel—the better to beat

2

and rob both himself and his passenger. He swung his whip with crazed abandon, shouting, "Go on! Go on!" And the team, sensing imminent danger, surged ahead across the slick stones. The brick was thrown, and crashed against the coach's side with the noise of splintering wood. "Go on!" the coachman cried out again, and kept the horses trotting until they'd left the murderous little beggars two streets behind.

The sliding partition behind the coachman's seat opened. "Driver," the passenger inquired, "what was that?" His voice was calm and steady—accustomed to giving orders, the driver thought.

"Beggin' your pardon, sir, but . . ." He glanced back over his shoulder through the partition, and saw in the dim interior lamplight the man's gaunt, pallid face, distinguished by a silvery, neatly trimmed beard and mustache. The gentleman's eyes were deepset, the color of burnished pewter; they fixed upon the coachman with the power of aristocracy. He appeared oddly ageless, his face free of any telltale wrinkles, and his flesh marble white. He was dressed in a black suit and a glossy black top hat, and his long-fingered hands in black leather gloves toyed with an ebony cane topped by a handsome sterling silver head of a cat—a lion, the coachman had seen—with gleaming emerald eyes.

"But *what*?" the man asked. The driver couldn't peg his accent.

"Sir . . . it's not too very safe in this neck o' town. You look to be a refined, respectable gentleman, sir, and it's not too many of those they gets down here in this part o'—"

"Just concern yourself with your driving," the man advised. "You're wasting time." He slid the partition shut.

The coachman muttered, his beard heavy with rain, and urged the team onward. There was just so much a man would do for a gold eagle! he thought. Then again, it sure would buy some fine times at the bar rail.

Sandy Welsh's Cellar, a bar on Ann Street, was the first stop. The gentleman went in, stayed only a few moments, and then they were off again. He stayed barely a minute in the Peacock, on Sullivan Street. Gent's Pinch, two blocks west, was worth only a brief visit as well. On narrow Pell Street, where a dead pig attracted a pack of scavenger dogs, the coachman reined his team up in front of a run-down tavern called the Muleskinner. As the gentleman in black went inside, the coachman pulled his hat low and pondered a return to the potato fields.

Within the Muleskinner, a motley assemblage of drunkards,

gamblers, and rowdies pursued their interests in the hazy yellow lamplight. Smoke hung in layers across the room, and the gentleman in black wrinkled his finely shaped nose at the mingled aromas of bad whiskey, cheap cigars, and rain-soaked clothes. A few men glanced in his direction, sizing him up as a profitable victim; but the strong set of his shoulders and the force of his gaze told them to look elsewhere. The rain and humidity had put a damper on even the most eager killer's energies.

He approached the Muleskinner's bar, where a swarthy gent in buckskin was drawing a mug of greenish beer from a keg, and spoke a single name.

The bartender smiled thinly and shrugged. A gold coin was slid across the rough pinewood bar, and greed flickered in the man's small black eyes. He reached out for the coin—and a cane topped by a silver lion's head pressed his hand to the wood. The gentleman in black spoke the name again, calmly and quietly.

"In the corner." The bartender nodded toward a man sitting alone, absorbed in scribbling something by the light of a smoking whale-oil lamp. "You ain't the law, are you?"

"No."

"Wouldn't want to get him in no trouble. He's the Shakespeare of America, y'know."

"I wouldn't know." He lifted his cane, and the other man's hand crawled like a spider upon the coin.

The gentleman in black strode purposefully to the solitary man writing by lamplight. On a scarred plank table before the writer were an inkpot, a scatter of cheap pale blue foolscap, a half-drained bottle of sherry, and a dirty glass. Wads of discarded paper littered the floor. The writer, a pale, slight man with watery gray eyes, was scribbling on a piece of paper with a quill pen gripped by a slender, nervous hand. He stopped writing to press his fist against his forehead, and then he sat without moving for a moment, as if his brain had gone blank. With a scowl and a bitter oath, he crumpled the paper and flung it to the floor, where it bounced off the toe of the gentleman's boot.

The writer looked up into the other man's face; he blinked, puzzled, the sheen of fever-sweat glistening on his cheeks and forehead.

"Mr. Edgar Poe?" the gentleman in black asked quietly.

"Yes," the writer replied, his voice slurred from sickness and sherry. "Who're *you?*"

"I've looked forward to meeting you for some time . . . *sir*. May I sit down?"

Poe shrugged and motioned toward a chair. There were dark blue hollows beneath his eyes, his lips were gray and slack, and the cheap brown suit he wore was blotched with mud and mildew. The front of his white linen shirt and his tattered black ascot were dappled with sherry stains; his frayed cuffs shot out of the coat like a poor schoolboy's. He radiated the heat of fever, and as he shivered in a sudden chill he lay down his pen and put a trembling hand to his brow; his dark hair was damp with sweat, and tiny beads of moisture in his thin dark mustache glinted with yellow lamplight. Poe gave a deep, rattling cough. "Forgive me," he said. "I've been ill."

The man put his cane on the table, careful not to disturb papers or inkpot, and sat down. At once a corpulent barmaid waddled over to ask him what his pleasure might be, but he waved her away with a flick of his hand.

"You should try the amontillado here, sir," Poe told him. "It fans the flames of the intellect. At the very least it provides warmth in the stomach on a wet night. Excuse my condition, sir; I've been working, you see." He narrowed his eyes to try to keep the gentleman in focus. "What did you say your name was?"

"My name," the gentleman in black said, "is Hudson Usher. Roderick Usher was my brother."

Poe sat very still for a moment, his mouth hanging half open; a small sigh escaped it, followed by a chuckle squeezed through a moan. He let out a high burst of laughter, and laughed until his eyes teared, laughed until he began coughing, until he knew he was in danger of choking and his hand clutched the black cloth of his ascot.

When he could control himself again, Poe wiped his eyes, caught back another spasm of coughing, and poured more sherry into his glass. "That's a fine joke! I commend you, sir! Now you may return your plumage to the costume shop and tell my dear *friend* Reverend Griswold that his attempt to give me a lung seizure very nearly succeeded! Tell him I won't forget his kind efforts!" He swallowed a mouthful of sherry, and his gray eyes gleamed in the sickly, pallid face. "Oh, no—wait! I've more to let you share with Reverend Griswold! Do you know what I'm writing here, my good 'Mr. Usher'?" He grinned drunkenly and tapped the few pages he'd finished. "My *masterpiece*, sir! An insight into the very nature of God! It's all here, all here . . ." He gripped the pages in one hand and brought them to his chest, a crooked grin on his mouth. "With *this* work, Edgar Poe will stand alongside Dickens and Hawthorne! Of course, we may all be eclipsed by that literary solaristarian, Reverend Griswold—but I think not!"

Poe waved the pages in front of the other man's face. They appeared to be a mess of ink blotches and sherry stains. "Wouldn't he pay you a pretty penny to see this for him? To *spy* for him, and help his plagiarizing pen along its confused course? Begone, sir! I've nothing more to say to you!"

The gentleman in black hadn't moved during Edgar Poe's tirade; he held the other man with a hard, steely stare. "Are you as hard of hearing as you are drunk?" he asked in his strange, melodious accent. "I *said* my name is Hudson Usher, and Roderick was my brother—a man you maligned with poisonous gall. I am in this American bedlam on business, and I chose to take a day to locate you. I first went to the *Tribune*, where I learned of your country cottage from a Mr. Horace Greeley. Your mother-in-law provided me with a list of—"

"*Muddy?*" Poe gasped. A page of his work slipped to the floor and lay in a puddle of spilled beer. "You went to see my Muddy?"

"—a list of taverns in which you might be found," Hudson Usher continued. He placed his black-gloved hands on the table and folded his fingers together. "I understand I just missed you at Sandy Welsh's Cellar."

"You're a liar!" Poe whispered, his eyes wide with shock. "You're not . . . you can't be who you say you are!"

"Can't I be? Well, then, shall we explore the facts? In 1837 my anguished older brother was drowned in a flood that destroyed our home in Pennsylvania. My wife and I were in London at the time, and my sister Madeline had recently run off with a traveling actor, leaving Roderick alone. We salvaged what we could, and we now reside in North Carolina." Usher's ageless face seemed drawn as tightly as a mask, his eyes glittering with long-repressed rage. "Now imagine my discomfiture, Mr. Poe, when five years later I happen to be shown a volume of despicable little figments called *Tales of the Grotesque and Arabesque*. Grotesque, indeed. Particularly the tale entitled— But you're well aware of the title, I'm sure. In it you make my brother out to be a madman and my sister a walking corpse! Oh, I've looked forward to meeting you finally, Mr. Poe; the *Tribune* mentions you frequently, I understand, and you were the literary lion of a few seasons past, weren't you? But now . . . well, fame's a tenuous commodity, isn't it?"

6

"What do you want of me?" Poe asked, stunned. "If you've come to demand money of me, or to drag my name through the dirt in a libel case, you're wasting your time, sir. I have very little money, and before God I never intentionally libeled your family's name or honor. There are hundreds of people named Usher in this country!"

"Perhaps there are," Usher agreed, "but there is only *one* drowned Roderick, and only *one* maligned Madeline." He spent a silent moment examining Poe's face and clothes. Then he smiled thinly, a humorless smile that showed the even white points of his teeth. "No, I don't want your money; I don't believe blood can be squeezed from a stone, but if I could, I'd confiscate every copy of that ridiculous tale and set them all blazing. No, I wanted to see what kind of man you were, and I wanted you to know what kind of man *I* am. The House of Usher still stands, Mr. Poe, and it *shall* stand long after you and I are dust in the earth." Usher produced a silver cigar case, from which he took a prime Havana; he lit it at the lamp and put the cigar case away. Then he blew gray smoke in Poe's face. "I should have your skin stretched and nailed to a tree for besmirching my family name. You should at the least be confined to a lunatic asylum."

"I swear I . . . I wrote that tale as fiction! It mirrored . . . things that were in my mind and soul!"

"Then, sir, I pity your soul in the hereafter." Usher pulled at the cigar and leaked smoke through his nostrils, his eyes narrowing to slits. "But let me try to guess how you stumbled onto this foul idea. It was never a secret that my brother was mentally and physically tormented; he'd been unbalanced since our father died in a mine cave-in before we came to this country from Wales. When Madeline left the house he must've felt totally deserted.

"In any event, Roderick's mental state—and the deterioration of the house I'd left him to protect—was not unnoticed by simpletons who lived in the villages around us. Small wonder, then, that his death and the ruin of our house in a flood should be the source of all kinds of vicious rumors! I suggest, Mr. Poe, that the seed of your tale came from some establishment like this one, where drink loosens the tongue and inflames the imagination. Perhaps you heard mention of Roderick Usher in a tavern between Pittsburgh and New York, and your own besotted brain invented the details. I blame myself for leaving Roderick alone at a crucial point in his sanity; thus you must see how your dirty little tale stabs me like a spike through the heart!"

Poe lowered his pages to the table and caressed them as if they were living flesh. He gave a soft whimper when he noticed the page lying in filth on the floor, and when he carefully picked it up he wiped the residue on his sleeve. He spent a moment trying, with shaking hands, to put the edges of the pages in true. "I . . . haven't been well for a while, Mr. Usher," he said softly. "My wife . . . recently passed away. Her name was Virginia. I . . . I know very well the pain of separation from a loved one. I vow to you before God, sir, that I never set out to sully your family's name. Perhaps I . . . did hear mention of your brother's name somewhere, or I read about the circumstances in a newspaper article; it's been so long now, I forget. But I am a writer, sir! And a writer has the defense of curiosity! I beg your forgiveness, Mr. Usher, but I must also say that as a writer I am compelled to view the world through my own eyes!"

"Then," the other man said coldly, "it seems the world would've been the better if you had been born blind."

"I've said all I possibly can." Poe reached for his glass of sherry again. "Is your business with me finished, sir?"

"Yes. I've had my look at you, and one look is all I can bear." Usher submerged his cigar in Poe's inkpot. There was a quick hiss as it went out, and Poe stared blankly at Usher with the glass of sherry at his lips. Usher took his cane and rose to his feet; he dropped a coin upon the table. "Have another bottle, Mr. Poe," he said. "It seems your brain thrives on such inspiration." He waited, watching, until Poe had picked up the coin.

"I . . . wish you and your family a long and profitable existence," Poe said.

"And may *your* fortunes continue their course." Usher touched the brim of his hat with his cane, then stalked out of the Muleskinner Bar. "The De Peyser Hotel," he told the soggy coachman as he slipped into the coach's black satin interior.

As the coach rumbled away from the curb, Usher lowered the interior lamp's wick to rest his eyes, and took off his top hat. From a widow's peak on his high forehead, his hair was luxuriant and glossy silver. He was satisfied with the day's events. He would have the deed to the De Peyser Hotel tomorrow afternoon, and his curiosity about Edgar Poe had been slaked. The man was obviously indigent, a madman with one foot in the grave. Poe knew nothing of any significance about the Usher family; the tale had been simply fiction that carved a bit too close. Within five years, Usher assured himself, Edgar Poe would be bones in a box and the tale he'd written would blow away in yellow dust like all other minor attempts at "literature." And that would be the end of it.

Rain hammered at the coach's roof. Usher closed his eyes, his hands gripped around the cane.

Oh, he thought, if Edgar Poe only knew the *rest* of the story! If he only knew the real nature of the madness that brother Roderick had harbored! But Roderick had always been weak; it was he, Hudson, who'd inherited the brute strength and determination of his father, the sense of survival that had passed down through the ages from the ancient Welsh clan of Ushaars. An Usher walks where he pleases, he mused, and takes what he wants.

The Usher name would be seared into the tapestry of the future. Hudson Usher would make certain of it. And God help those, he thought, who tried to resist the force of the Usher will.

The coach's team clattered across slick cobblestones. Hudson Usher, who at the age of fifty-three looked barely thirty, smiled like a lizard.

II

"The De Peyser Hotel, please," the tall, blond man in a brown tweed suit said as he climbed into a Yellow Cab on East Sixtieth Street, less than three blocks from Central Park.

"Huh?" The cabbie frowned. He was a Rastafarian with red dreadlocks and amber eyes. "Where's that, mon?"

"Canal Street. On the corner of Greene."

"You got it, mon." He slammed the cab into gear, pressed his palm against the horn, and nosed into the afternoon traffic, letting out a curse when a Bloomingdale's delivery truck almost sideswiped him. He fought his way to Fifth Avenue and headed south through a sea of taxis, trucks, cars, and buses.

The man in the back seat loosened his tie and unfastened his collar button. He realized numbly that his hands were trembling. The sound of a curbside jackhammer pierced his brain, and he wished he'd had one more bourbon at La Cocotte, the small French restaurant where he'd just eaten lunch. One more might have smoothed out the kinks in his head. But he was going to be all right, he decided. He was a survivor, and he could take the bad news that had just been dished out to him.

The blast of a truck's horn behind the cab almost startled him out of his skin. His head had started throbbing like the raw ache of a rotten tooth. A bad sign. He gripped his thighs and sat stiff-spined, trying to concentrate on the steady tick of the cab's meter. He found himself staring fixedly at an earring the cabbie wore—a tiny skeleton wearing a top hat, dangling from the Rasta's left lobe. It danced back and forth with the cab's jerky motion.

I'm getting worse, the man told himself.

"You're a professional, Rix," Joan Rutherford had told him less than an hour before at La Cocotte. "And it's not the end of the world, anyway." She was a sturdy woman with dyed black hair, and she chain-smoked Kools through a discolored ivory cigarette holder. One of the foremost literary agents in the business, she had handled his three previous horror novels and had just delivered the jarring truth about his fourth effort. "I can't see any future for *Bedlam*, not the way it's constructed now. It's too episodic, there are too many characters, and it's hard as hell to follow what's happening. Stratford House likes you, Rix, and they want to publish your next book, but I don't think it's going to be this one."

"What do you propose I do? Toss the book into the trashcan after I've spent over sixteen months working on it? The damned thing is almost six hundred pages long!" He had heard the note of pleading in his voice, and stopped until he could control himself again. "I've done four rewrites on it, Joan. I can't just throw it away!"

"*Bedlam* isn't the best you can do, Rix." Joan Rutherford looked at him with her level blue gaze, and he felt a trickle of sweat under his left armpit. "You've got characters crawling out of the woodwork, a little psychic blind boy who can see into the past or something, and a crazy doctor who carves people up in an apartment house basement. I still can't figure out what was going on. You've got a six-hundred-page novel that reads like a telephone directory, Rix."

The food he'd eaten lay like sawdust in the pit of his stomach. Sixteen months. Four agonizing rewrites. His last book, a moderate best-seller titled *Fire Fingers*, had been published by Stratford House three years before. The money he'd made from it was all gone. The movie deals had dried up and blown away. An iron band of pressure had settled across the back of his neck, and he'd begun having nightmares in which his father's voice told him with relish that he had been born to fail.

"Okay," Rix had said, staring into his second bourbon. "What am I supposed to do now?"

"You put *Bedlam* away and start on another book."

"Easily said."

"Oh, come on!" Joan stabbed out her cigarette in the little ceramic ashtray. "You're a big boy now, you can take it! If pros run into problems, they just backtrack and start again."

Rix had nodded and smiled grimly. His soul felt like a graveyard. In the three years since his best-seller, he'd tried writing several different books—had even gone to Wales to do research on an idea that hadn't panned out—but the plots had collapsed like houses of cards. When he'd found himself sitting in an Atlanta bar, pondering a *Fire Fingers* sequel, he'd known he was in trouble. The idea for *Bedlam* had come to him in a nightmare of shadowy corridors, distorted faces, and corpses hanging on hooks. Halfway into the writing, it had come apart like so much flimsy cloth. But to give it up after all this time! To strike the scenes and sets like tawdry cardboard, to cut the characters off from the umbilical of his imagination and let them perish! It seemed as cold as murder. Joan Rutherford had said "start on another book" as if it were as simple as changing clothes. He was afraid he could never finish another book. He felt wrung out by useless exercises of the mind, and he could no longer rely on his instinct to plot out decent stories. His health was continuing to weaken, and in him now was a fear he'd never experienced before—fear of success, fear of failure, fear of simply taking a chance. Over the tumult that raged within him he could hear the mocking note of his father's laughter.

"Why don't you try some short pieces?" Joan had asked as she signaled for the check. "I might be able to get something placed in *Playboy* or *Penthouse*. And you know I've said many times that using your real name might be a help, too."

"I thought you agreed Jonathan Strange was a good pen name."

"It is, but why not capitalize on your family name, Rix? There's no harm in letting people know you're descended from the Ushers that Poe wrote about. I think it'd be a plus, particularly in the horror genre."

"You know I don't like to do short stories. They don't interest me."

"Does your career interest you?" Joan had asked, too sharply. "If you want to be a writer, you write." She'd produced an American Express card and given it to the waiter after carefully going over the check. Then she'd narrowed her eyes as if looking at Rix Usher for the first time. "You didn't eat very much of your lunch. You look like you've lost some weight since the last time I saw you. Aren't you feeling well?"

"I'm okay," he'd lied.

When the check was paid, Joan had said she'd mail the manuscript back to him in Atlanta. He stayed behind, nursing his drink, as she left the restaurant. The slash of light that came in when she opened the door stung his eyes, though the mid-October day was heavily overcast.

One more drink. Down the hatch. Time to go.

Near Washington Square, the cabbie said, "Shit, looka that!"

A maniac was playing a violin in the middle of Fifth Avenue.

The Rasta leaned on his horn, and Rix Usher felt its treble scream like sandpaper on his spine.

The mad violinist—a stoop-shouldered elderly man in a long black coat—continued to saw at his instrument, snarling traffic in the intersection.

"Hey, freak!" the cabbie yelled from his window. "Get outta the way, mon!" He slammed his hand against the horn and sank his foot to the floor. The cab jerked forward, inches away from the violinist, who closed his eyes and kept right on playing.

Another cab suddenly spurted into the intersection, swerved to avoid the madman, and was sideswiped by a *Times* delivery van. The second cab, with a shouting Italian at the wheel, missed the violinist by less than a foot and plowed into the Rastafarian's left front fender.

Both cabbies leaped from their vehicles and began screaming at each other and at the lunatic. Rix sat frozen, his nerves jangling. His headache had turned vicious; the voices of the drivers, the blare of horns, and the violin's dissonant wail were for him a symphony of pain. His fists clenched so tightly that his fingernails cut into the flesh of his palms. I'll be all right, he told himself. Just need to stay calm. Stay calm. Stay—

There was a noise like a sizzle of grease, followed by the sound of a fingernail drawn slowly down a blackboard. The sounds repeated twice more before Rix realized what it was.

Rain.

Rain hitting the windshield, rolling down the glass.

His pores began leaking oily sweat.

"You crazy old fart!" the Italian shouted as the violinist played on. Rain started peppering down, plunking off roofs and hoods and windshields of vehicles caught at the intersection. "Hey, you! I'm talkin' to you!"

"Who's payin' for my cab, mon!" the Rastafarian demanded from the other driver. "You hit my cab, you pay for it!"

Rix heard raindrops strike the roof above him like cannonballs. Every blast of a horn felt like an icepick inserted more deeply into his ear. His heart throbbed mercilessly, and as the rain popped and

12

sizzled along the windshield, he knew he would lose his mind if he stayed in this maelstrom of noise. Beyond the drumming thunder of the rain he heard another sound—a deep, basso booming that was getting louder and louder, more terribly out of control. Rix put his hands to his ears, his eyes burning with tears of pain, but the booming noise was like a hammer striking the top of his head. A chorus of car horns pierced him. The razor-blade siren of an approaching police car slashed at his nerves. He realized the booming noise was his own heartbeat, and he was one breath away from panic's edge.

With a moan of pain and terror, Rix leaped out of the cab and started running through the rain toward the sidewalk. "Hey!" the Rastafarian shouted, in a voice that gripped the back of Rix's neck like a steel claw. "What about my goddamn fare, mon!"

Rix ran on, his head pounding, the sound of his runaway heartbeat dogging his steps. Rain on awnings along the sidewalks sounded like artillery explosions. He slipped on the remnants of a Danish and went down against a wire-mesh trash container, tipping it and spilling its contents all over the curb. Black motes spun before his eyes, and suddenly the dim gray light was so harsh he had to squint to see; gray buildings shimmered with light, the wet gray sidewalk glistened like a reflecting mirror. He tried to rise and skidded in trash, blinded by the riotous colors of cars, signs, people's clothing and skin. An orange scrawl of graffiti on the side of a city bus dazzled him senseless, like something from an alien world; a multicolored umbrella opened in the steady drizzle radiated laser beams of pain; the electric-white WALK at the corner seared into his eyes. When some well-meaning pedestrian tried to help Rix to his feet, Rix shrieked and pulled away; the man's hand on his shoulder had seemed to burn right down through the tweed to his flesh.

The Quiet Room—he had to get to the Quiet Room!

Bombarded from all sides by light, color, and noise, Rix struggled up and ran like a wild animal; he felt the pulse of human body heat as if the people around him were walking furnaces, and added to his own tumultuous heartbeat were theirs—a universe of heartbeats, functioning at different rhythms and intensities. When he screamed, his voice repeated itself in his head over and over again, like a crazy taped echo-loop. He ran across the street as blinding yellow, red, green, and blue shapes wailed around him, snorting at his heels. Tripping over a curb, he ripped his sleeve and scraped his knee, and as a vague glowing figure with a thundering heartbeat paused over him, he screamed not to be touched.

The rain fell harder, hitting the pavement around him with the sound of crashing boulders flung from a catapult. Each drop that hit his face, hair, or hands seemed to blister his skin like caustic acid. He had no choice but to keep running, half-blinded, south toward the safety of the De Peyser Hotel.

Finally, against the white glare of the pulsing sky loomed the Gothic spire of the De Peyser Hotel; its windows streamed and seethed with reflected light, and the tattered red awning above the hotel's Greene Street entrance shouted at Rix's ravaged senses. As he ran across the street, the screech of brakes and the horrendous cacophony of horns brought another scream of anguish from him, but he dared not slow his pace. His hands clasped to his ears, he threw himself into the De Peyser's revolving door and then across the long, moldy-smelling lobby with its garish carpet of red and gold interlocking circles. Heedless of whoever might be watching, Rix punched the button for the single elevator again and again, each contact of flesh and plastic bringing a scorch of pain. He could hear gears turning far above, the thick slapping of cables as the elevator descended. When it came, Rix stepped inside and punched the door shut before anyone else could enter. He depressed the button for the eighth floor, the De Peyser's highest level.

The elevator ascended with excruciating slowness. As it rose, Rix heard water gushing through pipes, televisions and radios blasting game shows, rock music, and disco; human voices filtered through the old walls like dialogue from nightmares, heard but impossible to understand. Rix crouched on the floor in a corner, his head tucked forward between his knees, his eyes tightly shut.

The door slid open. Rix ran for his room at the end of the dank, dimly lit corridor, fishing frantically for his door key. He burst into the suite, which had a window—now fortunately curtained—overlooking Greene Street. The light that leaked in around the cheap fabric was painfully incandescent. From another pocket Rix produced an antique brass key that had turned a greenish brown over the years; he plunged it into the lock of a white door near the bathroom, twisted it, and pulled open the heavy, rubber-coated door to the windowless Quiet Room.

With an involuntary cry of relief, Rix started to step across the threshold.

And a skeletal thing with bleeding eyesockets suddenly swung down into the doorway to block his path. Its bony arms were reaching out for him, and as Rix staggered backward he thought wildly that the Pumpkin Man had finally found him.

14

A familiar burst of laughter echoed through the suite. Rix fell to his knees, shaking and covered with sweat, and looked up into the face of his brother, Boone.

III

Boone was grinning. In the smeary light of Rix's tortured vision, Boone's long white teeth and craggy, rough-hewn face gave him the appearance of a predatory beast.

"Gotcha, Rixy!" he said in a harsh, booming voice that made Rix shudder. He started to laugh again, but then he realized his younger brother was enduring an attack and the grin froze solid on his face. "Rix? Are . . . are you okay?"

"Sick," Rix whispered, huddled on the floor at the Quiet Room's threshold. The cheap plastic life-sized skeleton dangled before him, held in place by a hook above the door. "Hit me out there . . . I didn't have time to . . . get to a quiet place . . ."

"Jesus!" Boone backed away from him a few steps, fearing that his brother was about to vomit. "Wait a minute, hold on!" He opened the door to the bathroom, where he'd been sitting and reading a *Rolling Stone* when Rix had come crashing into the suite, and drew Rix a plastic glass of tap water. It held a tint of rust that was hidden when Boone poured in some of the Canadian Club he'd bought from the liquor store around the corner. "No ice," he said, as he bent to offer Rix the drink. "Sorry."

Rix drank it down. The Scotch and bourbon in his system waged war in his stomach for a moment, and Rix squeezed his eyes shut so tightly that tears oozed out. When he opened his eyes again, the light was dimmer; Boone's expensive-looking dark blue suit didn't glow at him like a sapphire-painted lightbulb anymore, and even the wattage of his brother's teeth had ebbed. The noises of the hotel were quieting, as was the thump of his heartbeat. His head still throbbed savagely, and his eye sockets felt as if they'd been gouged, but he knew he was coming out of it. Another minute or two. Calm down, he told himself. Breathe deeply. Take it easy. Breathe deeply again. Christ Almighty, that was a bad one! He shook his head slowly from side to side, his fine sandy blond hair plastered down with rain and sweat. "It's almost over," he told Boone. "Wait a minute." He sat on his haunches, waiting for the low hum of overworked brain circuits to die down. "I'm better now," he rasped. "Help me up, okay?"

"You're not gonna puke, are you?"

"Just help me up, damn you!"

Boone took Rix's outstretched hand and pulled him to his feet. When he was standing, Rix punched his brother in the face with all the strength he could summon.

It was no more than a weak slap to the jaw. Boone stepped back, his grin returning with full force as he recognized the look of black rage on Rix's face.

"You dumb bastard!" Rix seethed. He started to rip the plastic skeleton with the bloody eyeholes—red paint, poorly applied—from its hook and throw it to the floor, but his hand stopped in midair. For some reason, he couldn't bear to touch it. He let his hand fall. "What's the idea of *that?*"

"A joke, that's all. Thought you'd enjoy it, seein' as how it's right up your alley." He shrugged and took the skeleton down, sitting it upright in a chair across the room. "There we go. Looks pretty real, huh?"

"Why did you hang it inside the Quiet Room? Why not in the bathroom, or a closet? You knew there'd be only one reason I'd open this door!"

"Oh." Boone frowned. "You're right, Rixy. I didn't think of that. Seemed to be a good place to hang it, is all. Well, it all turned out fine, didn't it? Shit, yes! That damned thing probably scared the attack right out of you!" He let out a braying laugh and pointed at Rix's crotch. "Ha! There you go, Rixy! Peed your pants, didn't you!"

Rix went to the chest of drawers for another pair of trousers and a clean shirt.

Boone sprawled his six-foot-two frame in an overstuffed easy chair and put his feet up on an Art Deco coffee table with blue glass legs. He massaged the side of his jaw where Rix's fist had stung him. He'd rubbed his brother's face in the North Carolina mud for much less an offense. "Smells like a wet dog in this hotel. Don't they ever shampoo the rugs?"

"How'd you get in here?" Rix asked as he changed clothes. He was still shaking.

"Everybody jumps around here when you tell 'em your name's Usher," Boone said. He crossed his ankles. He was wearing beige lizardskin cowboy boots that clashed with his conservative suit. "Know what I've heard about this place? That some of the bellboys have seen a man dressed in black, wearing a black top hat and a white beard, and carrying a cane. Sounds like old Hudson himself, don't it? Poor bastard's probably doomed to spend eternity walking the corridors of the De Peyser. They say his presence makes the air freezin' cold. Hell of a place to spend your afterlife, huh, Rixy?"

"I've asked you not to call me that."

"Oh. Beggin' your pardon. Shall I call you Jonathan Strange? Or what's your name this week, Mr. Famous Author?"

Rix ignored the barb. "How'd you get into the Quiet Room?"

"Asked for the key. They've got a whole boxful in a safe downstairs. Old green things that look like they open mausoleums. Some of 'em have got black fingerprints on the metal. I wonder how many Ushers used 'em? Me, I wouldn't spend one damned night in this old crypt. Jesus, why don't we get some light in here!"

Boone stood up and walked across the room to the window; he pulled aside the curtain, allowing in dim gray light through the rain-specked glass. He stood for a moment looking down at the traffic. His broad, handsome face was almost free of lines, though he was only three months shy of his thirty-seventh birthday; he might easily have passed for twenty-five. His full, wavy hair was a darker shade of brown than his brother's, and his clear, deepset eyes were amber with dark green flecks. He was husky and broad-shouldered, and he looked in the prime of health. "Sorry about your attack," he told Rix. "I wouldn't have pulled such a stupid trick if I'd been thinkin' right. I saw the thing hangin' in a magic shop's window on the way over here, and I thought . . . I don't know, I thought you might get a kick out of it. Do you know I haven't had an attack for over six months? And the last one wasn't too bad—it was over in about three or four minutes. Maybe I've forgotten how bad they can be." He turned away from the window to look at his brother—and froze.

It was almost a year since he'd last seen Rix, and he was stunned at the way his brother had changed. In the light, all the fine wrinkles and lines on Rix's face resembled cracks in porcelain. Rix's pewter-colored eyes were red-rimmed and weary, his high forehead deeply furrowed. Though Rix was four years younger than Boone, he appeared to be at least forty-five. He looked emaciated and sickly, and Boone saw that gray was spreading at his temples. "Rix," he whispered. "God Almighty! What's happened to you?"

"I've been sick," Rix replied, but he knew that wasn't all of it. In truth, he didn't exactly know what was happening to him—other than that his attacks were vicious and unpredictable, his sleep was continually jarred by nightmares, and he felt seventy years old. "I guess I've been working too hard." He eased himself down into a chair—carefully, because his bones were still throbbing.

"Listen. You need to start eatin' steaks to build up your blood." Boone puffed out his chest. "I eat a steak a day, and look at me! Healthy as a stud hoss."

"Great," Rix said. "How'd you know I was here?"

"You called Katt and told her you were flying up from Atlanta to meet with your agent today, didn't you? Where else would you stay but this old dump when you're visiting New York?"

Rix nodded. The De Peyser Hotel had been purchased in 1847 by Hudson Usher, when it was a magnificent Gothic showplace towering over the rough harbor city. As Rix understood it, Hudson Usher's gunpowder company, based near Asheville, North Carolina, shipped tremendous quantities of powder and lead bullets to Europe through New York City; Hudson had wanted to keep an eye on the middlemen, and had outfitted this suite with a rubber-walled Quiet Room, in case he was stricken with an attack. The Quiet Room had remained virtually unchanged, used by generations of Ushers, as the suite gradually became more tawdry. Rix surmised that his father, Walen, was only holding on to the De Peyser until he got a good offer from a co-op builder. The family rarely left Usherland, their rambling estate twenty miles north of Asheville.

"You shouldn't work so hard. When's your next book coming out?" Boone poured himself another drink of Scotch and sat down again. When he lifted the glass to his mouth, light sparkled off the large diamond pinky ring he wore. "It's been a long time since *Fire Fingers*, hasn't it?"

"I've just finished a new book."

"Oh yeah? When's it comin' out?"

"Maybe next summer." He was amazed that the lie came so easily.

Boone propped his feet up again. "You ought to write a real book, Rix. You know, something that could really happen. That horror shit is junk. Why don't you write a book you'd be proud to sign your real name to?"

"Let's don't get into that again, okay?" Every time he got near Boone, he wound up defending his choice of subject matter.

Boone shrugged. "Suits me. Just seems to me there must be somethin' a little wrong with people who write shit like that."

"I know you didn't come here to discuss my literary career," Rix said. "What's going on?"

Boone paused to take a swallow of his drink. Then he said quietly, "Momma wants you to come home. Daddy's taken a turn for the worse."

18

"Why the hell won't he go to a hospital?"

"You know what Daddy's always said. 'An Usher can't live past the gates of Usherland.' And lookin' at you, brother Rix, makes me think he's been right about that. There must be somethin' in that North Carolina air, because you've broken down pretty badly ever since you left it."

"I don't like the estate. I don't like the Lodge. My home is in Atlanta. Besides, I've got work to do."

"Oh? I thought you said you'd just finished another book. Hell, if it's anything like those other three, no amount of work can save it!"

Rix smiled grimly. "Thank you for the encouragement."

"Daddy's dying," Boone said, a quick flicker of anger like lightning behind his eyes. "I've tried to do all I could for him. I've tried to be what he wanted, all these years. But now he's askin' to see *you*. I don't know why, especially since you turned your back on the family. But I think he's holdin' on because he wants you at his side when he dies."

"Then if I don't come," Rix told him flatly, "maybe he won't die. Maybe he'll get up out of that bed and start making deals for laser guns and germ-warfare bombs again, huh?"

"Oh Christ!" Boone rose angrily from his seat. "Don't play that worn-out, holier-than-thou routine with me, Rix! The business brought you up on the finest estate in this country, fed you and clothed you and sent you to the best business school in America! Not that it did a damned bit of good! And who says you have to go to the Lodge if you come home? You always were scared shitless of the Lodge, weren't you? When you got yourself lost in there and Edwin had to bring you out, your face looked like green cheese for about a—" He stopped speaking abruptly, because Rix looked for a second as if he might leap across the table at his brother.

"That's not how *I* remember it," Rix said, his voice strained with tension.

They stared at each other for a few seconds. The image came to Rix of his brother tackling him from behind when they were children, planting a knee in the small of his back so the breath was squeezed out of him and his face was pressed into Usherland dirt. *Get up, Rixy*, Boone had taunted. *Get up, why can't you get up, Rixy?*

"Well." Boone reached inside his coat and brought out a first-class Delta ticket to Asheville. He dropped it onto the table. "I've seen you and said what I was supposed to. That's from Momma.

She thought just maybe you'd have enough heart to come see Daddy on his deathbed. If you don't, I guess that's your little red wagon." He walked to the door, then stopped and turned back. The hot light had returned to his eyes, and there was a curl to his mouth. "Yeah, you run on back to Atlanta, Rixy," he said. "Go on back to that fantasy world of yours. Shit, you're even startin' to look like somethin' out of the grave. I'll tell Momma not to expect you." He left the room and closed the door behind him. His lizardskin boots clumped away along the corridor.

Rix sat staring at the plastic skeleton across the room. It grinned at him like an old friend, the familiar symbol of death from a thousand horror movies Rix had seen. The skeleton in a closet. Bones buried under the floor. A skull in a hatbox. A skeletal hand reaching out from beneath a bed. Uneasy bones, digging free from the grave.

My father's dying, he thought. No, no; Walen Usher was too stubborn to give in to death. He and death were friends of long standing. They had a gentlemen's agreement. "The business" kept death's stomach swollen—why should it bite its feeder's hand?

Rix picked up the airline ticket. It was for a flight leaving around one the next afternoon. Walen dying? He'd known his father's condition had been deteriorating for the past six months, but *dying?* He felt numbed, stranded between a shout and a sob. He'd never gotten along with his father; they'd been strangers to each other for years. Walen Usher was the kind of man who insisted that his children make appointments to see him. He had kept his sons and daughter on short leashes—until Rix gnawed himself loose, earning his father's undying hatred.

He wasn't even sure if he loved his father, wasn't sure if he even knew what love felt like anymore.

Rix knew that Boone had always been a great practical joker. "Dad's not dying," he told the skeleton. "It's just a story to get me back there." The plastic bones offered a grin, but no advice. As he stared at the thing, he saw the cab driver's skeleton earring swinging back and forth in his mind. His skin crawled, and he had to call maid service to get the thing out because he couldn't force himself to touch it.

He made a second call, to Usherland's Gatehouse in North Carolina.

Four hundred miles away, a maid answered, "Usher residence."

"Edwin Bodane. Tell him it's Rix."

"Yes sir. Just a minute, please."

Rix waited. He was feeling better now. He'd been overdue for an attack; the last one had hit him in the middle of the night a week ago, when he was listening to a record from his collection of jazz albums in his Atlanta apartment. After it was over and he could move again, he'd broken the record to fragments, thinking that the music might have helped trigger it. He'd read somewhere that certain chord progressions, tones, and vibrations could cause a physical response.

The attacks, he knew, were symptoms of a condition called—in several medical journals—Usher's Malady. There was no cure. If his father was dying, it was the advanced stage of Usher's Malady that was killing him.

"Master Rix!" the warm, refined, slightly sandpapery voice said from North Carolina. "Where are you?"

"In New York. At the De Peyser." Hearing Edwin's voice had released a bounty of good memories for Rix. He visualized the man standing tall in his Usher uniform of gray blazer and dark blue slacks with creases so sharp you could slice your hand on them. He'd always felt closer to Edwin and Cass Bodane than to his own parents.

"Do you want to speak to your—"

"No. I don't want to talk to anybody else. Edwin, Boone was here a little while ago. He told me Dad's condition is worse. Is that true?"

"Your father's health is deteriorating rapidly," Edwin said. "I'm sure Boone told you how much your mother wants you to come home."

"I don't want to come. You know why."

There was a pause. Then, "Mr. Usher asks for you every day." He lowered his voice. "I wish you'd come home, Rix. He needs you."

Rix couldn't suppress a strangled, nervous laugh. "He's never needed me before now!"

"No. You're wrong. Your father's always needed you, and now more than ever."

Rix paused, torn by emotional crosscurrents. He'd fought for a life of his own, apart from the Usher clan. Why should he expose himself to the mental games that would now be in motion within Usherland's gates?

"He needs you, Rix," Edwin said softly. "Don't turn your back on your family."

The truth sank in before he could block it out: Walen Usher, patriarch of the powerful Usher clan and perhaps the wealthiest man

21

in America, was on his deathbed. Even though his feelings about the man were tied into tormented knots, Rix knew he should attend his father's passing. He asked Edwin to meet him at the airport when his flight arrived, then hung up before he could change his mind. He would stay at Usherland for a few days, he told himself. No longer. Then he had to get back to Atlanta, to get his own life in order, somehow come up with another idea and get to work on it before his entire writing career collapsed under the weight of lethargy.

A Hispanic maintenance man with bags under his eyes came up to the room. He was expecting another dead rat, and was relieved when Rix told him to take the plastic skeleton away.

Rix lay down and tried to sleep. His mind was disturbed by images of Usherland: the dark forests of his childhood, where nightmarish creatures were said to stalk through the undergrowth; the looming mountains black against an orange-streaked sky, clouds snagged like gray pennants on their rocky peaks; and the Lodge—it always came back to the Lodge—immense and dark and silent, holding its secrets like a closed fist.

A skeleton with bleeding eye sockets swung slowly through his mind's eye, and he sat up in the leaden light.

A recurring idea had snapped on in his brain again. It was the same idea that had sent him to Wales, the same idea that had made him enter genealogy rooms in libraries from New York to Atlanta, in search of the Usher name in half-forgotten record books. Sometimes he thought he could do it, if he really wanted to; at other times he realized it would be a hell of a lot of work, probably for nothing.

Maybe now is the time, he told himself. Yes. He certainly needed a project, and he was going back to Usherland anyway. A smile flickered across his mouth; he could hear Walen's shout of outrage over four hundred miles.

Rix went into the bathroom for a glass of water, then picked up the copy of *Rolling Stone* that Boone had folded and left on the tiles. When he took it back to bed to read, the fist-sized tarantula that Boone had carefully wrapped up within it dropped onto his chest, scuttling wildly across his shoulder.

Rix leaped out of bed, trying to get the thing off him. The attack that crashed over him like a black tidal wave drove him into the protection of the Quiet Room. With the door closed, no one could hear him scream.

Boone had always been a great practical joker.

22

One

USHERLAND

"Tell me a story," the little boy asked his father. "Something scary, okay?"

"Something scary," the man repeated, and mused for a moment. Outside the boy's window, the darkness was complete except for the moon's grinning orb. The boy could see it over his father's shoulder—and to him it looked like a rotting jack-o'-lantern in a black Halloween field where no one dares to walk.

His father leaned closer toward the bed. "Okay," he said, and the low light gleamed in his glasses. "I'll tell you a story about a dying king in his castle, and the king's children, and all the kings that came before them. It may go off in different directions and try to trick you. It may not end like you want it to . . . but that's the way this story is. And the scariest thing about it—the most scariest thing—is that it might be true . . . or it might not be. Ready?"

And the boy smiled, unaware.

—The Night Is Not Ours by Jonathan Strange,
Stratford House, 1978

1

As Rix walked off the Delta jet and into the airport terminal seven miles south of Asheville, he saw Edwin Bodane's head above the group of people who'd come to meet other passengers. Edwin stood six feet four, aristocratically thin, and was definitely hard to miss. He grinned like an excited child and rushed over to embrace Rix— who didn't fail to catch the almost imperceptible wince on Edwin's face when he saw how much Rix had aged in the past year.

"Master Rix, Master Rix!" Edwin said. His accent was old-blood Southern and as dignified as polished silver. "You look—"

"Like hell on a Popsicle stick. But you look great, Edwin. How's Cass?"

"She's as fine as ever. Getting feistier with the years, I'm afraid." He tried to take the garment bag that Rix was carrying, but Rix waved him off. "Did you bring any more luggage?"

"Just a suitcase. I don't plan on staying very long."

They stopped at the baggage check for the suitcase, then walked out into the cool breeze and sunlight of a beautiful October afternoon. At the curb was a new limo, a maroon Lincoln Continental with tinted windows and a sunroof. The Usher passions included mechanical as well as thoroughbred horsepower. Rix stored his luggage in the cavernous trunk and sat on the front seat, seeing no need to ride separated from Edwin by a plate of plexiglass. Edwin put on a pair of wire-rimmed sunglasses and then they were off, driving away from the airport and toward the dramatic line of the Blue Ridge Mountains.

Edwin had always reminded Rix of a character in a favorite tale—Ichabod Crane in Washington Irving's Headless Horseman story. No matter how precise the cut of his gray blazer, Edwin's wrists

27

always jutted from the coatsleeves. He had a beak of a nose that Boone said a hat could be hung from. His softly seamed face was square-jawed and held luminous, kindly blue-gray eyes. Under the black chauffeur's cap that he wore was a lofty forehead topped by a fragile crown of white hair. His large ears—true masterpieces of sculptured flesh—again invited comparisons to Irving's poor schoolmaster. In his eyes was the dreamy expression of a boy who still longed to join the circus, though Edwin Bodane was in his late sixties. He'd been born into service to the Usher family, continuing the long tradition of the Bodanes who'd acted as confidants to the Usher patriarchs. Wearing his gray blazer with gleaming silver buttons and the Usher emblem of a silver lion's head on the jacket pocket, his dark trousers carefully pressed, his black bow tie in place and his oxfords spit-shined, Edwin looked every inch the chief of staff of Usherland.

Behind that comical, unassuming face, Rix knew, was an intelligent mind that could organize anything from simple housekeeping duties to a banquet for two hundred people. Edwin and Cass had the responsibility of overseeing a small army of maids, laundry staff, groundskeepers, stable help, and cooks, though Cass preferred to do most of the cooking for the family herself. They were answerable only to Walen Usher.

"Master Rix, Master Rix!" Edwin repeated, relishing the sound of those words. "It's so good to have you home again!" He frowned slightly, and immediately tempered his enthusiasm. "Of course . . . I'm sorry you have to return under these circumstances."

"Atlanta's my home now." Rix realized he sounded too defensive. "This is a new limo, I see. Only three hundred miles on the odometer."

"Mr. Usher ordered it a month ago. He could get around then. Now he can't leave his bed. He has a private nurse, of course. A Mrs. Paula Reynolds, from Asheville."

The maroon limo glided through Asheville, passing tobacco warehouses, bank buildings, and shopping malls. Just beyond the city's northeastern boundary line stood a large gray concrete structure that resembled a bunker and covered almost twelve acres of prime commercial property. It was surrounded by a chain-link fence topped with barbed wire. The only windows were horizontal slits placed equidistantly from one another below the roof, like gunports in a fortress. The parking lot, full of cars, stretched another three acres. Set on the side of the building facing the highway were black metal letters that read USHER ARMAMENTS, and beneath that, in

28

smaller letters, ESTABLISHED 1841. It was the ugliest building Rix had ever seen, and it looked more repellent every time he passed it.

Old Hudson would be proud, Rix thought. The gunpowder-and-bullets business begun by a Welshman in 1841 had culminated in four ammunition and weaponry plants that bore the Usher name: in Asheville, in Washington, D.C., in San Diego, and in Brussels, Belgium. "The business," as it was referred to in the family, had supplied gunpowder, firearms, dynamite, plastic explosives, and state-of-the-art weapons systems to the highest bidder for more than one hundred and fifty years. "The business" had built Usherland, had made the Usher name known and respected as creators of death. Rix wondered how many people had been killed by those weapons for every one of the thirty thousand acres in Usherland, how many had been blown to pieces for every dark stone in the Lodge.

When he'd left Usherland almost seven years before, Rix had told himself he'd never return. To him, Usherland was awash with the gore of slaughter; even as a child, he'd felt the brooding presence of death in those tangled forests, in the ornate Gatehouse and the insane Lodge. Though his heritage of blood sickened him, he found himself haunted over the years by his early memories of Usherland, almost as if something within him was unfulfilled and Usherland was calling him back, time and again, with whispered promises. He had returned several times, but only for a day or two. His mother and father remained as remote and impassive as always, his brother seemed locked in time as a strutting bully, and his sister did all she could to avoid dealing with reality.

They left the building behind and turned onto a wide, winding highway that climbed into the mountains. Spectacular scenery greeted Rix; the craggy hills and carpets of woodland blazed with deep scarlet, purple, and gold. Beneath the cloudless blue sky the land was a panorama of blood and fire.

"How's Mom taking this?" Rix asked.

"She's coping. Some days are better than others. But you know how she is, Rix. She's lived in a perfect world for so long that she can't accept what's happening."

"I thought he'd get better," Rix said quietly. "You know how strong he is, and how stubborn. Who's the doctor you mentioned over the phone?"

"Dr. John Francis. Mr. Usher had him flown down from Boston. He's a specialist in cell degeneration."

"Is . . . Dad in much pain?"

Edwin didn't answer, and Rix understood. The agony that Walen

Usher would be enduring—the final stages of Usher's Malady—would make Rix's attack in New York seem like a mild headache.

Edwin turned off the main highway onto a narrow but well-kept country road. At an intersection ahead, a sign pointed in different directions to the communities of Rainbow, Taylorville, and Foxton. He drove east, toward Foxton. A town of some two thousand people, mostly farmers, Foxton and its surrounding tobacco fields had been owned by the Usher family for five generations.

The limo glided through Foxton's streets. The community was growing steadily, and Rix saw changes since he'd last come this way. The Broadleaf Cafe had moved to a new brick structure, there was a modern Carolinas Bank building, and colored pennants popped in the breeze over a used-car lot. The Empire Theater's marquee advertised a Halloween double bill of vintage Orlon Kronsteen horror flicks. Still, the old Foxton lingered: a couple of elderly farmers in straw hats sat on a bench in front of the hardware store enjoying the sunshine; a beat-up pickup truck rumbled past, loaded with bundles of tobacco leaves; a group of men standing idly by the Woolworth's store turned to watch the limo pass, and Rix could see the resentment in their eyes like low-burning coals. They quickly turned away. Rix knew that their voices would tighten as they talked about the Ushers; perhaps they would even whisper, fearful that anything said about old Walen would be heard across the dense forests and ridges of stone separating Foxton and Usherland.

Rix glanced toward a small, rough stone structure housing the *Foxton Democrat*, a weekly newspaper that served the "tri-city" area. He could see the reflection of the limo in the plate-glass window, and then he was aware that a woman with dark hair was standing behind the window, close enough that her face almost touched the glass. He imagined that for a second or two her eyes were fixed right on him, but he knew she couldn't see through the limo's tinted glass. Still, he looked away uneasily.

Outside Foxton, the forest rapidly thickened again, looming close to the road like impenetrable walls. The beauty of the mountains became savage, as jagged rock thrust up from the earth like the gray bones of grotesque, half-buried monsters. An occasional rutted dirt trail wound up into the forest from the main road, leading into remote territory where hundreds of hillbilly families clung tenaciously to the values of the nineteenth century. Their stronghold, Briartop Mountain, stood on the northern edge of Usherland, and Rix had often wondered what those people—who had occupied the mountain for generations—thought of the acres of gardens, rolling hills, fountains, and stables in the alien world beneath them. They were distrustful of all but their own, and rarely came down to trade in Foxton.

Rix suddenly felt the back of his neck prickle. If he'd been looking at a map of property lines, he wouldn't have known with any greater certainty that they had entered the Usher domain. The forest seemed darker, the autumn leaves of such deep reds and purples that they appeared to shimmer with an oily blackness. The black canopy of leaves overhung the road, and tangles of briars—the kind that could gash to the bone and snap off—twisted in ugly corkscrews as dangerous as barbed wire. Massive scabs of stone clung to the hillsides, threatening to slide down and smash the limo into junk. Rix realized his palms were sweating. The wilderness seemed to be a hostile environment unsuited for a civilized human being—yet this was the land that Hudson Usher had fallen in love with. Or, perhaps, seen as a challenge to be broken. In any case, it had never been Rix's cup of thorns.

In traveling this way over the years, though infrequently, Rix had never failed to catch a sense of brutality in the land, a kind of soulless crushing power that made him feel weak and small. It was little wonder, he thought, that the people of Foxton considered Usherland a place best avoided, and had created folktales to emphasize their fear of the dark, forbidding mountains.

"Pumpkin Man still in the woods?" Rix asked softly.

Edwin glanced at him, then smiled. "My God! Do you still remember that story?"

"How could I forget it? Let's see, how did that rhyme go? 'Run, run as fast as you can, 'cause out in the woods walks the Pumpkin Man.' Is that it?"

"Near enough."

"I should put the Pumpkin Man in a book someday," Rix said. "What about the black panther that walks like a man? Any new sightings?"

"Yes, as a matter of fact. In August the *Democrat* said some lunatic hunter swore he'd seen it up on Briartop. I suppose stories like those sell newspapers."

Rix scanned the tangled forest on both sides of the road. A knot of tension had thickened in his stomach as he recalled the tale told to him by Edwin about the Pumpkin Man, a creature the locals said had lived in the mountains for more than a hundred years and stole away children who roamed too far from home. Even now, as an adult, Rix still thought of the Pumpkin Man with childlike dread, though he knew the story had been concocted by the hillbillies to keep their children from getting lost in the woods.

Around the road's next curve stood a formidable granite wall that held an intricately fashioned pair of wrought-iron gates. Scripted in iron on a granite arch above the gates was the name USHER. Edwin reached over to the dashboard and switched on a small device that triggered the radio-controlled locks. As the gates swung open, Edwin never even had to lift his foot from the accelerator.

Rix looked over his shoulder when they were through and saw the gates locking themselves again. The design on them had always reminded him of a spider's web.

At once the landscape changed. Though there were still places of deep, wild forest, there were also lush greenswards and meticulously kept gardens where roses, violets, and sunflowers grew amid prancing statues of fauns, centaurs, and cherubs. A tall glass roof sighted through orderly rows of pine trees signaled the conservatory where one of Rix's ancestors had grown a variety of cacti and succulents. Honeysuckle, tall maiden grass, and English ivy boiled up from the forest. Rix saw several gardeners at work, trimming hedges and pruning trees. In one garden stood a huge red Baldwin locomotive mounted on a stone pedestal. It dated from the early days of the railroad pioneers and had been the first piece of equipment purchased by his great-great-grandfather Aram, Hudson's son. At one time the Ushers had operated their own railroad—the Atlantic Seaboard Limited—to haul freight of gunpowder, ammunition, and weapons.

Several thousand acres of the Usher estate had never been mapped. The land encompassed mountains, slow-moving streams, wide meadows, and three deep, peat-filmed lakes. As always, Rix was struck by the sheer beauty of Usherland as Edwin drove toward the Gatehouse. It was a magnificent, breathtaking estate worthy of American royalty. But then, Rix thought grimly, there was always the Lodge—the sanctified cathedral of the Usher clan.

Edwin slowed the car as they neared the Gatehouse's porte-cochere. The mansion, of white limestone with a red slate roof, was surrounded by colorful gardens and huge, ancient oak trees. It held thirty-two rooms, and had been built by Rix's great-grandfather Ludlow as a guesthouse.

The limo stopped. Rix dreaded stepping into that house. He paused as Edwin started to get out of the car, then felt Edwin's hand on his shoulder.

"It'll be all right," Edwin assured him. "You'll see."

32

"Yeah," Rix replied. He forced himself to get out, and took his garment bag from the trunk as Edwin carried his suitcase. They climbed a flight of stone steps, walked across a tiled patio with a goldfish pond at its center, and stopped at a front door that looked like an oak slab.

When Edwin pressed the doorbell, they were admitted by a young black maid in a crisp pale blue uniform. Another servant, a middle-aged black man in a gray suit, welcomed Rix home and took his bags, crossing the wide parquet-floored foyer to the sweeping central staircase. Rix saw that the house was becoming more like a damned museum every time he returned. The perfect furnishings—Persian rugs, antique French tables and chairs, gilded turn-of-the-century mirrors, and medieval tapestries of hunting scenes hanging from the walls—seemed meant to be admired at a distance. The Louis XV chairs would never feel human weight; brass and ceramic objets d'art would be tickled with a duster but never touched. All the things in the house seemed as cold to Rix as the people who had chosen them.

"Mrs. Usher and Mr. Boone are in the living room, sir," the young maid said, and waited to escort him.

Edwin said, "Good luck," and left to drive the limo around to the garage.

The burnished walnut living room doors were set in tracks. The maid slid them open for him. Rix paused on the threshold for a second, noticing a sickly sweet smell that had suddenly come wafting out of nowhere.

He realized it was human decay. Coming from upstairs.

His father's room.

He braced himself and walked into the living room to face his brother and the matriarch of the Usher family.

2

Nudging the logs in the marble fireplace with a brass poker, Boone glanced up at the sound of the opening doors and saw Rix in the gilt-framed mirror above the hearth. "Ah!" he said. "Here's the famous horror author, Momma!"

Margaret Usher sat in a high-backed Italian armchair, facing the fire. She'd been chilly all day, and she couldn't drive the cold from her bones. She did not turn to greet her son.

The doors slid closed behind Rix, gently but still with the faint *click*! of a trap snapping shut. Now he was alone with them. He wore faded jeans and a pale blue shirt under a beige sweater—a good enough outfit for anywhere but here, he thought. Boone was dressed in a pinstriped suit, his mother in an elaborate blue and gold gown. "Hello, Mother," Rix said.

"I'm cold." She spoke as if she hadn't even heard. "It's very cold in this house, don't you think?"

"Want me to get you a sweater, Momma?"

She paused, her head cocked slightly to one side, pondering Boone's question. "Yes," she said finally. "A sweater would do nicely."

"Sure thing. Momma, show Rixy those pearls I brought you from New York." He put a finger under her chin to persuade her to lift her head. The strand of pearls glowed, catching golden light that filtered in through the large picture window overlooking the azalea garden. "Nice, huh? They cost four thousand dollars."

"Very nice," Rix agreed. "Boone brought me a couple of gifts in New York, too, Mother."

Boone laughed without humor. "How about that thing, Rixy? I thought you'd like it! Pet shop two blocks from the De Peyser had just what I was looking for. Fella who sold it to me said it was just like the ones they use in monster flicks."

"I figure I screwed things up for you. You probably wanted me to find that thing first, and you thought the shock might trigger an attack. Then, when I went into the Quiet Room, I'd stumble into your second surprise."

"Don't say that word." Margaret was staring fixedly into the fire. " 'Screwed' is not a decent word." Her voice was calm and throaty—the voice of a woman used to giving commands.

"It's not the kind of word a famous author ought to use, is it, Momma?" As always, Boone leaped on every opportunity to score points with their mother against Rix. "Now you just sit right there and I'll run get you a sweater." When he passed Rix on his way to the door, Boone flashed a quick, tight smile.

"Boone?" Margaret called, and her older son paused. "Make sure the sweater won't clash, dear."

"Yes, Momma," Boone replied, and left the room.

Rix walked toward her. As he neared, he again caught a whiff of that foul aroma, like a dead rat moldering in one of the walls. Margaret picked up a can of Lysol pine air freshener from a table beside her chair and began to spray clouds of mist around her. When she was through, the room smelled like a pine woods full of dead animals.

Rix stood beside his mother. She was still trying to stall time. At fifty-eight, Margaret Usher was desperately fighting to remain thirty-five. Her hair was cut stylishly short and dyed a coppery auburn. Several trips to a California plastic surgeon had left the skin stretched so tightly over her sharp cheekbones that it looked as if it were about to rip. Her makeup was thicker than Rix recalled, and the shade of lipstick she'd chosen was much too red. Tiny lines were creeping around her mouth and nesting in the corners of her pale green eyes. Her body remained sleek except for a bit of heaviness around the hips and stomach, and Rix remembered Katt telling him his mother feared unsightly flab like the Black Plague. On her slim, graceful hands she wore a stunning variety of rings—diamonds, rubies, and emeralds. Pinned to her gown was a brooch whose diamonds glittered in the firelight. Sitting motionless, she appeared to Rix as yet another perfect furnishing of the Gatehouse, never meant to be touched.

Her expression was disconsolate and helpless. A feeling of sadness for her came over Rix. What price had she paid, he wondered, to live as the mistress of Usherland?

Suddenly she turned her head and looked at him. It was the same kind of vague stare one would give a stranger. "You've lost weight," she noted. "Have you been sick?"

"I've felt better."

"You look like a walking skeleton."

He shrugged uneasily, not wanting to be reminded of his physical ailments. "I'll be all right."

"Not living the way you do. Hand to mouth in a distant city, without your family. I don't see how you've stood it this long." A light glimmered in her eyes, and she reached out to take his hand. "But you've come home to stay this time, haven't you? We've needed you here. I've had your old room readied for you. Everything's just as it used to be, now that you're home to stay."

"Mom," Rix said gently, "I can't stay. I just came for a few days, to see Dad."

"Why?" Her grip tightened. "Why can't you stay here, where you belong?"

"I don't belong at Usherland." He knew it was pointless to be drawn into this discussion yet again. Inevitably there would be an argument. "I've got to get back to work."

"You mean that writing you do?" Margaret released his hand and stood up to admire her new pearls in the mirror. "I'd hardly call that work, Rix. At least not the kind of occupation you're capable of. Did you see these pearls your brother brought me? Aren't they nice?" She frowned and ran a finger beneath her chin. "My God, I'm looking like an old woman, aren't I? I should sue that last doctor who tucked my chin. I should sue him right out of business. Aren't I just the ugliest old woman you've ever seen?"

"You look fine."

She regarded herself and smiled wanly. "Oh, you don't remember what I *used* to look like. Do you know what my daddy always called me? The prettiest girl in the whole of North Carolina. Puddin' thinks she's pretty, but she doesn't know what real beauty is." Margaret mentioned the name of Boone's wife with an undisguised disgust. "I used to look like Katt. I used to have fine skin, just like hers."

"Where is Katt?"

"Didn't your brother tell you? She's gone down to the Bahamas somewhere on an assignment for a magazine. It was something she couldn't get out of. She hoped to get back either tomorrow or the day after. Do you know what they're paying her now? Two thousand dollars an hour. They're going to put her on the cover of *Vogue* next month. I used to look like Katt when I was her age."

"And what about Puddin'?"

"What about her?" Margaret shrugged, uninterested. "She's up in her room, I suppose. She sleeps all the time. I've tried to tell Boone his little beauty-queen wife is beginning to drink a bit too much, but will he listen? No. He goes running off to the stables to clock the horses." She picked up the Lysol can and misted the air again. "At least you're a free man. Your brother's made a mess of his—"

The doors slid open and Boone entered, carrying a pale gold sweater. The way Margaret immediately closed her mouth and stiffened her spine was a clear message that she'd been discussing him. Boone wore his toothy grin like a mask. "Here's your sweater, Momma." He draped it around her shoulders. "What mischief you two been talkin' about?"

"Oh, nothing that concerns you," Margaret said sweetly, her eyelids at half-mast. "Rix was just telling me about all the ladies in his life. He's playing his cards right."

36

Boone's mouth stretched wider, and Rix could almost hear the flesh crack. In his eyes was a familiar warning glint; Rix had seen it many times when they were children, just before Boone attacked him for some imagined slight. "What Momma means to say, Rixy, is that I'm the disgrace of the family—next to *you*, that is. Because I've been divorced twice and I've married a young chickie, Momma seems to think I ought to go through life carrying a ball and chain. Isn't that right, Momma?"

"Don't make a fool of yourself in front of your brother, dear."

"Know why Rixy's got so many ladies, Momma? 'Cause none of 'em go out with him a second time. His idea of a fun date is to amble over to the nearest graveyard and hunt up the spooks. And let's don't forget that little lady of Rix's who decided to take a nice warm—"

Rix wheeled toward him. He felt the rage contorting his face. Boone stopped dead. "Don't say it," Rix whispered hoarsely. "If you say it, you bastard, I'll have to kill you."

Boone stood like stone. Then he laughed, the note sharp and short—but there was a tremor in it.

"*Boys,*" Margaret chided softly. "Is there a draft in this room?"

Boone ambled over and warmed his hands before the hearth. "Know what, Momma? Rix says he's finished another book."

"Oh?" Her voice was stiff with frost. "I presume it's another disgusting bloodfest. I swear, I don't know why you write those things! Do you actually think those books of yours *please* people?"

Rix had a headache. He touched his temples, fearing an attack. My God, why did I come home? he asked himself. Boone's reference to Sandra had almost sent him over the edge.

"You've got to understand Rixy, Momma," Boone offered, his gaze flicking back and forth between them. "He was always scared of his own shadow when we were kids. Always seein' the Pumpkin Man under his bed. So now he writes horror books so he can kill off the bad ol' demons. And he thinks he's Edgar Allan Poe. You know, the sufferin' art—"

"Hush!" she said sharply. "Don't you dare mention that name in this house! Lord knows, your father would have a fit if he heard it!"

"Well, it's true!" Boone insisted. He grinned at Rix, rubbing his hands together. "When are you gonna write somethin' about *us*, Rixy? That's about what I'd expect of you next."

From the corner of his eye, Rix saw his mother blanch. He responded with a smug smile of his own. "You know, brother Boone, that might be a fine idea. I could write a book about the Ushers. The history of the family. How about that, Mom?"

She opened her mouth to reply, then abruptly clapped it shut. She sprayed the air again, and Rix smelled the new, almost over-powering stench that had crept in under the doors.

"It's so hard," Margaret said as she followed the mist around the room, "to keep an older house fresh and clean. When a house reaches a certain age, it starts to fall to pieces. I've always cared about keeping a good house." She stopped spraying; it was clear the disinfectant wasn't strong enough. "My mother raised me to care," she said proudly.

Rix had delayed the moment as long as possible. "I'd better go up and see him now," he said resignedly.

"No, not yet!" Margaret clutched his hand, a tight false smile across her mouth. "Let's sit down here together, both my fine boys. Cass is making a Welsh pie for you. She knows how much you like them."

"Mom, I have to go upstairs."

"He's probably sleeping. Mrs. Reynolds says he needs his sleep. Let's sit down and talk about pleasant things, all right?"

"Oh, let him go on upstairs, Momma," Boone said silkily, watching Rix. "After he sees what Daddy looks like, he can go write himself another one of those horror—"

"*You shut your mouth!*" Margaret whirled toward him. "You're a cruel boy, Boone Usher! At least your brother wants to pay his respects to Walen, which is more than you'll do!" Boone looked away from his mother's wrath, and muttered something under his breath.

Rix said, "I'd better go up." Tears glinted like tiny diamonds in his mother's eyes, and he reached out to touch her cheek.

"Don't," she said, quickly pulling her head back. "You'll muss my hair."

He slowly withdrew his hand. It never changes here, he thought. They draw you in some way or another, and then they try to crush the feelings out of you, like stepping on a bug. He shook his head and walked past her, out of the living room and along the hallway to the central staircase. It wound upward to bedrooms and parlors that had been used by Teddy Roosevelt, Woodrow Wilson, Herbert Hoover, and a score of government and Pentagon luminaries, both famous and infamous.

As he climbed the stairs, dread at seeing his father gnawed at

38

his insides. He didn't know what to expect. Why did Walen want to see him, he wondered. The old man hated him for leaving Usherland, and Rix despised what Usher Armaments stood for. What could they possibly have to talk about now?

On the second floor, the smell of decay was stronger. He passed by his old room without pausing to look inside. Brightly colored flowers and greenery were placed in crystal vases all along the corridor, in a vain attempt to mask the stench. Moody oil paintings—including *War Clouds* by Victor Hallmark, *After the Battle* by Rutledge Taylorson, and *Blood on the Snow* by George H. Nivens—lined the walls as testimonial to Walen Usher's bleak taste in art. At the end of the corridor, another staircase ascended to a single white door—the Gatehouse's Quiet Room.

Rix stood at the foot of the stairs, gathering his courage. The odor of decomposition drifted around him, a foul miasma. Nothing that smelled like that, Rix thought, could still be alive.

The last time Rix had seen his father, Walen Usher had been the tall, ramrod-straight figure of authority that Rix knew from his childhood. Age had done nothing to diminish the power of his gaze or the strength of his voice, and his rugged, rough-hewn features might have been those of a man in his early forties except for swirls of gray at his temples and a few deepening lines across his high, aristocratic forehead. Walen Usher's jaw jutted like the prow of a battleship, and his mouth was a thin grim line that rarely broke into a smile.

Rix had never been able to understand how his father's mind worked. They had no common ground, no means of easy communication. Walen ran the estate and the business with a dictator's firm control. He had always kept his various business projects a secret from the family, and when Rix had been a child, there were long periods of time when Walen locked himself into his study and didn't come out. Rix knew only that a lot of military men visited his father behind locked doors.

When Walen was around, he treated his children as if they were soldiers in his private army. There were predawn military-style inspections, strict codes of conduct, dress, and manners, and savage verbal attacks if his children failed in any way. His most vicious assaults had been against Rix, when the boy was deemed lazy or uncooperative.

If Rix "talked back," failed to keep his shoes brightly polished, was late to the dinner table, or committed some other infraction of the unwritten rules, then the broad leather strap that his father called the Peacemaker raised red welts across his legs and buttocks—usually with Boone smirking in the same room, behind Walen's shoulder. Boone, on the other hand, was a master at playing the perfect son, always dressed immaculately, always neat and clean and fawning around his father. Kattrina had learned the art of bending to whatever wind Walen blew, and so escaped much of the abuse. Margaret, ever busy with planning parties and charity events, knew it was best to stay out of Walen's way, and had never taken Rix's side against him. Rules, she would say, were rules.

Once, Rix had seen Walen knock a servant to the floor and kick him in the ribs for some imagined dereliction of duty. If Edwin hadn't intervened, Walen might have killed the man. Sometimes, late at night when the rest of the house had gone to sleep, Rix had lain in his bed and heard his father walking the corridor outside his room, pacing back and forth in some mindless expenditure of nervous energy. He feared the night when his father would throw open his door and set on him, rage burning in his eyes, with the same fury that had made him break the servant's ribs.

But in mellow moods, Walen would summon Rix to his huge bedroom, where the walls were painted dark red and the furnishings were heavy black Victorian monstrosities brought from the Lodge, and order Rix to read to him from the Bible. What Walen wanted to hear were not chapters that had to do with spiritual things, but instead were long, tongue-twisting lineages: who begat who begat who. He demanded them over and over again, and sometimes the ebony cane he carried would smack the floor with impatience when Rix stumbled over the names.

When he was ten, Rix had run away from home after a particularly nasty meeting with the Peacemaker. Edwin had found him at the Trailways bus station in Foxton; they'd had a long talk, and as Rix collapsed into tears, Edwin held him and promised that Walen would never hit him again, so long as Edwin lived. The vow had remained intact for all these years, though Walen's taunts had increased. Rix was still the failure, the black sheep, the weakling who whined that the Ushers had thrived and gotten fat on generations of the dead.

Rix's heart was pounding as he forced himself up the steps. A hand-lettered sign had been taped to the door: TAP QUIETLY. Beside the door was a table bearing a box of green surgical masks.

He put his hand on the doorknob and then abruptly drew it back. Corruption oozed out of that room; he could feel it, like furnace

40

heat. He didn't know if he could take what was waiting in there for him, and suddenly his resolve slipped away. He started back down the stairs.

But in another second the decision was made for him.

The knob turned from the other side, and the door opened.

3

A uniformed nurse with a surgical mask over the lower half of her face peered from the Quiet Room at Rix. She wore skintight surgical gloves as well. Above the mask her eyes were dark brown and set in webs of wrinkles.

A wave of decay rolled out of the Quiet Room and struck Rix with almost tangible force. He gripped the banister tightly, his teeth clenched.

Mrs. Reynolds whispered, "A mask should help," and motioned toward the box.

He put one on. The inside was scented with mint, but it was not much help.

"Are you Rix?" She was a big-boned woman, possibly in her mid-forties, with curly iron-gray hair cut short. Rix noted that her eyes were faintly bloodshot.

"Of course it's Rix, you damned fool!" came the hoarse, barely human rasp from the darkness. Rix stiffened. His father's melodic voice had degenerated to an animal's growl. "I told you it would be Rix, didn't I? Let him in!"

Mrs. Reynolds opened the door wider for him. "Quickly," she said. "Too much light hurts his eyes. And remember, please keep your voice as soft as possible."

Rix stepped into the high-ceilinged, rubber-walled room. There were no windows. The only light came from a small green-shaded Tensor lamp on a table next to the chair where Mrs. Reynolds had been sitting. It cast a low-wattage circle of illumination that extended for only a foot or so into the room. He had an instant to see his father's grim bedroom furniture arranged in the room before Mrs. Reynolds closed the heavy rubber-lined door, sealing off the corridor's light.

He'd seen his father's canopied bed. There had been something lying in that bed, within a clear plastic oxygen tent. Rix thanked God the door had closed before he'd been able to see it too well.

In the darkness he could hear the soft chirping of an oscilloscope. The machine was just to the left of his father's bed; he saw the pale green zigzag of Walen Usher's labored heartbeat. His father's breathing was a pained, liquid gasping. Silk sheets rustled on the bed.

"Do you need anything, Mr. Usher?" the nurse whispered.

"No," the agonized voice replied. "Don't shout, goddamn it!"

Mrs. Reynolds returned to her chair, leaving Rix to fend for himself. She continued where she'd left off in her Barbara Cartland novel.

"Come closer," Walen Usher commanded.

"I can't see where I'm—"

There was a sharp inhalation. "*Softly!* Oh God, my ears . . ."

"I'm sorry," Rix whispered, unnerved.

The oscilloscope had started chirping faster. Walen didn't speak again until his heartbeat had slowed down. "Closer. You're about to stumble into a chair. Step to your left. Don't trip over that cable, you idiot! More to the left. All right, you're five paces from the foot of the bed. Damn it, boy, do you have to *stomp*?"

When Rix reached the bed, he could feel the fever radiating from his father's body. He gripped one of the canopy sheets and felt sweat trickling down under his arms.

"Well, well," Walen said. Rix could sense himself being examined. The silk sheets rustled again, and a form slowly shifted on the bed. "So you've come home, have you? Turn around. Let me look at you."

"I'm not a prize horse," Rix mumbled to himself under his breath.

"You're not a prize son, either. You don't fill out those clothes, Rix. What's wrong with you? Doesn't writing put enough food on your table?"

"I'm all right."

Walen grunted. "Like hell you are." He was silent, and Rix heard the gurgling of fluid in his lungs. "I'm sure you recall this room, don't you? It used to shelter you, Boone, and Kattrina whenever you had attacks. Where do you go now?"

"There's a closet I use in my apartment. I've got egg cartons stapled to the walls to muffle sound, and I've fixed the door so light can't get in."

42

"I'll bet you've got it looking like a womb. Something about you always craved a return to the womb."

Rix let the remark go. The darkness and smell of corruption pressed on him. The sickening heat from his father's body glared in his face like sunlight off metal. "Where do Katt and Boone go, now that you've moved in up here?"

"Boone's built his own Quiet Room, a chamber next to his bedroom. Katt's cut a hole in the wall behind her closet. They don't have many attacks. They don't understand what I'm going through in here, Rix. They've always lived at Usherland, where it's safe. But you—you understand what hell can be like, don't you?"

"I don't have that many attacks."

"No? What would you call that experience you endured yesterday in New York?"

"Boone told you?"

"I heard him telling Margaret, down in the living room last night. You forget how much I *can* hear, Rix. I heard you talking downstairs with them. I heard you climbing the stairs. I can hear your heartbeat right now. It's racing. Sometimes my senses are more acute than at other times; it comes in waves. But you understand what I mean, don't you? Ushers can't survive for very long beyond the gates of Usherland; it's a fact I'm sure you're beginning to appreciate."

Rix's eyes were getting used to the darkness. Lying on the bed before him, beneath the folds of the oxygen tent, was something that looked like a brown stick-figure, horribly emaciated. It lay motionless—but when one bony, shriveled arm reached out to draw the silk sheet closer, a shiver rippled up Rix's spine. A little more than a year ago, Walen Usher had stood over six feet and weighed one hundred eighty-five pounds. The shape on the bed couldn't possibly weigh more than half that.

"Don't stare at me," Walen rasped. "Your time'll come."

A knot clogged Rix's throat. When he could find his voice, he said, "It doesn't appear that living at Usherland all your life has made a difference for you, one way or the other."

"You're wrong. I'm sixty-four years old. My time is almost up. Look at yourself! You could be my brother instead of my son. Every year you live outside the gates of Usherland, your health will continue to erode. Your attacks will get worse. Soon that little womb won't be enough. You'll try to hide in there one day, and you'll realize too late you've overlooked a chink of light. You'll go blind and mad in there, with no one to help you. Before this"—his voice dripped with disgust—"I hadn't suffered an attack for five years. Hudson Usher knew that the air here, the peace and solitude, would be a balm to the Malady. He built this estate so his ancestors could live long, full lives. We have our own world here. You're insane to want to live anywhere else—or you're intent on committing slow suicide."

"I left because I wanted to make my own way."

"Of *course*." There was a liquid rush and gurgle from beneath the bed. Bodily waste, Rix realized. Walen was hooked up to tubes that carried his fluids away. "Yes, you've certainly 'made your way.' You wrote advertising copy in some Atlanta department store for a while. Then you took a job selling books. And after that you were a copy editor on some local tabloid. Magnificent occupations, one and all. And let's not forget the progress of your personal life. Shall we discuss your misbegotten marriage and its aftermath?"

Rix's jaw clenched. He felt as if he were a child again, and being whipped by the Peacemaker.

"I'll spare you that, then. Let's talk about your literary achievements. Three pieces of jibbering nonsense. I understand that last book of yours was on the best-seller lists for a short time. As they say, if you put a monkey in a room with a typewriter long enough, he'll eventually produce Shakespearean sonnets." He paused, letting the pain of the lashings sink in. As a child, Rix had fought against crying when the Peacemaker was in use, but the pain ultimately won. *Had enough?* Walen would ask, and when Rix remained stubbornly silent the belt would whistle again. Walen said offhandedly, "Those books of yours probably drove your wife to suicide, you know."

Rix felt his control snap like a splintering bone. His mouth twisted under the mask, and the blood roared in his ears. "How does it feel to be dying, Dad?" he heard himself ask in an acid voice. "You're about to lose everything, aren't you? The estate, the business, the Lodge, the money. None of it will be worth a damn when you're dust in a box, will it?" The oscilloscope had begun singing, and across the room Mrs. Reynolds nervously cleared her throat. Rix went on, "You're going to be dead soon, and no one's going to care—except maybe those bloodsuckers in the Pentagon. You deserve each other. God knows, the Usher name makes me sick to my stomach!"

The skeleton on the bed hadn't moved. Suddenly, Walen lifted his skinny arms and softly clapped his hands together twice. "Very

44

dramatic," he whispered. "Very heartfelt. But don't you worry about my dying, Rix. I'll let go when I choose, not before. Until then, I'll be right here."

"I just can't seem to learn that things never change here, can I? I think I've stayed for too long already." He started to move away from the bed.

"No. Wait." It was a command, and in spite of his anger, Rix obeyed. "There's something more I have to say."

"Say it, then. I'm leaving."

"As you please. But you've misjudged me, son. I've always had your best interests at heart."

Rix almost laughed. "*What?*" he asked incredulously.

"I *am* a human being, no matter what you think. I have feelings. I've made mistakes. But I've also understood my destiny, Rix, and I've prepared for it. Only . . . it's come upon me so fast, so fast." He paused as more fluids rushed through the tubes. "The indignity of death is the worst of it," he said softly. "I watched my father die like this. I knew what was ahead for me, as well as for my children. You can't turn your back on your Usher heritage, no matter how hard you try."

"I'm going to do my best."

"Are you? *Really?*" Walen's hand came out from under the sheet and moved to a small panel beside the bed. He began pressing buttons, and a series of television screens lit up on a console that had been built into the wall. The screens' contrast and brightness had been turned very low, so as not to hurt Walen's eyes, but Rix could make out the interior of the estate's Roman-styled natatorium, the indoor tennis courts, the helipad and the helicopter hangar behind the Gatehouse, the interior of the garage with its collection of antique automobiles, and a view of Usherland's front gates. The closed-circuit cameras panned slowly back and forth. "The Usher life doesn't have to be unpleasant," Walen said. "Look what we have here. Our own world. The freedom to do as we please, when we please. And we have influence, Rix—influence you've never even dreamt of."

"Do you mean the power to blow whole countries off the map?" Rix asked sharply. In the increased illumination he saw the smiling skull of his father's face from the corner of his eye. He dared not look too closely.

"Come now. Ushers only design and build the weapons. We don't aim them. It's nothing that Colt didn't do, or Winchester, or

45

a hundred other men with vision. We've just taken the process a few steps further."

"From flintlock muskets to laser guns. What's next? A weapon to murder babies in their mothers' wombs? Something to kill them before they grow up to be enemy soldiers?"

The skull grinned. "You see? I always knew you were the most creative of my children."

"I'll stick to writing."

The television screens began to go dark. "Your mother needs you," Walen said.

"She's got Boone and Katt."

"Boone has other concerns. That wife of his has made him unstable. And Katt may pretend to be tough, but her emotions are like crystal. Your mother needs a shoulder to lean on right now. Jesus Christ! What's that hissing noise I keep hearing? It sounds as if it's coming from somewhere downstairs!"

"Mother's spraying Lysol." Rix was amazed that his father could detect the distant noise.

"It aggravates the piss out of me! Tell her to stop it. She needs *you*, Rix. Not Boone or Katt. You."

"What about Cass and Edwin?"

"They have the estate to look after. Damn it, boy! I won't beg you! This is the last thing I'll ever ask of you! Stay here, for your mother's sake!"

Rix had been caught off guard; he hadn't expected such an open appeal from his father. But here he was, back at Usherland, with the run of the estate and time on his hands—what better opportunity, then, to pursue the idea that had sparked in his mind in New York? The Gatehouse had a large library; there might be something of use in there. He would have to be careful. Though he'd mentioned his idea casually to Cass the last time he'd been home, he didn't want anyone knowing he was seriously considering it.

"All right," Rix agreed. "Only a few days. I can't stay any longer."

"That's all I ask."

Rix nodded. The skeleton on the bed shifted painfully. There was something on the bed beside him. Rix stared at it for a moment before he realized it was the Usher cane with the silver lion's head, the symbol of the Usher patriarch. Walen's crablike hand closed around it.

"You can go now," Walen told him shortly.

My appointment's over, Rix thought. He turned abruptly away

46

from the bed and groped to the door. Mrs. Reynolds put aside her book and rose to let him out.

The muted stairway light stung his eyes. He ripped the surgical mask from his face and dropped it into a stainless-steel trashcan. His clothes reeked of rot.

He descended the stairs on shaky legs, but halfway down an overwhelming dizziness struck him. He had to stop as the world spun around. There were cold specks of sweat on his face, and he braced for an attack. But then it passed, and he took several deep breaths to clear his head.

When he was ready to walk again, he went along the corridor and found Edwin waiting for him. Edwin didn't have to ask about his reaction to seeing Walen; Rix's face looked like a sheet of waxed paper.

Edwin cleared his throat. "Have you seen your room yet?"

"No. Why?" The last time he'd slept in there, it was comfortable but nothing special. All his old furniture had long since been taken out to make way for an elaborate bed, a chest of drawers, a rosewood dresser, and a marble-topped table brought from the Lodge.

Edwin opened the door for him.

Rix stopped as if he'd walked into a glass wall.

The room had been changed back again. The ostentatious furniture had departed. In its place was a familiar, battered pinewood desk topped with a green blotter and a beat-up Royal typewriter— his first typewriter, the one he'd pounded out monster stories on when he was ten years old; his own chest of drawers, decorated with a hundred decals from airplane model kits; his bed, with the carved headboard that he'd pretended was a spaceship's instrument panel; even the dark green rug that looked like forest moss. It was all the same, right down to the brass lamps on the desk and bedside table. Rix was amazed. He had the eerie sensation of stepping backward in time, and thought that if he opened the closet door he might find Boone—a smaller Boone, but no less tricky—crouched in there among the boy-sized suits and shoes, waiting to leap out and scream *"Pumpkin Man!"* at the top of his lungs.

"My God," Rix said.

"Your mother insisted that all these items be taken out of storage in the Lodge and returned," Edwin said with a helpless shrug.

"I can't believe this! It's exactly the way the room looked when I was ten years old!"

"She wanted to make sure you were comfortable. It was all done overnight."

Rix entered the room. Everything was the same. Even the blue and green checked bedspread. "How did she remember what was in here? I didn't think she ever paid that much attention to my room."

"Cass and I helped her."

Rix opened the bottom drawer of the chest, half hoping to find the three stacks of vintage Batman comics he'd saved and then, stupidly, thrown away when he thought he'd outgrown them. The drawer was empty, as were all the others. The smell of mothballs wafted out. Atop the chest was something Rix had all but forgotten— a small carved wooden box. Rix opened it and felt like a kid again; inside was an assortment of polished stones, marbles, and old coins. His collection had remained intact over the years. He gently closed the lid of what he'd called his "treasure box" and went to the closet. His garment bag and suitcase were inside.

"Is it all right? Your mother wants to know."

"I guess it's fine. I still can't believe this! She went a little overboard, didn't she?"

"It's her way of showing you how pleased she is that you're back," Edwin said. "And I am too, Rix. Cass and I have missed you more than you'll ever know." He touched Rix's shoulder gently.

"Is Cass in the kitchen? I'd like to see her."

"No, she drove over to the farmer's market in Foxton for some fresh vegetables. She's making a Welsh pie for you tonight. Uh . . . you did bring a coat and tie, didn't you?"

Rix smiled thinly. "I knew that if I didn't I wouldn't be allowed to eat." His mother barred from the dining room anyone who wasn't wearing what she considered civilized clothing. "She'll never change, will she?"

"Your mother was brought up to be a lady," Edwin said diplomatically. "She has certain standards. But please, Rix—remember that she's under a terrible strain right now."

"I'll be on my best behavior," Rix promised.

"We'll talk later, then. I want to hear about your newest book. What's its title? *Bedlam*?"

"Right." He had explained the plot of *Bedlam* to Edwin one night during a long telephone call about six months before, and he remembered Edwin's silence when he had gone into detail about the carved-up bodies hanging in the apartment building's basement. Edwin did his best to be enthusiastic about Rix's writing projects, though Rix knew his taste ran to American history and biographies.

When Edwin had left him, Rix put his suitcase on the bed and opened it. Inside, amid the clothes, were a dozen bottles of vitamins. He'd begun consuming megadoses more than three years ago, when he'd looked in the mirror and seen himself aging almost supernaturally fast. He thought that if he took enough vitamins his appetite would pick up. Still, he ate barely enough to keep a bird alive. He thought that they were doing some good, though. At least his hair had stopped falling out in clumps.

In the bathroom, he drew tap water into a glass and downed several capsules from each bottle.

"Welcome home," he said to the old man in the mirror.

Two

THE
MOUNTAIN
BOY

4

The sun was descending in an orange slash across the horizon. A chilly wind had strengthened, whispering through the pines, scarlet oaks, and dense whorls of inch-long thorns on Briartop Mountain.

A fifteen-year-old mountain boy named Newlan Tharpe stood on the smooth, jutting boulder he knew as The Devil's Tongue. In each hand he held a plastic bucket brimming with blackberries. His fingers, lips, and chin were stained vivid blue; his alert, dark green eyes were fixed on the vista almost seven hundred feet below.

The thick forests and black lakes of Usherland were dappled with deep shadow and orange light, like an intricate quilt woven with Halloween colors. And on an island at the center of the largest lake stood the biggest house in the world. Usher's Lodge, it was called. New had decided long ago that the whole town of Foxton could fit inside it, and there'd still be room for a horse ranch. His ma said even the Ushers themselves couldn't stand to live in it, and the house had been empty for a long time—except for the thing that dwelled in it, all alone, in the dark.

But what that thing was, she would not say.

For a few minutes now, the dying sun would paint the Lodge's walls the color of fire. New could see the sparks of light on the dozens of weathervanes and lightning rods mounted on the slanted slate roofs. On a granite ledge running beneath the roofs were statues of lions, some resting, some stalking. When the sun caught them just right, as it did now, the tawny marble cats seemed to stretch and move, pacing the ledge as if guarding their territory.

New watched a flock of six wild ducks feeding in the high weeds on the lake's northern shore. The lake was ebony even in bright sunlight, and in all the many times he'd come to this place to look down, he'd never seen a fish jump from its surface.

The Lodge took up almost the entire island. A stone bridge over the lake connected it to one of Usherland's paved roads. Once, after a particularly hard rain, New had come here and seen the water lapping against the Lodge's foundations. He let his mind wander over the blue mountains that were the boundary of his world, and he always came back to the same question: What would life have been like, he wondered, if his ma had been an Usher instead of a Tharpe? What if he'd been able to roam those forests, ride horses across the gentle green slopes, see that massive Lodge from the inside? Sometimes he felt a stirring of envy when he saw figures on horseback down there, riding the forest trails. Though he lived on the northern edge of Usherland, he knew he might as well be a hundred miles away. He saw the Lodge in his dreams, and his yearnings to enter it were getting stronger; he never told his ma about the feelings, though. She forbade him and his ten-year-old brother, Nathan, to follow any of the meandering paths from Briartop deeper into Usherland. It was a haunted place, she said. The Ushers were a depraved breed best left alone.

With the Pumpkin Man and his black familiar running in the woods, New kept his curiosity about the Lodge in check. Though he'd never seen any of them, he knew the tales by heart. There were things in the woods that roamed at night, things that should be avoided at all costs. He'd found large, bestial footprints in the soil before, and once on a cold January night he'd heard something big moving on the cabin's roof. He'd taken a flashlight and Pa's shotgun outside—because now he was the man of the house, no matter how scared he was—and had shone the light up on the roof, but there was nothing there at all.

Suddenly he saw the ducks flap their wings and rise from the lake almost as one. They made a V formation and began to fly across the lake, passing the Lodge.

Fly faster, New thought. *Faster.*

The ducks gained altitude.

Hurry, he urged them mentally. Hurry, before it wakes up and—

The ducks' formation was suddenly disturbed, as if by turbulence in the air. Four of them flapped wildly as they began to spin in a confused whirlpool. The other two dropped lower, skimming across the surface of the lake.

Hurry, he thought, and held his breath.

The four ducks veered off course, toward the Lodge's mountainous north face.

54

One after the other, they smashed into the wall and cascaded down in a shower of feathers, where they lay amid the rotting carcasses of other birds and wildfowl.

New heard the distant calling of one of the ducks that had escaped—then silence, but for the prowling wind. The Lodge had no windows; all of them—hundreds, in what had been every conceivable shape and size—were bricked up. New guessed why: over the years, birds had probably smashed all the glass out, and the Ushers had decided to seal them over.

"Gettin' dark," Nathan said, standing beside his brother. He carried a single bucket heaped with blackberries, and he kept snapping that doggoned blue whistling yo-yo that Ma had bought him in Foxton. "Better be gettin' home, or Ma'll pitch a fit."

"Yep," New replied, though he didn't retreat from the Tongue's edge. He kicked a loose stone off into space. They'd been picking blackberries for the better part of the afternoon. Ma used them in the pies she baked for the Broadleaf Cafe in Foxton. They hadn't had to pass near The Devil's Tongue, but New had wandered this way, and had been standing here for ten minutes, staring down at the Lodge. Corpses of birds lay like snow on the many balconies. Perched atop the Lodge, among the chimneys and turrets, was something that looked like a huge discolored lightbulb, opaque and dirty. Why was that house so godawful big, he wondered, and why did he feel the need to come here, day after day, as if in answer to the dreams that beckoned him at night? He saw one of the ducks still jerking at the base of the house, and turned away. The image of the Lodge, bathed in fading sunlight, stayed in his mind. "Okay," he said. "I guess we'd best get home."

"Gotta hurry, too. Gettin' dark."

They left the Tongue—New looked back for only a few seconds—and started walking along the narrow, rocky path that would eventually lead them home, about a mile and a half away. They were supposed to have been home long before dark, and they would have been, New realized, if he hadn't wanted to stop at the Tongue. Some man of the house, he thought.

The families who lived on Briartop's winding dirt roads had been there for generations. Nestled in shady hollows or clearings where the wilderness had been forced back were several hundred clapboard cabins, just like the one owned by the Tharpes. Briartop was a massive mountain with a rocky peak collared by a jungle of thorns. Those thorns, some said, could creep around you when your back was turned, could trap you so you'd never find your way out again. It was well known that many hunters who'd gone out after the deer on Briartop had been seized and buried by the thorns, and even their bones were swallowed up.

Briartop was part of Usherland, and stood on the northern edge of the thirty-thousand-acre estate. The families inhabiting it were of hardy Scots-Irish stock; they protected their privacy and lived on an abundant supply of deer, rabbits, and quail. Outsiders—anyone who did not live on the mountain—were quickly run off by a few warning shots, but then again, outsiders had no use for the mountain, either. The hardships of mountain life were understood, and taken as part of life. Still, the people stayed away from untrodden paths, and made sure their doors were bolted after sundown.

"I woulda got as many berries as you if I'da had another bucket!" Nathan said as they walked. "I coulda filled up three buckets!"

"You cain't carry but one bucket without spillin' the other," New told him. "Like last time."

"Can so!"

"Cain't."

"Can so!"

"Cain't."

The yo-yo, Nathan's prized possession, whistled impudently.

New noted that their shadows were getting longer. Darkness was going to catch them, for sure. They should've started for home an hour ago, he thought, but they'd eaten a lot of the blackberries as they picked them, and the sun had felt so good on their backs that they'd forgotten about time. It was harvest season—and that meant the Pumpkin Man might be near.

He comes out when the pumpkins are on the ground, New's ma had told him; he can ride the wind and slither through the brush, and he comes up on you so fast you'll never know he's there until it's too late . . .

"Let's walk faster," New said.

"You got longer legs than me!"

"Quit playin' with that damn yo-yo!"

"I'm gonna tell Ma you cussed!" Nathan warned.

A strong cold wind had risen, sweeping past the boys and stirring the thick foliage on either side of the path. New shivered, though he was wearing his brown sweater, patched jeans, and a brown corduroy jacket that used to be his pa's. The man-smell was still in it, the aroma of bay rum and a corncob pipe.

56

New was tall for his age. He looked a lot like his father, lean and rawboned, with a sharp nose and chin, a scatter of freckles across his cheeks, and reddish brown hair that curled over his ears and collar. His eyes were large and expressive, and at the same time curious and wary. He was at an awkward age, and he knew it. Standing at the gate of manhood, New couldn't decide whether he wanted to rush through or back away. Nathan, on the other hand, resembled their mother more. His frame was smaller, and he had a pale complexion, except for two ruddy spots on his cheeks. The kids at the school on the other side of the mountain picked on him because he was little, and New had busted more than one boy in the chops for taunting his little brother.

New stopped to wait for him. "Come on, Christmas!" He was trying to keep his voice calm, though unease was tickling his belly. The darkness was spreading like a blanket over Briartop. Ma said the Pumpkin Man had eyes that shone in the dark.

"Quit walkin' so fast!" Nathan complained. "If we hadn't stayed so long at the—"

There was a sharp squeaking cry. Suddenly the air around Nathan's head was filled with fluttering forms that had burst from the underbrush. The smaller boy let out a startled holler and dodged, dancing in a circle. Something was in his hair. He cried out, "Bats!" and flung the blackberry bucket at them in scared desperation. They scattered and wheeled into the sky.

New had been almost startled out of his britches, but now he watched the things flying away and laughed at his own quick jig of fear. "Quail," he said. "You scared up a covey of 'em!"

"They were bats!" Nathan insisted defiantly. "They got in my hair!"

"Quail."

"Bats!" He wasn't going to admit that a few measly quail had made his heart knock like a woodpecker. "Big ones, too!" He still had the yo-yo in his hand, but suddenly he realized he'd flung the blackberry bucket into the woods. "My berries!"

"Oh Lordy. I bet you threw blackberries from here to Asheville." They were all over the path.

"Ma'll skin me if I don't bring that bucket home!" He started searching through the brush, saying "ouch" every time a thorn nicked his fingers.

"No, she won't. Come on, we've gotta get—" He stopped when Nathan looked at him. His brother was about to cry from frustration;

he'd worked hard all afternoon, and now a few quail had made him mess everything up. Life took a mischievous delight in tormenting Nathan. "All right," New said, and set his buckets down. "I'll help you look."

The shadows were deepening. New pushed into the brush, thorns jabbing at his clothes. "Why'd you do that?" he asked angrily. "That was a stupid thing to do!"

" 'Cause they was bats and they was tanglin' in my hair, that's why!"

"*Quail*," New said pointedly. He saw something a few feet away and approached it. Snagged in the thorns was a bleached-out piece of cloth. It looked as if it might once have been a shirt. A thorn scraped New's cheek, and he swore softly. "I don't know where the thing went! It might've gone to the doggone moon, the way—"

He took another step forward, and the ground went out from under his feet.

He fell, his body tearing through kudzu vines, dense weeds, and ropes of thorns.

He heard Nathan cry out his name, and then he heard the sound of his own screaming.

He'd stepped over the edge of the mountain, he realized. He was going to fall to his death.

Then he was rolling over and over, his flailing hands being torn by thorns. The back of his head smashed into something hard—*a rock . . . hit a rock . . . damn it, my head!*—and he didn't know anything else until he heard Nathan calling his name from above.

New lay still. He was gasping for breath, and there was blood in his mouth.

". . . hear me, New? Can you hear me?" Nathan's voice was frantic.

Tears of pain coursed down New's cheeks. He couldn't see, and when he tried to wipe his eyes he couldn't get his arms free. He was hung in something. There was the strong odor of earth—and a sharper, sweeter smell. The aroma of something dead, very close to him.

"Nathan?" he called. Didn't think he'd spoken above a whisper. "*Nathan?*" Louder.

"You all right?"

Just fine, he thought, and almost laughed. Every joint in his body was on fire. He wrenched his right arm as hard as he could, and heard cloth rip; then he wiped the wetness and gummy dirt from his eyes, and he saw in the faint purple light where he was.

He hadn't stepped off Briartop, but only into a hollow that had

58

been hidden by underbrush. It was about thirty-five feet deep, he figured, with steeply sloping dirt walls, and angled down into darkness. New was caught in a barbed-wire prison of thorns that had tangled around his chest and legs, manacling his left arm at the wrist. Ugly, inch-long barbs curled all around him, in loops and coils and knots. If he moved, he realized with a shock of fear, they might grab him even tighter.

But the worst part was what lay caught in the thorns with him.

There were moldering carcasses in various stages of decay, from fresh bloat to yellow bone. A stag's skeleton reared its rack of horns toward the sky, hopelessly tangled. There were raccoon, skunk, fox, snake, and bird bones everywhere. A fresh deer carcass was tangled on his right; it had recently burst open. As New twisted his head to the left, barbs scraped across his neck.

Not six feet away, enmeshed in the tangle, was a human skeleton. It wore the rags of a red flannel shirt, fringed buckskin pants, and boots. Its mouth gaped wide, as though in a final gasp or scream. Thorns grew along the spine, kudzu vines burst through cracks in the skull. The skeleton's right arm was twisted backward at a sharp angle, the bone clearly snapped. Several feet away was a rusted rifle, and the hunter wore an empty knife sheath around his waist.

New struggled violently to free himself. The coils snaked more firmly around his chest.

"Help!" he shouted. "Nathan! Go get help!" His head throbbed mercilessly.

Nathan didn't respond for a few seconds. Then: "I'm scairt, New. I thought I heard somethin' just then. Somethin' walkin'."

"Go get help! Get Ma! Hurry, Nathan!" A thorn was spiked deeply into his cheek.

"I *heard* somethin', New!" The boy's voice was shaking. "It's gettin' closer!"

The moon was rising. Like a pumpkin, New thought—and he went cold inside. "Run," he whispered. Then he shouted, "Run home, Nathan! Go on! *Run home!*"

When Nathan's voice came floating back, there was new determination in it. "I'll run get Ma! I'll save you, New! You'll see!" There was the sound of him struggling through the brush, and then a faint cry—"*You'll see!*"—and silence.

The wind moved. Dead leaves floated down into the hollow. New listened to the sound of his own harsh breathing. The smell of death wafted around him.

He didn't know how much later it was, but he suddenly shivered as a terrible, aching cold passed through his bones. Something was watching him—he could sense it as surely as a hound on the track of a redtailed fox. He looked up toward the lip of the pit, his heart pounding.

Touched by moonlight, a figure stood thirty-five feet above him, on the pit's edge. It was shrouded in black, and carried something that looked like a sack under its right arm.

New almost spoke—almost—but his blood had turned icy, and he knew what he was looking at.

The thing was motionless. New couldn't tell what it was, but it seemed . . . vaguely human. Whatever was under its arm didn't move, either, but New thought for a terrifying instant that the moonlight shone upon a white, upturned face. The face of a small boy.

New blinked.

The thing was gone. If it had ever been there. It had slipped noiselessly away in the space of a heartbeat.

"Nathan!" he shouted. He continued to call his brother's name until his voice was reduced to a weary whisper. In his soul he felt the same black despair as when he'd watched Pa's coffin being lowered into the ground.

Run, run as fast as you can, 'cause out in the woods walks the Pumpkin Man . . .

A shuddering cry of anguish left his lips. Around him, bones rattled when the cold wind swept past.

5

Rix was dressing for dinner. As he knotted his tie in front of the oval mirror above his chest of drawers, a gust of wind that scattered blood-red leaves against the north-facing windows caught his attention. The trees parted for an instant, like a fiery sea opening, and Rix saw the high roofs and chimneys of Usher's Lodge in the distance, tinted orange and purple in the fading light. The trees closed again.

He had to reknot his tie. His fingers had slipped.

When he was barely nine, he'd gone into the Lodge for the first and last time. Boone had goaded Rix into playing hide-and-seek inside. Rix had to do the seeking first. It was dark in there, but they'd had flashlights. Boone laid down the ground rules: there would be hiding only on the first floor in the main house, no use of the east and west wings. Close your eyes now, count to fifty! Rix had started hunting him when he reached thirty. There was no electricity in the Lodge because it had been uninhabited since 1945, and it was as silent as winter in there. And *cold*—the deeper he'd gone, the colder it had been. Which was strange, since it was the first of October and still warm outside. But the Lodge, he was certain now, repelled heat. It clutched within its winding corridors and maze of rooms the frozen ghosts of one hundred forty years of winters. It was always deep January inside the Lodge, a world of icy, remote magnificence.

Malengine, Rix thought. It was a word he'd been mulling over to use as the title of a book someday. It meant "evil machination" or, more literally, something constructed for an evil purpose. The Lodge was a malengine, built with the spoils of destruction, meant to shield the generations of murderers that Rix called his ancestors. If Usherland could be compared to a body, the Lodge was its malignant heart—silent now, but not stilled. Like Walen Usher, the Lodge listened, and brooded, and waited.

It had trapped him in its maw for almost forty-eight hours when he was nine years old, like a beast patiently trying to digest him. Sometimes Rix's mind slipped gears and he was back in that nine-year-old body, back in the Lodge's darkness after the weak batteries that Boone had put in his flashlight flickered out. He didn't remember very much of the ordeal, but he remembered that darkness—absolute and chilling, a monstrous, silent force that first brought him to his knees and then made him crawl. He hadn't known it then, but two hundred rooms had been counted in the Lodge, and due to the madness—or cunning—of the floor plans, there were windowless areas that could not be reached by any corridor yet discovered. He thought he recalled falling down a long staircase and bruising his knees, but nothing was certain. All shadows that he tried to keep behind a bolted door.

He'd awakened in bed several days later. Edwin had gone inside, Cass told him afterward, and had found him wandering up on the second floor in the east wing. Rix had been all but sleepwalking through the Lodge, banging into walls and doors like a wind-up toy robot. God only knew how he'd kept from breaking his neck. From that time on he'd never stepped into the Lodge again.

The image of the bloody-eyed skeleton on its hook swung slowly through Rix's mind. He quickly shunted it aside. His head was aching dully. Boone had deliberately lured him into the Lodge and gotten him lost.

It amused Rix that Walen would let Boone have nothing to do with Usher Armaments. Boone had never even toured the plant, and Rix had no desire to. Though the racehorses seemed to be his primary occupation, Boone owned a talent agency with offices in Houston, Miami, and New Orleans. He was closemouthed about his business, but had bragged once to Rix that he handled "about a dozen Hollywood starlets so pretty they'd melt your pecker off."

If that was so, Rix had wondered, then why didn't Boone have an office in California? Rix had never visited any of his brother's offices—and was unlikely to be invited—but Boone apparently made a good deal of money from his agency. At least he dressed and talked the role of a successful businessman.

Nothing but writing had ever been even moderately successful for Rix. He had a few thousand dollars in savings, but he knew it would be gone soon enough. Then what? Find another poorly paying job that would last four or five months at the most? If he couldn't write another book—a best-seller—everything that Walen had ever said about his being a failure would turn out to be true, and he'd have to come crawling back to Usherland.

Rix tried to put his uncertainties out of his mind. He put on his tweed jacket and inspected a tear under his right sleeve, caused when he'd tumbled to the sidewalk in New York. Some of the lining was ripped, too, but he decided his mother wouldn't notice. He was as ready as he would ever be. He went downstairs.

On his way to the living room, he stopped to peer into the game room, with its two large billiard tables and antique aquamarine Tiffany lamps. Everything was still the same—except, he noted, for two new additions: Wizard's Quest and Defender arcade games. They were shoved discreetly into a corner, probably there for Boone's pleasure. He went through the game room into the "gentlemen's room," a high-ceilinged, oak-paneled parlor that still smelled faintly of cigar smoke. Oil paintings of hunting scenes adorned the walls, along with the stuffed heads of moose, rams, and wild boars. Standing in a corner was a seven-foot-tall grizzly bear that Teddy Roosevelt had supposedly shot on the estate. A grandfather clock with a beautiful brass pendulum struck softly seven times.

A pair of sliding oak doors stood on the other side of the gentlemen's room. Rix walked across to open them. His father's library lay beyond.

But the doors were securely locked.

"Have you seen your brother?"

Rix jumped like a child caught with his hand in the cookie jar. He turned toward his mother, who was wearing a shimmering gray evening gown. Her makeup and hair were perfect. "Nope," he said easily.

"I suppose he's gone over to the stables again, then." She frowned with disapproval. "If he's not spending his time clocking the horses, he's playing poker with those friends of his at the country club. I've told him time and again that they're ganging up on him to cheat him, but does he listen? Of course not." Her gaze sharpened. "Were you looking for something to read?"

"Not particularly, just poking around."

"Your father keeps the library locked now."

"It wasn't locked the last time I was here."

"It's locked," she repeated, "now."

"Why?"

"Your father was doing some research . . . before he got sick, I mean." There was a quicksilver flicker of distress in her eyes, then it was gone. "He had some books brought over from the Lodge's library. Evidently he doesn't want them to deteriorate any more than they already have."

"Research on what?"

She shrugged. "I have no earthly idea. Doesn't your brother know that we eat dinner at seven-thirty *sharp* in this house? I don't want him sitting at my dining room table smelling of horse perspiration!"

"I'm sure he'll smell like his nice malodorous self."

"Sarcasm never won any popularity contests, son," she told him firmly. "Well, I have to know if that little wife of his is going to join us tonight or not. She's gone a straight week of eating her dinner in bed."

"Why don't you just send a servant up to ask her?"

"Because," Margaret said icily, "Puddin' is *Boone's* responsibility. I won't have my servants bowing to her like she's a princess! I don't give a damn if she's too lazy to get out of bed to use the commode, but Cass would like to know how many places to set."

"I can't help you with that." He glanced once again at the library door's brass handles and then directed his attention to an elk's head on the wall above the fireplace.

Margaret said, "I trust you'll be on time for dinner. You look as if you can use a good, filling meal. A needle and thread would do wonders for that shabby coat, as well. Take it off after dinner and I'll have it fixed for you."

"Thanks."

"Come along when you're ready, then. We eat at seven-thirty in this house."

Left alone, Rix contemplated the locked doors again, and then went back the way he'd come to the main corridor. He walked past the living room and dining room, heading for the rear of the house.

In the large Gatehouse kitchen, where copper pots and utensils hung in orderly precision from hooks on the spotless, white-tiled walls, Rix stood at the doorway. He watched a short, rotund woman with gray hair checking a number of simmering pots on one of the ranges while she gave orders in a soft but firm voice to the two subordinate cooks who bustled about. An amazing warmth spread through him, and he realized at once just how much he'd missed Cass Bodane. One of the cooks glanced over her shoulder at him— and didn't recognize him—but then Cass turned toward him and froze.

Rix was prepared. Her oval, ruddy-cheeked face registered shock for only a fleeting second, and then a smile like sunshine took its place. Rix was sure Edwin had told her how bad he looked.

"Oh, Rix!" Cass said, and embraced him. The top of her head came only to his chin. Her warmth was as welcome as a cheerful hearth on a winter's night, and Rix felt his bones beginning to glow. Without this woman and her husband, Rix knew his life at Usherland would have been truly bleak. They lived in a white house behind the gardens and garage, and many times when he was a little boy, Rix had wished he could live in that house with them. Though they had an enormous responsibility, they'd never been too busy to spend a while listening to him, or giving him encouragement.

"It's so *good* to have you home again!" She pulled back to look at him; her clear blue eyes only flinched a fraction.

"If you say I look wonderful, I'll know you've been hitting the cooking sherry," he said with a smile.

"Don't you tease me!" She pushed affectionately at his chest, then took his hand. "Come sit down. Louise, bring two cups of coffee to the nook, please. One with cream and sugar, one with sugar only."

"Yes ma'am," one of the cooks said.

Cass led him out of the kitchen, through a door to the small room where the servants took their breaks. A table and chairs were set up here, and a window looked out toward the gardens, now illuminated by low-level floodlights. They sat down, and Louise brought their coffee.

"Edwin told me you were upstairs," Cass explained, "but I knew you needed your rest. How was New York?"

"Okay, I guess. Pretty noisy."

"Were you up there on business? Researching a new book?"

"No, I . . . had some things to take care of with my agent."

When she smiled, the deep lines surfaced around her eyes. She was a lovely woman at sixty-one, and Rix knew she had been a real knockout when she was a girl. He'd seen an old photograph Edwin carried in his wallet: Cass in her twenties, with long blond hair, a flawless complexion, and those eyes that could stop time. "Rix, that's so exciting!" she said, and covered his hand with her own. "I want to hear all about your new book!"

Bedlam was dead, he knew. There was no sense in trying to stir it from the grave. "I'd . . . like to tell you what I'm going to work on next," he said.

Her eyes brightened. "A new thriller? Oh, goody!"

"We talked about it before, the last time I was home." He braced himself, because he remembered her reaction. "I still want to do the history of the Ushers."

Cass's smile faded. She was silent, averting her gaze and toying with her coffee cup.

"I've been thinking about this for a long time," Rix continued. "I've even started the research."

"Oh? How?"

"I went to Wales after I finished *Fire Fingers*. I remembered that Dad told me Malcolm Usher owned a coal mine in the early 1800s. It took me two weeks, but I found what was left of it, near a village called Gosgarrie. It was boarded up, but a records clerk in the village dug up some documents on the Usher Coal Company. There'd been an explosion and cave-in around 1830. Malcolm, Hudson, and Roderick were touring the mine when it happened, and they were trapped in there." He expected her to look up at him, but she didn't. "Hudson and Roderick were rescued, but their father's corpse was never recovered. Evidently they were so torn up about his death that they came over to America, with Madeline."

Still, Cass didn't respond. "I want to know what my ancestors were like," Rix persisted. "What motivated them to create weapons? Why did they settle here, and why did they keep building onto the Lodge? Edwin's told me things about grandfather Erik, but what about the others?" Their portraits hung in the library, and he knew their names—Ludlow, Erik's father; Aram, Ludlow's father and Hudson's son—but he knew nothing of their lives. "What were the Usher women like?" Rix pressed on. "I know researching the book would be tough. I'd probably have to use my imagination on a lot of it, but I think it could be done."

She drank from her cup and held it between her palms. "Your father would put your head on top of a flagpole," she said softly.

"Don't you think people would like to know about the Usher family? It would be a history of the American weapons industry, too. Don't you think I could do it?"

"That's not the point. Mr. Usher has a right to privacy. Your entire family has, including your deceased ancestors. Are you sure you'd want strangers knowing everything that's gone on at Usherland?"

Rix knew Cass was referring to his grandfather Erik, who had a penchant for throwing wild parties where nude women served as centerpieces. At one party, Edwin had told him, all the guests rode horses inside the Lodge, and Erik required the servants to wear suits of armor and joust on the lakeshore for entertainment.

"Pardon me if I'm wrong," Cass said, and finally raised her eyes to his, "but I think you want to write that family history because you see it as striking out against your father and against the family business. You've already let him know how you feel. Can't you see how he respects you for daring to break the mold?"

"Are you kidding?"

"He's a proud man, and he won't ever admit that he's been wrong about you. He envies your independence. Mr. Usher could never break away from Erik. Someone had to take control of the business after Erik died. You shouldn't hate him because of that. Well . . . do as you please. You will anyway. But my advice is to let sleeping lions lie."

"I could write that book," Rix said firmly. "I know I could."

Cass nodded absently. It was clear she had something more to say, but she didn't know how to begin. Her mouth pressed into a tight line. "Rix," she said, "there's something you need to know. Oh dear, how can I say this?" She gazed out toward the gardens.

"There are so many changes in the wind, Rix, so many things in a state of passage. Oh hell! I was never any good at making speeches." Cass looked directly at him. "This is the last year for Edwin and myself at Usherland."

Rix's first impulse was to laugh. Surely she was kidding! The laugh stuck in his throat when her expression remained serious.

"It's time for us to retire." She tried to smile, but it wouldn't come. "Past time, really. We wanted to retire two years ago, but Mr. Usher talked Edwin out of it. Now we've saved enough money to buy a home in Pensacola. I've always wanted to live in Florida."

"I can't believe I'm hearing this! My God! You've been here all my life!"

"I know that. And it goes without saying that you've been like a son to us." There was pain in her eyes, and she had to pause for a moment to gather her thoughts. "Edwin can't get around the estate like he used to. Usherland needs a younger man's touch. We want to enjoy the sun, and Edwin wants to go deep-sea fishing. I want to wear sun hats." She smiled wistfully. "If I get bored with doing that, Edwin says I can open a small bake shop. It's time, Rix. It really is."

Rix was so stunned he could hardly think. What would Usherland be without Edwin and Cass? "Florida's . . . so far away."

"Not that far. They do have telephones down there, you know."

"But who'll take your places—as if anyone could?" Rix knew it had been a tradition, ever since Hudson's day, for the chief of staff of Usherland to be a Bodane. But since Cass and Edwin had no children, the next chief of staff would have to be an outsider.

"I know what you're wondering," Cass replied. "There's always been a Bodane in charge of Usherland. Well, Edwin wants to keep the tradition going. You've heard him mention his brother Robert, haven't you?"

"A couple of times." Edwin's brother had left the estate when he was a young man, but had settled on the other side of Foxton. Rix knew that Edwin visited him occasionally.

"Robert has a grandson named Logan. He's nineteen, and he's been working at the armaments plant for two years. Edwin believes he has the potential to take the job."

"A nineteen-year-old chief of staff? That's crazy!"

"Edwin was twenty-three when he took over from his father," Cass reminded him. "He's talked to Logan about this, and he believes Logan can do it. Mr. Usher has given his approval. Edwin's going to bring Logan here tomorrow or the day after to begin his training. Of course, if Logan decides he doesn't want to stay, we'll advertise for an outsider. And if there's any problem at all, he leaves."

"Have you met this kid?"

"Once. He seems to be intelligent, and he has an excellent work record at the plant."

Rix caught a trace of reticence in her voice. "Are you sold on him?"

"Honestly? No, I'm not. He's a little unpolished. I think he'll have to prove himself. But he's agreed to try it, and I think he should have the chance."

A buzzer went off in the kitchen. It was almost seven-thirty, and Margaret was summoning the servants to the dining room.

"I have to go." Cass rose quickly to her feet. Rix sat staring out at the gardens, and Cass touched his shoulder. "I'm sorry if this came as a shock to you, Rix, but it's for the best. It's the way things are. You'd better run along now. I've got a good, rich Welsh pie in the oven for you."

Rix left Cass working in the kitchen, and walked dazedly to the dining room. His mother was waiting alone at the long, gleaming mahogany table.

As one of the many clocks struck seven-thirty, and others echoed it, Boone strode through the doorway. His face was flushed, and there was racetrack dust in his eyebrows, but he'd dressed for dinner in a dark blue suit and striped necktie. "You look like crap on a cracker, Rixy," Boone said as he took his place across from Rix.

"Both of my fine boys are home," Margaret said, with a strained note of cheer. She bowed her head. "Let us give thanks for what we are about to receive."

6

The Pumpkin Man was in the woods.

He wore a funeral suit of black velvet and a black top hat. His face was as yellow as spoiled milk. He carried a scythe that glowed electric blue in the moonlight, and with a wave of one skeletal hand he parted the underbrush before him. Those who had seen him and lived to tell the tale said his eyes shone like green lamps; his face was split by a cunning grin, his teeth sharpened to tiny points.

The Pumpkin Man was used to waiting. He had all the time in the world. Sooner or later a child would wander from a familiar path, or chase a rabbit into a place where shadows slanted like tombstones. Then there would be no more going home, ever again.

He carried his weapon in an easy grip, and sniffed the night wind for the human scent. A small animal tore away through the weeds. The Pumpkin Man stood like a statue, his only movement the slow sweep of his gelid gaze through the darkness.

He looked toward the Gatehouse, where the Usher boy was sleeping. The Usher boy had come home again. If the Usher boy didn't come out to play tomorrow evening—then there would always be the next. Or the next. He stood beneath the Usher boy's window, staring upward. Come out, come out and play, he whispered in a voice like the wind through dead trees. You're the one I want, little Usher boy—

When Rix forced himself awake, his nerves were jangling like fire alarms. He sat up in bed. The walls of his room were crisscrossed with shadows—tree branches, outlined by moonlight. He'd never had such a vivid nightmare about the Pumpkin Man before. The thing had looked like a picture he'd seen of Lon Chaney in *London After Midnight*, all hypnotic eyes and vampire teeth. Got to cut down on those damned late-night "Creature Features," he told himself. They're not too good for the old beauty sleep, are—

A floorboard creaked.

There was a shape standing over his bed. Watching him.

Before Rix could react—he was about to cry out like a child—a smoky feminine voice that dripped with honey whispered, "Shhhhh! It's me, sugah!"

He found the switch to the bedside lamp after much fumbling, and turned it on. Squinting in the light, he looked up at Puddin' Usher, his brother's wife.

She wore a diaphanous pink gown that clung to her body as if she'd been poured into it. Showing through the filmy material were the dark circles of her nipples and the darker vee between her thighs. She was about as naked as a woman could be without taking off her clothes. Her heavy blond mane cascaded around her bared shoulders. Puddin' wore full makeup, including bright red lipstick and champagne eyeshadow. Her eyes were dark brown, as unfathomable as Usherland's peaty lakes. She'd put on perhaps ten pounds since Rix last saw her, but she was still beautiful in a wild, coarse way. Her figure, stuffed into a red swimsuit a size too small, had won her the title of Miss North Carolina several years ago. In Atlantic City, she had twirled flaming batons in the talent competition, and she hadn't even made the finals. Her full-lipped, sexy mouth always made her look as if she was begging to be kissed—the harder, the better. But now her mouth had a bitter twist to it. Her face was taking on a hardness. Her eyes were vacant, disturbed. Rix smelled a wave of perfume—Chanel No. 5?—coming off her, but underneath that fragrance was a complex aroma of bourbon and body odor. In fact, Puddin' smelled as if she hadn't taken a bath in a week or more.

"What are you doing in here? Where's Boone?"

"Gone bye-bye," she said, and her mouth twisted again as she smiled. "Gone to that club of his to play poker till all fuckin' hours."

Rix looked at his wristwatch on the bedside table. A quarter of three. He rubbed his eyes. "What happened? You two have a fight?"

She shrugged. "Me and Boone have fights sometimes." She spoke with a thick backhills whang. "He left around midnight. They let him sleep at that club after he's lost his money and he's too drunk to drive home."

"Do you make a habit of sneaking into people's rooms? You scared the hell out of me."

"I didn't sneak. Sneakin' is when a door's *locked*." There were no locks on the doors to Rix's, Boone's, or Katt's bedrooms. Puddin' frowned at him. "You're lookin' kinda puny. You been sick or somethin'?"

"Or something. Why don't you pour yourself into your room and go to sleep?"

"I want to talk. Please. I've got to talk to somebody, or I'll go right fuckin' out of my bird!"

Same old Puddin', Rix thought. When she was drunk, she could swear a truck driver's face blue. "What about?" he asked, against his better judgment.

"If you was a gentleman, you'd ask me to sit down."

He motioned reluctantly toward a chair. Puddin' chose to sit on the edge of the bed. Her gown hiked up over her thighs. There was a heart-shaped birthmark on her left knee. Damn, Rix thought; his body was responding, and he raised his knees under the sheet to make a tent. Puddin' picked at a long, copper-painted fingernail for a moment. "I cain't talk to nobody 'round here," she whined. "They don't like me."

"I thought you and Katt were friends."

"Katt's too busy for friends. Either she's out ridin' on the estate, or she's on that telephone. One time she talked to a guy in Venice for two whole fuckin' hours! Now who in hell can talk on a phone *that* long?"

"Do you also listen in on people's phone conversations?"

She tossed her head impudently. "I get bored. There ain't a whole hell of a lot to do, y' understand? Boone pays more attention to those goddamned horses than he does to me." She giggled. "Maybe if I put a saddle on my back, he'd get a hard-on, right?"

"Puddin'," Rix said wearily, "what's this all about?"

"You've . . . always kinda liked me, ain't you?"

"We hardly know each other."

"But what you know, you like. Don't you?" She touched his hand.

"I guess so." Though he knew he should, he didn't move his hand. His groin stirred.

Puddin' smiled. "I thought so. A woman can tell. You know, the gleam in a man's eye and all. You should've seen those men judges in Atlantic City sit tall when I come out on stage. You could almost hear their cocks thump against the bottom of that desk. Old stuck-up bitches was the ones voted against me."

"I think you'd better go back to your room." He wrinkled his nose. "When was the last time you had a bath?"

"Soap causes cancer," she replied. "I heard it on the news. There's something in soap that gives you cancer. Know what's best for your skin? Gelatin. Know what that is? It's Jell-O. I put Jell-O in the bathtub and let it sit until it gets real firm. Then I get in and wiggle around. Orange is best, 'cause it's got vitamin C in it too."

He wanted to ask her if she was losing her mind, but didn't. Maybe she *was* losing her mind. Living in this house would certainly do it.

"I know you like me," Puddin' said. "I like you, too. Really. I always thought you were cute and smart and all. You're not like Boone. You're . . . well, a gentleman." She leaned closer to him, the valley between her breasts opening. Bourbon fumes rolled into his face. She whispered, "Take me with you when you leave here. Okay?"

When Rix paused, taken off guard, Puddin' plowed on: "Everybody hates me 'round here! Especially the dragon lady! That mother of yours has got eyes in the back of her head! She just *loooooves* to tell lies about me! Katt's all hung up on bein' a model and a celebrity and all. Edwin and Cass watch me all the time. I cain't even drive alone to Asheville to go shoppin'!"

"I don't believe that."

"It's *true*, damn it! They won't let me out the front gate! See, I tried to run off in August. Had a gutful of this fuckin' place, and took off in the Maserati. They sent the *cops* after me, Rix! State trooper pulled me over right outside Asheville, hauled me to the jailhouse on a charge of car theft! Had to sit there all night till Boone came for me!" She scowled bitterly. "He *lied* to me to get me to marry him. Said he was a world traveler, and a billionaire to boot. I didn't know I'd be a prisoner here, and that he didn't have one cent of his own to spend!"

"Boone's got his talent agency."

"Yeah. *That.*" Puddin' laughed sharply. "It was paid for with old Walen's money. Boone's still payin' him back, with interest. Boone ain't got a pot to pee in!"

"He *will* be rich," Rix said. "After our father dies"—the realization sank in as he said it—"the family business will belong to Boone."

"Oh no. You're wrong. Boone wants it, but so does Katt. And Boone's scared shitless the old man's gonna hand everything over to her, lock, stock, and fuckin' barrel!"

Rix pondered that for a moment. All the Usher children had attended the Harvard School of Business, with a stipulation that they return to Usherland every weekend. Boone had flunked out after a year, Rix had quit to study English Lit at the University of North Carolina, but Kattrina had graduated with honors. She'd always been interested in fashion and modeling, and had opened her own agency in New York when she was twenty-two. After a couple of years, she'd sold the agency for a profit of almost three million dollars; then she'd decided to free-lance for herself, at the rate of two thousand dollars an hour. Her golden, healthy look was enormously popular in Europe, where her face sold everything from fur coats to Ferraris.

"Katt's happy," Rix said. "She's not interested in the business."

"Boone knows she wants it. He says your daddy's been talkin' to her in secret. That's why old Walen's never let Boone handle any of the decisions."

"That doesn't mean anything. He's never let any of us handle decisions." He smiled. "So Boone's champing at the bit, is he?"

"Sure. Just like *you* are."

"Sorry. I don't want a damned thing to do with it."

"That ain't what Boone says. He says you're pretendin' not to be interested. He says you're waitin' for the old man to die, just like everybody else. Know what Boone told me when we got married?" She blinked her heavy lids. "He said the business was worth about *ten* billion dollars, and that every time somebody even thinks there's gonna be a war, the millions come rollin' into those factories by the truckload. He says that's because nobody in the world, not even the Germans, makes weapons better than the Ushers. Now you look me straight in the eye and say you don't want a piece!"

"I don't," he said firmly, "want a piece."

"Bullshit." Her breasts were about to spill from her gown, the nipples peeking over like brown, crosseyed eyeballs. "Only a god-damn idjit wouldn't want a cut of ten billion bucks! That's all the money in the world! Look, I know you protested V'etnam when you was in college, but you ain't a hippie no more. You're a grown man." Her voice trailed off, and for a moment she appeared to be about to keel over. Then she clutched his arm. "I cain't *stand* this place no more, Rix. It's creepy around here, 'specially at night. The wind blows so hard when it gets dark. Boone goes off and leaves me alone. Now, with the old man in that room right over my head . . . I cain't stand the *smell* of him, Rix! I want to be with people who like me!"

"Have you tried talking to Boone about—"

"Yes, I've tried," Puddin' snapped, her face reddening. "He don't listen! He just laughs! Boone . . . don't want to be around me no more." Tears came to her eyes, but Rix couldn't tell whether she was forcing them or not. "He says he . . . cain't go to bed with me. *Me!* Head majorette at Daniel Webster High School! A beauty con-test winner! Hell, I used to have football players wantin' to just sniff my panties! Boone's got a cock like a wet noodle!"

It took a moment for that to sink in. "Boone's . . . impotent?" Rix asked. The last time he'd been home, Boone had taken him to a club called the Rooster Strut, where topless dancers gyrated in the harsh, hot lights and the beer tasted like dishwater. Boone had made a big show of calling all the girls by their first names, of bragging about how many he'd laid. He remembered the way Boone had grinned, his teeth flashing in the strobe lights.

"You like me, don't you?" She wiped one eye and left a trail of mascara. "I could go to Atlanta with you. They'd let you take me, they wouldn't try to stop you. Boone's scared of you. He told me so. I'd be real good for you, Rix. You need a woman, and I wouldn't be like that last one you had. I wouldn't get crazy and cut my—"

73

"Go back to your room," he said. He'd been jolted by the memory of Sandra in the bathtub, and all that blood. The razor on the scarlet tiles. Blood on the walls. Her curly, ash-blond hair floating in the water like an open flower.

Puddin' popped her breasts out of the gown. They hung inches away from his face. "Take 'em," she whispered huskily. "You can, if you want to." She tried to guide his hands.

He made a fist. "No," he said, and knew he was the biggest fool who'd ever lived.

"Just touch one. Just one."

"*No.*"

In an instant her face crumbled like wet cardboard. Her lower lip swelled. "I . . . thought you liked me."

"I do, but you're my brother's wife."

"Are you queer?" There was a nasty hint in her voice.

"I'm not gay, no. But you and Boone have a problem. I'm not getting in the middle of it."

Her eyes narrowed into slits. Her mask of perfection fell off, and the real Puddin' was hiding behind it. "You're just like the rest of 'em! You don't care 'bout nobody but your own damn self!" She stood up, tugging drunkenly at her gown. "Oh, you play so high and mighty, but you're just another goddamned Usher, through and through!"

"Keep your voice down." Walen might sure as hell be getting a kick out of this!

"I'll shout if I want to!" Still, she wasn't drunk enough to want to rouse Margaret Usher. She marched to the door, then turned back. "Thanks for your help, Mr. Usher! I sure do appreciate it!" She left the room in a proud fury, but the door closed with a bump instead of a slam.

Rix lay back in the bed and grinned. So all of Boone's sexual crowing was just hot air! What a laugh! Boone's afraid of me? he thought. No way!

But he will be, before I'm through with him.

Ten billion dollars, he mused, as sleep began to pull at him again. With that much money, a man could do anything he pleased. He could have undreamed-of power. There'd be no more struggling at the typewriter, alternately playing God and Satan over paper characters.

—no more hassles no more books no more agents' dirty looks—

The strange singsong had come unbidden, a soft, seductive voice from the deepest recess of his mind. For an instant he was lulled by it, and he pictured himself stepping out of the limousine and striding toward the open doors of the armaments plant. Inside, military men, beautiful secretaries, and smiling sycophants were waiting to welcome him.

No, he thought—and the image faded. No. Every cent of that money was tainted with blood. He would make his own way in the world, on his own strengths. He didn't need any blood money.

But when he switched off the lamp and settled back to sleep, his last conscious thought was

—ten billion dollars—

◆ ◆ ◆

An hour or so later, Puddin' was awakened from an uneasy sleep by the noise of rushing wind around the Gatehouse. She looked toward the door—and saw a shape interrupt the light that crept in from the corridor. She held her breath, waiting. The shape paused, then went on. Puddin' clutched her silk sheet; for some reason, she dared not open that door to see who walked the Gatehouse at this dead hour. She could smell Walen's stink in the room.

Puddin' squeezed her eyes shut, and, as she drifted toward darkness, she called in a hoarse whisper for her momma.

7

The sun was rising, tinting the sky scarlet. New Tharpe had ceased his struggling.

Every time he'd tried to fight free during the long night, the thorny coils had clasped him tighter. They dug into his flesh in a dozen places. He'd cried a couple of times, but when he realized that crying sapped his strength—and he was going to need that strength, or he was as good as dead—he stopped sobbing as if he'd been slapped in the face.

Red light was beginning to tumble into the hollow. The wind, so violent during the night, had died to a furtive whisper. He could still see his breath, but his bones were thawing. He'd never been so cold in his life.

Twice during the night he thought he'd heard his name called, far in the distance. He'd tried to shout for help, but his voice was weak and raspy, and his head rang with pain. Then, when the moon started sinking, he'd heard something moving up at the edge of the pit. He'd looked up as high as possible, though there was a band of thorns around his throat, but seen nothing. Whatever it was, judging from the sound of crackling brush, it was very big. New had thought he'd heard rumbling breathing. The forest had fallen silent. In the next rush of wind, New had smelled the musky scent of an animal—a cat on the prowl.

Greediguts, New had thought as he kept perfectly still. Greediguts was up on the lip of the hollow. Greediguts was smelling him, and *wanting* him, but even the monstrous black panther itself wouldn't come down into those thorns.

After a while, the rumbling had faded away. The beast was gone, to find easier prey.

Every time he'd closed his eyes, New had seen that black figure standing up there with the limp sack under its arm. He could tell nothing about the figure—man or woman? young or old? human or not?—but he'd known who it was. His heart had stuttered, his flesh crawling. It was the thing his ma had warned him about all his life, the thing that had taken the Parnell girl the third week in September, and little Vernon Simmons last harvest season.

Sometimes he thought it was only a tale the mothers and fathers of Briartop Mountain had made up to scare their children, to keep them from getting lost in the woods.

But now he knew different. The moonlight had told him so.

Got to get out of here! New screamed inwardly. He fought again, trying to pull his left arm and right leg loose. The thorns dug into his throat, drawing pinpricks of blood. They clutched his chest like little claws.

Settle down. Easy, easy. Thorns'll choke you. Got to *think* your way out.

He carefully turned his head. The hunter's skeleton beside him was on fire with early light. He saw that it still wore a rotting leather powder horn. The dead man had been here for a long, long time.

His gaze followed the kudzu vines that trailed along the skeleton's broken right arm. The green finger bones were pointed like an arrow into the bleached leaves that gathered around the cadaver's legs.

New stared at the empty knife sheath.

Where was the knife?

Had it been lost in the hunter's fall? New looked again at the grasping finger bones. Then toward the mound of leaves.

He swung his left leg out, digging the toe of his boot into leaves, shoveling them aside. Black beetles scurried away. The odor of a damp grave drifted up. Barbs plunged into him as he tried to strain farther to the left. He moved his foot, tried again in a different place, and uncovered white leaves, worms, and bugs.

Hissing with pain as the thorns gouged his throat, New dug his toe down into the leaves just beneath the skeleton's hand. He shoveled his foot back and forth. A nest of brown spiders fled in all directions.

One of them scrabbled along the staghorn handle of a bowie knife, sunk to its hilt in the damp earth.

The hunter had been straining for his knife as he died.

A crow cawed from above the hollow. It sounded like cruel laughter. The knife might as well be a mile away; with only one arm and leg free, New couldn't possibly retrieve it.

"Help!" he tried to shout in desperation. His voice came out in a rattle. His mother would be looking for him by now, he knew. So would other people. They'd find him, eventually. *Sure,* he thought grimly. Just like somebody had found the hunter.

New caught back a sob. He stared fixedly at the knife. Have to get it, he told himself. Somehow. Or I might die right here.

You're the man of the house now, he thought. It was what his ma always told him. His pa had died in February, at the garage where he'd worked in Foxton. A freak accident, Sheriff Kemp had said. Bobby Tharpe was repairing a pickup truck's tire. It blew up in his face. Didn't feel no pain, Kemp had said. He went right on the spot.

You get yourself in trouble, his ma told him, you get yourself out of it, too.

New had loved his father very much. Bobby Tharpe had married Myra Satterwhite late, when he was in his mid-thirties; he'd been fifty-two when he died. New's father had had eyes the color of emeralds, just like New's own. He'd been a quiet, peaceful man—but sometimes New could tell that he was troubled, and New didn't know why. New's father had stayed to himself a lot.

Get the knife. *Somehow.*

He imagined the way it would feel in his hand. He tried to dislodge it with his boot, but only drove it deeper into the ground. In his mind, his hand curled around the cool staghorn handle, and he could feel every groove and dent. The knife's weight tugged at his grip.

The Pumpkin Man had taken his little brother. His flesh and blood. Had stood at the pit's edge, and been grinning all the time.

Anger crackled like lightning behind New's eyes. He was staring at the bowie knife.

If you want something bad enough, his father had said once, you can get it. But only if you want it with heart and soul and mind, if you want it with every pore in your skin and hair on your head, and you know it's the right thing . . .

The Pumpkin Man had been grinning. Laughing at him, laughing as he stole Nathan away into the wild depths of the forest . . .

New's heart was beating hard. Red light stung his eyes. He strained toward the knife as much as he could; the thorns tore his skin mercilessly. They were not going to let him get away.

The Pumpkin Man had taken his brother, then had laughed at him in the dark.

A surge of rage ripped through him, filling him with bitter fire. It was an anger he'd never known before, and in it was not only the Pumpkin Man but also the cheap pine box that had held his father's body, and the truck tire that had exploded with no warning, and the thorns and Briartop Mountain and the rundown cabin where his taciturn mother cooked her blackberry pies. All of it came through his pores in a yell of sweat.

I WANT IT! he shouted in his head.

The bowie knife stirred and withdrew from the earth with a quiet hiss. It hung three inches off the ground, then fell back into the leaves again.

New cried out in amazement.

For a second he'd felt, actually *felt*, the knife clutched in his right hand. It had been burning hot.

He watched it to see if it would move again, but it didn't. Still, it was free of the ground. He hooked his foot out and dragged it closer. Spiders crawled over his boot.

I want it . . . *now*, he said mentally, concentrating on feeling that knife in his hand again. On curling his fingers around the staghorn handle. On feeling its weight.

The knife jumped like a fish. Then lay still.

He was in a dream, floating. His head throbbed where he'd bumped it against a rock in the fall. There was a pressure like an iron band squeezing his temples. He'd never felt this way before, as

78

if his mind were separating from his body, becoming disjointed, out of kilter. His heart was racing, and for a moment the pain in his head was so bad he thought he was going to pass out.

But he didn't. The knife was still on the ground at his feet. Its blade was veined with rust, but the edge gleamed in the red, raw light.

New could feel its sharpness. A pulse of power beat between him and the knife, connecting them like a charge of electricity.

And New understood what it was.

Magic.

There was magic in that knife. It had lain so long in Briartop earth that it had absorbed some of Briartop's magic. There was magic in it, and the magic was going to help New escape.

I want it, he commanded.

It didn't move.

Now. I want it now. He visualized the knife rising from the ground—slowly, slowly, coming through the air toward his open hand—felt the cool staghorn handle against his skin, closed his hand around it. Now. I want it *right now.*

The knife jumped, jumped.

Now. Right now. *Now, damn it!* Again, rage sizzled through his bones.

As if obeying his command, the knife jumped high and hung, spinning, three feet off the ground. It began to move toward his fingers, but fell to the ground again. The next time was easier, but again it fell. Now it was on the ground beneath his right hand.

Come up, New commanded. Come up and into my hand. He almost giggled: Wait'll Nathan hears about *this*! But the memory of Nathan came and went. He saw white moonlight on Nathan's up-turned face, and mentally screamed.

The magic knife spun up from the ground, higher, higher, whirling like a top, and its handle slid into New's grasp as if he'd been born with it.

Quickly he started sawing at the thorns that held him. The coils around his chest parted with a brittle snapping sound, and leaked yellowish fluids. He cut his left arm free, and saw a bracelet of wounds around his wrist. The thorns around his neck were the hardest to cut loose, because some of them were in pretty deep, and he didn't want to slash his throat.

By the time he'd cut away enough thorns to pull free, the light that filtered through the trees was warm and golden. He fashioned footholds in the dirt wall and, climbing up by grasping bushes and roots, pulled himself slowly to the rim. At the top, with the magic knife still clutched in his fist, New turned his grimy, blood-streaked face toward the hollow and shouted, "Die, damn you!" His voice was a weak croak, but it carried his anger sufficiently.

Then he made his way back to the path, where his blackberry buckets were being picked at by crows, and started running for home.

He never saw the thorns down in the hollow begin to turn black, wither—and die.

8

"Penny for your thoughts," Margaret Usher said brightly.

Rix snapped himself back. "Just wandering," he told her, and took another bite of sausage from his breakfast plate. In fact, he'd been thinking about what a gorgeous morning it was; they were sitting on the glass-enclosed breakfast porch at the rear of the Gatehouse, and from here the panorama of the gardens and the western mountain peaks was an unbroken blaze of color. Though it was only eight o'clock, a black gardener in a straw hat was already hard at work, sweeping stray leaves from the fieldstone paths that crisscrossed the gardens. Marble statues of cherubs, fauns, and satyrs pranced through the flowers.

The sky was blue and clear. A squadron of ducks flew across Rix's field of view. The breakfast was good, the coffee strong, and Rix had enjoyed a restful sleep after Puddin' had left last night. When he'd taken his vitamins this morning, he'd looked in the mirror and seen that the bags under his eyes didn't look quite as severe. Or was that only his hopeful imagination? Anyway, he felt fine, and even his appetite had picked up, because he was finishing all of his breakfast. He'd missed Cass's cooking in the year that he'd been away.

"I heard Boone come in this morning," Margaret said. Today she wore only a light coating of makeup, to accentuate her cheekbones. "About five, I think it was. You'd be surprised what I can hear when the house is quiet."

"Really?" Instantly, Rix was on guard. Did she mean she'd heard him and Puddin'? Probably not. Her room was at the far end of the hallway, with many rooms between them.

"I can certainly hear Boone and that woman fighting like cats and dogs." She shook her head, her red lips pressed together in disgust. "Oh, I *told* him not to marry her! I told him he'd be sorry, and you know I'm never wrong. Well, he's sorry all right."

"Why doesn't he divorce her like he did those two others, if he's so unhappy?"

She carefully folded her napkin and placed it beside her plate. A maid came in and began to carry away the dirty dishes. "Because," Margaret said after the maid had gone, "there's no telling what that trollop would say about us if she was let off this estate. She's a drunken little fool, but she's been an Usher now for two years, four months, and twelve days. That's two years longer than either of the others. She knows . . . things about us that might find their way into print if she was allowed to run wild."

"You mean the Malady?"

Margaret's eyes clouded over. "Yes, that. And more. Like how much money we're worth, and what our real-estate holdings are. She knows about the Caribbean island we own, the casino in Monte Carlo, the banks and the other companies. Boone has a mouth as big as a mountain. Can you imagine the headlines if there was a divorce? That little trollop wouldn't accept an out-of-court settlement, like the other two. She'd go straight to the *National Enquirer* with all sorts of lurid lies."

"And lurid truths?" Rix asked.

"You have a very bad attitude about your family, Rix. You should be proud of who you are, and of the contribution your ancestors have made to this country's survival."

"Right. Well, I've always been the black sheep, haven't I? I think it's too late to act like a star-spangled drummer boy."

"Please don't mention flags," she said coldly. She was remembering, Rix knew, a photograph that had been in several North Carolina newspapers. In it, Rix had been wearing a Jefferson Airplane T-shirt and waving a black flag; his hair was down to his shoulders, and he was walking in the front row of a crowd of Vietnam war demonstrators at the University of North Carolina. The picture had been snapped just minutes before the police waded in to break up their peace rally. Before the fighting was over, nine kids had broken bones and Rix sat in the gutter with a knot the size of a hen's egg on his head, watching a sea of legs flow and ebb around him.

The photograph had also appeared on the front page of the weekly *Foxton Democrat*, with a circle around Rix's head.

Walen had gone through the roof like a Roman candle.

81

"You'd do well to study the achievements of your ancestors," Margaret suggested. Rix listened politely, with no trace of surprise on his face. "They'd teach you a thing or two about family pride."

"And just how would I go about doing that, pray tell?"

She shrugged. "You might start by reading some of those books that Walen brought from the Lodge's library. He's been studying the family documents for the past three months."

"*What!*" Rix's heart gave a kick.

"Family documents. That's what Walen had the servants bring out of the Lodge. Dozens of old ledgers and diaries and things, from the collection of family records. There's a library in the Lodge's basement with thousands of them. I've never seen it, of course, but Edwin's told me about it."

Rix was stunned. Family documents? Right here in the Gatehouse? "I thought you said you didn't know what those books were."

"Well, I don't know *exactly* what they are, or why Walen's been reading them. But I do know they came from the Lodge's library."

"You saw them?" Steady, he told himself. Don't act too interested!

"Of course I saw them. I was here the morning they were brought in. Some of them are so mildewed they smell like dead fish."

My God, Rix thought. He leaned his chin on his hand to keep from grinning. Family documents in the Gatehouse library! He'd hoped he could find something in there worth his attention, but this was a godsend! No, hold on a minute. There was a rip in the silver lining. "The library's locked," he reminded her. "Even if I wanted to browse through those old books, I couldn't get in, could I?"

"Well, Walen *has* insisted that he wants it kept locked. But, of course, Edwin has the set of master keys. We do have to get in to dust and vacuum, don't we? If we didn't, the smell of mildew from that room would take over the house." She blinked suddenly, and Rix knew she was thinking about Walen's reek. "That was a nice breakfast, wasn't it?" she asked, recovering quickly. "Boone's going to be sorry he missed it."

Rix was about to ask her more about the Lodge's basement library when he heard a faint, steady whining sound. Birds burst from the trees. The whining noise grew louder. He looked toward the sky as a gleaming silver Bell Jetcopter streaked over the Gatehouse, circled slowly, and then settled down out of sight on the helipad.

"Oh, that might be your sister!" Margaret rose from her chair, craning to see. "Kattrina's home!" she trilled.

But it wasn't Katt who came up the pathway. There were two men, one wearing a military uniform and the other in a dark business suit. The one in the business suit wore sunglasses and carried a black briefcase.

"It's just them again," Margaret said, sitting down. She sighed softly. "They're here to see Walen."

The two men walked briskly through the gardens, then around the Gatehouse toward the front entrance.

"Who are they?" Rix asked.

"One's from the Pentagon. I think you've met him before, but maybe not. General McVair. The other man is Mr. Meredith, from the armaments plant. Dr. Francis told your father he should have absolute rest, but Walen doesn't listen." She smiled at Rix, but her eyes were vacant. "When your father pulls out of this thing, we're going on a vacation. Perhaps to Acapulco. That would be lovely in January, don't you think?"

"Yes," he said, watching her carefully, "it would be."

"It's sunny all the time in Acapulco. Your father needs a nice vacation. He needs to get out in the sun and laugh."

"Excuse me." Rix stood up. "I think I might take a walk. Enjoy the fresh air."

"It's a lovely day for a walk, isn't it? You could go for a horse-back ride, if you like."

"I'll find something to do. Thanks for the breakfast." He left his mother sitting on the porch; he couldn't bear the realization that she was living in a twilight world of false hopes and dreams, waiting for her husband to kick off the shroud and dance down the staircase like Fred Astaire. Her next trip would be to the Usher cemetery, on the eastern edge of the estate.

But right now he wanted to find Edwin. He wanted to get that master key and see for himself what was beyond the library's door. He'd have to be very careful; he didn't want anyone knowing what he intended to do, and now he regretted even telling Cass about it. If Walen ever got a hint he was going to shake some Usher coffins, the documents would be whisked back to the Lodge's basement. He stopped a maid and asked if she'd seen Edwin, but she told him she hadn't.

Rix went out of the Gatehouse. The sparkling air smelled like a fine, crisp white wine. Edwin might be any of a dozen places on the estate, commanding the hundred routine duties that went on every day. He walked through the gardens, taking the pathway that would lead him past the tennis courts to the Bodane house.

He passed the garage, a long, low stone structure with ten wooden doors that each slid upward to allow a car into its separate stall. At one time the garage had housed Usher carriages and coaches; now it held Boone's red Ferrari, Katt's pink Maserati, the new limo, a second limo in case the first had mechanical trouble, a red '57 Thunderbird, a robin's-egg-blue '52 Cadillac, a white '48 Packard, a gray '32 Duesenberg, a Stutz Bearcat, and a Model T Ford in perfect condition. Those, anyway, were the cars that were in there the last time Rix had looked; the assemblage might have been upgraded during the past year.

The Bodane house, tiny compared to the Gatehouse, but itself a two-story Victorian manor, was tucked back amid the trees. Next to it was a small white garage that held the Bodanes' Chevy station wagon. Rix walked up the steps to the front door and pressed the buzzer.

The door opened. Edwin stood there, capless, but wearing his uniform. "Rix," he said, and smiled—but there was pain in his eyes. "Please come in."

"I'm glad I caught you." Rix entered the house. At once a wave of nostalgia crashed over him. This house, like his bedroom, hadn't changed a bit: the walls were of softly glowing wood, adorned with samplers and needlepoint that Cass had done; the parlor floor was covered by a burgundy rug—threadbare in places—trimmed in gold; cozy, overstuffed chairs and a sofa were arranged around a red brick hearth where a small fire flickered; above the hearth was a wreath made of pine cones and acorns. The parlor's two large bay windows looked directly toward the Gatehouse.

Rix had sat on that rug and dreamed before the hearth, while Cass read him stories, either Aesop's Fables or Hans Christian Andersen fairy tales. Cass could break your heart with "The Brave Tin Soldier," or make you laugh at the greedy fox who wanted all the grapes. Edwin made the best hot chocolate in the world, and his hand on your shoulder felt as strong as courage. Where had all the years gone, Rix wondered, as he looked around the parlor. What had happened to the little boy who sat in front of that fireplace with dreams in his eyes?

He had been swept into the furnace of reality with his ballerina bride, and all that remained was scorched metal.

"Did you want me for something?" Edwin asked, breaking the spell.

"Yes, I—" Something on the mantel caught his attention. He

walked across the rug to it, and stood staring at a small framed photograph of himself at about seven or eight, wearing a suit and a bow tie, with his hair slicked back. On either side of him, holding his hands and smiling, were a much younger Edwin and Cass. A servant had taken that picture, he recalled. It was done on a hot July day—his birthday! His father and mother had gone to Washington on business, and taken Boone with them. Edwin and Cass had hosted a birthday party for him, inviting all the servants' children and Rix's friends from his private school in Asheville. He picked up the photograph and looked closely at it. Everyone was so happy then. The world was happy. There were no wars, or rumors of wars. No black banners or demonstrations or police riot batons. Life was stretched out like a red carpet.

"I'd forgotten about this," Rix said softly. He looked from one face to the next, as Edwin came up behind him. Three happy people with linked hands, Rix thought. But there was another presence in the picture, something he'd never realized before.

Over Rix's left shoulder, jutting above the full summer trees, was one of the Lodge's towering chimneys. The Lodge had crashed his birthday party without his even knowing it.

Rix returned the photograph to its place on the mantel. "I'd like to get the library key from you," he said, turning away from the hearth. "Dad's offered me the use of the materials in there."

"Do you mean . . . the documents that your father brought out of the Lodge?"

"Actually, I'm just looking for something about Wales. And coal mining." Rix smiled. He felt his insides writhe. If there was anything on earth he hated to do, it was to lie to Edwin Bodane; but he feared that Edwin, out of loyalty to Walen, would balk at giving him the key if Rix told him the real reason. "Do you think there's anything in the library on coal mines?"

"There should be." He was searching Rix's eyes, and for a few seconds Rix felt that Edwin was seeing right through him. "I think there's a book on every subject under the sun in there." Then he crossed the room to a shelf with a number of clay jars on it. One was marked CARS, another GROUNDSKEEPING, a third HOUSEHOLD, a fourth RECREATION—and the final three jars were all marked LODGE. He took the HOUSEHOLD jar down, opened it, and brought out a large ring of keys in all sizes and shapes. He found the key he wanted and started working it off the ring. "What's your next book idea about? Wales?" he asked.

"That's where it's going to be set. It's about—don't laugh, now— vampires who live down in the old coal mines." Lie was following lie.

"Lord!" Edwin said. An amused grin spread across his pliable features. "How in the *world* did you come up with that one?"

Rix shrugged. "That I can't tell you. Anyway, I've just started my research. It might work out, or it might not."

Edwin got the key off, returned the ring to the jar, and placed the jar on the shelf. As he offered it to Rix, he said quietly, "Cass told me, Rix."

Oh Christ! "She did, huh?"

"Yes. We talked about it last night."

"Okay, then," Rix said. "What's your opinion?"

Edwin frowned. "Opinion? Well, if you put it that way, my opinion is that Logan will do a fine job, once he learns some patience and discipline."

"Logan?"

"That's who we're talking about, isn't it? Cass told me last night that she let you know about our retirement. I was going to tell you myself, on the ride from the airport, but I didn't want to burden you with anything else."

Rix slipped the key into his trouser pocket, relieved. "In other words, he's impatient and undisciplined?"

"Logan is a young man," Edwin answered diplomatically. "He doesn't put a high value on responsibility yet." He stepped past Rix to straighten the photograph on the mantel. "He doesn't quite understand the meaning of tradition. One generation of Bodanes building for the next, ever since Hudson Usher hired a mountain man named Whitt Bodane as an assistant groundskeeper. Within four years, Whitt was Usherland's chief of staff. I'd hate to see that long tradition disrupted."

"So you think you can teach a nineteen-year-old boy everything you know?"

"When I began as chief of staff, Usherland employed more than three hundred servants. Now there are fewer than eighty. I'm not saying he won't make mistakes. Maybe I'm not even saying that I'm certain he'll work out. But I'm going to do my damnedest to make Logan understand the importance of that tradition."

"I can't wait to meet him," Rix said with something less than enthusiasm.

"Good." Edwin glanced at his gold pocket watch. "I was just

cleaning his room upstairs. I'm to pick him up in an hour, at Robert's farm. I could use the company, if you'd like to go."

Rix wanted to get into that library, but his curiosity burned about the young man who was to take Edwin's place. He decided it would be too risky to search through the documents in broad daylight. They could wait until night. "All right," he agreed. "I'll go."

Edwin took his cap from a hatstand in the foyer and put it on. Then he and Rix went out into the warm morning sunlight, got into the tan station wagon, and drove away from Usherland.

9

Rix gazed out his window at a vista of tobacco fields. In the distance a farmer urged a horsedrawn wagon along a dirt road, the rising dust leaving a shimmering haze in the air. Edwin was driving toward Taylorville at a leisurely pace, enjoying the beautiful scenery—scarlet forests, meadows ripe for the scythe. They passed heaps of pumpkins in one field, being loaded into the back of a truck for market in Asheville. For some reason they made Rix think of a picture he'd seen of a Vietnam battlefield: disembodied heads piled up and rotting in the sun.

The question was in Rix's mind again. He'd asked it of Edwin before, and had always gotten the same answer. Asking it meant walking on swampy ground that could pull him down without warning at any second. Still, he had to.

"Edwin," he said finally, "when you . . . talked to Sandra that night, are you sure she didn't . . . you know . . . sound like she was . . ." He trailed off.

"Disturbed?" Edwin asked mercifully.

"Yes. Disturbed."

"No, she didn't. Not at all. She sounded very happy. She told me you'd sold *Congregation* to Stratford House, that you had just finished *Fire Fingers*, and that you and she were going out to celebrate the next night. I had no idea that anything was wrong."

"There was nothing wrong. Oh, maybe a few little things. Money was tight, the dishwasher was broken down, the car's transmission was slipping, she was under some pressure at the insurance company—but Sandra was a strong woman, Edwin. Strong mentally. We'd gotten through tough times before. Hell, she was the one who kept me going." His hands had become fists, and when he opened them, they were stiff with tension.

"Sometimes people do things for strange reasons. I never met your wife, of course, but whenever we spoke on the phone, she sounded very happy and very much in love with you." His gray brows knitted together. "You have to let go of it, Rix. It's the past."

"I can't let go of it!" His voice cracked, and he had to wait a minute before continuing. "I've tried. There was nothing wrong, Edwin. She wasn't crazy. She wasn't the type of person who just gives up and cuts her wrists in a bathtub!"

"I'm sorry," Edwin said gently. "I wish I could tell you that she did sound disturbed, if that would help you. But when we spoke on the phone that night, Sandra seemed very happy. I was as shocked as you were when it happened."

Rix had telephoned Edwin at Usherland four years ago, when he'd found Sandra lying in the bathtub. All that blood, all that blood! The water was red, and Sandra's head had slipped down so her hair floated like the petals of a bruised flower. The razor she'd used lay on the tiles, smeared with blood where her veins had jetted.

Rix was in a state of mindless shock, and Edwin had told him to call the police and not to touch anything until they got there. He had flown down to Atlanta the next morning to be with Rix, and had stayed through the funeral.

Afterward, Rix's nightmares of being lost in the Lodge again grew worse, and the attacks descended upon him with a new virulence.

The night before it happened, she'd told him that Edwin had called while he was out. They'd talked for a while about Rix and his writing, about the new book he was starting, about the possibility that they would come to Usherland for Christmas. She seemed happy about the future, and hopeful that she could continue to help Rix deal with the guilt he felt over his family's business. He'd always told her that she was his safety valve, that without her he might never be able to channel his feelings into another book. There had been many long nights of talks about his childhood at Usherland and his need to make something of himself apart from the family. She encouraged him in his writing, and had an uplifting optimism.

Four years after her suicide, Rix still couldn't make sense of it.

He'd loved her very much, and he'd thought she loved him. In his brooding over her death, Rix found only one possibility—that somehow he had contaminated her, had driven her into a depression that was carefully and tragically masked.

"She'd told me before how much you meant to her," Edwin offered. "I believe that whatever drove her to take her own life was in her mind long before you met her. I think it was unavoidable. You're not to blame, Rix. No one is."

"I wish I could believe that."

Edwin slowed the station wagon and turned off the main highway, following a dirt road that wound through the tobacco fields. On a hill stood a curing barn and a modest white house. Next to the house was a small clapboard shed. A white-haired woman in a gingham dress sat on the house's front porch, shelling peas into a metal pan. The screen door opened as Edwin stopped the car, and a tall, balding elderly man with a luxuriant white mustache came out. He was wearing overalls and a flannel workshirt, but he carried himself with Bodane dignity.

Rix got out of the car with Edwin as Robert Bodane approached. His wife set aside her peas and came down from the porch on plump legs.

The two brothers shook hands. "Do you remember Rix?" Edwin asked the other man. "I think he was about this tall the last time you saw him." He motioned with his hand about four feet off the ground.

"*Rix!* This is that same little boy? My Lord!" Robert looked stunned. His face was heavily weathered, and he was missing a couple of lower teeth. When Rix shook his hand, the strength of the man's grip amazed him. "I guess you don't remember meetin' me, do you? I came out to visit Usherland."

Rix didn't, but he smiled anyway and said, "I think I do. It's good to see you again."

Robert Bodane introduced his wife, Jeanie, and talked to Edwin for a minute or two about the bumper crop he was expecting this year. "Ought to go into farmin' yourself," Robert said with a sly grin. "Get some good dirt under those fingernails, makes a man out of you."

"I expect to have Florida sand under my feet in about three months, thank you. Is Logan ready?"

"His bags are packed. I s'pose the boy's wandered off somewhere. Hard to keep track of a rounder like that one. Hey, Logan!"

he shouted toward the forest that edged up behind the house. "Edwin's here for you!"

"Prob'ly off runnin' with Mutt," the elderly woman said. "He's taken a shine to that dog."

"Hey, Logan!" Robert shouted again. Then he shrugged and said, "Y'all come on up and sit on the porch awhile. He'll show up directly."

A young man with curly hair the color of burnished brass peered out the window of the toolshed as his grandparents and the other two men walked to the porch. He knew the tall old dude in the suit was Edwin; the younger one might be somebody else who worked at Usherland. It wasn't nine-thirty yet. Edwin was here early. Well, the young man thought, he could just fuckin' wait, then.

Logan turned back to the worktable to regard the job he'd been doing. He was wearing the old man's barbecuing apron, the one that had *I Ain't Pretty, But I Sure Can Cook* written on it above the caricature of a chef burning hot dogs on a grill. He had done a very good job, he thought. It was something he'd been meaning to get around to for a long time. He replaced the hammer and hacksaw in their places on the tool rack, then carefully wiped his hands on a rag.

He took the apron off and draped it over the worktable. Then, satisfied, he left the toolshed, closed and latched the door behind him, and ambled slowly up to the house.

Rix saw the young man approaching, and instantly he decided he wouldn't trust Logan Bodane to shine his shoes, much less take over Edwin's duties at Usherland.

Logan walked with an arrogant swagger, his hands thrust into the pockets of his faded blue jeans. He wore a beat-up leather jacket over a gray workshirt, and he kicked at an errant stone with one of his scuffed boots. His longish hair framed a lean, ruddy face with sharply angled cheekbones, and as he came nearer, Rix saw that his deepset eyes were a chilly shade of blue. His gaze was remote and unconcerned—almost bored. He flicked a glance at all of them as he stepped up onto the porch.

"Been callin' you, boy," Robert said. "Where'd you go?"

"Toolshed," Logan replied; he had a deep, rough voice that grated on Rix's nerves. "Just messin' around in there."

"Well, don't just stand there. Shake hands with Edwin and Mr. Usher."

The young man turned his attention to Rix. When he smiled,

only one side of his mouth hitched up, so the smile was more like a sneer. "Yeah?" he asked. "Which Usher are you?"

"*Mr.* Usher," Rix said.

"Are you gonna be my new boss?"

"No. Edwin is."

"Got it." Logan extended his hand toward Rix, who saw a red crust around the fingernails. Logan's smile faltered a fraction, and he drew his hand back. "Been workin' in the shed," he said. "Got some woodstain on me, I guess. Ought to be more careful."

"You ought to be."

Edwin rose from his chair to shake Logan's hand. Logan was almost as tall as he was, but much broader; the young man had wide, thick shoulders and the large hands of a laborer. "We should be getting back to Usherland," Edwin told him. "Are your bags ready?"

"Just take me a few minutes. Pleased to meet you, Mr. Usher." He smiled—the smile of a cunning animal, Rix thought—and then went into the house.

Edwin was watching Rix carefully. "You're wearing your opinions like a red scarf," he said. "Give him a chance."

"Logan's a fine boy, Mr. Usher," the old woman offered, shelling her peas. "Oh, he's got his rough edges, but then again, all boys his age do, don't they? He's a smart one, though, and he's got a strong back."

"He's a rounder," Robert said. "Reminds me of myself, when I was his age."

"That was long before I straightened him out." She winked quickly at Rix, then let out a sharp whistle. "Mutt! Here, boy! Come on! Where'd that dog get off to? Heard him barkin' fit to bust before sunup."

"Chasin' squirrels again, most likely."

Rix stood up as Logan came out of the house, carrying two suitcases. Edwin took one of them for him. Rix said it had been a pleasure to meet the Bodanes, then walked on to the station wagon and climbed in.

Logan and Edwin slid the suitcases into the rear, then the young man took his place in the back seat. He rolled down his window as Edwin started the car.

"You be a good boy!" Mrs. Bodane called to him. "Pay attention to what Edwin tells you, now!"

"Hey, Gramps," Logan said, "I was doin' some work in the shed and forgot to clean up. I left kind of a mess, I suppose."

"I'll get it. You listen to Edwin and you make us proud of you, hear?"

"I'll make you real proud," Logan said, and rolled his window back up.

Edwin drove away from the house as Logan waved to his grand-parents from behind the glass. "This thing got a radio?" he asked.

At the toolshed door, Robert Bodane stopped to watch the station wagon out of sight.

"Fresh peas for lunch!" the woman called. "You want some potatoes to go with 'em?"

"That'd be fine," he replied. The dust was already settling. He unlatched the door and went into the toolshed. The work his grand-son had been doing was covered with an apron atop the workbench. There was a strong smell in the place.

He lifted the apron.

It took him a moment to realize that the mess on the workbench had once been a dog. Mutt had been decapitated and disemboweled, the intestines laid out in pools of thick, congealing blood.

He heard his wife calling the dog again, and he started looking for something to scrape the remains into.

10

Parked in front of the Gatehouse was a new silver-gray Cadillac. From the back seat of the station wagon, Logan whistled apprecia-tively, breaking the silence that had descended on the drive back from Taylorville.

"That car belongs to Dr. Francis," Edwin told Rix. He stopped the station wagon under the porte-cochere. "I'll show Logan around the estate. You'd better find out what's going on."

As Rix started to get out, Logan said, "It was good meetin' you, Mr. Usher." Rix glanced back into the young man's chilly smile, and told himself that Logan Bodane wouldn't last a week. Then he went up the steps to the Gatehouse, where a servant told him that his mother was looking for him and wanted him at once in the living room.

He hurried along the corridor and slid the living-room doors open. ". . . destructive cellular activity," were the only words he heard before the man who was seated and speaking to Boone and Margaret stopped to look across the room at him.

Margaret said, "Dr. Francis, this is our younger son. Rix, come in and sit down. I want you to hear what the doctor has to say."

Rix sat in a chair behind and to the left of Boone, where he could watch Dr. Francis as the man spoke. John Francis was a trim, middle-aged man with dark brown, gray-flecked hair receding from a widow's peak. He wore tortoiseshell-framed glasses, behind which his dark, intense gaze was fixed firmly on Margaret. He had the artistic hands of a fine surgeon or a concert pianist, Rix noted, and he was dressed immaculately in a herringbone suit with a brown striped tie.

Dr. Francis continued from the point of interruption. "The destructive cellular activity in Mr. Usher's tissue samples was increased by radiation. That tells us that the traditional treatments for cancer—to which this condition seems related on a cellular basis— are not going to work." He removed his glasses and polished the lenses with a paisley handkerchief. There were dark hollows of fatigue beneath his eyes. "His blood pressure has shot into the stratosphere. The fluids in his lungs build up as fast as we drain them. I'm afraid his kidneys are going to shut down at any time. The sensitivity of his nervous system, of course, increases every day. He's complaining that he has trouble sleeping because of the noise of his own heart."

"What I want to know," Margaret said, "is when Walen will be well again."

There was a moment of dead silence. Dr. Francis cleared his throat and put his glasses back on. Boone suddenly rose from his chair and crossed the room to the sideboard where the bar glasses and decanters of liquor were kept.

"Mrs. Usher," the doctor said finally, "one thing is very clear, and I thought you understood: Usher's Malady—at this point—is an incurable deterioration of the body's cellular structure. White blood cells are consuming the red. His digestive system is feeding on the tissues of the body. Brain cells, connective-tissue corpuscles, cartilage, and bone cells are being broken down and devoured. I don't pretend to understand why or how it's happening."

"But you're a doctor." There was a faint quaver in her voice. Her eyes were getting glassy, like a madwoman's stare. "A specialist. You should be able to do something." She flinched when Boone clacked ice cubes into his glass.

"The tranquilizers have helped him rest, and the painkillers have had some effect, too. Mrs. Reynolds is a fine nurse. Our research on the tissue samples is going to continue. But I can't do very much more for him unless he consents to enter a hospital."

"Walen's never been inside a hospital in his life." Her face was stricken. "Publicity. There would be . . . such *awful* publicity."

Dr. Francis frowned. "I think publicity should be the least of your concerns. Your husband is dying. I can't make it any clearer; I cannot adequately treat him up in that room."

"Could you cure him if he was to go to a hospital?" Boone asked, stirring his Scotch with a finger.

"I can't promise that. But we could run more thorough tests on him, and take more tissue samples. We'd be better able to study the degenerative process."

"Use him like a guinea pig, y'mean?" Boone took a quick slug of his drink.

Rix saw the frustration in the doctor's eyes, and a hint of red surfaced across the older man's cheeks. "How can you treat something, young man, if you don't know a damned thing about it? As I understand, the physicians who've attended other generations of your family were just as puzzled as I am. Why does it occur only in your family? Why does it begin almost overnight, when the subject is in otherwise perfect health? Why is the nervous system superhumanly enhanced while the other bodily functions crash-dive? In the past, your family prohibited autopsies as well." He glanced quickly at Margaret, but she was too dazed to react. "If we ever hope to cure this thing, we've got to first understand it. If that means making your father into a 'guinea pig,' is that such a terrible thing?"

"The press would tear that hospital apart, lookin' for him," Boone said.

"Walen's always been so healthy," Margaret said in a soft, feeble voice. She looked at Dr. Francis, but was staring right through him. "He's never been sick before. Never. Even when he cuts himself shaving, the wound is gone the next day. I've never seen him bleed more than a drop or two. Once, when we were first married, Walen took me to the stables to show off a new Arabian stallion. The horse threw him, and he . . . he landed on the back of his head. I'll never forget the sound of his skull hitting the ground. I thought his neck was broken . . . but then Walen stood up, and he was just fine. He doesn't get hurt, and he's never been sick before."

"He's sick now," Dr. Francis said. "I can't help him if he won't go to a hospital."

She shook her head. Her vision cleared, and her mouth became a firm, hard line. "No. My husband doesn't want to leave Usherland. The publicity would be terrible for the whole family. Bring your equipment here. Bring your entire hospital staff. But Walen has made it clear he won't leave the estate."

Dr. Francis looked at Boone and Rix. "How about you two? Would you enter a hospital for tests?"

"What for?" Boone asked nervously.

"Blood and tissue samples."

Boone downed his Scotch with one quick, jerky movement. "Listen, doc, I've never had a sick day in my life. Never set foot in a hospital and never intend to."

"What about you?" Dr. Francis turned to Rix.

"I'm not too keen on hospitals, either. Anyway, I'll be leaving here in a few days." He felt his mother glance at him.

The doctor sighed, shook his head, and rose from his chair. "I don't think you people fully understand what's at stake here. We're not only talking about Walen Usher's life. We're talking about yours, and about those of the children who come after you."

"My husband is your patient," Margaret said. "Not my sons."

"Your sons will be, Mrs. Usher," he replied firmly. "Sooner or later, they will be."

"I'm very tired now. Will one of you boys show Dr. Francis to the door, please?"

Boone busied himself by pouring a second drink. Rix escorted the doctor out of the living room, along the corridor, and to the entrance foyer.

"How long does my father have?" Rix asked him in a guarded voice at the front door.

"His bodily systems may shut down within a week. Two weeks at the most." When Rix didn't respond, Dr. Francis said, "Do *you* want to die like that? Odds are you will, you know. It's a grim fact you're going to have to face. In the meantime, what are you going to do about it?"

Hearing a stranger tell him how long his father had to live had numbed Rix. "I don't know," he said dully.

"Listen to me. I'm staying at the Sheraton Hotel in Asheville, near the medical center. If you change your mind about those tests, will you give me a call?"

Rix nodded, though his mind was made up. Walen had impressed upon him and Boone at an early age that hospitals were full

95

of quacks who experimented on dying patients. As far as Rix knew, Walen had never even taken prescription drugs.

Dr. Francis left the Gatehouse and walked down to his Cadillac, and Rix closed the Gatehouse door behind him.

When he returned to the living room, he found Boone alone, nursing his drink in a chair before the fireplace. "It's shit, ain't it?" Boone commented. "A real heap of shit."

Rix poured himself a bourbon, added ice cubes, and swallowed enough to make his throat burn.

"What's wrong with *you*? So happy you can't talk?"

"Meaning what?"

"Meanin' just what I said. This should be your happy day, Rixy. The doc says there ain't a shred of hope to pull Daddy through this thing. That should put a real glow in your heart."

"Knock it off."

"It ain't no secret that you've always hated Daddy," Boone said sharply. "And I know the real reason you've come home, too. You want some of that money in your claws, don't you?"

"Are you talking to the mirror?"

Boone stood up, and Rix sensed that he was in a dangerous mood. A lock of hair had fallen untidily over his forehead, and his face was ruddy with anger and alcohol. "You don't care about Daddy! You're just perched on a limb, waitin' for him to die!" He advanced a few steps. "I oughta throw you out that goddamned window!"

Rix knew his brother was looking for a punching bag. In the silence that stretched between them, Rix heard the telephone begin to ring out in the corridor. "You invited me here, remember?" Rix asked calmly.

"I didn't invite you! Momma sent me lookin' for you! Hell, I didn't really think you'd show your face around here a—" There was a knock at the door, and Boone shouted, "What the *hell* is it?"

A scared maid, the same young black woman who'd met Rix at the front door yesterday, peered inside. "Mr. Usher, suh? There's a woman named Dunstan on the telephone. She say she's callin' from the *Foxton Democrat*, suh."

Boone's face contorted with rage. "Hang up in her fucking face!" he roared. "Don't you have a lick of sense in your head?"

The maid disappeared like a rabbit down a hole.

"Idiot!" Boone muttered. He drank the rest of his Scotch, scowled, and lumbered toward the decanters again. "Move out of my way," he told Rix, who stepped aside to let him pass.

"Mind telling me what's going on? Who's the woman on the phone?"

"A nosy little bitch from that rag in Foxton, that's who."

"Is she after a story?"

Boone snorted. "I don't know what she's after, but she ain't gonna get it from *me*! If it ain't her callin' here, it's her father, old Wheeler Dunstan. That bastard should've been thrown into a nuthouse years ago!" Boone poured his glass full, this time not bothering with the ice. Some of his steam had been vented at the maid, but anger still hung around him like noxious fumes.

"Wheeler Dunstan?" That name rang a bell. "Doesn't he own the *Democrat*?"

"Yeah, owns it. Writes in it. Publishes it. Wipes his ass with it too, I guess, like everybody else in the county."

"I didn't know he had a daughter."

"Bitch has been away, in Memphis or somewhere. Wish it had been the moon. Daddy said nobody was to talk to any newspaper, 'specially not the *Democrat*. We keep changin' our number, and it's unlisted anyway, but somehow they keep findin' out what it is. Wait a minute." He focused his bleary eyes on Rix. "I thought you knew by now. About the book. Don't you?"

"No. What book?"

"What book? Jesus Christ in a sidecar! That crazy Dunstan bastard is writin' a book about *us*, Rixy! About the Usher family! He's been workin' on the damned thing for years!"

Rix's glass fell to the carpet.

"Dropped your glass, stupid," Boone said.

"I . . . didn't know about this." Rix's tongue felt like a plate of lead jammed into his mouth.

"Hell, yes! Bastard's diggin' up all kind of dirt about us. Used to call all hours of the day and night, till Daddy sent a lawyer to see him. That settled his dust some, but Dunstan told the lawyer we were public figures, and Daddy couldn't legally stop him from writin' that book. Ain't that a hell of a note?"

"Who knows about this besides Walen?"

"Everybody. Except you, until now. Well, why should you? You've been gone too long."

"Is . . . this book finished yet?"

"No, not yet. Daddy was puttin' together a court case when he got sick. Anyway, Daddy thinks the book'll never get finished. How's old Dunstan gonna research the thing, when all the family records and stuff are down in the Lodge's basement? Except for what Daddy brought to the Gatehouse, I mean, and no way in hell Dunstan's gonna get to *those*. So Daddy figures that sooner or later he'll give it up." He put down another few swallows of alcohol, and his eyes watered. "Edwin went over to Dunstan's house, tried to see the manuscript. Dunstan wouldn't show it to him. Daddy thinks the old bastard's probably given up on it and chucked what he had in the trash."

"If that's true, why's his daughter still calling the house?"

"Who knows? Daddy said not to talk to her, to hang up in her face. That's just what I do."

Rix picked up his glass and returned it to the sideboard. He felt unsteady, weak, and a tense laugh kept trying to escape through his teeth. Cass hadn't told him about this when he'd mentioned his idea to her. Why? Because she feared he might collaborate with Wheeler Dunstan? Smuggle secrets to the enemy camp? "How long has this been going on?" he asked.

"Seems like forever. I guess it's been about six years. That's when Dunstan called the first time. He wanted to meet with Daddy and discuss the idea. Daddy thought he was a first-class fool, and told him so."

"Six years?" Rix repeated incredulously. For six years an outsider had been probing the Usher lineage? How had Dunstan come up with the idea to begin with? What had made him think he could write such a book? And—most important—how far had he gotten with his research?

"You look sick," Boone said. "You're not fixin' to have an attack, are you?"

He didn't think so; his head was clear, and there was no pain. His stomach, however, had sunk down to the level of his kneecaps. "No."

"If you are, go throw up somewhere else. I'm gonna sit in here and get drunk."

Rix left the living room and went upstairs. He closed the door and slid a chair against it to keep Puddin' from wandering in, and then he lay down on his back on the bed. He could smell the odor of Walen's decay in the room, permeating his hair and clothes. In a frenzy, he suddenly jumped up and tore his clothes off, then turned the bathroom's shower on and stepped into the cleansing flood.

He was horrified to realize, as he dried himself off, that his father's reek had settled into the pores of his skin.

11

Night had descended over Usherland, and with it the wind had risen, sweeping down from the mountains and rattling the Gatehouse windows in their frames.

It was almost midnight when Rix left his bedroom, still clad in the suit he'd worn to dinner, and went downstairs. The corridor lights were on, pools of shadow standing around them like ink puddles. Wind whined around the house with the sound of angry hornets. Rix reached into his pocket and brought out the library key.

He went through the game room and the gentlemen's smoking room and stopped at the library door. The key fit easily into the lock, but the sound of the lock disengaging seemed loud enough to make him wince. As he stepped into the library and switched on the lights, the grandfather clock in the smoking room chimed the quarter hour.

It was one of the largest rooms in the house, its walls lined with book-packed shelves. On the hardwood floor lay a magnificent black and crimson Oriental rug, and from the high, oak-beamed ceiling hung a large wrought-iron chandelier. The library was furnished with several Black Angus–hide easy chairs, a black leather couch, an ornately carved walnut writing desk, and a worktable with a chair and green-shaded high-intensity lamp. Above a black marble fireplace hung the Usher coat of arms: three silver lions on a sable field, separated from one another by red diagonal bands called bendlets.

The room was permeated with the musty aroma of history. On the walls between the bookshelves hung oil portraits of the past masters of Usherland. Rix's grandfather—stocky, athletic Erik Usher—sat astride a beautiful chestnut stallion with the Lodge at his back. His reddish blond hair was pomaded and parted in the middle, his small dark eyes keen behind wire-rimmed spectacles, his mustache neatly trimmed. Across his knees lay the lion-headed cane.

Erik's father, Ludlow Usher, was blond and frail in the next portrait. He was depicted standing in a shadowy room, staring out one of the Lodge's windows toward the forest. He wore a black suit, and most of his pale, sharply chiseled face was shrouded in shadow as well. Behind him, a shard of light glinted off the pendulum of a grandfather clock much like the one in the smoking room. Ludlow was supporting himself on the lion-headed cane.

The following portrait showed Aram Usher, Ludlow's father. Aram was youthful and vigorous, his hair a mass of sandy blond curls, his lean and handsome face almost radiating light. He wore a gunbelt with two gold pistols, and behind him lay a phantasmagoric scene of thundering locomotives, stampeding horses, wild Indians, and flame-snorting buffalos. The lion-headed cane was propped gallantly against his right shoulder.

Hudson Usher, dour and silver-bearded, glowered down at Rix from his gray-tinted picture. His eyes were Rix's metallic shade of pewter, and they held a power that crackled over the generations. He sat in a high-backed, thronelike chair with a scarlet cushion. His right hand was clenched firmly around the lion-headed cane, and his gaze challenged anyone to take it away.

Rix turned to regard the most recent portrait, hanging across the room from Erik's. Walen Usher, broad-shouldered, aristocratically handsome, with wavy reddish blond hair, was dressed in a gray suit and vest. Behind him lay the Lodge—grown dramatically since Erik's portrait—and the blue peaks of surrounding mountains. He gripped the lion-headed cane with both hands, clutching it close to his body.

The next space was reserved for Usherland's new master. Boone would want to be captured in riding silks on a racehorse, Rix mused; he'd probably have that damned cane clenched between his teeth. But what if it was Katt, there on the wall? He could imagine the old bones and mummy dust out in the Usher cemetery writhing with indignation.

Examples of Usher weaponry also decorated the library walls: the Usher 1854 Buffalo Rifle; the 1886 Mark III revolver, which had been adopted by the Chinese navy; the 1900 recoil-operated cavalry pistol; and others, including the Enforcer, a seven-shot, .455-caliber revolver of 1902, used by police officers from Chicago to Hong Kong. The Enforcer could blow a man's head off at ten yards, and was used by the British as a field pistol during World War I.

Several cardboard boxes lay stacked around the worktable. Rix looked into one of them, and found a hodgepodge: yellowed letters wrapped in rubber bands, bundles of bills and checks, what looked like old ledgers and journals—most of them tainted with grayish green streaks of mildew. He picked up a brown leatherbound book, and as he lifted it from the box, old photographs drifted out and to the floor like dead leaves.

They were sepia-toned pictures of the Lodge. Rix put the photo album aside and bent down to retrieve them. In one, Erik Usher stood in a tweed suit and cap, smiling defiantly at the camera while, in the background, workmen crawled over scaffolds attached to the Lodge. In another, Erik sat on a white horse on the carriage bridge; again, construction was in progress on the massive house behind him. He did not smile with his eyes, Rix noted; they were intense and chilling, fixed on the camera in a haughty, challenging stare. His idea of a smile was apparently to simply crook his thin mouth to one side or the other.

Most of the photographs showed various angles of the Lodge. In many of them, workmen were present as blurred forms on spidery scaffolds. They were expanding the Lodge, Rix realized. The photos depicted a variety of seasons: the full halos of summer trees; the same trees skeletal in winter, with snow on the Lodge's roofs and smoke trailing from the chimneys; new buds bursting forth in spring. And still the workmen were there, hammers and chisels in hand, hoisting up slabs of granite or marble, building the framework of an even larger house.

Why was Erik building the Lodge bigger? What was the point, when it was already the largest house in the country? Rix looked back at the two pictures of Erik and suddenly realized something was missing.

The cane.

Erik didn't have the lion's-head cane in those two pictures.

One of the other photographs caught his eye as he started to return it to the album. It was a long shot of the Lodge, probably taken from the lakeshore. Against the massive gray face of the house was a figure in white, standing on one of the upper balconies of the east wing. A woman, Rix thought as he looked closely. A woman in a long white dress. Who was it? One of Erik's many mistresses? Walen's mother?

He dug into the box again, and uncovered a treasure of old blueprints that had been rolled up and secured with brittle rubber bands. Spreading some of them out on the worktable, Rix switched on the high-intensity lamp. The blueprints were items from Usher Armaments' black bag of tricks, circa 1941. Shown in breakaway detail were an antitank mine, a handheld rocket launcher, a flamethrower, and various machine guns.

The next thing that caught Rix's curiosity was a small, battered black book, veined with mold. He opened it under the lamp, and loose pages threatened to spill out. The paper was mustard-colored with age, and in danger of crumbling. Rix carefully turned the pages. His bewilderment mounted. Scribbled in the book were mathematical formulas, some of them going on for page after page; there were strange sketches of what looked like horseshoes with their open ends upward, supported on pedestals. The formulas continued, so dense that Rix couldn't make heads or tails of them.

Then the formulas changed into musical notations: groups of chords, bars of music. More horseshoe drawings, and then sketches of long rods with round, half-moon, or triangular shapes at their bottoms. The last pages of the book were water-stained and too moldy to decipher. Puzzled, he returned it to the box and sat for a moment staring at the wealth of documents in all the other boxes.

How in God's name could he ever hope to make sense of all of it? Months of research would be involved, and the actual writing would be a bitch. Besides, he had no control over these documents; at any time Walen might decide to return them to the Lodge, and then they'd be lost to Rix—because he could never set foot in that house again. But *why* had Walen brought them out? What was he looking for?

The story of the Ushers, who'd built a multibillion-dollar empire out of bullets and bombs, lay in those cardboard boxes—certainly not all the story, Rix knew, but enough to start with. How many skeletons and scandals were buried in those moldy graves? The material was all right here, if he could only figure out how to put it together.

He imagined the horror that was his father, lying up in the Quiet Room. His thoughts turned toward the silent Lodge, brooding at the center of Usherland, and its twisting corridors that had drawn him deeper and deeper.

The skeleton with bleeding eyes swung slowly through his mind. Logan Bodane's cunning smile—so much like Boone's, Rix thought—surfaced in his memory.

Wheeler Dunstan had been working on the Usher history for six years. *Six years.* Wouldn't he at least have the framework assembled by now? Wouldn't he know how the generations linked together? And what other secrets might he know, as well?

Rix wished he could get his hands on Dunstan's manuscript—if indeed one existed. He'd never met the man, but he'd heard his mother fume about Wheeler Dunstan before. The *Foxton Democrat* had evidently been owned by the Dunstan family for generations, and though it was only a weekly county tabloid, it delighted in running stories about the Ushers, and editorials on how Usher money had ruined the competitive tobacco market in the Rainbow-Taylorville-Foxton area. The Ushers had subsidized almost every large tobacco farm in the country, and owned every square block of Foxton except for one: the land on which the *Democrat* office stood.

Rix rummaged through one of the other boxes, and found a scrapbook full of newspaper clippings about the opening of the Usher factories in San Diego and Washington, an old ledger containing notations and monetary figures written in strong, ornate letters, and a brown book inside a manila envelope.

He opened the brown book, and an aroma like dusty roses drifted out. He found himself looking at graceful feminine handwriting. It was a diary, the dates clearly marked before each entry. He began to read the entry dated November 5, 1916:

"Mr. Usher sat across from me at the dining table. While he and Father were occupied in discussion about the war and the economy, I could feel his eye upon me. He commented on the new blue dress I was wearing, and inquired as to whether I enjoy the horse races. I told him yes, if the winning horse belongs to St. Clair Stables. Mr. Usher curls his lip when he smiles.

"In the candlelight he appeared handsome, though I have seen photographs of him in the news journals, and in them he looks like a schoolyard bully. He is in his late twenties or early thirties, I believe, and he has the build of a sportsman. His eyes are very dark, but in the light I thought I could detect a spark of color in them, like the glint of a copper coin. Mr. Usher has a laugh like a bassoon, which Father encouraged by telling him dreary business anecdotes.

"For all his coarseness, Mr. Usher does possess a certain appeal. He has a strong, uncompromising face. I noted he was wearing bay rum. Was that for my benefit? No, silly! Mr. Usher only came because he was interested in buying some of the new colts. Over dessert, Father inquired about the health of the elder Mr. Usher, and a change came over our guest. He said his father was in fine health, but he seemed to bite the words off with his teeth, and I wonder if Mr. Usher doesn't wish his father were ill. The strained mood soon passed, however, as Mr. Usher began telling Father about a new automatic pistol his company was producing. Mother and I were dismissed from the table, while Mr. Usher and Father took their brandy and cigars in the parlor."

Rix looked ahead to the next entry with Erik Usher's name in it, dated the eleventh of November: "Amazed at Mr. Usher's generosity. Today arrives a wagonload of red roses. *For me!* Father said that Mr. Usher was quite taken with me, and I should write him at Usherland to say thank you for his attention."

On November thirteenth: "Mr. Usher has interesting taste in gifts. This afternoon a gilded carriage, pulled by four of the finest white Arabians I have ever seen, came up the drive. Inside it were more than a hundred fishbowls full of Japanese goldfish. It was testimonial to the carriage and horses that none of them had spilled out. A letter from Mr. Usher—he wants me to call him Erik, dear diary—said he hoped I would enjoy the fish, and that I would use the carriage and stallions to visit him at Usherland for Christmas. Mother says I shouldn't go unescorted, but Father got angry and said all those things written about Erik Usher were simply lies, and that he is a fine, upstanding Christian businessman."

Right, Rix thought. He pulled the wool over your daddy's eyes, didn't he, Nora?

This diary belonged to Nora St. Clair Usher—Erik's only wife, Walen's mother, his own grandmother.

The grandfather clock in the smoking room chimed out one o'clock. For a moment Rix listened to the wail of wind, moving past the Gatehouse's walls.

He could start with this diary, he told himself. At least it might help him get a better understanding of Erik Usher, and certainly of Nora St. Clair Usher, whom Walen rarely talked about. Then he might begin to make sense of some of the other material.

Rix returned everything to the cardboard boxes and left the library, taking the diary with him. He switched off the chandelier and locked the door again, then climbed the stairs to his bedroom. The house, but for the noise of the raging wind, was quiet.

In his room, Rix sat at his desk and began to read where he'd left off. On the first day of 1917, Erik had asked for Nora's hand in marriage. Nora was indecisive. Her mother told her she'd have to make up her own mind, but Erik was the catch of a lifetime. Nora's father said that only a fool would pass up such a sterling opportunity.

They were married at the First Methodist Church of Charlotte on the second of March, 1917. Ludlow Usher did not attend the ceremony. Details of the wedding night were omitted. The next entry was a week later: Erik had left on a business trip to England, and Nora was alone in the Lodge.

Old bastard, Rix thought.

A spark of light caught his attention, and he looked up from the diary.

There was nothing but darkness beyond his window; then, lasting for only a second, there came the glint of a light, out in the forest between the Gatehouse and the Lodge. It did not reappear.

Rix sat watching for several minutes longer. The darkness was absolute. Had he imagined a light out there, or not? Christ! he thought. Thinking you saw a light in a dark forest past midnight was the oldest horror-fiction cliché in the book! At this point, in his books at least, the gallant—and stupid—hero would go out there to investigate and get turned into walking hamburger. But this was real life, and Rix was no hero. He knew no local thief would be prowling across Usherland in the dark; you couldn't find one man in the whole county who'd set foot on the estate after nightfall, not with all the stories that circulated about the Pumpkin Man, the black panther, the hag who supposedly lived in the depths of one of the lakes, and all the other beasties roaming about.

There was nothing out there, anyway. Nothing except Erik's zoo, and that lay in ruins.

Still—had he seen a light, or not?

There was no light now, if he had. If some fool had fallen into the empty alligator pit, he'd still be there with a broken leg in the morning.

Rix returned to his reading, but every now and then he glanced into the darkness.

The Lodge was out there. A malengine, waiting for someone to turn the key again, set it thundering. Waiting for Katt? Or for Boone?

Ten billion dollars, he mused. Then he submerged himself into the life of Nora St. Clair Usher.

Three

---◆◆◆---

RAVEN

12

She'd been in some rough places before, and right now she wished she were back at any one of them. The narrow dirt road that led her yellow Volkswagen Beetle up Briartop Mountain was so littered with loose stones and muddy potholes that she feared from one moment to the next either a blowout or a stuck wheel. She'd climbed more than a mile in first gear, and she kept thinking she smelled the transmission burning. Since leaving the Perry cabin, way down at the foot of Briartop, a bone-jarring forty-minute drive away, she'd seen not a living soul and only a few cabins all but hidden in the thick woods.

Clint Perry had told her to look for a clapboard house with red shutters and two big oaks that sprawled above the roof. He'd warned her not to put the Volkswagen in any of the ditches alongside the road; hard to get a tow truck up some of them trails that pass as roads, he'd said. Get stuck in a ditch and you won't get your car down till after New Year's.

She definitely didn't want to spend any more time than necessary on Briartop Mountain. She was surrounded by the densest forests she'd ever seen, and though it was almost ten in the morning, even the bright golden sunlight failed to penetrate the overhang of foliage. An occasional bird called from a treetop, but otherwise all was quiet. The wind, so vicious last night that it had awakened her constantly, had died to a still, soft whisper. Yellow and red leaves drifted down from the trees, forming a colorful carpet across the road.

The Volks jarred over a series of potholes. Hope the damned suspension holds! she told herself. She passed a rickety-looking cabin with a smoking stone chimney and saw a big red dog lying in front of it in a splash of sunlight. The dog's ears perked up at the sound of the car's straining engine, but the animal was obviously too lazy even to bark. It watched her go by, its tongue hanging out like a pink towel.

The road ascended at a still steeper angle. She was torturing the engine, but if she shifted down to second gear it wouldn't pull. Not going to make it, she thought grimly.

And then she came around a wooded bend and nearly ran right over an old man in rags, who was slowly crossing the road with the aid of a gnarled walking stick.

For an instant she knew she was going to hit him. She could almost hear the crunch of bone. Then her foot moved toward the brake and the car stopped so suddenly she was jerked forward against the steering wheel.

The old man continued on his way, his shoes—old orange fisherman's boots—shuffling through the dead leaves. He was emaciated, his head bowed by the weight of a long yellowish gray beard, his bony shoulders stooped. His cane probed carefully ahead for potholes.

She stuck her head out the open window. "Excuse me." He didn't stop. "Mister, excuse me!"

Finally the old man paused, but he didn't look in her direction. He was waiting for her to speak.

"I'm looking for the Tharpe house." She spoke with a Southern accent that still carried faint hints of a Scots-Irish brogue. "Is it near here?"

He cocked his head to one side, listening; then, still silent, he continued crossing the road and began moving away into the woods.

"Hey!" she called, but the forest had closed behind him like a multicolored door. "Some great hospitality up here," she muttered, and gunned the Volkswagen onward and upward. It came to her then that the car had stopped an instant before she'd put her foot to the brake. Or had it?

Going screwy, she thought, and breathed a sigh of relief as she saw the cabin with the red shutters ahead. It was set about thirty feet or so off the road, and in the front yard there was a beat-up old pickup truck with a green fender, a brown door, a red roof, and rusted-out bumpers. A discarded hand-crank washing machine lay on its side in high weeds. What looked like a truck engine lay over there as well, gathering rust.

She pulled her car off the road and behind the pickup truck. As she was getting out, the cabin's screened front door opened and a

110

skinny middle-aged woman with lank brown hair and wearing faded jeans and a pale yellow sweater stepped out onto the front porch.

"Mrs. Tharpe?" the younger woman inquired as she approached.

"Who might you be?" It was asked sharply, brimming with suspicion.

"My name is Raven Dunstan. I've come from Foxton to see you."

"What about?"

"I talked to Sheriff Kemp yesterday afternoon. He told me your youngest son's been missing since night before last. Can I come up and talk to you for a few minutes?"

Myra Tharpe crossed her arms over her chest. She'd been a pretty woman once, a long time ago, but the years had been unkind to her; the harsh weather of Briartop Mountain had etched deep lines along the ravines and crests of her sallow face, and her small dark brown eyes were ringed with wrinkles. Now they were puffy from the crying she'd been doing. Her mouth was a thin, grim line, and her chin ended in a sharp point. She regarded her visitor with a bitter, unyielding stare. "Nobody called the sheriff," she replied. "Nobody told him about Nathan."

"Clint Perry did, yesterday. He's a part-time deputy, you know."

"Nobody asked an outsider to butt in," Myra said. "It's nobody's business." She examined the other woman: a city woman, dressed in corduroys and a dark blue jacket over a white blouse. City woman, through and through. Maybe about twenty-five, tall, with a curly mane of black hair that spilled around her shoulders. She had clear, pale blue eyes and a fair, smooth complexion that showed she sure didn't work in the weather. She wore almost no makeup, and she was pretty, but something was wrong with her left leg because she limped when she walked. As Raven came closer to the porch steps, Myra saw a white scar slashed through her left eyebrow, hitching it upward. City woman. Even her hands were white and smooth. What was she doin', way up here on Briartop?

"I'd like to talk to you for a few minutes about Nathan," Raven said. "May I come in?"

"No. I'll hear what you've got to say right here."

"I'm from the *Foxton Democrat*." Raven brought her wallet out of her shoulderbag and showed her press card, but the other woman didn't look at it.

"That newspaper? I don't never read it."

111

"Oh. Well, Mr. Perry told the sheriff that a search party went out looking for your two sons the night before last, and that one of them—is Newlan his name?—came home the next morning. He said the search party went out again yesterday, but they didn't find a trace of Nathan. Are they going to look again today?"

"A few men are out in the woods right now," she replied. "If my boy *can* be found, they'll find him."

Something in the way she said that put Raven on guard. "Don't you think they'll find him, Mrs. Tharpe?"

"If he's to be found."

She'd been prepared for resistance. Her father had told her about the mountain people. But what Raven felt from this woman was direct hostility. "May I talk to Newlan, then?"

"No. New's sleepin'. He got hurt in the woods."

"Nothing serious, I hope."

"Cuts and bruises. He'll be all right in a few days."

"Who are the men who've been searching for Nathan, Mrs. Tharpe?"

"Men," she said, her eyes narrowing. "You wouldn't know 'em, you bein' an outsider and all."

"Why didn't you go to the sheriff about this?" Raven asked. "He would've organized a proper search—"

"Is this gonna be in that newspaper? You writin' a story about my boys?"

"No. This is for my own information."

"I see," Myra said, nodding. "Well then, I've said about all I can say."

Raven asked, "All you can say . . . or all you *will* say?"

"Both." She turned away and started to go back inside.

"Mrs. Tharpe?" Raven called. "I'd like to talk to you about the Pumpkin Man."

The other woman stopped dead. Raven saw her shoulders tense; then Myra turned around again, and this time her face was squeezed with emotion, the cheeks splotched with color. "Get off my land, city woman," she said.

"You're familiar with the Pumpkin Man, then?"

"I'm through talkin'."

"Why? Because you think the Pumpkin Man's listening? Come on, Mrs. Tharpe! Talk to me! Let me come in and see Newlan."

"I said get off my land. I won't say it again."

"What's wrong with you people?" Raven's voice was tinged with frustration. "What are you trying to hide? My God, Mrs. Tharpe!

112

Your son's been missing for two nights! You don't even report it to Sheriff Kemp! What are you people afraid of?"

Myra Tharpe whirled and entered the house. She came back a moment later, carrying a shotgun. Without hesitation she swung it up, pointing its barrel toward Raven. "I'll give you a minute, city woman," she warned quietly. "If you ain't off my land in a minute, I'll blow your fancy ass into the trees."

Raven began carefully backing away from the porch. "All right," she said. "I'll go. Don't get nervous."

"I'll nervous a hole straight through your head."

Raven reached the car—damn, her leg was aching!—and climbed in. Myra Tharpe was still aiming the shotgun as she started the Volks, put it in reverse, and eased back onto the road. Then she drove away down the mountain, having to ride the brakes to keep the tires from slipping. Her hands were clenched hard around the wheel.

◆ ◆ ◆

"Damned fool," Myra Tharpe muttered as she lowered the shotgun. It was an Usher gun, and had been Bobby's pride and joy before the accident. As she turned to go inside, she saw New standing behind the screen. There were bandages on his neck and across the bridge of his nose. His eyes were swollen, and beneath them were deep blue hollows. Bandages were wrapped around his raw, scraped fingers.

He stepped back as his mother entered the house and closed the door behind her. She crossed the small parlor and returned Bobby's shotgun to its rack near the stone fireplace. The house was simply constructed, with only two rooms and a kitchen in addition to the parlor; the plank floors in some places rose and tilted like a sea in motion, and the thin wooden roof often dripped rainwater like a sieve. Most of the pinewood furniture had been handmade by Bobby in a shed out back, near the outhouse, and cheap rugs helped cover the water stains on the floor. Now the house smelled of cooking blackberries and rich pastry. Mr. Berthon, owner of the Broadleaf Cafe, was expecting his pies today.

"So," Myra Tharpe said, looking at her son, "how much of that did you hear?"

"Most all."

"You shouldn't be out of bed. Run on, now."

"Why wouldn't you let that woman in to talk to me, Ma?" New asked quietly.

" 'Cause our business is our business, that's why! She's an out sider, a city woman. You can tell that just by lookin' at her."

"Maybe so," New agreed, "but I think she wanted to help."

"*Help.*" She said it like a sneer. "We don't need no help from an outsider, boy! That's fool talk. Now you run on back to bed where you belong." She started toward the kitchen, the floor creaking under her steps.

"Ma?" New said. "I *saw* him. Up on the edge of that pit. I saw him, and I heard his black cat prowlin'—"

"You didn't see or hear *nothin'*!" she snapped, turning on him. She advanced a few steps, but New stood his ground. Myra reddened to the roots of her hair. "Do you *understand* me, boy?" She started to reach out and shake him, but he said, "Don't do that, Ma," and an undercurrent in his voice stayed her hand. She blinked uncertainly; he was growin' up *so* fast! She dropped her hand to her side, but her eyes flashed anger. "You didn't see or hear a *thing* out there!"

"He took Nathan." New's voice cracked. "He bundled Nathan up under his arm, and he took him off into the woods. I know, Ma, because I saw him and nobody can say I didn't."

"It was dark and you were a-layin' in them thorns all cut and busted up! You got a knot on the back of your head as big as a man's fist! How do you know what you saw out there?"

In his pale, scratched-up face, New's eyes were fiery, dark green emeralds. "I saw the Pumpkin Man," he said steadfastly. "He took Nathan."

"Don't you say that name in this house, boy!"

"That woman was right. You *are* afraid. Of what, Ma? Tell me."

"Outsiders ain't never right!" Tears welled up in her eyes. "You don't understand a thing, New. Not a single blessed thing. You don't talk to outsiders—especially not about *him*. We don't want outsiders on Briartop Mountain, askin' their fool questions and pokin' their noses into every gully. We take care of our own."

"If I didn't see him," New replied, "then what happened to Nathan, Ma? How come none of those men have found Nathan by now?"

"Nathan got hisself lost in the woods. He took a wrong path somewhere. Maybe the thorns got him. I don't know. If he's to be found, they'll bring him back to us."

New shook his head. "They won't find him. You know that, and so do I. If they were gonna find him, they would've by now. And Nathan wouldn't have gone off the path, Ma. Not in the dark."

Myra started to speak, then stopped; when her voice came, it was an anguished whisper: "Don't beg trouble, son. Don't go seekin' it. Lord knows, I'm just about to go crazy inside over Nathan, but . . .

114

you're all I got now. You have to be the man of the house. We've got to be strong, and go on with our lives. Do you understand that?"

New didn't. Why had his ma prevented him from talking to the newspaperwoman? Why had she not even let him talk to the local men who'd volunteered for the search party? But he saw how close she was to breaking down, and he said, "Yes, ma'am."

"Good." She forced a weak, crooked smile, but her eyes were tortured. "That's my good boy. Now you get on back to bed. You need your rest." She paused for only a moment, her lower lip trembling, and then she went back to the kitchen to tend to her pies.

New returned to the room he'd shared with Nathan. There were two cots, divided by a rickety pine desk. The room had no closet; New's and Nathan's clothes were hung on a metal rod bolted to one of the walls. A single window looked toward the road, and it was through this that New had seen the newspaperwoman drive up.

New closed the door and sat down on his cot. He smelled the medicine his mother had used on his cuts: tobacco juice and iodine. It had stung him like the Devil's pitchfork.

He'd dreamed of the Lodge again last night. The house was ablaze with lights, the brightest thing New had ever seen in his life, and as he'd watched, he'd seen figures pass back and forth behind the windowglass. They moved slowly, with stately cadence, as if they were dancing at a huge party. And in the dream, as it usually happened, he'd heard his name called as if from a vast distance, the whispering, seductive voice that he thought sometimes lured him to the edge of The Devil's Tongue.

Questions about the Pumpkin Man plagued him. What was the thing, and why had it taken Nathan? Better to ask the moon why it changed shape, he thought. The Pumpkin Man lived in the wind, in the trees, in the earth, in the thorns. The Pumpkin Man came out from his hiding places to snatch the unwary away. If I hadn't fallen into those thorns, New told himself, Nathan would still be here. He looked at Nathan's cot. I could've saved him . . . somehow. I'm the man of the house, and I could've done *something*.

Couldn't I?

His pa would've let him talk to that woman, he knew. His pa wasn't afraid of anything. And now he was the man of the house, and Nathan's cot was empty.

New lifted his cot's thin mattress and took out the magic knife.

He'd brought it home hidden inside his jacket, tucked up his sleeve out of sight. It was a trick his pa had shown him once; you put a knife up your sleeve, and when you want it you just straighten your arm out real fast and it slides right into your hand. Pa had been a hard drinker a long time ago, before he'd married Ma, and New suspected his father had used that trick to protect himself in some of the rough backhills honkytonks.

The magic knife was his secret. He hadn't shown it to his mother, and he didn't know exactly why, but he knew he wanted to test it further before he told her.

He laid it on Nathan's cot and then sat back down again.

I want it, he said in his mind, and held his bandaged hand out.

The knife didn't move.

He had to want it harder. He focused all his attention on urging the magic knife to come to him. I want it now, he thought.

Maybe the knife shivered—and maybe it didn't.

The image of the dark shape with Nathan under its arm came to him unbidden. He saw the moonlight on his brother's face, felt the thorny coils holding him tight as he tried to struggle, saw in his mind a hideous grin spreading across the Pumpkin Man's malformed head.

He took a deep breath.

I WANT IT NOW!

The magic knife flew up from the cot with a suddenness that amazed him. It spun in midair, gathering speed, and then came end over end toward his hand.

But it was too fast, faster than he could control, and he realized that the knife might go right through him and into the wall.

And then his mother opened the door to tell him she was sorry she'd lost her temper, and she was looking into the room when the knife curved in the air, inches away from his body, and slammed violently upward into the ceiling, three feet above her head.

She gasped, the breath shocked out of her.

The knife stuck in the ceiling and stayed there, quivering with a sound like a broken fiddle string.

13

Rix awakened in the embrace of his grandmother's ghost.

The room was a hazy gold, filled with sunlight that streamed through the trees outside. It was after ten o'clock; Rix was ravenously hungry, and he regretted that no one had awakened him for breakfast. Lunch wouldn't be served until twelve-thirty.

He rose from the bed and stretched. This morning he'd read in Nora Usher's diary until almost two o'clock, and scenes of Usher life in 1917 and 1918 stayed in his mind as vividly as the old sepia-toned photographs he'd found in the library. After the wedding, Nora's entries in her diary had become more and more terse and erratic. He could sense a change in her personality, from that of a sheltered child to that of a bewildered but awesomely wealthy woman. Whole months went by without a notation, or sometimes a month was summed up simply in a phrase describing a dinner party or some other activity. It was clear that Nora was bored out of her skull at Usherland, and that Erik—once he had her under his thumb—had tired of her very quickly indeed.

Rix washed his face with cold water in the bathroom, and with a finger traced the deep lines around his eyes. But were they less deep than the day before? Was his complexion less pale, his eyes less weary-looking? He knew he felt fine, but he took his vitamins anyway.

There was a knock at his bedroom door, and Rix opened it.

"Rise and shine," Cass said, bringing in a tray of scrambled eggs, sausage patties, grits, and a small pot of coffee.

"Good morning. Sorry I overslept breakfast."

"I saved you some. Were you up late last night?" She set the tray down on his desk—right beside, Rix realized, the open diary of Nora Usher.

"Yes. Pretty late."

If she noticed the diary, Cass didn't react to it. Her smile was broad and sunny. "Your mother wanted to wake you up. She had to eat alone this morning, but I persuaded her to let you sleep."

"Thanks. The food looks great. Where was Boone this morning?"

"I don't think he came home before sunrise." Before Rix could reach the diary, Cass had turned and was pouring him a cup of coffee. "His love of poker is bad for his bank account. What's this?" She nodded toward the open book.

"Just . . . something I'm reading."

"It looks very old." Rix saw her eyes flicker across the page, and she stopped pouring. "Where did you get it, Rix?" she asked, and he heard from her tone of voice that she knew what it was. He didn't respond for a few seconds, trying to think of a good story, but then she faced him and he knew he couldn't lie to her.

"Edwin gave me the library key."

"Oh. Then . . . you know about the books that were brought from the Lodge."

"That's right, and I also know about the Usher history that Wheeler Dunstan's writing. Cass, why didn't you tell me about that?"

She set the pot aside, avoiding Rix's gaze. "I don't know," she said with a soft sigh. "I guess I just . . . didn't think it was important."

"Not *important*?" he asked incredulously. "Some stranger's been working for six years on a history of the family, and you don't think that's important? Come on, Cass! When Boone told me about it, I almost hit the ceiling! If anybody should write that book, it should be me. Not a stranger."

"Dunstan will never finish it," she said calmly, and lifted her eyes to his.

"But it seems to have worried Dad enough to send a lawyer after him."

"Your father values his privacy. He wants to protect the Usher name. Can you blame him?"

Rix paused. On Cass's face was such firm resolve that he felt tugged toward her point of view. "No," he said. "I guess not."

"Right now," she continued, "any press coverage would be bad for your family's situation. Sooner or later the reporters are going to find out your father's dying. They'll swarm all over Usherland—God forbid. But I hope that'll be after the estate is settled and the business has changed hands."

Rix grunted, picked up his cup, and sipped at the coffee. "Who's Dad got his eye on?" he asked, trying to sound casual about it. "Boone or Katt?"

"I can't say. Edwin thinks Mr. Usher favors your sister. She has the better education."

Rix shook his head. "No, I can't see her wanting it. She's too happy doing what she does now." The next question came out before he could stop it: "Is she staying straight?"

"As far as I know," she replied, and shrugged. "She's sworn off everything but an occasional glass of wine. She still smokes too much, though—just regular cigarettes, none of that funny stuff. After what happened in Tokyo, well—" She left the rest unsaid.

Katt had been caught entering Japan on a modeling assignment several years ago with twelve grams of high-grade coke and an ounce of Maui Wowie stashed in jars in her makeup case. The Japanese

118

police had crashed down hard on her, and the mess had dragged on for almost a month. Rix, at that time busy working on a novel about witches, called *Congregation*, had seen the stories in the papers; in one front-page picture, Katt was wan and unkempt, being supported between her father and Boone as they entered a limo in front of a police station. Walen's cane was raised threateningly toward the photographers, and Boone's mouth curled in a snarled curse.

"So"—Cass motioned toward the diary—"are you reading that for pleasure . . . or research?"

"If I tell you that I really do intend to write the book, will you go to Edwin or Dad?"

She frowned, two lines deepening between her eyes, and thought for a moment. "I took an oath of loyalty to your father, Rix," she said finally. "Just as Edwin did. I'm bound by that oath to tell him if I feel something's going on he should know about."

Suddenly Rix was struck by a horrifying thought. Cass might not even have to tell Walen. If his hearing was sharp enough to pick up voices in the living room, he could certainly hear this conversation right now! Still, Walen wouldn't completely understand what they were talking about—or would he? "He can hear us, can't he?" Rix asked in a nervous whisper, his heart pounding. "Is that what you wanted, for him to hear?"

"No. He can't hear. I took Mrs. Reynolds her breakfast an hour ago, and he was asleep. She'd given him his tranquilizers, because he had a restless night."

Cass had never lied to him, and he could see in her face now that this was the truth. Still, he was wary. "Will you tell him?" he asked, keeping his voice low. Before she could answer, he grasped her hand. "Please don't, Cass. I'm begging you. Give me a chance. Ever since . . . Sandra died, things haven't been going too well for me. I can't make my ideas work anymore; everything comes out scrambled and screwed up. Sandra helped me talk things out, and she kept me going. Without her . . . I just can't get a handle on anything anymore." He squeezed her hand. "I have to start working on another book, Cass. If I don't, Dad will have been right about me— I'll be nothing but a hack who had a stroke of good luck."

"Why are you so sure you could write a family history? It seems to me that writing a novel would be so much easier."

"I'm not sure, but I've got to try it. The research will be hard, yes, but the story's already written! All I have to do is put it together. What if Wheeler Dunstan does finish it first? He's got a six-year head start on me! If I lose my chance, I don't know what I'll do."

Her face was a mirror of her conflicting emotions. "I . . . took an oath."

"You and Edwin are about to retire. You'll be long gone by the time I finish the book. All I'm asking of you is that you give me some time. If you tell Dad, he'll send all the documents back to the Lodge, and if that happens there's no way I can get to them. *Please.* Time is all I'm asking for."

Cass pulled her hand free. "I'll have to think about this. I can't promise you one way or the other."

Rix felt clammy, and his heart continued to pound.

"Are you all right?" Cass asked. "You look pale."

He nodded. "I need some breakfast, I guess."

"Well, eat it before it gets cold." She walked to the door and paused before she went out. "You've put me in a bad spot, Rix," she said quietly. "I love you—but I love Mr. Usher, too."

"Whom do you love more?" he asked.

Cass left the room without answering.

Rix felt slimy inside; asking her to make a choice like that was a manipulation his father might have used. If she told Walen about his idea, though, he might as well forget about it. The idea rightfully belonged to him, not to a stranger! He touched his temple and felt a sheen of cold sweat.

The skeleton with bloody eye sockets swung back and forth, back and forth in his mind. Droplets of blood ran down the white cheekbones. Sandra's hair floated in the red water.

"Failure," he heard his father say. "You're nothing but a damned failure . . ."

Rix gripped the edge of the desk. His nerves were on fire.

The golden light that filled the room began to grow harshly yellow, so bright that it stung his eyes. He heard water gurgling through the Gatehouse pipes. Boone's snoring sounded like the rumble of a chainsaw through the wall. A noise like a mosquito's hum grew steadily louder. The hum became a whine. It was the Jetcopter, approaching Usherland.

He had to find a place to hide. The nearest Quiet Room was Boone's, but he'd have to get through Puddin' to use it. There was a closet in Katt's room, Walen had said. He'd have to hurry to get there before the full force of the oncoming attack hit him. His head was hammering as he stumbled toward the door and reached for the knob.

120

But as his arm stretched out for it, the doorknob changed. It was no longer a large octagon of cut crystal; now it was fashioned of polished silver, and embossed on it was the face of a roaring lion.

Rix pulled his hand back as if he'd been burned. A whipstrike of pain seared through his head, and at that instant he saw an emaciated body laying in darkness on a bed, and he realized it was not his father but himself, rotting in the Quiet Room.

And then it was over. The attack had passed, leaving him sweating and shivering, with his forehead pressed against the door. The intensity of the light faded, as did the Gatehouse sounds.

He looked at the cut-crystal doorknob. The silver lion's-face was gone. But he'd seen that silver doorknob before. He couldn't recall where. Perhaps, he wondered, in his recurrent nightmares of the Lodge?

He asked himself why the attack had stopped. The sweat was drying on his face, and his heartbeat was returning to normal. Usually, by now, he'd be crawling on his belly. Was what Walen said about Usherland true? he wondered. Now that he was back, was he getting better?

Still shaky, Rix dressed in a pair of khaki trousers, a white shirt, and a brown pullover sweater. In his closet had materialized three new suits in his size, pants, sweaters, and a dozen starched dress shirts. He sat down at his desk and ravenously ate the food Cass had brought.

Then, feeling a lot better, he paged through the diary.

He had no idea what Nora St. Clair Usher had looked like, but he remembered the photograph of the woman in white, standing on a balcony. She'd held herself with regal dignity, though there'd been something terribly sad about that picture: a single figure, standing alone against the grandeur of the Lodge, staring out across the black, solemn lake. He envisioned Nora as a woman of her time—childlike, innocent, maybe a little spoiled, but certainly beautiful. In his imagination he gave her a slender frame, ringlets of light brown hair brushed back from a high forehead, the large gray eyes of a curious waif. Surely she was a stylish woman, or Erik wouldn't have gone after her so ardently. She was charming, able to chat amiably with any of the guests Erik brought to Usherland, and probably a model hostess.

Rix drank his coffee and poured himself a second cup. He was feeling much stronger now. The breakfast had helped.

He stopped at what was written in the diary under "July 5,

1919." It was the first entry in more than six months. The handwriting was shaky, marred with untidy smears and blotches. Nora's strain was showing.

The first line read, "He is a murderer."

As he read, Nora St. Clair Usher began to speak to Rix over the decades. Her words sparked his imagination; they roamed over time and space, and suddenly he was attending the Fourth of July Gala held at Usherland more than thirty years before his birth.

◆ ◆ ◆

A thousand Japanese lanterns winked with rainbow colors in Usherland's trees. Long tables covered with fine white Irish lace had been set up on the lakeshore for Erik Usher's guests. More than six hundred people had come to be fed on roast pig, thick slabs of Chicago beef, New England lobster, veal, lamb, and platters of raw oysters on ice, flown up from Florida. There were pickled quail eggs, pheasant's tongue in vinaigrette, smoked Peking duck, and Alaskan king crabs as big as Rolls-Royce wheels. Blazing torches embedded in the ground illuminated the scene as an army of waiters in red tuxedos scurried around the tables, pouring champagne into crystal goblets. On a white bandstand decorated with American flags, a brass band played regimental marching music. Cicadas hummed in the trees, and every so often a lion or some other big predator roared from Erik's private zoo.

Small American flags were placed beside every plate. The guests had dressed in accordance with a request on their gold-embossed invitations: all of them, from Washington diplomat to Asheville bank president, wore red, white, and blue.

At the head of the longest table, Erik Usher suddenly rose to his feet. Broad-shouldered and hulking, he wore a flaming red suit, a white bow tie, and a blue shirt. He lifted a megaphone to his lips, torchflame sparkling in his eyeglasses. "A toast!" he bellowed, and raised his champagne glass.

The brass band stopped in mid-cadence. The noise of six hundred eighty-four people talking, eating, and drinking faded to a soft mutter. Waiters were stumbling over each other, trying to fill all the upraised glasses. Corks popped like firecrackers.

"Well?" Erik shouted through the megaphone. "*Stand up,* damn it!"

The guests rose as if at attention before the President of the United States—whose aide, Mr. Conyers, was placed beside a stunning, white-silk-clad Nora Usher. She wore blue gloves, and there were red ribbons in her hair. As Nora stood up, she saw the drunken gleam in her husband's eyes. He'd had too much champagne. If this party was like others Erik had hosted, it might continue for days, until people passed out on the ground or swam naked in the estate's fountains. She lifted her glass with the others. Across the table from her, Harry Sanderson—a middle-aged tobacco magnate from Winston-Salem—belched up a breath of crabmeat and garlic sauce.

"To the Fourth of July," Erik roared, "and to the principles on which this great nation was founded! Long may our flag wave over a country where any man can roll up his goddamned sleeves and make himself a millionaire!" Behind him, across the flat surface of the lake, the Lodge glowed with light. It was an awesome sight, and still Erik ordered the workmen to continue building. In the darkness that was Briartop Mountain, a few specks of light could be seen through the trees.

"My great-great-grandfather came here from Wales with his pockets full of coal dust!" Erik said. "But he had an idea. He designed a rifle that would knock a redskin from Kansas City into Canada, and that sonofabitch *worked*! The Usher Repeating Rifle opened this country's frontier, and without it we might be eating corn soup instead of roast beef, and jingling beads in our pockets instead of silver dollars!"

There was a murmur of laughter. Down the table, a young floozy who'd arrived hooked on the arm of a rich, elderly gunpowder merchant giggled like a hyena.

Nora was not a drinker. She detested the taste of alcohol, and so there was only icewater in her glass. Cigar smoke wafted through the air like a blue fog, irritating her sinuses. Over Erik's shoulder, she suddenly saw a shape move past the glass walls of the cupola that stood on the highest roof of the Lodge. Erik's father, Ludlow, had become all but a hermit in the two years she'd been an Usher's wife. She rarely saw him, and he never spoke to her. He stayed up in that glass cupola for the most part, but sometimes at night she could hear him walking the corridor outside her bedchamber. She could tell it was him, because she heard the cane tapping on the hardwood floor.

Suddenly, Erik put down his glass and grabbed Nora's arm, pulling her toward him. She stumbled, spilling water all over her dress. He smelled of the horses that he ran, hour after hour, day after day, on the estate's racetrack. "And I've got an announcement for you people!" he told them. "I'm gonna be a *father*!" There was a hearty round of applause and shouts of bravo. Erik patted Nora's stomach, and she felt her face burn. "Gonna be a father in February or March, the doctor says! So this toast is to the future, too, and all the Ushers who are yet to be born. Everybody can drink now!"

Nora pulled away from him and sat down. She'd planned on sending out announcements to a select group of friends, and thought Erik had agreed. By morning, the item would be in the Asheville newspaper, she knew. She caught Mrs. Van Doss watching her with a cold smile on her weasel features. Across the table, Harry Sanderson lit another of his seven-inch-long Havana cigars and shouted for more champagne.

The fireworks display began with an ear-cracking boom that echoed across the lake and back again off the walls of the Lodge. The sky lit up with fiery colors, red rockets, blue star-shells, gold pinwheels. The display, which had cost Erik more than sixty thousand dollars, went on for more than a half hour; when it was over and the last cinder had hissed into the lake, Nora was a trembling bundle of raw nerves. Erik grinned gleefully. The lights had gone out, Nora saw, in the glass cupola.

After the applause had died away and Nora forced herself to converse with an elderly Asheville social queen named Delilah Huckabee, Sanderson clapped his hands and called out, "Fine show, Erik! Damned fine! Couldn't have done better myself!" His blue bow tie was crooked, his eyes red-rimmed. His wife was trying to control him, but having little effect.

"You know the Ushers, Harry," Erik replied, cutting another slab of beef from the platter before him. "We always entertain with a bang."

"How much your daddy give you to put on that show, Erik?"

Erik glanced up. There was a thin smile on his grease-filmed mouth, but his eyes were like chunks of granite. "You're drinking too much, aren't you, Harry?"

"The hell I am, boy! See, I came to your daddy's fortieth birthday party, right here at Usherland. Now *that* was one hell of a party! Old bastard must've shot off a hundred thousand bucks' worth of fireworks! How much did he give you to buy yours?"

Sanderson was probing a sore spot, and he knew it. Erik Usher was still on his father's payroll. Though Ludlow's health was unsteady, the old man held the purse strings—and Nora had heard Erik rage like a madman over what he considered a paltry allowance.

124

"Yeah," Sanderson continued, with an exaggerated wink at Nora, "that old Ludlow really knew how to throw a party. Made people sit up and take notice, he did. When you went to one of *his* parties, you never forgot it. He must've spent a hundred thousand bucks on those fireworks. Went on for a goddamned hour, they did."

"Is that so?" Erik asked. Flames glinted in his glasses. About thirty people were listening to this exchange, and none of them but Nora knew what was seething inside her husband. "So you like fireworks, Harry?"

"Went on for a goddamned hour," he said. "Champagne over here, waiter!"

Erik slowly stood up. His chest was thrust forward like a fighting rooster's. Nora recognized it as a dangerous sign. "If it's fireworks you like, Harry . . . then it's fireworks you'll get. Enjoy the party. Drink up. And smile. Mr. Conyers, will you attend to my wife for a while, please? I'll return shortly." Before Nora could ask him where he was going, Erik strode briskly across the lawn to the cars parked along the drive. He slid into a Rolls-Royce limousine and it turned around, heading out of Usherland.

The band played on, and for the next hour or so Nora talked to Mr. Conyers about the social scene in Washington. Harry Sanderson progressively slid lower in his seat. A formally dressed couple leaped into the lake. Someone produced a pistol and began to shoot out the hanging lanterns.

Nora's conversation was interrupted by the rumble of engines. Headlights stabbed through the woods. Three Usher trucks, each towing something covered with green tarpaulins, were approaching the Lodge. They stopped on the road, thirty yards from the tables. She heard a man shouting; it sounded like Erik's voice, but she wasn't sure. Other figures began to scramble out of the trucks. Erik materialized from the gloom, walking toward his guests, and Nora rose from her seat.

Erik's face was flushed, and as he walked right past Nora she heard him breathing hard, like an enraged animal. "Harry?" he asked, and the drunken man looked up, unable to focus. "I've brought you a present, Harry. Something to help you remember my party."

"Thass damn fine," Harry mumbled, and grinned stupidly.

The tarpaulins were being whipped back. Nora saw the men from the trucks straining to pivot the objects around. It took Nora a moment to make out what the tarpaulins had uncovered.

Guns. Usher field howitzers, similar to one in a battlefield photograph Erik had once proudly shown her.

"Fireworks," Erik said, smiling. People were already starting to leave their seats. The guns were being aimed right at the crowd.

"Ready, Mr. Usher!" one of the gun crewmen called out.

"Erik," Nora began, stunned. "My God, you can't—"

"Hope you like the show, Harry." Erik turned regally toward the trucks and shouted, "Fire!"

The first howitzer went off. Its shell streaked over the tables with a noise like a freight train, up into the air above the Lodge, and toward Briartop Mountain.

There was a roar such as might be made by the damned souls of Hades as party guests scrambled wildly away, crashing into each other, knocking over tables, food, and champagne. The other cannons began to fire, each blast shaking the earth, the concussion knocking scores of people to their knees. Mr. and Mrs. Sanderson flew out of their chairs like ragdolls, and Nora went down clinging to Mr. Conyers. Champagne bottles exploded in their cases. The Japanese lanterns swung wildly back and forth. As the shells continued to flash overhead, the sky was lit up with an eerie, pulsating red glow.

Still the blasts went on. Her head ringing, Nora sat dazedly on her knees, watching people in tuxedos and evening dresses running for the safety of the woods, being knocked down by the shockwaves, getting up and fleeing again. The air reeked of gunpowder. The band had left their instruments behind when the entire bandstand collapsed like cardboard. Some of the shells had been coated with phosphorus, and Nora watched one of them flare over the Lodge and into the night like a shooting star—and then she saw the red explosion on Briartop Mountain.

My God, she thought in horror. The cannons are aimed toward the mountain! He's firing toward people's houses!

And then she found her voice, and though she couldn't hear herself over the noise, she screamed, "Stop it you bastard stop it stop it you murderer stop it!"

The artillery pieces were razing the mountainside. She saw leaping tongues of fire where the shells hit. Standing up, she groped through the descending pall of smoke, bumping into people, tripping over dazed bodies. A shape approached through the haze, and only when she was right in front of him did she realize it was Erik. "Why?" she screamed. "*Why?*"

He stopped, blinked at her. His smile was hanging lopsided from his mouth. "Because," he said, and it was then that Nora realized the cannonfire had ended, "*I can.*"

Then he brushed past her, like a sleepwalker, into the thickening whorls and eddies of smoke.

She stood watching the fires burn on Briartop Mountain, and she began to sob. At her feet, tiny American flags blew across the ground in the scorched turbulence that the howitzers had created.

◆ ◆ ◆

Someone knocked at Rix's door.

"What is it?" he snapped, looking up from the diary.

The door opened with no warning.

"You don't have to bite my head off," Kattrina Usher said with a pout.

14

"Tell us more about that party on the yacht," Margaret urged Katt. In her voice was a girlish excitement. "That sounds so wonderful!"

Katt shrugged, quickly glancing across the dining room table at Rix. "Well, it was just a party. There were about a hundred people aboard, I suppose. Most of them work in the fashion industry, and there were other models there, too. We sailed around the islands in the moonlight. There were little twinkling lamps all up in the rigging. The breeze was fresh and clean, and when you looked out at the water you could see fish swimming around the boat, because they leave these beautiful blue-green trails behind them. It has something to do with the microscopic life in the water. Anyway, we had a great time. The next day we finished the shoot, and I came home."

"But didn't you meet any exciting men?" Margaret looked disappointed. "Surely there were all kinds of wealthy bachelors at that party."

"Mom," Katt said, smiling gently, "I've told you a hundred times I don't need to get involved with any wealthy bachelors. Anyway, I was in Barbados to work."

"Sounds like you were really breakin' your back, too," Boone commented. His eyes were still puffy from sleep, but he was dressed for lunch in a pinstriped suit and silk tie. He plunged his fork into his salad and filled his mouth with lettuce. "Could have got yourself killed, too. Sailin' around at night like that. Ever heard of reefs? Boat runs up on a reef, tears the whole bottom out of it."

"Don't talk with your mouth full," Margaret said. When she looked at her daughter again, her eyes sparkled. "Where will you be going next, Katt?"

"I'm not sure. Maybe Sweden in November for a shoot in the icebergs. I promised I'd do something for Stephano's coats."

"Freeze your ass up there," Boone said. "You get frostbite, you can wave that modeling career of yours good-bye."

Rix smiled as Katt rolled her eyes. He was, as always, stunned by her beauty. She had the finely sculpted face of a Celtic queen; her skin—now only lightly tanned from the Caribbean sun—was silken and free of all but the most gossamer of lines. They surfaced in the corners of her eyes when she smiled. Her hair, cut short and layered, was pale blond with hints of strawberry in it, and her brows were thick and blond as well. As striking as her bone structure was, her eyes were the feature that the cameras fell in love with: they were large and expressive, but slightly almond-shaped and mysterious, as if with a trace of Oriental blood. Boreal lights—green, amber, pewter—sparkled in her eyes. Today she wore very little makeup, just a trace of pale lip gloss, but her beauty had never relied on artifice, anyway. Though she was thirty-one years old, she could easily pass for twenty.

Rix had seen her face dozens of times on magazine covers. When he'd gone to Wales, Katt's face had adorned the cover of the airline magazine stuck in the seat pocket in front of him. She'd smiled at him across the Atlantic. Rix recalled seeing her on the cover of *Sports Illustrated*, modeling a zebra-striped swimsuit, in the supermarket checkout line an hour or so before he'd found Sandra dead in the bathtub.

Katt had come in from the airport by way of the Jetcopter. Her white suitcases and traveling bags had just been delivered, and the family had sat down for lunch. Again, Rix noticed, there was no place set for Puddin'. The room had been misted with Lysol, but every so often Rix could smell his father. If Katt did, she wouldn't show it.

Rix loved her very much, but they'd seen little of each other in the past seven years. Whenever Rix had come to Usherland for a short visit, Katt was usually off for a few days on an assignment in some foreign country. Though she was a wealthy woman, she took jobs now as favors for designer friends and simply to keep her face before the public. Katt called Rix regularly, though, and she'd read all his books. She thought of herself, Rix knew, as the president of his fan club—as if there were such a thing—and she was always encouraging him to come to Usherland for an extended stay.

Her youthfulness was amazing. Rix knew she played tennis, swam, jogged, rode horses, fenced, skied, worked out with weights, and sky-dived. He hoped her troubles with drugs were over; the clarity of her eyes seemed to indicate that they might be.

"That's enough about me," she said. Her voice was low and quiet, a genteel Southern accent. "I want to hear about you, Rix. How was New York?"

"Full of surprises." He glanced at Boone, who was stuffing his face. "But fairly productive, I guess."

"Did they buy your new book? What's the title of it? *Bedlam?*"

"That's the one. Well . . . they're still considering it."

"*What!*" Margaret put down her fork. "Do you mean to say it's uncertain whether your next work is going to be purchased or not?"

"They'll buy it," Rix said defensively. "Publishers just take their time about things."

"Ought to write a spy book," Boone told him. "That horror crap is too unrealistic."

"But it's fun to read," Katt offered quickly. "Especially on airplanes. Rix's books make the time pass. I mean . . . that's not the only reason I read them, Rix. Your best one was *Congregation*. I liked the idea of a witch coven in a Southern town, and you made it so real you'd believe it could really happen."

"Right," Boone laughed harshly, "and the Pumpkin Man's out in the woods, too."

Katt looked at him and lifted her eyebrows. "He might be. You never know."

"Rixy thinks he's got somethin' to prove." Boone glanced quickly at his mother. "He probably couldn't write real books, could he, Momma?"

The repeated sarcastic use of his childhood nickname, particularly in front of Katt, finally snapped Rix's temper. He felt his face reddening, and he stared across the table at Boone. "Why don't you grow up, you dumbass? If you say something, be man enough to say it without getting Mom to agree with you!"

Boone grinned, his eyes cunning and cold. It was the same grin Rix had feared as a child, but now it only made him want to smash his brother in the face. "I'll say what I please, any way I please, Rixy.

You're a goddamned failure and a disgrace to this family. Is that clear enough for you?"

"Don't talk about failures, Boone. Puddin' can tell us about failures, can't she?"

Boone froze. Slowly his lower jaw dropped, and he blinked as if slapped.

"Boys," Margaret chided softly. "Let's be friends at the dinner ta—"

"*What did you say?*" Boone's voice was choked with anger, and he half rose from his seat.

Rix almost stood up as well, his blood boiling. One punch, he thought. Just let me get in one good punch.

But then he saw the blood bleach from his brother's cheeks, and Boone let out a soft, small gasp. He was staring over Rix's shoulder. Rix twisted around to look.

"Hi, y'all," Puddin' Usher said in a slurred voice.

She was standing in the doorway, dressed in a floor-length, pearl-studded white evening gown with a bright red sash wrapped around her neck. Her posture, as she supported herself against the doorframe, was insolent and whorish, her hips thrust out to one side, her breasts about to overflow the plunging neckline. Thick makeup covered her face, and her hair had been sprayed into a brass helmet, decorated with bits of gold glitter. It was immediately obvious that she had on not a stitch of underwear, because the gown stuck to her body like white paint. She wore bright red cowboy boots adorned with rhinestones.

When Boone stood up, he almost knocked his chair over. At the head of the table, Margaret's mouth was an O of surprise. "What are you doin' down here?" Boone snapped.

"Why, Boone, honey, I live in this house, too. I got tired of eatin' in my room, and I wanted to come say hello to Katt." Puddin' smiled tightly. " 'Lo, Katt."

"Hi."

She sashayed into the dining room, swinging her hips as if she were onstage in Atlantic City. She was reliving her finest hour for an audience of three. "Looky here," Puddin' said. "Ain't no place set for me, is there?"

When Margaret Usher spoke, the room became a deep freeze. "Young woman," she said, almost strangling, "you have overslept luncheon by twenty minutes. Luncheon in this house is served at twelve-thirty, and not a moment afterward. You may eat in your room or you may go hungry, but you shall not eat at this table."

Puddin' leaned closer to Margaret. The older woman blanched and put a lace napkin to her face. Puddin' whispered in her best Southern-belle imitation, "Bull . . . fuckin' . . . *shit.*"

"Boone!" Margaret shrieked, trying to turn her head away from the fumes. "Do something with this woman!"

He moved as if he'd started the hundred-yard dash, and caught her arm from behind. "You're drunk. Go back to your room."

She jerked free. "No. I'm stayin' right here."

"You heard what I said! Get back to that room or I'll strop the whine out of you!"

"She *smells!*" Margaret moaned. "Oh Lord, get her out of here!"

"Come on!" Boone grabbed her wrist and twisted her arm, trying to drag her through the door. She fought him wildly, her free hand flashing toward his face. He ducked her fingernails, but she broke free and staggered against the table, knocking a glass of iced tea to the floor. Boone, livid with rage, gripped her hair and pulled at her gown as Margaret rose to her feet, screaming for help.

"Leave her alone!" Rix shouted. He was coming around the table. "Get away from her, Boone!"

"Oh Jesus!" Katt said disgustedly, and laid her fork down on her plate.

Boone and Puddin' grappled. He flung her against the table so hard that the breath whooshed out of her. Then he grabbed her around the neck and started dragging her out; she clung to the tablecloth and pulled plates, glasses, and utensils off in a mad clatter. A maid appeared at the door but didn't know what to do.

"Edwin!" Margaret screamed at the top of her lungs.

Rix caught his brother's shoulder. "Cut it out, Boone! Come on, damn it! Cut it—"

Boone snorted like an animal and backhanded Rix across the side of the face so fast he had no time to duck. The blow stunned him and made his eyes water; he was knocked backward a few steps.

"Bastard!" Puddin' was shrieking. "You cockless, freak-lovin' bastard!"

White-hot anger crackled through Rix. He felt something under his right hand, and he closed his fist around it. Then he brought it swiftly up. Even though he knew it was only a table knife, he meant to drive it into Boone's back with all his strength.

"*Rix!*" It was Katt's voice, penetrating through the din. "*Don't!*"

Something in Katt's shout made Boone twist wildly to one side. The knife snagged his coat, but was too dull to do much damage. Then Boone, still holding on to a writhing and cursing Puddin', saw

131

the knife and the look in his brother's eyes. He swung his wife in front of him as a shield and started backing away. "He's tryin' to kill me, Momma!" he yelled, his voice shaking. "Get him away from me!"

In another instant, Rix's anger had evaporated. He stared at the knife in his hand, amazed at how quickly the urge to kill had come over him. Boone kept shouting, even as Rix opened his hand. The knife fell to the floor.

Cass pushed the frightened maid aside and stood in the door-way. "What's going on? Who's trying to kill who?"

"Take that insane woman out of here!" Margaret commanded. There was iced tea all over her lap as she stood up. "She's out of her mind!"

"Rix!" Puddin' said, and terror sparked in her watery eyes. "Don't let him take me upstairs! He'll strop me with his belt, Rix! Don't let him do it!"

But Rix was staring at his empty hand, working it into a fist and then opening it again.

"Cass?" Katt asked calmly. "Will you help my brother with his wife, please? I think she needs a cold shower."

"Yes, ma'am. Come on, Puddin'. No one's going to hurt you."

Puddin' tried to fight free again, but this time Boone had a firmer hold. "Y'all ask him about that talent agency!" she cried out as Cass and Boone wrestled her out of the room. "Just *ask* him what kind of—" And then Boone clamped his hand over her mouth; her shouting became incomprehensible.

Margaret slammed the door shut and stood trembling, unable to speak. Finally she patted her hair into place and smoothed her stained dress before she turned toward her children. "That woman," she announced, "belongs in an insane asylum."

Rix closed his hand, opened it, closed it again. Pain stirred in his head. He stared at the knife on the floor, unable to believe that a moment ago he'd tried to stab his brother. My God! he thought, as the cold sweat gathered on his face. I tried to kill Boone! If that knife had been sharper, it might've gone right through Boone's coat and into his back!

"Rix?" Katt asked carefully. "Are you all right?"

I wasn't really going to stab him, Rix thought. I was only going to scare Boone. I knew the knife wasn't sharp. I knew it. He bent, retrieved the knife, and laid it on the table. Margaret was watching him with an incriminating stare. Was I really going to stab my brother in the back? he asked himself.

132

Yes . . .

Rix trembled. The answer had come in a soft, sibilant whisper that flowed like freezing water through his veins.

"Rix?" Katt asked.

"I'm okay," he said, still looking at the knife. He feared the pain in his head was going to strengthen, but instead it was ebbing. He picked up a napkin and wiped the beads of sweat from his cheeks and forehead. "I'm okay," he repeated.

Margaret moaned, "My dress is *ruined!* Just look at it! Oh, that foulmouthed little lunatic!"

Someone knocked at the dining room door, and when Margaret opened it, one of the elderly black butlers said quietly, "Excuse me, Miz Usher, but Mr. Usher say he'd like to see Miss Kattrina."

"I'll go up in a minute, Marcus," Katt told him, and the dignified old man went off along the corridor. "Well," she said, looking at the shambles of the dining room, "I guess I'd better go up and see Dad."

"You haven't eaten your lunch yet!"

"He wouldn't like to wait," Katt reminded her. She came up close to Rix and searched his face. "You sure you're all right?"

"Yeah." He smiled tightly. "Peachy."

Katt left the room. When his mother started raging about her ruined dress again, Rix hurried after Katt. "Has everybody in this house forgotten what it means to be *civilized?*" Margaret called from the doorway.

Rix and Katt climbed the stairs together. An occasional whiff of decay floated past.

"I don't know why I did that," Rix said. "Jesus Christ! I really wanted to hurt him!"

"No, you didn't. I saw you turn your arm so you wouldn't stab him. I think you wanted to scare him, and it worked. His eyes were as big as dinner plates."

"I'm not a violent person. But he taunts me, Katt. You know how he's taunted me before. I just can't take it anymore. Christ, I don't know why I came back here! I thought things would be different. But they never change here, do they?"

"Things *will* change here," Katt said as they reached the second floor. "Very soon."

Her tone of voice was firm and knowing. Rix asked, "What do you mean?"

"Dad and I have been talking, probably more lately than we've talked in our entire lives. I think he wants me to take over the business. Oh, he hasn't come out and said so, but that's my impres-

133

sion. He's been letting me know about some of the current projects. If I do get control of the business, I'm going to make some changes."

"Like what?"

"With the business comes ownership of the estate," she said as they walked along the corridor. "I'm going to send Boone packing. Then I'm going to start research in some new directions."

"But I thought you enjoyed what you were doing! You don't seriously want the responsibility of the business, do you?"

"The vice-presidents and research teams would have to run the show for a while, until I could figure out what was going on. But I like challenges, Rix. I like to go where I don't belong. And who else is there to take it over? Not Boone; the way he manages his own money, he'd break Usher Armaments within five years. And you certainly don't want it."

Rix couldn't believe what he was hearing. "You don't want to be responsible for more death and destruction, do you?"

She stopped at the foot of the stairs that led to the Quiet Room, and turned toward him. In her angelic face, her eyes seemed dark and haunted. "Rix, you're not being very realistic, are you? I wish to God that our family made toys or thimbles or electric plugs. But that's not how things are. You and Boone seem to think of yourselves as the only Ushers, but you're wrong. I'm an Usher, too. I regret what the family business is, but I'm not ashamed of it. Someone has to make the weapons. If *we* don't, another company will."

"There are better ways to make money."

"Yes, there are," she agreed. "But not for us."

At that instant, Rix looked at his sister as if she were a stranger. He'd never suspected she was even remotely interested in Usher Armaments, and now he wondered how well he really knew her. What had happened to the little girl who used to tag along behind him and drive him crazy with silly questions? "I never knew you felt that way," he said.

"There are probably a lot of things you don't know about me." She held his gaze for a few seconds longer, then said, "I'd better go up and see him now." She climbed the stairs to the Quiet Room, paused to put on a surgical mask and a pair of rubber gloves, and entered the chamber.

Rix got away from the staircase before a fresh wave of his father's stench could reach him. He walked along the corridor toward his room, pondering Katt's attitude. There was a hidden part of her, he realized—a dark part that he'd never seen. Nobody in his right

134

mind would want to create the kind of destruction that Usher Armaments manufactured!

Ahead of him, a telephone on a table in the hallway began to ring. The elderly butler, Marcus, was coming toward him, and stopped to pick up the receiver on the second ring. "Usher residence."

Rix had started to pass by when Marcus said, "I'm sorry, miss, but I'm not to relay any of your calls to the family." He began lowering the receiver.

Dunstan's daughter, Rix thought. And suddenly he turned to grasp the phone before Marcus could hang up. "I'll take it," he said quietly, and then, into the phone, "This is Rix Usher. Why do you keep harassing my family?"

There was shocked silence on the other end.

"Well?" Rix prompted. "I'm listening."

"I'm sorry," the woman said, with a smoky Southern accent. "I didn't expect an Usher to answer the phone."

"I'll take care of it," Rix told Marcus, and the old man moved away. "What can I do for you, Miss Dunstan?" he asked, when Marcus had gone.

"I'm surprised you know who I am. You've been living away from Usherland for seven or eight years, haven't you?"

"I'm sure you didn't call here to ask about me. You know, there's a law about harassing people over the telephone."

"All I want is the answer to one question: What's Walen Usher's condition?"

"His condition? What are you talking about? My father's fine."

"That's strange to hear," she said, "especially since Walen hasn't gone to the plant in almost two months. A silver-gray Cadillac, rented to a Dr. John Francis from Boston, goes back and forth from Usherland three or four times a week. Dr. Francis is a cell-disease specialist. If Walen Usher isn't ill, who is?"

Hang up on her, he told himself. But as he started to put the receiver down, he realized the power of his position. This was the daughter of the man who'd been working on an Usher history for six years. She needed information, and Rix did, too. The chance might not come again. Rix asked quietly, "Is there a place we can meet?"

Again, she was cautiously silent.

"Hurry and decide. I'm taking a hell of a risk as it is."

"The Broadleaf Cafe," she said. "In Foxton. Can you meet me this afternoon?"

135

"If I'm not there by three, I won't be coming. Good-bye." He returned the receiver to its cradle, and instantly felt a twinge of shame. Was what he was about to do a betrayal of his family's trust, or simple cold practicality? Information about Walen's condition might be the key he needed to get close to Wheeler Dunstan, to find out how he was researching the book and how much of it was finished. He wanted to see that manuscript, and if he had to divulge something that would have to come out sooner or later anyway— so be it.

As he passed Boone's door, he heard Puddin' sobbing. Boone cursed—a muffled, brutal sound—and then there was the crack of flesh striking flesh.

Bastard! Rix thought grimly. Boone was going to get his own reward one of these days—and Rix ardently hoped he'd be around to see it happen.

What was it Puddin' had said downstairs? Rix asked himself. Something about Boone's talent agency? Maybe all wasn't as it seemed, he thought. And maybe it would be to his advantage to find out.

The sound of the next blow made him wince. He reached toward the doorknob, intending to interrupt the beating—but suddenly that shining silver circle with the roaring lion's face was before him, and he couldn't bear to touch it. Within an instant, it had faded again.

Something in the Lodge? he thought. *What?* A doorknob? What door, and leading where?

All shadows, hidden in the past.

He pulled his hand back and went on.

15

Sitting in a booth at the back of the Broadleaf Cafe, Raven Dunstan checked her wristwatch. It was seven minutes after three. A couple of farmers sat at the counter, drinking coffee and eating stale doughnuts. The waitress, a skinny woman in a yellow uniform, with platinum-blond hair heaped up in a tight bun, sat on a stool behind the counter, reading an old copy of *People* magazine. Hazy afternoon sunlight filtered through the windows that faced the street. A pickup truck rattled past. Two kids on bikes, pedaling furiously, rocketed by the windows.

She'd decided to give him five more minutes, and then she would leave. She'd been here for over an hour, had consumed a piece of blackberry pie with vanilla ice cream and three cups of the black sludge that passed as coffee. A copy of last week's *Democrat* lay on the seat beside her, covered with circles of red ink where she'd marked typos, inconsistencies or headlines that she felt could've been better. After talking to Rix Usher, she'd called her father to find out more about him. Wheeler had said he was the middle child, about thirty-three or thirty-four years old. He was the black sheep of the family, Wheeler had told her, and had been arrested in 1970 for participating in an antiwar demonstration at the University of North Carolina. Wheeler said he understood Rix had been living in the deep South somewhere, but didn't know how he'd been making a living.

The door opened, clanging a small cowbell over it, and Raven looked up. A burly man in a plaid jacket and brown cap came in, took his seat at the counter, and ordered a ham sandwich and fries. Definitely not Rix Usher, she told herself.

Raven had been calling Usherland every day for the past two weeks, trying to find out more about Walen Usher's condition. Once she'd gotten a maid to admit that the man was very ill, but then someone had grabbed the phone and slammed it down. Usually she could tell when an Usher answered, because there was a moment of stony silence before the telephone crashed down. The Ushers had changed their number several times, but Raven had ferreted out the new numbers with the help of an old high school friend who worked for the phone company in Asheville. Her father had impressed upon her his belief that if a bull charged a barn door enough times, either he would knock the door off its hinges or somebody would open the door to stop the damned banging.

In this case, Raven thought, Rix Usher had opened that door.

The cowbell clanged.

A tall, lean blond man in khakis and a brown sweater had entered the Broadleaf. Raven saw he had the Usher appearance of haughty aristocracy: a displaced Welsh prince, perhaps, who dreamed of returning triumphantly to the ancestral castle. He was very pale and almost too thin, as if he'd been sick and hidden away from the sunlight. If this *was* Rix Usher, then her father had been wrong about his age. This man was in his late thirties or early forties. In spite of her feelings about the Usher clan, her heart was beating harder. She sat stiffly, watching him approach her table. He was a handsome man, though something about him seemed almost fragile.

He looked at her through wary eyes the color of silver coins, and Raven felt herself shift uneasily.

"Miss Dunstan?" Rix asked.

"That's right." She motioned toward the other side of the booth, and Rix slid in.

The woman was certainly younger and more attractive than Rix had imagined. In fact, he was pleasantly surprised. There was strength in the set of her jaw, intelligence and curiosity in her light blue eyes. She wasn't a beautiful woman in the classic sense—her mouth was too wide, her nose too sharp and slightly crooked, as if it had been broken and poorly set—but the combination of her fair complexion, black hair, and piercing blue eyes was riveting. To mask his interest, Rix picked up a menu and looked over the items. "Anything good here?" he asked.

"The pie, if you like apple, persimmon, or blackberry. I won't recommend the coffee."

The waitress ambled on over. Rix said he'd just take a glass of water; she shrugged and went to the counter to get it.

"I understand you've been disturbing my family," Rix said.

"I suppose that's part of my job."

"Is it? A court of law might not see it that way. As a matter of fact, I don't understand why my family doesn't bring a harassment suit against you and that paper you work for."

"I've wondered that myself," she replied, her direct gaze challenging him. "But I think I know why. Your father's very ill. He doesn't want the least bit of publicity. Zero. Nil. He knows that if he starts something with the *Democrat*, other papers are going to take notice."

The waitress brought Rix's water, and he sipped at it thoughtfully. "You've got an inflated opinion of the *Democrat*, Miss Dunstan. It's only one of a dozen county newspapers in the state. What makes you think it's so important?"

"Because it is. The *Democrat* was being published in these hills thirty years before the first stone was laid at Usherland. My great-great-great-grandfather brought the hand press with him on his back from Dublin, and the paper started out as a bulletin for the tobacco farmers. My family has edited it, written in it, and published it for over a hundred and sixty years. Sure, there are plenty of county papers, but the *Democrat* is the oldest—and we've been monitoring you Ushers since old Hudson himself settled here."

"Watching us, you mean."

She smiled faintly. Rix looked at the scar that cut through her left eyebrow and wondered how she'd gotten it. "Someone has to. Your family owns controlling interest in at least seven Southern newspapers. God only knows how many television and radio stations you own. If you want to go to court, Mr. Usher, a nice case might be made out of monopoly and conflict of interest, don't you think?"

"No one wants to go to court," he said. "Especially not over a tabloid like the *Democrat*."

"You don't have a very high regard for the paper, do you? Well, it might interest you to know that your father offered mine over two hundred thousand dollars for the *Democrat*, four years ago. He refused, of course. The *Democrat* is distributed statewide and has a paid subscription of forty-five thousand."

"And I'd say that most of those people read it because they're looking for news about the Ushers—or, I should say, hints of scandal. I've never met your father, but I'm sure he'd agree that the Ushers have helped sell his newspaper."

"It's not his newspaper anymore," Raven said. She folded her hands before her on the table. "It's mine. I've owned it and published it since the first of August, when I took it over from my father."

"Oh. I see. Then I guess Wheeler's spending his retirement working on that book of his? The one about the Usher family?"

"He works on it every day, yes."

Jesus Christ! Rix thought. He willed himself not to show emotion. "My family's not too happy about it. They'd like to know where he's getting his research materials."

"From sources," she said enigmatically.

"When's he going to be finished with it?"

"Maybe next year. He wants to make sure all the facts are correct."

"I hope they are, for both your sakes. My family won't go to court over the *Democrat*, but they'll come down on you like a brick snowstorm over this book."

Raven's eyes searched his face. "How much longer does Walen have to live? And who's the estate going to pass to after he dies?"

Rix swirled the ice cubes around his glass. He should get up and leave, he told himself. He should never have agreed to meet her! But then the instant of inner turmoil passed, and he was in control again. "Why are you so sure my father's dying?"

"The presence of a cell specialist seems pretty serious. Dr. Francis won't talk to us, either. But the real clincher is that you've come back to Usherland. I think the clan's gathered to see a successor named."

"And you want the story before the big-league papers and TV people get it, right?"

"Breaking a story like this would be a major coup for the *Democrat*. We'd go with a special edition and make it available statewide. It would probably triple our circulation, and give us real respectability."

"You must have big plans for your paper's future."

"It's not going away, if that's what you mean."

Rix nodded and smiled faintly. He waited a moment, then said, "Okay. Let's say, for the sake of speculation, that I do know who's going to take over the estate and business. I realize how much that would be worth to you." He looked directly at her. "But I want something, too."

"What?"

"A look at your father's manuscript. And I want to know where he's getting his research materials."

Raven frowned. She hadn't expected to have to trade information, like a couple of secret agents. Rix Usher was waiting for her reply. "It's my father's book, not mine. I can't—"

"If you can't help me," he interrupted, "then I won't help you."

"Maybe I'm stupid for asking," Raven said, "but why *should* you help me? Your family and mine haven't exactly been on the best of terms for the last hundred years or so. Why should you suddenly want to help me out?"

"I'm curious. I want to see what your father's written."

"So you can report back?"

"No one knows I'm here," Rix said firmly. "I said I was going out for a drive and took one of the cars. Whatever your father shows me, it won't get back to Usherland."

Raven paused uncertainly. In her estimation, the Ushers were as slippery as snake oil. But now here was the black sheep of the Usher family, offering her vital information. Why? What did he have to gain by seeing her father's work? "I don't know," she said finally. "I don't think I can agree to anything like that."

"Why not?"

"Because my father guards his work *very* strictly. *I* don't even get to see it." Again she searched his eyes, trying to decide whether this was one of Walen's tricks. "I'll have to talk to him about it. Can we meet again?"

140

"Where and when?"

"How about right here? At three o'clock tomorrow afternoon?"

"I have to be careful. If anybody from Usherland saw me with you, word might get back to Walen."

"What would he do?" She lifted her eyebrows. "Disown you for collaborating with the enemy?"

"Something like that." He thought of the documents in the library; at the merest hint of collusion, Walen would send them back to the Lodge, and his hopes would be finished. "Okay. Three tomorrow." He stood up from the booth, relieved that his first meeting with Raven Dunstan was almost over.

Raven wasn't satisfied. There was something too simple about this. "Mr. Usher," she said, before he could get away, "why does seeing my father's book mean so much to you?"

"As I said, curiosity. I'm a writer myself." Careful, he cautioned himself.

"Oh? What sort of things do you write?"

"Horror novels," he explained, figuring it would do no harm to tell her. "Not under my real name, though. My pseudonym is Jonathan Strange."

Raven had never heard the name before and wasn't familiar with the books, but she didn't say it. "Interesting choice of a profession," she commented. The cowbell clanged again, and Raven glanced toward the door.

Myra Tharpe and her son had just come in. The woman was carrying a large wicker basket, which she laid on the counter near the cash register. The waitress looked through a door into the kitchen and called for Mr. Berthon.

Raven rose from her seat. The Broadleaf Cafe's manager, a thickset Foxton man with curly brown hair and a fleshy, bovine face, came out of the back to see the pies Mrs. Tharpe had brought.

"Well," Rix said, "I'll meet you to—" But then Raven had walked right past him, and he watched her approach the raggedy woman and boy. He noticed that Raven walked with a limp, and he wondered what had hurt her leg.

"Hello, Mrs. Tharpe," Raven said. Myra looked at her and blinked, a cold curtain of suspicion and dislike descending over her eyes. Raven regarded the handsome young boy at the woman's side. On his cheek and forehead were thin bandages, and Raven could smell— what was it?—the sharp odor of tobacco juice. "You must be Newlan. I'm Raven Dunstan."

"Yes, ma'am. I saw you this mornin', through my window."

"I came up to talk to you, but your mother wouldn't let me. I wanted to ask you some questions about—"

"Listen, you!" the other woman snapped. "You just leave us be, you hear?"

Berthon frowned. "Miz Tharpe, you're talkin' to the owner of the—"

"I *know* who I'm talkin' to, thank you!" Her eyes blazed at Raven, and she flicked a glance at Rix as he came up behind her. "My son don't want to be bothered. Is that spelled out clear enough for you? I'll take the usual price for my pies, please, Mr. Berthon."

Raven looked at the boy. He had the greenest eyes she'd ever seen, and right now they were troubled and confused. "You're old enough to speak for yourself," she said. "I'd like to know what happened to you and your brother the night before last."

"Go out to the truck, New!" Myra told him sharply. She extended her palm toward Berthon, who was counting a few bills and change from the register.

"New?" Raven's voice stopped the boy from leaving. "Look at that poster on the wall over there." She motioned with a tilt of her head.

New looked at it, and so did Rix. Near the kitchen door was a yellow poster showing the pictures of four children—three boys and a girl, all about nine or ten years old. Stenciled above the pictures were the words REWARD FOR INFORMATION—HAVE YOU SEEN THESE CHILDREN? ALL REPLIES IN CONFIDENCE.

At the bottom of the poster was written CALL THE FOXTON DEMOCRAT, followed by a phone number. Rix had no idea what the poster meant, but he studied each photograph with a growing sense of unease.

"Two of those children," Raven said, "have been missing for more than a year. The little girl vanished the first of this month. The other boy went out hunting with his father two weeks ago, and neither one of them came home. Sheriff Kemp has a stack of folders in his office, New. Each one of them represents a child, aged from six to fourteen, who disappeared into thin air—just as your brother did. I'm trying to find out how and why."

New stared at the poster. His eyes narrowed slightly, but he didn't speak.

Myra took her money and clasped her son's shoulder to guide him out of the Broadleaf—but he resisted her as if he'd suddenly grown roots through the floor. She flashed a cutting glance at Raven, then seemed to see the man behind her for the first time. *"You,"* she whispered in an acid tone. "You're an Usher, ain't you?"

Oh Christ! Rix thought. Berthon and everybody else in the place were listening.

"I *know* you're an Usher. You've got the Usher look about you. Are you with this woman, Mr. Usher?"

Rix knew there was no use in lying. "Yes, I am."

"City woman," Myra said mockingly, "what you're lookin' for is right under your nose. You ask anybody hereabouts what goes on at night at Usherland. You ask 'em about that Lodge, and what kind of thing lives inside there, all alone, in the dark. New! We're goin' now!"

In his mind, New could see Nathan's face up there with the others. He should let this woman know what he'd seen, he told himself. He was the man of the house now, and telling her would be the right thing to do. His mother's hand tightened on his arm. *"New,"* she said.

The raw tension in her voice broke the spell. He looked at Raven Dunstan and wanted to tell her, but then his mother pulled at him and he let himself be led out the door. Feeling utterly helpless and frustrated, Raven watched through the door's glass as Myra Tharpe slid behind the wheel of their pickup truck. The boy got into the passenger side, and then the truck backed away from the curb and rattled down the street toward Briartop Mountain.

"Damn it!" Raven swore softly.

"Don't mind her, Miz Dunstan," Berthon said. "Myra Tharpe's one of them folks who stay to themselves, up on the mountain. Her husband died around the first of the year. She don't know nothin'."

That's where you're wrong, Raven thought.

Rix pulled his attention away from the poster. "What was all that about?"

"Something I'm working on." She didn't elaborate, because she didn't want to discuss it with everyone in the cafe listening.

Rix was in a hurry to leave. He could feel the stares fixed to the back of his neck. As Raven paid her check, Rix glanced again at the children's faces.

Disappeared into thin air, Raven had said. *Just as your brother did.*

He abruptly turned away and went out to stand in the bright

sunlight. He'd parked the red Thunderbird around the corner, where it wouldn't be seen from Foxton's main street.

"What was she talking about?" Rix asked Raven when she came out. "She mentioned the Lodge."

Raven looked off into the distance, where Briartop Mountain's peak was lost in filmy clouds. This mention of the Lodge from Myra Tharpe wasn't the first insinuation Raven had heard; she'd discounted the tales as mountain superstition—but now she wondered whether, as with all superstition, there might not be a grain of truth in it. "The people around here believe that someone—some*thing*—is living inside Usher's Lodge. When was it closed up?"

"After my grandfather died, in 1945. All the rooms have been left as they were then, but nobody lives there."

"Are you *sure* about that? Could some vagrant be hiding in there? Maybe a poacher?"

"No. There's no electricity, no lights. The windows are bricked up, and no one could find his way around in the dark."

"Is the Lodge locked?"

He shook his head. "My family's never seen the need to lock it. We've never had trouble with poachers before."

"But you don't know for sure that the Lodge is uninhabited, do you?" Raven asked pointedly. "With all those rooms, someone could hide very easily."

Rix didn't answer. He realized she was right; there were hundreds of places in the Lodge where a vagrant could hide, and with a gun one could easily feed off the land.

"I have to get back to the office," Raven said, checking her watch. "I'll meet you here tomorrow."

Rix watched her limp away. In his mind he saw the pictures of those children on the poster, their faces smiling and unaware. The afternoon light was turning bloody. He hurried around the corner to his car.

As he drove away from Foxton, a storm of troubled thoughts whirled through his head. *Disappeared into thin air . . . Have You Seen These Children? . . . Sheriff Kemp has a stack of folders in his office . . . Disappeared into thin air, just as your brother did . . .*

Pumpkin Man's in the woods, he thought suddenly. No, no; that was a story to scare children, a Halloween tale for a chilly October night.

The skeleton swung through Rix's mind in awful slow motion,

its eyeholes dripping gore. In the next instant, Rix had to jerk the wheel to the right because he'd been drifting over the center line.

A mile from Foxton, Rix glanced in his rearview mirror and noticed a battered brown van on the road behind him. It followed him around the next curve, then abruptly turned off onto a dirt road before he crossed over into Usherland. Moonshiner, Rix thought; he could use a good slug of mountain brew about now.

When the red Thunderbird was out of sight, the brown van stopped, turned around, and headed toward Foxton again.

16

As the wind whooped and wailed outside the Gatehouse, and tree branches clawed at the moon, Nora St. Clair Usher slowly gave up her secrets to Rix.

It was almost one o'clock, and Rix had been reading through her diary since before eleven, when he'd excused himself from the game room after Katt had whipped his tail in chess. She'd been thoughtful and precise in her moves, and had given no indication of what she and Walen had talked about that afternoon. Boone had come in and played darts by himself, trying to stir up some trouble by inquiring as to where Rix had gone riding, but Rix had successfully staved him off. After dinner, Boone had gone to the stables to check on the horses for the night. Rix had lodged a chair and a suitcase against his door to keep Puddin' from barging in.

Now Rix sat at his desk before the window, carefully turning the brittle pages. Nora's handwriting was clear, her prose direct and without flowery excess. Some of the pages were too faded to be legible, but the story of her life at Usherland was coming together in Rix's mind like a delicate watercolor. He could see the Lodge as she described it: the rooms, corridors, and chambers spotless, filled with priceless antiques from around the world, the hardwood floors waxed and shining, the myriad windows in all shapes and sizes framing only Usher earth. By January 1920, she was resigned to the constant presence of workmen—who started promptly at dawn and worked until dusk. The Lodge spread to even larger proportions.

On lazy spring afternoons she enjoyed boating across the lake, usually in the company of Norris Bodane, and watching the wild swans that nested on the northern shore. It was during one of those outings, in April 1920, when Erik was in Washington on business, that she noted a peculiarity about the Lodge. The workmen had cut away a stand of pines from the northern face of the house in order to erect their scaffolds, and there in the Lodge's stones, from roof to foundation, was a jagged crack, filled with mortar, at least two feet wide.

When she inquired, Norris had explained in his distinctive North Carolinian accent that the weight of the Lodge was making it slowly sink into the island. The crack had been there for years, and Erik was making sure it didn't widen by having the workmen balance the Lodge with new additions. Not to worry, he said; the Lodge would be standing for little Walen's great-great-grandchildren.

Nora had her own suite of rooms in the east wing, from which she rarely ventured. She'd been lost several times in the Lodge, and had wandered hopelessly through the maze of rooms until she'd been lucky enough to find a servant. Sometimes days passed without her even seeing Erik, and Ludlow was no more than a ghost heard long after midnight as he walked the corridors.

Rix was fascinated by her. He was watching a little girl become a woman. Her voice was breathless when she described banquets for three hundred people; seething when she berated Erik for flying the captured German Fokker—shipped over from England after the Great War—past the nursery windows and upsetting the baby; loving and tender when she wrote about little Walen.

Little Walen, Rix thought grimly. Oh, Nora, if you could only see him now!

Wind thrashed the trees outside. He was nearing the end of her diary. He was Nora's confidant, her final companion, and as he read, time shifted, cracked open, drew him into its whirlpool of people and events.

◆ ◆ ◆

Nora stood on her balcony in her long white dress and watched the surly May sky. Rainclouds were rolling across the mountains like freight trains, each carrying a heavier load than the one before. Threads of dark purple veined the sky, and in the distance danced quick flashes of lightning. When raindrops began to ripple the lake's surface, Nora went into her bedroom and closed the balcony doors. Thunder boomed, shaking the windows in their frames.

She left her room and walked down the hallway to the nursery, where Maye Bodane was tending the infant Walen. The child played happily in his crib. Maye, a lively young Irishwoman with curly golden hair, stood at the large bay window, watching curtains of rain flap across the lake.

"How's my angel this morning?" Nora asked brightly.

"He's fine, mum." She came over to the crib and smiled at Walen. A lovely woman with calm gray eyes, she had a young son of her own whom she'd named Edwin. "Happy as a lark, he is."

Nora gazed down at her beautiful boy. Erik was already talking about having another child, but Nora was reluctant. In bed, Erik was cold and rough. She remembered her father's advice: "Stay with him, Nora. Give him time. If you let this chance slip through your fingers, you'll regret it for the rest of your life."

Walen was gurgling, playing with a new toy.

As Nora saw what it was, her face became a mask of shock.

The toy was an infant-sized, silver pistol.

She reached in and snatched the thing away. Instantly, Walen began bawling. "What is *this*?" she demanded. "You know how I dislike guns, Maye!"

"Yes, mum," she said nervously, "but when I came in this mornin', it was right there in his crib. Walen seemed so taken with it, I thought—"

"Who put this thing in there with him?"

"I don't know. Oh, he's awful upset, mum!" She picked up the squalling child and began cooing to him.

Nora's hand was gripped tightly around the offending toy. She'd told Erik that she didn't want her son associating with weapons—toy guns included—until he'd had a chance to see how destructive guns were. She was enraged that he had so openly flaunted her wishes. "Damn it to hell!" she snapped, and Maye looked at her openmouthed. "I won't let him treat me like this!" Storming out of the nursery, she stalked along the corridor toward the stairway that would take her up another level and into Erik's private domain.

Rain slammed against the leaded windows and streamed off the balconies. As Nora climbed the stairs a flash of lightning dazzled her, and thunder crashed so close to the house that she imagined she could feel the entire Lodge tremble like a ship in a tempest.

On the third floor, dim light filtered through the thick stained-glass windows, giving this section of the Lodge the atmosphere of an unholy church dedicated to some pagan god of war. On the walls were all makes of Usher rifles, pistols, and machine guns. Artillery pieces stood mounted in the wide corridors. A menagerie of stuffed animals—bears, stags, panthers, lions, tigers—crouched in the shadows. Their glass eyes seemed fixed on Nora as she passed them, and more than once she turned to make sure none were tracking her. The hallways took her to the left, then to the right—and led her to doors that opened on stone walls, narrow staircases that ascended into total darkness. From far up in the attic drifted down the staccato rhythm of the workmen's hammers, like a laboring, never-ceasing heartbeat.

Thunder sounded like the cannonfire of that terrible July night almost a year ago. "Erik!" Nora shouted, and her voice rolled down the halls, distorting, echoing back to her in a whisper.

Within another few minutes, Nora realized she'd taken a wrong turn somewhere. Nothing was familiar. Lightning struck again, and harder still. A dozen crystal owls mounted on pedestals on the walls trembled; one of them fell and shattered on the floor with the sound of a gunshot.

"Erik!" she called, a note of rising panic in her voice. She continued on, this time searching for a staircase down. She saw no servants, and the windows she passed were covered with sheets of water. Still, the hammering went on and on, ebbing and fading, almost in cadence with the booming of thunder.

She was lost. Predators growled silently at her, and ahead a stuffed lion blocked her path. Its green, gleaming eyes challenged her to approach. She took another corridor, this one lined with perhaps a hundred suits of armor and medieval weapons. At the end of it was a heavy door; she pulled it open and called for Erik again. There was no reply but the hammering, now even louder.

A wrought-iron spiral staircase ascended to a white door twenty feet above her head. She looked upward, the noise of hammers about to split her skull. If that door led to the attic, she told herself, she could at least get one of the workmen to help her find her way. She climbed the stairs, being careful of her footing, and reached out to open the door.

But then she stopped. The door was covered with thick white rubber, its brass handle discolored by sweat. When she touched it, a thrill of cold coursed up her arm. But the door was locked. She was about to pound on it and try to call for help above the cacophony of thunder and hammers when the lock disengaged with a metallic *click*.

Slowly the door began to open. Nora stepped back. The sickly-sweet aroma of decay was oozing through the door's widening crack. Within, all was blackness.

A soft, hoarse voice whispered, "What is it?"

"Oh," Nora said. "You startled me." She couldn't see a thing inside there. The hammers, the hammers! Why wouldn't they stop?

"Please," the voice implored, "speak as quietly as you can."

"I . . . didn't mean to disturb you." Realization dawned on her with a shock. "Is that . . . Mr. Usher?"

There was a silence. Then: "Are you lost again?"

She nodded. "I was . . . trying to find Erik."

"Erik," Ludlow Usher repeated softly. "Dear Erik." The door opened wider, and a hand curled around its edge. The fingers were withered, the nails long and ragged. The flesh looked unhealthy and mottled. It had been more than two months since she'd last seen Ludlow, and she'd assumed he was still living up in the glass cupola. She'd never seen this room before. "I'd welcome a visitor," he said. "Won't you come in?" When she hesitated, he asked, "You're not afraid, are you?"

"No," she lied.

"Good. You've got guts. I always admired you for that. Come in and we'll talk . . . just you and I. All right?"

Nora paused. To flee now would make her look foolish. And what did she have to fear from Ludlow Usher, anyway? He was an old man. At least he could tell her how to get down from this awful place. She entered the room, and Ludlow, an indistinguishable shape in the gloom, closed the door behind her. She caught her breath as the lock clicked shut.

"Don't be afraid," he whispered. "I'm going to take your hand and lead you to a chair." His hand embraced hers, and she restrained the urge to jerk away. His flesh was cool and slimy. He led her across the room. "You can sit down now. May I pour you a glass of sherry?"

Nora found the chair and sat down. "No, thank you, I . . . can stay just a few minutes."

"Ah. Well, you'll forgive me if I partake, won't you?" A bottle was uncorked; liquid was poured.

"How can you *see* in here? It's so terribly dark!"

"Dark? Not at all. Not to me, that is." He sighed heavily. "For me, light leaks through the seams in these walls. It creeps from every pore of your body, Nora. Your eyes are ablaze. And the wedding ring on your finger is as incandescent as a meteor. I could sun myself

in its heat. Listen to those hammers, Nora. Isn't it a lovely music?"
It was said with cutting sarcasm.

She listened. In this room she couldn't hear the hammering at
all; instead, there was a different noise: a sound like soft, muffled
heartbeats. There were many heartbeats, some louder than others,
some more metallic, some crisper. The noises seemed to be coming
from all around the room, or even from the very walls themselves.
She heard the clicking of gears, the faint rattling of chains through
some kind of mechanism.

"My clocks," Ludlow said, as if he'd read her mind. "There are
sixty-two grandfather clocks in this room. I started out with more
than a hundred, but alas, they do break down. Listen, and you can
hear the air parting as the pendulums swing. The sound of time
passing is comforting to me, Nora. At least it helps to mask the
hammering and sawing. Oh, just listen to those workmen up in the
attic! And the storm, too!" He sucked in his breath suddenly. When
he spoke again, his voice was strained. "Lightning hit very close to
the house that time. The thunder's getting louder."

Nora couldn't hear a thing but the ticking of the clocks. This
room was windowless, and evidently the walls were several feet
thick. But exactly where the room was in the house, she couldn't
say.

"Of course you know I'm dying," Ludlow said flatly.

"Dying? Of what?"

"It's . . . a peculiar disease. Oh, I would've thought Erik might
have told you by now. He will. I won't spoil the surprise."

"I don't understand. If you're sick, why are you up here alone,
in the dark?"

"That, my dear, is precisely why I'm—" He stopped. "The thunder," he whispered urgently. "My God, didn't you *hear* that?"

"No. Not a thing."

He was silent, and Nora had the impression that he was waiting
for something. When it didn't come, he allowed his breath to hiss
between his teeth. "I despise storms as much as that damned hammering. It goes on night and day. Erik destroys a room and rebuilds
it. He constructs corridors that end at stone walls. He builds a staircase that ascends to empty air. All for *my* benefit, of course. Oh,
Erik's a sly one! He's trying to kill me, you know."

"Trying to kill you? *How?*"

"With noise, my dear," Ludlow said. "Incessant, nerve-racking,
demonic noise. The hammering and sawing that never stops. Even

150

that ridiculous display on the Fourth of July was for me. The sound of those cannons going off almost drove me to suicide."

"You're wrong. Erik's trying to balance the Lodge. There's a crack that runs up the north face of the—"

Ludlow interrupted her with a mirthless laugh. "Balance the Lodge? Oh, that's a good one! Perhaps that's what he's telling the workmen, but it's a lie."

"The Lodge is sinking into the island," Nora said. "I saw the crack myself."

"Oh, the crack's there, all right. I've seen it, too. But the Lodge isn't sinking, my dear. An earthquake damaged the Lodge in—when was it?—1892. Or 1893, I can't recall. We're in an area that's prone to tremors."

Nora thought of the crystal owls trembling on their pedestals, and the one crashing to pieces on the floor.

"Erik is trying to kill me," Ludlow whispered, "because he wants *this*."

Something touched her shoulder, startling her. She ran a hand along it, feeling the slick smoothness of the ebony cane that was always in Ludlow Usher's grip.

"He's on fire inside for it, Nora. Do you know why? It's *power*. Over the estate, the factories, everything. Even the future. I have no choice but to pass it to Erik, though I dread the consequences." The cane moved away from her shoulder. "Erik wants to hurry my death, you see, so he can—" She sensed his sudden tension, and he rasped, "The *thunder*! Oh God, the *thunder*!"

This time she heard it—a faint, distant booming, muffled by the stone walls. The storm, she knew, must be raging fiercely outside the Lodge.

"Wait," Ludlow breathed. "Don't move, just wait."

"What is it?"

"Quiet!" he hissed.

Silence stretched between them. Nora heard the sherry bottles clink together. In another few seconds she could feel a vibration in her chair, traveling upward through her body to the top of her skull. The wooden floor creaked and groaned. Around the strange room, chimes in some of the grandfather clocks tinkled, off key and dissonant. Then, just as suddenly, the vibration stopped.

"That fool draws the lightning with those rods on the roof," Ludlow said hoarsely. "Did you feel it? The tremor? It's gone now, but I'd say a good deal of the kitchen crockery is broken and a dozen windows shattered. That fool! He doesn't know what he's tampering with!"

He's insane, Nora thought. Ludlow was jabbering like a madman.

"That pistol, there in your hand. Why do you carry it? I thought you hated guns."

"Someone put it in Walen's crib." Her anger resurfaced. "Erik knows how I feel about exposing my son to weapons, and I won't lie down for this."

"I pity your son," Ludlow said. "Erik wants another child, I understand. He wants to breed children like fine thoroughbred horses. Resist him, Nora. For your own sanity, resist him."

"Why?"

"Why? Why? Why?" he mocked her savagely. "Because I *tell* you! Listen to me well; if you have two children, one of them is going to die. If three, *two* will perish. In the end, only one will be spared execution." She winced at the use of that word. "And that one," Ludlow whispered, "will inherit the gates of hell. Save yourself grief, Nora. Refuse to bear another child."

"You're . . . you're out of your mind!" Nora objected. The room's darkness was closing in around her, trapping and suffocating her. She smelled Ludlow's decay, like the aroma of damp green moss.

"Leave Usherland," he said. "Don't ask why. Leave today. This minute. Forget Walen, there's nothing you can do for him. You don't deserve to be dragged down into damnation!"

Nora rose from her chair, her face flushed with anger. She cracked her shin on a table, backed away, and hit another piece of furniture.

"Run, Nora. Get out of this house and never look back. Oh, the hammering, the hammering!"

It was clear to her that Erik was keeping his father up in this room because he was going insane. She groped toward the door, stumbled over a table, and kicked at it. Bottles tumbled off. When she reached the door, she fumbled for the lock but couldn't find it. She thought she heard him coming up behind her, and she said, "Keep away from me!" into the darkness. "Don't touch me, damn you!"

But Ludlow was still across the room. He gave a pained, soft sigh. "I didn't want to tell you this," he said, his voice almost kind, "but I will. It might save your sanity, and possibly your soul. God knows, I need to do a good deed."

"Let me out of here!" Nora fumbled for the lock.

"Erik doesn't love you," the old man said. "He never has. He needed a wife to breed children—the Usher future. And you came with an extra bonus. Erik's always been obsessed with his racehorses. Your father's stables have a sterling reputation. Erik and your father agreed on a *contract*, Nora. He bought you, along with four horses to be used in breeding a Kentucky Derby champion. Your father received three million dollars on your wedding day, and he will get an additional million for every child you breed for Erik."

Her hand was frozen on the lock. "*No*," she said. She remembered her father saying, "Stay with him, don't turn your back on this chance." Even though he'd known she was unhappy, he'd strongly urged her to stay with Erik Usher. *Why?*

"I signed the check that went to St. Clair Stables," the voice said from the darkness. "You're meat to Erik. Breeding flesh. When he has no more use for you, he'll cast you out to pasture. Believe me, Nora. I'm begging you to get away from Usherland!"

"This is my house," she told him bravely, though tears were stinging her eyes. "I am Erik Usher's wife."

"You're his *mare*," Ludlow replied. "And don't believe for a second that one inch of Usherland will ever belong to you."

She got the lock disengaged and wrenched the door open. The murky light that filtered in dazzled her eyes. She turned to look at Ludlow Usher.

He was emaciated to the point of freakishness, a skeleton in a black pinstriped suit and a gray ascot. His face was yellowish white but splotched with what appeared to be brown scabs. Thin gray hair curled over his shoulders, though the top of his scalp was bald. The Usher cane was clenched in his right fist. Staring at the master of Usherland, Nora felt a strange rush of pity—though she was horrified by the sight. Ludlow's deepset eyes were fixed upon her, and in them was a red glare like the depths of a blast furnace. "For God's sake," he said with a liquid rattle of phlegm, "get away from Usherland!"

Nora dropped the toy pistol on the floor and fled. She almost fell down the tricky stairs, then ran through the corridors and descended the first staircase she found. After about twenty minutes she came across a pair of gossiping maids.

At dinner that night, Nora sat at the long dining table and watched Erik consume his beef stew. It had spattered his coat and shirt. He rang for a second helping and a bottle of cabernet.

During a dessert of baked Alaska and sugared strawberries, Erik interrupted his feasting to tell her that the new colt he'd been working with, a fine chestnut stallion called King South, was already showing the kind of speed and determination that made Kentucky Derby champions. King South, he reminded Nora, had been sired by Donovan Red—one of the prizewinning stallions that her father had given them as a wedding gift. Erik, bits of stew clinging to his mustache, poured himself a glass of wine and vowed that the Usher stables would bring home the 1922 Derby cup.

A servant approached Nora with a silver tray. The object on it was covered with a white silk handkerchief. He set it down before her and left without explanation.

"What's that?" Erik asked. "What'd Foster bring you?"

Nora lifted the corner of the handkerchief. On the tray was the toy pistol she'd dropped in Ludlow's chamber. Beneath the gun was a folded piece of paper. She slid the toy to one side, picked up the paper, and opened it.

It was a canceled bank draft for three million dollars, dated the second of March, 1917. Ludlow Usher's spiky signature was on it. St. Clair Stables had received it.

"What's there, damn it? Don't keep secrets from me!"

Clutching the check in her fist, Nora took the toy pistol and slid it with all her strength down the long table. It spun toward Erik, glinting under the magnificent crystal chandeliers, and after a journey of some thirty feet it clinked against his plate.

"Explain that," Nora said, "you bastard."

Erik laughed. Laughed and laughed. When he was through, he lifted his glass in a toast. "To our second child," he said.

◆ ◆ ◆

And there Nora's diary ended. Rix closed it. There had to be another volume down in the library, he thought. Surely Nora's story continued somewhere, down in those cardboard boxes. The tale had left him with several unanswered questions: What was Nora's response after she learned that Ludlow was telling the truth? How did she stave off Erik's desire to have more children? And, especially, what was the meaning of Ludlow's strange warnings to her? In all probability, Rix mused, Nora had been correct about Ludlow being insane. It was obvious that living in the Lodge's Quiet Room had unhinged him, and his fear of thunder was simply due to his heightened senses—but what was all that stuff about earthquakes and a crack in the Lodge's north face? Rix decided he'd have to go over tomorrow and check it out for himself.

He took the diary and quietly went out into the hallway. He looked both ways, as if he were about to cross railroad tracks and expected a roaring diesel at any second. Then he went downstairs, through the game room and smoking room, and unlocked the library's doors.

Rix returned the diary to one of the boxes, then began browsing through more materials. A small leatherbound book he picked up fell to pieces in his hands, and he muttered, "Damn it to hell!" He bent down to gather the pages together and stuff them back into the binding.

"Well, well," the voice floated from behind him. "Found me a prowler, didn't I?"

17

New Tharpe sat alone in the cabin's front room. The fire had almost played itself out, but was kept alive by errant thrusts of wind that swooped down the chimney and fanned the coals. Atop the mantel, next to a framed snapshot of his father and mother, a single kerosene lamp held an unblinking eye of flame.

The wind blasted against the side of the cabin with fierce velocity, making shrill pipings as it found chinks in the walls. He was half expecting the thin old roof to tear away suddenly and spin upward into the sky like a top. The wind's whistling sounded all too close to the note Nathan's yo-yo had made. From around the bend he could hear the gruff barking of Birdie, the big red hound that belonged to the Claytons.

New couldn't sleep. His cuts were still bothering him, though they were healing nicely under the bandages. He'd tossed and turned for a long time on his cot, but rest eluded him. The city woman's face was on his mind, and the things she'd said to him at the Broadleaf haunted him. He kept seeing that poster on the wall; when he imagined Nathan's picture up there with the others, his stomach felt squeezed by a powerful hand.

He stared at the lamp on the mantel, and knew he would never see his brother again. The Pumpkin Man had taken Nathan; when the Pumpkin Man struck, there was no coming home, ever again.

But why did it have to be that way, he asked himself. What *was* the Pumpkin Man, and why had no one ever seen him? No one, New realized, except himself. He was the man of the house. Wasn't there something he could do, some way to strike back at the Pumpkin Man for stealing his brother away? He felt so helpless, so weak! His hands clenched into fists, and a lightning bolt of confused rage seemed to rip through his brain.

The kerosene lamp trembled, clinking against the stones.

New's eyes narrowed. Had the lamp moved, or hadn't it? In his room, the magic knife was hidden under his mattress. When it had hit the ceiling over his mother's head, Myra had stood like a statue, her face drained of color. She'd given a short, soft gasp, and New had seen a wet glint of fear in her eyes. Then she'd slammed the door shut and retreated to her own room, where New had heard her crying. She hadn't spoken to him for several hours after that. Then it was back to her baking pies in the kitchen, baking more of them than ever, and all the while chattering too merrily about how the men would eventually find Nathan, he would return home, and then everything would be like it was before, only better, because Nathan and New would've learned a valuable lesson about being on time.

Either he was going crazy, he decided, or the kerosene lamp had moved.

And if he had made it move . . . then was the magic in the knife—or in *him*?

He pushed away all thoughts of his mother, the Pumpkin Man, and Nathan. The whine of the wind became a whisper. *Move*, he commanded. Nothing happened. He wasn't doing it right, wasn't thinking hard enough. He didn't have magic! It was in the knife, after all! But in his mind he envisioned the lamp lifting from the mantel, lifting higher and higher until it was almost up to the roof. He clenched his hand around the chair's armrests, and thought, *Move!*

Like a bucking bronco, the chair began to jump under him.

He cried out in amazement and held on. The chair balanced on one leg and spun wildly, then crashed to the floor. As New scrambled up, he realized the light in the room had changed.

The lamp.

The lamp had risen from the mantel some three feet, and was hovering just under the roof.

"*Lord*," New breathed softly.

And then the lamp started to fall, to shatter on the mantel.

He thought of burning kerosene, the house on fire, and he said, *"No!"* The lamp wobbled, slowed its descent, and very gently clinked back onto the mantel.

He was going crazy, he thought. Crazy as a loon. Either that, or he'd been witched. One was just as horrible a prospect as the other.

Floorboards creaked. New turned to find his mother standing in the room, one hand up to her throat. She looked as though the merest breath of wind might cause her to crumble like a column of ashes.

"It ain't the knife," was all he could think to say. "It's me, Ma."

Her voice came in a strained whisper: "Yes."

"I made the lamp move, Ma. Just like I made the knife move. What's happenin' to me? How come I can do it?" A cold blade of panic pierced him. Witched! he thought. How? Why?

"I don't know," Myra said. Then she slowly dropped her hand from her throat and stood looking at the fallen chair. With an effort she shuffled forward and righted the chair, running her hands over the wood as if she expected to feel something alive in it.

"I'm witched. It must've happened when I fell into that pit, Ma. Whatever it is, that's where it started."

She shook her head. "No. That ain't where it started, New. And if you're witched . . . then so was your pa."

"Ma'am?"

"Your pa," she repeated. Her face was pale, her gaze unfocused. Wind shrilled down the chimney and made the coals glow like red lanterns. "I don't know why, I don't know how—but I know your pa was a strange man. He was a good man, New, a God-fearin' man, but there was strangeness in him all the same." She lifted her eyes to meet his. "He had a powerful temper. It took him over sometimes. One time he got mad at me for something—I forget what now, somethin' silly—and the furniture in this house started to jump like grasshoppers. I've seen him break windows without even touchin' 'em. One night I woke up and found your pa standin' outside in a drivin' rainstorm. The truck's headlights were a-flashin' off and on. New"—she blinked, her mouth contorting—"I swear to you that I watched the whole front of the truck lift off the ground like a rearin' horse. Then it set back down again, real slow and pretty as you please. It made the hair stand up on my head to think that your pa had it in him to do such things. He wouldn't talk much about it, 'cause he didn't seem to understand it hisself, but he did say he'd done things at school where he was raised— like makin' tables dance, or one time throwin' a bully into a fence just by *thinkin'* hard about it happenin'. He said he didn't know why he could, New, but that such things were easy for him, and had been since he was about eleven or twelve years old. 'Course, he didn't let everybody know about it, for fear of what people would say."

"What would they say," New asked, "if they knew about *me*, Ma? That I was cursed? Under a spell? How come it's happened to me all of a sudden? A couple of days ago, before I fell into that pit, I was just like everybody else." He shook his head, distraught and confused. "Now . . . I don't know *what* I am, Ma! Or why I'm able to do such a thing as make that lamp move without touchin' it!"

"That I can't say. Your pa worked on keepin' hisself under control. He said that the only time he let hisself go was when he came across a rusted lug nut or somethin' heavy that he couldn't lift just with his arm muscles." She nodded toward the lamp. "I saw what you did. I saw that knife this mornin', and I knew whatever was in your pa was in you, too. It may not have been in Nathan; but then maybe it was, who can say? I cried because it scared me so much, New. It took me back to rememberin' the things your pa could do. He was a good man, but . . . I think there was a part of him that wasn't so good."

New frowned. "Why?"

She walked to a window and looked out. Birdie was still barking, around the bend at the Clayton house. It was another moment before Myra answered. "He was troubled, New. I don't know why, and neither did he. It was more than the things he could move with his mind." She paused, and released her breath between her teeth. "He never slept so good," she said softly. "He got up in the middle of the night and sat in this room for hours—just like you were sittin' in here when I looked in. Bobby saw things in his head when he closed his eyes. He saw fire and destruction and death, so bad he couldn't bear to tell me about 'em . . . and I couldn't bear to listen. He saw the earth splittin' open and houses fallin' in, and people on fire. It was like the end of the world, he said. The end of the world was goin' on, right behind his eyes."

She turned toward him, and New was struck by how frail she

158

looked. There was more to be said; he could see it in the darkness of her stare. "He saw the Lodge in his mind, New. He saw it all lit up like a party was goin' on inside, a celebration or somethin'. And in his mind he was dressed in a suit, and he knew he lived inside that Lodge and he had everythin' he could ever ask for. Anythin' he wanted was given to him. He said he could feel that Lodge, pullin' at him day 'n night. And a voice in his head, New—the most beautiful voice in the world, callin' him to come down to Usherland. He said he wanted to go into that house more than anythin', but he knew that if he did, he'd never come back out again. At least, not the same as when he'd gone in."

New's spine had stiffened. He'd felt the Lodge pulling at him, too, and that was why he stopped at The Devil's Tongue every chance he got, to dream about living at Usherland. He'd thought they were just foolish daydreams, but now he wasn't sure.

"Usherland is a haunted place," Myra said. "And that Lodge is its evil soul. God only knows what's gone on inside there, over the years. I'll tell you this, New—Bobby followed what was callin' him, and he went down to Usherland. He stood on the lakeshore and looked at that Lodge for a long, long time. When he came back home, his face was dead white, and he told me that if ever he wanted to leave this house after dark, to hold the shotgun on him till he'd got hisself under control again. He was a brave man, New, but there was somethin' down in that Lodge that wanted him, and whatever it was, it scared Bobby so much he took to sleepin' with ropes tyin' him to the bed. He tried hard not to let you boys know how troubled he was. Whatever is down there kept on a-pullin' at him and a-tauntin' him." She brushed the hair away from her face with a trembling hand, and stared at the glowing embers. "He said . . . it was all he could do to keep from listenin' to what that Lodge wanted him to do."

New's throat was dry, and he swallowed. "What, Ma? What was it?"

"Kill us," she replied. "Every one of us. Burn this house to the ground. And then find the old man."

"The old man? You mean the Mountain King?"

"Yes. Him. Find the Mountain King and . . . not just kill him, New, but tear him into pieces. Put the pieces in a sack and take them to the Lodge. That's what would give him entry."

"The Mountain King? He's just a crazy old man . . . ain't he?"

Myra nodded. "Bobby planned to go up to the ruins to find the old man, but before he could, that tire blew up in his face at the garage. He wanted to talk to him, to see if maybe the old man knew somethin' about the Lodge; he never got the chance. I . . . never breathed this to a soul, New. And I'll never say it again. But I think . . . somehow it was the Lodge that killed your pa. It murdered him before he could get to the old man."

"No," New said, "it was just an accident. The Lodge . . . ain't alive. It's just made out of stone."

"You got to promise me," she begged, "not to *ever* go down to Usherland. Don't let nobody else know you can move things with your mind. And most of all, don't talk about the Pumpkin Man—especially to no damned outsider!"

He had no intention of going to Usherland, and he was too stunned by this new-found ability to even conceive of telling anyone about it; but the last point stuck in his craw. He felt that the Dunstan woman sincerely wanted to find out more about the Pumpkin Man, and maybe by telling her what he'd seen, he could, in some small way at least, help Nathan—or atone for his own guilt at having been unable to free Nathan from the creature's grasp. He was the man of the house; shouldn't he make his own decisions?

"Promise me," Myra said.

It took an effort for him to nod his head.

She seemed to breathe easier. "You ought to go on to bed now. Get your rest. Your hurts still botherin' you?"

"A little. They itch."

She grunted softly. "Your pa taught me how to make that medicine I put on you. Said it would take the sting out of just about anythin'." Wind rattled the window behind her, and again she peered into the darkness. Birdie's bark had changed to an occasional guttural baying. "Dog's makin' a lot of noise tonight, ain't he? It's the wind, I reckon, that's got Birdie spooked. Your pa knew a lot about the weather. He could sit and watch the clouds and say right to the minute when the next rain was comin'." Her voice had become wistful, and now she pressed the fingers of one hand against the cold glass. "Bobby was a good man. You know, he used to like to believe that his pa was a sailor. The captain of a ship. An admiral, even. At the school, when he was growin' up, he liked to read about the Pilgrims and such, all those folks who came over from England in boats. He used to dream about boats with big white sails stretched in the wind—though I don't think he ever saw the ocean, 'cept in pictures. He was a good man, and full of life."

160

Wind whined through the wall cracks once more, and in his mind New heard the whistling of his brother's toy.

"Wind's been risin' two nights in a row," Myra said. "Your pa always told me that meant rain three, four days away. Might be in for some bad weather." She glanced up at the roof. "Ought to get some new timbers and shingles up there before the cold hits, I reckon."

"Yes ma'am."

She looked at him for a few seconds, then said, "Better get on to bed."

"I will directly."

"We'll talk more about it tomorrow," she said, and they both knew what she meant. Then Myra turned away and left the room. New heard her door close behind her.

He sank down into the chair again. His insides were quaking, and his mind was a storm of confusion. Why had his pa been able to do such things? And why was *he* suddenly able to, when for years he'd just been as normal as anybody else? It was too much for him to grasp: a floating knife, a hovering lamp, dancing furniture, and a truck that reared like a wild stallion were things of witchcraft—the kind of sorcery, New thought, that only the Devil himself could command.

It was no secret that evil prowled Briartop Mountain in many guises, from the Pumpkin Man to the black panther known as Greediguts by the locals. They were never seen, but everyone knew they were out there in the darkness, waiting.

And now New had to wonder what kind of man his pa had really been. He looked at the picture on the mantel. It didn't tell the whole story. What kind of power had been hiding behind Bobby Tharpe's face? And what had been trying to lure him down to Usherland with the promise of wealth and luxury?

New felt as if his back were bending under the weight of his thoughts. After some more thinking that only took him in circles, he stood up and took the lamp off the mantel, then went back to his room. As he readied himself for bed and blew out the flame, he heard Birdie howl. The howling went on for almost a minute—then abruptly cut off. After that, New didn't hear Birdie anymore.

And in the dense woods across the road from the Tharpe cabin, the figure that had been standing there for more than an hour slowly turned away and disappeared into the night.

161

18

"Yes sir," Logan Bodane said, "it looks like you're into something you're not supposed to be in." He was leaning against the wall just inside the library door, and his sly, knowing grin was maddening to Rix. Logan had been outfitted with an Usher uniform—dark slacks, light blue shirt, striped tie, and gray blazer—but he was already asserting himself. The tie was missing, the shirt open down the neck, the blazer wrinkled where Logan had been careless with it. A curl of his copper-colored hair tumbled over his forehead, and above the grin his cold blue eyes were mirthless.

Rix had straightened up at the first sound of the voice. Around his feet were the pages that had fallen from the book. "What are you doing in here?" he demanded, anger taking over now that the scare was seeping away.

"I was out walkin'. Decided to come in and have a look-see around the house before I went to sleep. I saw the light on in that room with the pool tables, and I heard you messin' around in here."

"The Gatehouse is off limits to you," Rix snapped.

"Beggin' your pardon, sir, but that's not what I understand. The way I hear it, I've got the run of the whole estate. See?" He held up a ring of keys and jingled them. "Anyway, I figured you folks would appreciate my comin' in and checkin' around. Can't be too careful these days." He ambled around the library, examining the books on the shelves. His eyes flickered toward the mounted weapons, and he gave a low whistle. "These are old ones, aren't they? Antiques and all."

"Does Edwin know you're prowling around the estate?"

"Ain't prowlin'," he said, and smiled again. "Like I say, I'm checkin'." He reached up and lifted the Mark III pistol from the wall mount. "Heavy gun. Couldn't hit a damn thing with a gun this heavy."

"Maybe I'll just give Edwin a call and tell him you're making a nuisance of yourself." Rix reached toward the telephone on the walnut writing desk.

"You don't want to do that, Mr. Usher. You'll wake Cass and Edwin up for nothin'. Part of my job is makin' sure everything's

162

buttoned up good and proper for the night. That's why Edwin gave me these keys."

Rix paid no attention. He dialed Edwin's number and waited while it rang. Now maybe this cocky bastard would get his ass kicked out of Usherland. The phone continued to ring. Rix glanced at his watch. It was ten minutes before two.

"Go on, then." Logan shrugged, gave the revolver's cylinder a whirl, and then returned it to its mount. The spilled pages caught his eye, and he walked over to look down at the cardboard boxes. "Seems to me you're the one who might not be where he ought to be," Logan said. "Kinda peculiar to be studyin' books at two o'clock in the mornin', ain't it?"

Someone picked up the phone. Edwin said sleepily, "Bodane house."

At that instant, Rix realized he'd made a mistake. Of course it was Logan's job to make sure everything was locked up for the night, and the keys Edwin had given him said so. It was Rix who was in jeopardy, because how would he explain being in the library at this time of the morning, especially after Logan told of seeing Rix rummaging through the old documents? Edwin would know at once what Rix was up to, and might feel compelled by the vow he'd taken to report it either to Walen or to Margaret.

"Bodane house," Edwin repeated, with a trace of irritation.

Logan had picked up a volume out of one of the boxes, and was watching Rix sharply. Damn it! Rix thought. He put the telephone back on its cradle. "No answer," he said. "I don't want to wake them up because of *you*, anyway."

"Yeah, Edwin sleeps like a rock. I can hear him snorin' right through the wall." His gaze penetrated, and for a second Rix thought that Logan's expression indicated he saw through the lie.

"Just leave," Rix said, "and that'll be the end of it."

"What's all this stuff?" Logan nodded toward the boxes. "Scrapbooks?"

"Some of them are, yes."

"Edwin told me you write books for a livin'. What are you doin'? Research or somethin'?"

"No," Rix said, too quickly. "I just came downstairs for a book to read."

"You must be a night owl, like me. Hey! Pictures!" He reached down into one of the boxes and brought out a handful of yellowed photographs.

"Be careful with those. They're fragile."

"Yeah, they look pretty old and all." Still, he handled them as if they were as tough as tree bark. Rix could see that they were more views of the Lodge, the pictures creased and cracked, marred by the passage of time. "Big old place, ain't it?" Logan asked as he examined them. "Bet you could put about ten factories inside there. Edwin says nobody's lived in it for about forty years. How come?"

"My mother didn't choose to."

"Bet you could get lost in there," he said, and Rix tensed. "Bet it's got all kinds of secret rooms and stuff. You ever been inside?"

"Once. A long time ago."

"Edwin says he's going to take me in. Going to show me how you Ushers used to live. I've heard you people threw some mighty strange shindigs inside there."

How Edwin planned to smooth this cretin's rough edges, Rix didn't know. His manner of speech grated on Rix's nerves. He probably had, at best, a high-school education. It was ridiculous to think this boy could fill Edwin's shoes! "Why don't you leave now?" Rix asked him.

Logan put the photographs down on the desk and stared at him for a silent moment. Behind his shoulder, Rix saw, was Hudson's portrait. Both of them were staring at him. Then Logan blinked and said, "You don't like me very much, do you?"

"Right."

"Why not? Because Edwin wants me to learn the ropes?"

"You've got it. I don't think you're capable. You're arrogant, rude, and slovenly, and I don't think you give a kick about working on Usherland. I believe you saw this as a way to get off the assembly line. Within a month after Edwin retires, I think you'll take whatever you can get your hands on and run off with it."

"Now why should I do that? This looks to me like a pretty cushy job. Oh, there's a lot of work to be done and all, but it's mostly organizin' other people and makin' sure they're not layin' around. Edwin says the secret to success is in lettin' everybody know you're boss, but not pushin' too hard. He says the trick is *anticipatin'* problems, knowin' how to take care of them before they crop up. The pay's good, I get my own house and car, and I get to drive that big limo. Why should I run off from all that?"

"Because," Rix replied evenly, "you're not cut out for the job. I don't care if you're a Bodane or not. You haven't got Edwin's style or education. You know that as well as I do, and why Edwin can't see it I don't understand."

"I can do the job. Maybe I'm not as smooth as Edwin, but I can do it. I worked my ass off on that assembly line, and two years in a row I won the highest-production trophy. Nobody's ever accused me of not tryin'. Whatever Edwin teaches me, I'll learn, and I'll do a damned good job."

"That remains to be seen."

Logan shrugged; he'd said all he cared to say, and Rix's opinion clearly didn't concern him. He moved to the door, then stopped and glanced back. "If you go out on the grounds at night," he said quietly, "you'd best be real careful."

"What's that supposed to mean?"

"You never know what might be out there in the dark. I've heard that all kinds of animals run wild in them woods. Old Greed-iguts might decide he wants you for a midnight snack. Or you might run right into the Pumpkin Man. So if you want to go walkin' after dark—you'd best just call me first." He smiled thinly. " 'Night, Mr. Usher." And then he left the library, closing the doors behind him.

Rix scowled and uttered a soft curse. He knew that the local people referred to the mythical black panther that roamed Briartop as Greediguts; only a few hunters had ever glimpsed the thing, and they were so hysterical that their accounts—written up in the *Democrat*, of course—took on ludicrous proportions. The creature was supposed to be as big as a car, and to move so fast that it was only a blur. One poor soul who'd "seen" Greediguts at close range swore that it was not totally a black panther, but it was a weird combination of predatory cat and reptile. The thing supposedly had the tail of a rattlesnake, the cold, lidless eyes of a lizard, and a forked tongue that flashed like quicksilver from its mouth. If there *was* a panther up there, Rix thought, it was probably some old, broken-down descendant of the animals that had fled Erik Usher's zoo the night he had—for unknown reasons—set it aflame.

Rix, unnerved by Logan's intrusion, picked up a couple of books at random from one of the boxes. There were some old letters tied up with rubber bands, and he took those, too. Then he looked through the photographs Logan had set on the desk.

Included with the exterior views were pictures of some of the Lodge's rooms. They were massive chambers decorated with over-sized leather- or fur-covered furniture, medieval tapestries and suits of armor, hunting trophies, huge crystal chandeliers, and fireplaces large enough to park a truck in. On the backs of the photographs, identifications of the rooms were written in faded black ink: Guest's

Parlor, Breakfast Room, Second-Floor Sitting Room, and Main Gallery. The Nautical Room was filled with ship models, ship's wheels, portholes, and other maritime fixtures. Stuffed polar bears stood in menacing postures, and fake icicles hung from the white ceiling in the Arctic Room. On the walls of the cavernous Gun Room hung hundreds of examples of Usher pistols and rifles, and at the center of the room was a charging stuffed buffalo.

Rix came to the photograph—badly cracked and faded—of a little girl sitting at a huge white grand piano. Her fingers were poised over the keyboard, her face smiling toward the camera. The child was wearing a ruffled dress with long sleeves, her high-topped shoes dangling over the piano's pedals. She had long, shining dark hair and lively almond-shaped eyes that revealed her Oriental heritage. Her face seemed carved from a beautiful piece of ivory. On the back, in strong, even printing, was written simply "My Angel." Rix knew it had to be a picture of Shann Usher, Aram's daughter by an Oriental wife.

But it was the next photograph that fully riveted Rix's attention.

It showed Erik sitting in a chair covered with thick white fur. The ebony cane was propped against the chair, and Erik regarded the camera like a king facing a commoner. On Erik's left knee sat a boy who appeared to be four or five years old, dressed in a dark suit with a little striped bow tie. The child, blond and curly-haired, was smiling gleefully and reaching toward the lens.

And standing behind Erik was a tall blond woman with a lovely but strained face, her eyes dark and haunted, as though by some inner sadness. Her hair was upswept, secured by a diamond tiara. In her arms she cradled an infant, probably not more than a year old.

Rix turned the picture over. It was inscribed "Walen and Simms. August, 1923" in Erik's spidery handwriting.

My God! Rix thought. He could see his father's eyes in the little boy's face. The mass of curly hair glowed with light and health. But who was Simms? The infant in the woman's arms? Was that Nora St. Clair Usher, cradling a *second* child? Simms was an ambiguous name—was the child male or female?

It was the first time Rix had ever seen the name. Was this a picture, then, of Walen's younger sibling? Rix had always thought Walen was an only child. What had happened to this infant, and why had Walen never mentioned Simms?

The eyes of Nora Usher, if that was who this was, pierced him.

She was as beautiful as he had imagined, but something in her face was empty—drained of life. By contrast, Erik's gaze mirrored an indolent, self-satisfied boredom.

Rix slipped the photograph into one of the books he carried. He wanted to find out more about Simms. Was it possible he had a living aunt or uncle he'd never even heard of before?

The unanswered questions were multiplying, and Rix realized the immensity of sorting through all the materials for his research. He had to see Dunstan's manuscript! He switched off the lights and left the library, locking the door behind him. In the safety of his bedroom, he examined his father's beaming face in the photograph, and was amazed as a knot of sadness formed in his throat. Walen Usher was human, after all. He'd once been a smiling child, unaware of what the future held for him. What had turned him into the decaying monster that lay upstairs? Simply the passage of time—or something more?

When Rix finally slept—restlessly, jarred by the rush and call of the wind—the dreams came to him.

He was lost again in the winding hallways of the Lodge, and he could feel its immense tonnage poised over him like a fist about to smash down. Ahead in the gloom was a single closed door, and as Rix approached it he saw the floating silver circle with its embossed, roaring lion's face. He watched his arm telescope out, saw his hand close around the circle; it was freezing cold, and began to shrink in size.

The door came open, and inside, the skeleton with bloody eyeholes swung like a macabre pendulum, lit by a flickering reddish light. There was blood all over the floor, streaming in thick rivulets. Rix recoiled and tried to scream, but his voice wouldn't work anymore. He had the sense of something coming down the corridor behind him, something large and dark and monstrous, rushing toward him with hideous speed.

And then Boone pushed the plastic bones aside and peered through the door with a sadistic grin on his face. "There you go, Rixy!" he crowed. "Peed your pants, didn't ya!"

Rix sat up in the dark. There was a sweat on his face, and he was shaking. The wind bumped and growled outside the house. He got out of bed, bracing himself for an attack if it should come.

The noise of the wind changed, and in it Rix thought he heard his name called: a soft whisper, as of a parent to a child, and then

167

it was gone. He looked up and through the window, toward where the Lodge stood in the seething darkness.

Ten billion dollars, the voice in his mind whispered. *All the money in the world.*

He shivered; his head was aching, but the attack never came. I'm getting better, he thought.

Ten billion dollars.

When he was sure he was going to make it without an attack, he returned to bed—and then time slept in a dreamless void.

Four

THE MOUNTAIN KING

19

The Mountain King awoke when he smelled the sun coming up.

He had no idea what time it was. Time meant nothing to him anymore. For him the clock had stopped long ago, and all hours were the same, the present destroying the past, the future crowding the present. He only knew that the bitter, chilly wind had died to a whisper and the sun was rising over the eastern peaks, its golden light smelling like wild strawberries.

He'd been dressed in his long, tattered black coat and rubber-soled boots when he'd lain down to sleep on his mattress covered with rags and newspapers, and so he was dressed now, as he pulled himself up with the aid of his gnarled hickory walking stick. There were twigs in his long, unkempt, yellow-gray beard, and what was left of his angel-fine hair wisped on his liver-spotted scalp. Around him, in the remains of what had once been a structure with rough stone walls, was utter chaos: there was an untidy pile of empty food cans and soft-drink bottles, scattered newspapers and magazines, the remnants of an old washing machine and a discarded truck trans-mission, and a sphere of collected twine the size of a basketball. Dead leaves had drifted through gaping holes in the slate roof, and now crackled underfoot as the old man crossed the room. His cane tapped the dirt floor before him. He reached one of the structure's two windows—neither of which held a pane of glass—and turned his face toward the sun.

A network of deep scars and gouges covered most of his face, from high forehead to sharp, jutting chin. His right eye was missing, and in its place was a brown, puckered hole. A thin gray film covered the left eye, and the little that he could see was veiled in mist. His right ear was a stub. Though he was emaciated and walked with his head bowed, there was still a fierceness in his face that made those who visited him, bringing cans of food, bottled drinks, or string for his collection, avert their eyes from him until he'd turned away. Those who knew him as the Mountain King came up here, to the peak of Briartop Mountain, to pose questions, to ask for advice, or simply to touch him. It was well known to the mountain people that the old man—who, as anyone would say, had lived on Briartop's peak for a hundred years or more—could accurately forecast the weather to the last drop of rain or flake of snow, look deeply into a person's mind and sort out any trouble that might be lying there, and give advice that might at first sound like the ravings of a lunatic—but much later would blossom into clarity. He could forecast births and deaths, boom crops or busts, even tell who might have designs on a neighbor's wife or husband. For all this he asked only canned food—peaches were his favorite—and soft drinks, preferably Buffalo Rock ginger ale. A gift of twine could buy a rambling weather forecast or a prediction of how the giver's life would end on a rain-slick road; one took such chances in asking questions of the Mountain King.

Under his coat he wore three layers of ragged old sweaters that had been left for him down on the rock where all his gifts were received. No one came up into the ruins. It was a haunted place, the locals knew, and only the Mountain King dared live there.

He let the sunlight play across his face to warm him, and then he drew several deep breaths of the morning air. Outside, the last traces of fog were being evaporated from around the tumbles of dark boulders and thin evergreens. After a while he made his way out of the stone structure and across the bleak, rocky earth toward the mountain's edge. It was still cold, and he began shivering. Around him were the forms of other stone structures, most of them fallen to ruin and barely recognizable except as heaps of lichen-green rocks. Some of the stones were as black as coals.

The Mountain King stopped; he leaned on his cane and with his other hand supported himself against a misshapen tree whose wood was in a state of petrification. Then he stared down almost two thousand feet at the massive house, on its island at the center of a black, calm lake.

For a long time he stood without moving, and an observer might have thought the old man had grown roots. He seemed to be waiting for something, his head cocked slightly to one side, his single eye with its fading sight aimed like a gunbarrel at the Lodge below.

"I know you," he said in a soft, reedy voice. "What's your next trick gonna be?"

He looked across the great expanse of Usherland, his gaze returning to the house. "Wind before rain," he said. "Stones grindin' stones. You've got a crack in your grin this mornin'. What's your next trick gonna be?"

The wind stirred around him, lifting dead leaves off the ground and snapping them in the air.

"Is it the boy?" the Mountain King whispered. "Or is it *me* you still want?"

He saw birds on the wing far below. Ducks or pigeons, he thought. He watched as they veered from their course as if caught in a sudden riptide of air. They smashed against one of the Lodge's walls and spun to the earth.

"I can wait, too," he said. But inwardly he knew he could not wait very much longer. His back was giving him trouble, his sight came and went, and sometimes his legs were so stiff, particularly after a hard rain, that he couldn't walk. He had lost track of time, but his body had marked the years with painful regularity. A sweep of frigid wind came from Usherland, and in it the Mountain King smelled change like charred wood. What would the change be? he asked himself. And how did the boy fit into it?

He couldn't see the answers. The eye in his mind was going blind, too. He turned away from the mountain's edge and walked slowly back to his refuge.

But before he reached it he stopped again, and brushed dead leaves aside with the tip of his cane.

There were animal tracks in the earth. They came out of the woods, he saw, and up to within fifteen feet of the house. Then they curved around the house and back into the forest again.

He was being watched, he knew. It gave him a feeling of satisfaction, but the sight of those monstrous tracks—sunken at least an inch into the ground—troubled him as well. He hadn't known the thing was out here last night, and worse still was the realization that it had never before come so close to where he lay sleeping.

Gathering saliva in his mouth, the Mountain King spat on a set of the tracks and ground it in with his foot. Then he walked slowly back to his shelter for a breakfast of canned peaches and ginger ale.

20

Usherland's forests blazed with color in the strong late-morning sunlight. Leaves in the giant, ancient oaks had turned brilliant scarlet and deep purple; ash leaves gleamed like golden coins; chestnut trees held variegated patterns of green, gold, and violet.

Katt and Rix were on horseback, following one of the many trails that meandered through the woods. It had been a long time since Rix had hoisted himself into a saddle, but Katt had come to his door this morning and urged him to join her for a ride before lunch. The stablemaster, a burly, middle-aged black man named Humphries, had chosen a mild-tempered roan mare for Rix, while Katt had taken her favorite horse, a nimble white stallion with a black star on his forehead.

They were about a mile from the Gatehouse and heading eastward. Rix had the impression of being inside a tremendous cathedral roofed with tall, multihued treetops. Every so often the light breeze showered Rix and Katt with falling leaves. The sunlight filtered down as if through stained-glass windows.

Katt, wearing a tan crushed-velvet riding outfit, silently pointed into the woods off the trail, and Rix looked in time to see two white-tailed deer freeze for a second before they leaped into the cover of denser undergrowth.

If there was a God, He was at this moment on Usherland. The world seemed still and peaceful; a serenity that Rix hadn't known for years settled around him. The crisp air smelled pungent and earthy. Sandra would have enjoyed this perfect moment. She had been the rare type of person who found the silver lining in even the blackest cloud. Right up to the end, she'd encouraged Rix to try to purge himself of the old family hurts. He was especially halting in talking about his father, but Sandra had patiently listened and drawn him out. She'd even suggested she go to Usherland with him and stand by him as he struggled to strike a truce with his parents and brother. She was helping him feel that he was worth a damn—and then he'd walked into that bloody bathroom and almost lost his mind.

Rix blamed himself. He'd been too caught up in his own problems to sense a need in Sandra. Or, more horribly, maybe he'd expressed his emotions too well—and Sandra had been overcome by the ghosts of his childhood.

"Where are you?" Katt asked, checking her horse until Rix could catch up.

He blinked, returning from the haunted world. "Sorry. I was thinking how beautiful this is."

"Like old times, isn't it?" Katt's smile was radiant this morning. There was no trace of the cold practicality she'd displayed yesterday, when talking about the future of Usher Armaments. He was comfortable with her again. "I've missed having a riding partner."

"Doesn't Boone ride with you? I thought he was such a great horseman."

She shrugged. "He stays to himself most of the time. Usually he's over at the racetrack, clocking the horses."

Shades of Erik, Rix thought. He remembered Puddin's shouts as Boone pulled her out of the dining room. "What did Puddin' mean about Boone's talent agency yesterday?" he asked.

"I don't know. I thought she was drunk and babbling. Why?"

"Boone's the type who crows from dusk till dawn, but he doesn't talk very much about his work. Doesn't that strike you as odd?"

"I've never thought about it. I know it's a legitimate business, though. Dad put up the cash for it." She smiled mischievously. "What's on your mind, Rix?"

"Boone's too evasive when he should be beating his chest. Does he go to his club every night?"

"Just about."

"Good. I think I'll have a little talk with Puddin'."

"I wouldn't mess around with her if I were you," Katt warned. "She's trouble."

He nodded, but he hadn't heard her. As they continued along the trail deeper into the woods, Rix's thoughts turned toward the documents in the library. "Katt?" he said casually. "Why did Dad bring all those books from the Lodge?"

"Is your writer's curiosity working overtime?"

"Maybe. Has Dad been working on a special project or something?"

Katt hesitated a moment. "I don't know if I should answer that or not."

"Why not?"

175

"Because . . . you know, the security and everything."

"What do you think I'm going to do?" He grinned tightly. "Sell out to the Russians? Come on. What's the big secret?"

"Well, I don't suppose it would hurt. I don't know a lot about it, really, but Dad's told me he's working on something new for Usher Armaments. It's called Pendulum, but what it is and what it does, I don't know. General McVair and Mr. Meredith have been coming to see him a lot lately. It must be important to him, because he lets them use the Jetcopter."

"Pendulum," Rix repeated. "Sounds ominous." What new witch's brew was the business cooking up? he wondered. And what did the old documents have to do with it? The picture of the infant in Nora's arms flashed through his mind. The family cemetery was to the north, nearer the Lodge. It might take twenty minutes or so to get there from here. If Walen did have a brother or sister who had died as a child, wouldn't there be a grave and a headstone? "We're not too far from the cemetery, are we?" he asked Katt.

"Oh my God!" she said with mock horror. "Don't tell me Boone's right!"

"About what?"

"Boone says you missed your calling. He says you have a deep-seated desire to rob graves."

"Not exactly, though whenever I'm around Boone, I feel like digging a grave for *him*. No, really. I'm serious. I'd like to ride over and look around."

"To the cemetery?" She made a face. "What for?"

"Because it's a beautiful day. Because I'm crazy. Because I want to. Okay? Will you take me over there?"

"Boy, you sure know how to have fun!" she said, but she turned her horse northward at the next intersection of trails.

They came out of the forest onto a paved road, and crossed a small bridge spanning a dark, peat-laden stream connecting two lakes. On the other side of the bridge was Usherland's Memory Garden, two acres of sculpted grounds surrounded by eight-foot-high marble walls and a large bronze gate.

Rix and Katt left their horses tied to the lower branches of a pine tree and entered the cemetery. Inside, brilliantly colored trees shaded a phantasmagoria of intricate marble and granite monuments, obelisks, grotesque statues, and religious totems. Walkways intersected each other, cutting through manicured hedgerows to converge on the white marble chapel at the Memory Garden's center.

176

Elsewhere on the grounds were a Japanese rock garden, a manmade waterfall that spilled down several terraces into a pond stocked with goldfish, a Grotto of Solitude where one could meditate in a fake cavern in the presence of statues of the saints, and a collection of antique Baldwin steam engines from the early days of railroading. The Usher graves, Rix knew, were located near the chapel; on the outer edges of the garden were the graves of servants. There was even a section for pets, over near the steam engines.

Rix, followed at a distance by his sister, went along a walkway toward the chapel. He passed a series of statues that were at once fascinating and repellent: The first was a young child in vibrant health, the second a teenaged boy with his face toward the sky— and, grotesquely, the same figure was repeated every fifty feet or so, becoming progressively older and more infirm until the last statue. It was a skeleton with beckoning arms.

And near it was the twenty-foot-tall gilded pyramid that was the final resting place of Hudson Usher. A scrolled inscription in bronze letters read: HE SAW THE FUTURE. Hudson's date of birth was not given, but his death date was July 14, 1855. Ten yards away, beneath the statue of a nun with clasped hands, lay his wife, Hannah Burke Usher. A neat hedge and a row of limestone cherubs separated Hannah's grave from a simple black marble headstone that bore the name RODERICK. Whether the man's dust actually lay under that stone or not, Rix didn't know. There was no grave for Madeline Usher.

Rix had come to this place only once before, to seek peace after Sandra's suicide. He hadn't made it to the pond before he had to get out. There was something terribly decadent in the ostentatious monuments and statues of death angels. This place was almost a celebration of death, a shout of debased joy from the lips of the new generation over the graves of the old.

Aram Usher lay entombed in a marble cube ten feet high. At each corner stood a life-sized statue of a man standing at attention, holding what looked to be a dueling pistol. Each figure had different eyes: rubies, emeralds, jade, and topaz. Next to him, in a similar cube but without the figures, was Cynthia Cordweiler Usher. The legend on her stone read: ASHES TO ASHES, DEAD OCTOBER 8, 1871. Near their stones, surrounded by a wrought-iron fence, was a marble column topped by, of all things, a small grand piano of marble. The name SHANN was spelled out in wrought-iron letters.

Thirty feet or so away, Ludlow Usher was buried under a granite representation of the Lodge that had to weigh at least a ton. Erik's handiwork was all over this gravesite, Rix mused. The inscription read LUDLOW USHER, DEAR FATHER. Flanking him were the graves of two wives, Jessamyn Usher and Lauretta Kenworth Usher.

A rearing horse marked Erik's tomb, which was engraved with golden finials and studded with gemstones. He lay alone, without the protection of shade trees. There was no grave for Nora, and none for Simms.

A new section had been added since Rix's last visit. Freshly carved angels rose from a block of gold-veined marble. It bore the name of Walen Usher, with his date of birth. Nearby, a pink marble stone was inscribed MARGARET—MY LOVE.

"You ready to go now?" Katt asked from behind him. "This isn't my favorite place."

He stood looking at the two gravesites that were ready for his mother and father, and he felt very old. Seeing this stone brought home Walen's impending death even more than hearing what Dr. Francis had said. In a week—if that long—his father would be lying in the earth. How was he going to handle it? He was long familiar with the turbulence of intermingled love and hate, but now a sadness seeped into the tangle of contradictory emotions. "Yeah," he said distantly. "I'm ready."

But he stopped again, before Erik's tomb. A three-foot-high hedge stood beyond it, about twenty feet away. He could see the back of a small head—another statue on a monument. He walked toward it.

"Rix!" Katt called irritably. "Come on!"

He went through an opening in the hedge and around to the front of the gravestone, which was an angel strumming a lyre. Rix's heart kicked, and he said, "Katt? Come here for a minute, okay?"

She sighed and shook her head, but went over to him. She looked at the monument. "So what?"

"That's what." Rix pointed toward the stone. Etched into the lyre was SIMMS—OUR GOLDEN BOY.

"Simms? I never heard of anybody named Simms before."

"Maybe you weren't supposed to. Simms was Dad's brother. He must've died when he was a small boy, from the size of the grave."

"Dad's *brother*? Come on! Dad was an only child!"

"Maybe that's what he wanted us to think," Rix replied. "Why, I don't know."

"You're wrong. Simms must've been a servant's child. Have you gone off your rocker?"

"None of the servants or their children are buried up here," he reminded her. "These are all Usher plots. I can't tell you how I know, but I do. For some reason, Dad's kept Simms a secret all these years."

"Cut it out. You're making it sound creepy. I still say it's a servant's child. Christ, maybe it's a dog! Listen, I don't know about you, but I'm getting out of here. You coming or not?"

Rix bent down, running his fingers over the carved letters. SIMMS—OUR GOLDEN BOY. Whose sentiment was that? Nora's? There was no date on the stone, so conceivably Simms might have died as an infant. In that case, Walen would hardly have known his brother. When Rix stood up, he saw that Katt had stalked off. He didn't blame her; he must have sounded like a ghoul.

By the time he left the Memory Garden he was satiated with death imagery. Katt had taken her horse and gone. As he untied his horse and climbed into the saddle, he thought that Katt had better get used to death if she seriously wanted to control the business.

The road ran north and south. Going south would eventually return him to the stables. The northern path would take him past the Lodge. The sunshine was warm and strong, and Rix wanted a look at the massive crack that Nora had mentioned in her diary. He headed north.

Within fifteen minutes he saw the chimneys and lightning rods jutting above the trees. Before he was mentally prepared for the sight, the foliage cleared and he had reached the lake's southern shore and was looking across the smooth black water at Usher's Lodge.

It was a madman's dream, Rix thought. No emperor, tsar, or king had ever owned such an ungodly monument to the spoils of war. Rix gazed upward at the lions that stalked the roof, and then his eye found the discolored glass cupola that looked like a burned-out lightbulb. A breeze blew across the lake from the direction of the Lodge, and Rix shivered as if he were standing before a huge deep freeze. Water whispered against the shore through a mass of reeds and floating green algae.

The only way to the island was across the granite carriage bridge. Trying to follow the shoreline to the northern side of the Lodge was impossible, because over there the forest was impenetrable. Rix guided his horse toward the bridge. His heart had started beating harder.

Ten feet onto the bridge, Rix reined in sharply. The Lodge's shadow, bloated and monstrous, waited to engulf him.

He couldn't go any closer. The Lodge still held power over him. Even this far from the house, he felt disoriented and claustrophobic. As he turned the horse away, his palms were slick with sweat.

Rix guided the mare onto a path through the woods, intending to take a shortcut to the stables. The tension at the back of his neck eased only when the forest blocked his view of the Lodge. As he continued into the woods, the trees overhead cut the sunlight to a murky orange haze.

The mare suddenly tossed her head with such force that Rix almost lost the reins. She balked, neighing and snorting. After a minute or two of rubbing her neck, Rix got her settled down and moving forward again. He looked around to see what might have spooked her. The forest seemed tranquil. An occasional bird called in the distance, but otherwise the only sound was the wind whispering through the trees.

Again the horse jerked her head, her hindquarters dancing nervously. "Calm down, now," Rix said softly. From her throat came a quiet, ominous rumble, but she responded to the reins and kept moving forward.

They'd gone another thirty yards when Rix saw old, rusted gaslamp poles on either side of the path. From the gloom emerged a series of large wire cages, battered out of shape, some of them broken open. Dark green trails of kudzu snaked through them, and the odor of decay rose from rotting trees slimed with gray fungus.

It was the wreckage of Erik's private zoo. He had set it aflame in the 1920s, Margaret had told Rix, but she didn't know why he'd done it. Most of the lions, tigers, panthers, crocodiles, pythons, zebras, gazelles, and exotic birds had died in the fire, but some had burst out of their cages and fled into the woods. Every once in a while, some farmer in the area had sworn he'd seen a zebra running through his tobacco field, and an old, toothless leopard had been shot by a hunter in 1943. Of course, there was Greediguts, too; the story was that Greediguts was a mutant, the offspring of a black panther who'd escaped the conflagration and mated with another animal in the wilderness. Others said that Greediguts was as ancient as Briartop Mountain itself.

As he rode past the misshapen cages, the concrete crocodile pit now filled with rainwater and debris, the aviary a mass of twisted vines and hanging branches, Rix could almost hear the screams of the animals. The strongest ones must have thrown their bodies against the cages in a frenzy until they either killed themselves or broke loose. To Rix, this had always been a malevolent place. Boone had loved to come here as a boy and play among the cages, but Rix gave it a wide berth.

180

Once again the mare balked; she seemed confused about what direction to take. When he'd gotten her around the next bend, Rix saw what was spooking her.

Hanging on wires from low tree branches, suspended about five or six feet from the ground, were eight animal carcasses. There were three squirrels, two possums, a red fox, and two deer, all dangling by their legs. He could smell the blood that had pooled on the ground beneath them, and he knew his horse had smelled it long ago. Flies were abundant, merrily buzzing and plundering.

He moved as close to the carcasses as the horse would let him. The animals' throats had been deeply slashed, but other than that they seemed to be unmarked. Most of the eyes had been picked out by insects, and battalions of bugs feasted on the crusted blood. Rix waved away flies that darted around his head. "Christ!" he muttered.

He recalled the light he'd seen from his window. It had been in this area. Was this somebody's idea of a joke?

The carcasses swayed slightly on their wires, reminding Rix again of Boone's grisly surprise at the De Peyser Hotel. Surely Boone wouldn't be nuts enough to come out in the middle of the night and do this!

He guided the mare around the hanging trophies and left the zoo's ruins behind. Something about that scene disturbed him deeply, more than the cruel carnage.

It took him a few minutes to realize exactly what it was.

There had been no bullet holes in those carcasses, just the throat slashes.

How had they been hunted down?

He gave the mare a quick kick in the flanks, and she trotted back to the stable.

21

"What I'd like to know," Raven Dunstan said firmly, "is why you don't deputize about thirty men and take bloodhounds up on Briartop Mountain. Surely you've at least considered it!"

Sitting across the desk from her, in his Taylorville office, was Walt Kemp, the county sheriff. He was a thickset man with a gray crewcut and full gray sideburns. His square-jawed face was heavily lined, his dark brown eyes now bored with the interview, giving him the appearance of what he actually was: a man who worked in the weather, a well-to-do tobacco farmer with some law enforcement training who'd decided to run for county sheriff because the last man was just so damned lazy. He was in his second year in office, and he was ready to give it up. It wasn't that crime was so bad in the county—it wasn't, except for a few burglaries, auto thefts, and moonshine stills—but the paperwork was mountainous. His office was understaffed, his budget had been slashed, and now here was Raven Dunstan again, pursuing her favorite subject with the tenacity of a coon dog.

"I don't think I could find five men who'd want to hike up there," he replied, lighting a cigarette. "And yes, I've considered it. As a matter of fact, last year I did take two men up with hounds. And y'know what happened? Somebody shot one of the dogs with rock salt and started shootin' at us, too, before we'd hardly gotten out of our cars. I reckon they figured we were gonna find a still or something."

"So you gave up? Why?"

"We *didn't* give up. We just figured we couldn't search too well with rock salt in our asses, excuse my French." He took a pull from his cigarette and exhaled the smoke through his nostrils. "Those Briartop people are mean as hell, Miss Dunstan. They don't want what they call 'outsiders' on their territory—and I've found out that means me, too. You know, I deputized one man up there—Clint Perry. He's the only one who'd even listen to me when I tried to find volunteers. The rest of those mountain folks just don't want to be bothered."

She shook her head. "I can't believe this! You're the county sheriff. It's your job to 'bother' them!"

"They don't want my help." Kemp was trying to control his temper. Wheeler's daughter, he thought, could worry the warts off a toadfrog. "When they come at you with guns, what are you gonna do? When they fell trees across the road to block the way, what are you gonna do? Clint tries to help me out as much as he can, but he's just one man. And the folks up there treat him like he's poison for the help he does give me! I'm tellin' you, they don't want the law up there."

"I want to read something to you," she said, and brought out a notepad from her purse. "When I took the paper over from my father, I went back through the old copies of the *Democrat*. Dad keeps them bound in books at the house. I went over every reference to missing children that I could find, and I want to tell you what I came up with."

"Shoot," he offered.

"Since 1872," Raven said, "there have been three or four incidents every year except one, in 1893, the year of the Briartop 'quake. At *least* three or four. And those are the ones that were reported. How many others might there be? Add it up. It comes out to more than *three hundred*. Most of the incidents took place in October and November. Harvest time. Three hundred children, all aged between six and fourteen, all from an area that includes Briartop Mountain, Foxton, Rainbow, and Taylorville. Now don't you think that's worth 'bothering' somebody about?"

"You don't have to get sarcastic about it, now." Kemp drew so hard on his cigarette that he almost scorched his thick fingers. "When you came to me wantin' to see the missin' persons files and all that stuff, I thought you'd write stories about how hard I've been workin' on this thing—not articles takin' me to hell and back. I even gave you the name of that Tharpe boy as a favor."

"I appreciate the favor, but I don't see you doing a damned thing about it."

"What can I do, woman?" he said, more loudly than he'd wanted. The secretary's typing in the outer office suddenly silenced. "Move up to Briartop *myself*? Sure, something's goin' on up there! I ain't sayin' it's been goin' on since 1872, 'cause I wasn't around back then! And I'd say that figure you've come up with is probably a bit inflated, if those other Dunstans were anything like you and old Wheeler! Okay, we've got kids steppin' into thin air. And I *do* mean thin air, Miss Dunstan! There's not a trace of 'em left. Not a piece of clothing, not a footprint, *nothin'*! When you ask questions on Briartop, you get some damned hillbilly holdin' a gun in your face. What am I gonna do?"

Raven didn't reply. She closed her notepad and returned it to her purse. The sheriff was right, she knew. If all the others were as resistant as Myra Tharpe, how could any decent search be carried out? "I don't know," she said finally.

"Right." He stabbed the cigarette out with an angry thrust. Splotches of color burned on his jowls. "Neither do I. You know what I think?" He pinned her gaze with his own. "There's no such thing as the Pumpkin Man. It's a made-up story to scare the children. Whenever a kid goes wanderin' off into the woods and doesn't come home, it's supposed to be the Pumpkin Man got him. Well, what about the ones who just get themselves lost? Or the ones who run away from home? You know, those cabins up there ain't mansions. I'll bet plenty of kids run away to the city."

"Six-year-olds?" she asked pointedly.

Kemp folded his hands together on his blotter-topped desk. He looked more weary today, Raven thought, than she'd ever seen him. "I've gone up on Briartop a couple of times," he told her in a quieter tone of voice. "All by myself. Do you know how *big* it is? How thick those woods are? The thorns up there'll cut you like knives. You can walk ten feet off a path and get yourself so lost your head spins. There are caves and ravines and craters and God knows what-all. You know what's up at the very tiptop? A whole damned *town*, that's what."

"A town? What kind of town?"

"Well, it's just ruins, is all. But it *was* a town, a long time ago. Nobody lives there but one old crazy bird who calls himself the Mountain King." He picked at an offending hangnail for a few seconds. "And I'll tell you somethin' else," he decided. "Clint Perry says he wouldn't go up to those ruins if you paid him five hundred bucks."

"That's a brave deputy you've got. Is he afraid of one old man?"

"Hell, no! Listen, you're not puttin' all this in your newspaper, are you? I thought I made it real clear that what I say is off the record."

"It's clear," she agreed. If she didn't need the man's confidential information from time to time, Raven would have blasted him out of this office by now.

"The damned place is haunted," Kemp said. He gave a quick, crooked grin to let her know he didn't really believe it. "At least that's what Perry says. I've been up there once, and once was enough. Some of the old stone walls are still standin', but they're as black as soot—and I swear to God, you can see the outlines of people burned right into the walls. Now you can laugh if you want to."

Raven might have smiled wryly, but the expression in Kemp's eyes stopped her. He was dead serious, she saw. "People in the walls, huh?"

"No, I didn't say that. I said the *outlines* of people. You know, silhouettes. It'll give you the creeps to see 'em, I guaran-damn-tee it!"

"What happened up there?"

He shrugged. "Hell if I know, but I've heard all kinds of crazy stories about Briartop Mountain. Supposed to be that comets fell one summer night and set the whole mountain on fire. 'Course, you know about the black panther that's supposed to be roamin' around up there. Bastard gets bigger every year. Then there's the stories about the witches, too. All kinds of fool—"

"The witches?" Raven interrupted. "I hadn't heard that one."

"Yeah, supposed to be that Briartop used to be crawlin' with 'em. Gil Partain, over in Rainbow, says his grandmother used to talk about 'em before she died. Said that God Hisself tried to destroy Briartop Mountain. Guess it didn't work, though, 'cause it's still there."

Raven glanced at her wristwatch and saw that she was going to be late for her meeting with Rix Usher. This visit with Sheriff Kemp had been totally unproductive. She put her purse strap around her shoulder and rose to leave.

"I'll keep you posted," Kemp said, lifting his bulk from the chair. "I told you them stories by way of sayin' that you can't believe everything you hear. There ain't no Pumpkin Man. One of these days, somebody'll find that Tharpe boy's bones at the bottom of a cliff, or caught down in some thorns where he couldn't get loose."

"Then that just leaves us the other two hundred ninety-nine to find, doesn't it?" She left his office before he could reply.

Raven made the drive from Taylorville to Foxton in twenty minutes, and walked into the Broadleaf Cafe just after three. The place was almost empty, except for the bored waitress with the double-dip hairdo and a stocky, bearded man in overalls sitting at the counter with a doughnut and a cup of coffee. Rix Usher was waiting in the same booth they'd occupied yesterday.

"Sorry I'm late," she said as she slid in. "I was over in Taylorville."

"That's okay, I just got here." Again, he'd parked the red Thunderbird around the corner where it wouldn't be seen. After lunch, he'd sheltered himself in his room to look through some of the materials he'd taken from the library last night. The old account books were filled with scribblings and monetary figures, mostly illegible. The letters were more revealing; the majority were from bank presidents, gunpowder suppliers, and steel company presidents, and had to do with Erik's business affairs. A few of the letters, however, were from women. Two of those, still bearing a faint scent of lavender, were positively lewd, describing nights of bestial sex-

and-whipping sessions. At two-thirty, Rix had slipped away from the Gatehouse.

Raven waved the waitress away before she could reach the table. "I talked to Dad last night about your proposal," she said. "The first thing is that he doesn't trust you any more than he could run a hundred-yard dash. The second thing is that he wants to meet you."

Better yet, Rix thought. "When?"

"How about right now? My car's out front, if you want to leave yours here."

Rix nodded. In a few minutes he was sitting in Raven's Volkswagen as she drove out of Foxton and turned onto a narrow country road north of the town limits. He had the opportunity to settle back and really look at Raven Dunstan. She had strong, even features and thick, curly black hair that accentuated her fair complexion. She wore very little makeup, and Rix didn't think she needed any. She was naturally attractive, with a strong, earthy sensuality. There was strength in her eyes and in the set of her jaw, and Rix wondered what she'd look like when she laughed. She looked unafraid to go anywhere or do anything; she had guts, he decided. Otherwise, she never would have kept calling Usherland until she finally wore down the opposition. He realized that he actually liked her.

But in the next moment he shifted his position and looked away. His feelings for Sandra were still strong; until he could resolve the question of why she'd killed herself in that bathtub, he couldn't let her go.

Raven had felt him watching her, and glanced quickly at him. Though he appeared wan and tired, she thought he was a striking-looking man. He needed light in his eyes, she decided. They held an inner darkness that disturbed her.

"How'd you get involved with the *Democrat*? Why didn't you go after a job on a city newspaper, or get into television journalism?"

"Oh, I worked for a city paper for a while. I was a feature editor for almost three years with a paper in Memphis. But when Dad called me, I had to come home. The *Democrat*'s been in my family for a long time. Besides, Dad needed help with his book."

"Then you help him write it, too?"

"No. In fact, I've never seen any of the book. He won't even let me come around when he's working on it. My father's a very private person, Mr. Usher. And he's a very proud and stubborn man, as well."

"That's not exactly the opinion my father has of him," Rix

186

commented, and saw her smile faintly. It was a nice smile, and Rix hoped to see it again.

Raven took a left onto a long gravel drive. It climbed gently through pine woods to a gabled, two-story white house at the top of a hill, overlooking a magnificent vista of sky and mountains.

"Welcome to the homestead," Raven said. As he followed her up the steps to the porch, Rix almost asked her about her limp—but then the front door opened and he had his first glimpse of Wheeler Dunstan.

22

Rix's initial thought, macabre as it was, was that the old man's first name was appropriate. Dunstan was confined to a motorized wheelchair that he controlled by a lever in the armrest gearbox.

"That's far enough," Dunstan commanded in a voice like the grating of coarse sandpaper. "Let me look at you."

Rix stopped. The old man's brilliant blue eyes—almost the same shade as his daughter's, but much colder—examined him from head to foot, as Rix did the same to Wheeler Dunstan. He was probably in his early sixties, with close-cropped, iron-gray hair and the hard-bitten look of a Marine drill sergeant. He had a short gray beard and mustache that further enhanced his bristling appearance. Though the man's legs looked thin and shriveled in the jeans he wore, his upper body was knotty and muscular; his forearms, exposed by the rolled-up sleeves of a faded blue workshirt, were twice the girth of Rix's. His thick neck indicated that he'd been a man of some power before whatever happened to put him in that chair, and Rix guessed he might still be able to straighten out a horseshoe with his bare hands. Clenched between his teeth was a fist-sized corncob pipe, and blue smoke came from his mouth in quick, haughty puffs.

"I'm unarmed, if that's what you're looking for," Rix said.

Dunstan smiled just a fraction, but his eyes remained wary. "You've got the Usher look, all right. Quick, boy—what's the name of the police chief who threw you in the clink after that peace march?"

"Bill Blanchard. His nickname was 'Bulldog.' "

"Your mother goes to a plastic surgeon in New York. What's his name? Quick."

"Dr. Martin Steiner. And he's not in New York, he's in Los Angeles." Rix lifted his eyebrows. "Want me to name the winner of the '48 World Series?"

"If you can, I'll throw your ass off this porch. The real Rix Usher doesn't know shit about sports."

"I didn't realize I had to pass an oral exam."

"Yep," Dunstan replied. He puffed on his pipe, taking his time in sizing Rix up, then removed it from his mouth and motioned toward the door with a jerk of his head. "Come on in, then."

It was clearly a man's house, full of dark wood and functional, inexpensive pine furniture. An electric lift attached to the staircase was used to convey the wheelchair to the second floor. Shelves around the red brick fireplace in the large parlor held such found objects as smooth river stones, dried Indian corncobs, an intricately woven bird's nest, and an assortment of pinecones. A framed front page of the *Foxton Democrat* shouted, in three-inch-tall black letters, WAR DECLARED. Also on the walls were oil paintings of various barns.

"I did those," Dunstan announced, noting Rix's interest. "I've got a studio at the back of the house. I like the texture and look of barns. Painting 'em relaxes me. Sit down."

Rix settled into a chair with his back to the wall. The house smelled strongly of aromatic pipe tobacco. Light filtered in through a pair of ceiling-high bay windows that faced the mountain view. In the distance Rix could see the new bank building in Foxton, and the white steeple of the Foxton First Baptist Church.

Raven sat on the parlor couch a few feet away from Rix, where she could watch both him and her father. The old man's chair whirred forward until his knees were almost touching Rix's; for an instant Rix felt trapped, a traitor in the enemy's camp. Dunstan tapped his fingers on the armrests, his head cocked slightly to one side.

"What're you doin' here?" the old man asked, his eyes hooded. "You're Walen Usher's boy." The word *boy* was spoken with a sneer.

"I'm his son, but I'm not his 'boy.' If you know me as well as you pretend, you're aware of that."

"I know you've been the black sheep of the family. I know you've been livin' in another state for the last seven years. You look older than I expected."

"I'm thirty-three," Rix said.

"Well, time does things to people." Dunstan's hands wandered down to touch his crippled legs. "What's your story, then? Why'd you agree to come here?"

"I explained the deal to your daughter yesterday. For the information I've got about Walen and his successor, I want to see your manuscript and know where you're getting your research material."

"The manuscript's locked up," Dunstan said flatly. "I won't show my book to anyone."

"Then I don't guess we've got anything to discuss."

Rix started to rise, but the old man said, "Wait a minute. I didn't say that."

"Okay, I'm listening."

Dunstan glanced quickly at his daughter, then back to Rix. "I've put in six years on that manuscript. No way in hell am I gonna let *anybody* see it. But we might still strike a deal, Mr. Usher. Anything you want to know that's in the book, I'll tell you. And I'll show you how I'm writing it. But first you tell us what we want to know: What's your father's condition, and who's going to take over the business?"

Rix paused thoughtfully. Traitor, betrayer, turncoat—all the definitions applied. But then he thought of how Walen's belt had stung his legs, of how Boone had grinned before the fist had smashed down, of how the skeleton had swung in the De Peyser doorway. *When are you gonna write somethin' about us, Rixy?* And in that instant, Rix was certain of his true purpose in coming to this house: somehow he had to take control of the book that Wheeler Dunstan was writing. He hoped the flash of realization in his eyes hadn't given him away. But first he had to test the man. "No," he said firmly. "It won't work that way. You might not have a damned thing. I'm taking a chance being here. First you have to prove to me that you've got something I might be interested in knowing."

Now it was the old man's turn to consider. Smoke curled from his mouth. "What do you think?" he asked Raven.

"I'm not sure. I may be dead wrong . . . but I think we can trust him."

Dunstan grunted softly, his brows knit. "All right," he said. "What do you want to know?"

It came to him in the quick recollection of the angel strumming its lyre. "Simms Usher," Rix said. "Tell me about him."

Dunstan looked relieved, as if he'd been prepared for a heavier

189

question. "Simms was your father's younger brother. Nora St. Clair Usher's second child. There's not much to tell, really—except that he was retarded. Not severely, but enough so that Erik didn't have very much to do with him. Erik despised imperfection. Simms died when he was six years old. That's it."

That was all? Why had Walen never mentioned Simms, then? Was he ashamed of having a retarded brother? "How did he die? Something to do with his condition?"

"Nope," Dunstan said. "An animal killed Simms."

Rix's interest perked up. "An animal? What kind of animal?"

"A *wild* animal," the old man said dryly. "I don't know what kind." His pipe had gone out; he took it from his mouth to relight it with a match from his shirt pocket. "A gardener found what was left of the body. There wasn't much. Simms had wandered away from the Lodge, chasin' butterflies or something. An animal got him in the woods." His match flared. "When the locals heard about it, there were all kinds of opinions. Some said Erik wanted the boy to be killed. Others said the animal was one of those that escaped from the burnin' zoo about four years earlier. Anyway, it was never found. About two months after Simms died, Nora left Usherland and never came back."

"She left Walen with Erik? Where'd she go?"

"St. Augustine, Florida. She married a Greek who owned a fleet of fishing boats, and she started teaching retarded children in a school down there. She taught right up until the day she died, in 1966. They put a statue of her up in the front yard." He regarded Rix through a veil of smoke. "That's all about Simms. I thought you were gonna ask me about something nobody else knows."

If what Dunstan had told him was true, it was obvious the man knew his facts very well. But *how* had he gotten those facts? "I found Nora's diary in the Gatehouse library," Rix said. "Do you know about the deal Erik struck with St. Clair Stables?"

"Sure. Three million dollars bought Nora and four stud horses. Ludlow Usher signed the bank draft."

Rix remembered a bit of information from the diary which he could use to really test Dunstan's knowledge. "Erik had a particular horse in mind to win the Kentucky Derby. Do you know its name?"

He smiled faintly around his pipe. "King South. Erik scrubbed that horse down with beer and spent over a hundred thousand dollars on a special stall with fans and steam heating. He let the horse run free through the Lodge. Of course you know what happened at the 1922 Derby?"

Rix shook his head.

"King South was ahead by two lengths at the far turn when he staggered and hit the rail," Dunstan said. "He went down. The infield observers swore they could hear the leg break. Or it might have been the jockey's back they heard crackin'. In any case, King South had to be destroyed right on the track. Erik and Nora had watched the whole thing from their private box, though there's no record of Erik's response. They returned directly to Usherland. Around two o'clock the next morning, Erik went crazy and set fire to his zoo. A rumor is that Erik had the carcass of King South stuffed and mounted in his bedroom. A visitor from Washington supposedly found Erik stark naked, ridin' that stuffed horse and whippin' its flanks as if he were racin' in the Derby. Any truth to that?"

"I don't know. I've never been up to Erik's bedroom."

"Okay." Dunstan gave out one last puff of smoke and removed the pipe from his mouth. He leaned slightly toward Rix, his stare unyielding. "Let's hear it about Walen. What's going on?"

The moment of truth, Rix thought. An unfamiliar sense of family loyalty tugged at him. But who would he be hurting? And this man had something he desperately wanted—no, desperately *needed*. "Walen's dying," Rix said. "Dr. John Francis from Boston is attending to him, but he doesn't see much hope. He thinks Walen may go anytime."

"Raven already figured that out," Dunstan replied. "Francis is a specialist in cell degeneration. But there's no stopping the Malady's progress, is there? Old Walen must be locked in his Quiet Room by now." A flicker of pleasure passed across his face. "I'm surprised he's lasted this long. Goes to show he's a tough old bastard. Now tell us something we don't know: Who's going to control the estate and the business?"

Rix paused with the name on his lips. He was betraying family secrets for the sake of gaining the trust of Wheeler Dunstan; he told himself that if he didn't, he had no chance of getting his hands on that manuscript. Rix said, "Kattrina. My sister's going to take over the business."

Wheeler Dunstan was silent; then he gave a soft, low whistle. "Shitfire," he said. "I always thought it would be Boone. Then, when I found out you were comin' back, I assumed *you* were in the runnin'."

"I'm not. I despise the business."

"So I've heard, but ten billion dollars can change hate to love. That's about what Usher Armaments is worth, isn't it? Kattrina, huh? You sure about that?"

191

"Fairly certain. Dad's been talking with her a lot, alone. She wants the responsibility, and she's got a good record of success."

"The weapons business is a whole hell of a lot different from modelin'. Of course, she'll be surrounded by top-flight advisors and technical experts. All she has to do is sign her name to Pentagon contracts. Still . . . you wouldn't be tryin' to blow smoke in my face, would you?"

"No."

"Why would he lie?" Raven ventured to her father. "There's no point in it."

"Maybe," Dunstan said carefully. "I don't think Boone'll lie down and play dead, though. He's acted the role of Usher heir in every go-go joint in Asheville. He'll fight Kattrina for the power."

"But he'll lose. When Walen transfers everything to Katt, the papers will be ironclad."

Dunstan still wasn't convinced. "Kattrina's got a reputation for drug use. She's gone through everything from LSD to angel dust. Why would Walen pass the business on to a drughead?"

"She's off drugs," Rix said. Sullen anger burned in his stomach. Discussing Katt with a stranger like this was repellent. "Anyway, that's none of your damned business."

Dunstan's glance at Raven held a bit of triumph in making Rix lose his cool.

"You've got what you wanted," Rix told him. "Now I want *my* part. How are you doing your research?"

"I'll show you." The wheelchair whirred backward a few feet, and Rix rose from his chair. "My study's down in the basement. I'll even tell you the book title: *Time Will Tell the Tale*. That's the first sentence, too. Come on, then." He led Rix, with Raven following behind, through a short corridor and to a doorway that opened onto a gently sloping concrete ramp. They went down it and into a basement that looked like any other, full of odds and ends, old clothes, and broken furniture. Dunstan rolled toward a door on the far side of the basement and took a key ring with one key and a tiny brass charm in the shape of a typewriter from his shirt pocket. He turned a lock, then pulled the door open. "Come on, take a look." He returned the key ring to his pocket, reached in, and switched on the lights.

Dunstan's study was a small, windowless room paneled in pine, with a concrete floor and a tile ceiling. Metal bookshelves that took up almost every inch of wall space held thick leatherbound volumes. Books, newspapers, and magazines stood in stacks around Dunstan's desk; atop the desk, amid a scatter of books and papers on a worn-looking brown blotter, were a telephone, a green-shaded high-intensity lamp—and a word processor, hooked up to a daisy-wheel printer.

"On those shelves are one hundred and thirty years of the *Foxton Democrat*," Dunstan explained. "Every issue mentions the Ushers at least once. I've interviewed about sixty former Usher servants, groundskeepers, carpenters, and painters. Of course, Raven does my legwork for me."

"You're writing the book on a word processor?"

"That's right. Was doing the thing on a typewriter, but I bought this two years ago. It helps me with my research, too. A lot of libraries in major cities are hooked up to a computer network that lets you go through old genealogical records, rare-document collections, and church records. Whatever I need copies of, my friends at the Asheville library can get for me."

Rix looked at a stack of magazines next to the desk. There were back issues of *Time*, *Newsweek*, *Forbes*, *Business Week*, and others—all containing, Rix assumed, some fact, fiction, or fancy about the Ushers. On the man's desk were a few musty-looking books and some yellowed pieces of paper covered with ornate, feminine handwriting.

Letters, Rix thought. He pretended to be examining the word processor, but his glance veered toward the letters. He caught the words "Dearest Erik" on one piece of paper.

"That's the tour," Dunstan said suddenly. His voice betrayed an edge of tension, as if he realized what Rix had seen.

Rix heard the wheelchair motor whine as Dunstan approached him; but by then Rix had picked up the letter and sniffed at the paper. The scent of faded perfume was familiar. Lavender. The letter was from the same woman who'd adored Erik's whipping techniques. "Where did you get this?" Rix asked, turning toward Wheeler Dunstan.

"From an ex-servant who kept some of Erik's documents. The man lives in Georgia." He reached up to take it, but Rix held the letter away from him.

"That's bullshit. All the family records, documents, and letters are kept locked in the Lodge's basement, and they've been down there for years. No servant would've dared to keep anything that belonged to the family." He stopped, realizing the truth from Dunstan's grim, haughty expression. "You got this from Usherland, didn't you?"

Dunstan's chin lifted a few notches higher. "I've shown you what you wanted to see. You can leave now."

"No. This letter—hell, *all* these letters!—came from Usherland. I want to know how you got them off the estate." As Dunstan stared at him defiantly, Rix felt a hammerblow of realization. "There's a spy on the inside, isn't there? Collecting letters and whatever else he can get his hands on? Who is it?"

"You don't really want to know," Dunstan replied. "Not really. Now leave, why don't you? Our business is over."

"What are you going to do? Call the sheriff to *make* me leave?"

"Rix," Raven said, "please—"

"I knew it was a damned fool mistake to let him come here!" Dunstan raged to his daughter. "We didn't need him! Shitfire!"

"You'll tell me who it is," Rix demanded.

Dunstan's face tightened. In his eyes was scorching fury. "Don't you *dare* use that tone of voice to me, boy!" he shouted. "You're not at Usherland now, you're in *my* house! You don't snap your fingers and make me jump, you little—"

"Dad," Raven interrupted, putting both hands on his knotty shoulders. "Calm down, now, come on."

"You don't order me around," Dunstan told Rix, though his voice had lost some of its power. "You hear me?"

"The name." Rix continued as if the outburst had never happened. "I want it."

"I know all about your childhood, boy. I know things about you that you'd rather forget. I know how Boone used to beat you up, and how Walen whipped you with a belt till you bled." His eyes had become fierce slits. "I know you hate Walen Usher as much as *I* do, boy. You don't really want that name. Just go. Take the letters, if you want 'em."

"The name," Rix repeated.

When it was spat out to him, Rix's knees almost buckled.

23

Late-afternoon shadows were deepening across Usherland as Rix walked from the garage to the Bodane house. He knocked heavily at the door and waited for an answer.

Edwin looked dapper and fresh, though he'd put in a full day's work. He was wearing neither his cap nor his gray blazer, but instead a pinstriped blue shirt with his dark, razor-creased trousers. The shirt was open at the neck, showing a wisp of white hair. "Rix!" he said. "Where have you been all afternoon? I was looking for—"

"Is Cass here?" Rix interrupted.

"No. She's over at the Gatehouse, cooking dinner. Is something wrong?"

Rix stepped into the house. "How about Logan? Is he around?"

Edwin shook his head. "He's been working at the stables today. I expect him here in about fifteen minutes, though. What's going on?" He closed the door and waited for Rix to explain.

The younger man walked across the parlor to warm his hands before a small fire that crackled in the hearth. Alongside Edwin's favorite easy chair was this afternoon's edition of the Asheville paper. A mug of hot tea steamed on the little oak table beside the chair, and there was a scratchpad and a pen. Edwin had been doing the crossword puzzle.

"It's going to be cold tonight," Rix said; his voice sounded hollow in the large room. "The wind's already started to pick up."

"Yes, I noticed. Can I get you something? I've got some jasmine tea, if you'd—"

"No. Nothing, thank you."

Edwin walked to the table, picked up his mug, and sipped at the tea. Over the rim, his eyes were alert and watchful.

"I know about Wheeler Dunstan," Rix finally said. "Damn it, Edwin!" His gaze flared. "Why didn't you tell me you were helping him research that book of his?"

"Oh." It was spoken in a whisper. "I see."

"I don't. Dunstan told me you've been bringing him materials from the Lodge's library since August. And there I sat, telling Cass about how I wanted to do a history of the family, and she was talking about vows of loyalty!"

"Loyalty," Edwin repeated softly. "That has an ominous sound, doesn't it? Rather like the sound of a key turning in a cell door. Cass doesn't know, Rix. I don't want her to know, ever."

"But what was all that crap about tradition? About ties to the past and all that? I don't understand why you're helping Dunstan!"

Edwin suddenly looked very tired and old, and the sight of him standing in the fading golden light almost broke Rix's heart. Edwin took a long, deep breath and eased himself into his chair. "Where shall I begin, then?"

"How about the beginning?"

"Easily said." He smiled bitterly. The lines around his eyes were deep. He stared into the fire, focusing on nothing. "I'm sick," he said. "I'm sick to death of . . . dark things. *Evil* things, Rix. Hurts and secrets and rattling bones in chains. Oh, I knew what went on here when I was a boy. It didn't bother me then. I considered it exciting. See, I was just like Logan. Just as arrogant, just as . . . stupid, really. I had to learn for myself, and, oh God, what an education I've gotten!"

"What kind of dark things? What do you mean?"

"Spiritual darkness. Moral darkness. Blasphemy and decay." His eyes closed. "Poe's tale may have been fiction, Rix, but it cut very close to the bone. The Ushers have everything. *Everything.* But they are dead in their souls. I've known it for a long time, and I cannot take that knowledge very much longer." His voice cracked; he paused, gathering strength to speak again.

"I still don't understand."

Edwin's eyes opened. They were as red as the embers in the fire. "When your father passes away," he said, "the Usher empire is going to be torn to pieces. Walen will die soon. Perhaps a matter of days. Or hours. He wants to pass the estate and business to Kattrina; I'm sure you know that by now. Boone expects it to go to him. He'll fight Kattrina in court. It'll be a prolonged, messy affair. Boone can't win, of course, but he'll do everything in his power to discredit Kattrina. He's money-mad, Rix. He loses upwards of five thousand dollars every night in poker games. He bets twenty-five thousand dollars on one play of a football game. It doesn't mean a damned thing to him, because he knows he can always get more. Mr. Usher gives him an allowance of three hundred thousand a year, and whenever Boone wants an advance, he simply writes out an IOU to your father. But Boone gambles it all away. In court, he's going to smear your sister with her drug problems. He'll go to every smut-sheet in this country, trying to ruin her."

When he picked up the mug again, his hand was unsteady. "Kattrina can't take that kind of pressure, Rix. She thinks she can, but she's wrong. I know. I've watched her grow up. By the time Boone is finished with her, Kattrina will be ready for an institution— or a coffin."

"Are you suggesting that Dad should change his mind and give the estate and business to Boone?"

"No! God, no. Boone would destroy the business. He shouldn't be allowed to run loose. Of course, Puddin' doesn't help matters. She's a further complication in a very sticky web."

"What does all this have to do with Wheeler Dunstan's book?" Rix asked.

"I'm explaining my frame of mind. Please be patient. In any event, Usher Armaments is on the verge of total disaster. Without a guiding hand, it'll be ripped apart by other arms companies and conglomerates. They're waiting in the wings right now. The family will never be poor, but without the business they'll be stripped of power."

"That might be the best thing that ever happened to us."

"It might be," Edwin agreed. "Though if Usher Armaments is lost, so is a great chance for world peace."

"*What?* Surely you don't believe that."

"Yes," he said, "I do. Most strongly. The Usher name stands for power and reliability. In itself, it is a great deterrent to hostile foreign countries. If the production of weapons systems using Usher technology is stopped and the older systems are outdated—which they most certainly will be—then the world may be primed for disaster. I'm no weaponry expert, and I abhor war as much as any man alive, but the question remains: Do we dare to *stop* producing the missiles and bombs? I used to have faith in mankind, Rix. That was when I was much younger and more foolish. Listen to me go on! I must sound like a total damned idiot."

"The book," Rix reminded him. "Why are you helping Dunstan research it?"

"Because I'm tired of pretending that I have no eyes nor ears, nor mouth to speak. I'm tired of being an appliance, or a coatrack, or a piece of furniture. I'm a human being!" He announced it with dignity, though his eyes were glazed. "I've seen many things in my lifetime, Rix. Most of them I could do nothing about, though they turned my stomach and made my blood freeze." He leaned forward in his chair. "I'll tell you what happened to my loyalty, if you like. If you really want to hear it."

"Go ahead."

"All right." He folded his hands before him, lost in thought. "You've seen Wheeler Dunstan. He's crippled. His daughter—a lovely woman—has a scar across one eyebrow, and she walks with a limp. I know how that came to be."

"I'm listening."

"Good. I *want* you to listen. I want you to understand what

197

happened to my loyalty. In November of 1964, Wheeler Dunstan and his daughter and wife were involved in an automobile accident on the Interstate south of Asheville. They'd gone to visit the wife's family for Thanksgiving, as I recall. In any event, the accident was . . . very bad. A diesel truck swerved into their lane, skidded on ice, and slammed into the car. Dunstan's spine was injured, the little girl's leg and arm were broken, the wife suffered numerous internal injuries and fractures. But the worst part is that the car had gone up *underneath* the truck. It was pinned there, and the police couldn't get them out. As I understand it, Dunstan's wife was in hideous agony. The little girl was crushed against her, and had to listen to her mother sob and scream for hours, until the wreckage could be unsnarled. Dunstan's wife lingered in the hospital for several days before she died. He went through months of therapy before he could even use a wheelchair. I suppose Raven came out the best, though God only knows what she sees in her nightmares."

Edwin stared at Rix. "It was an Usher Armaments truck that swerved into their path," he said. "The driver—just a teenager—was so full of pills he didn't even know what state he was in. Wheeler Dunstan initiated a lawsuit against your father. Walen offered to settle out of court, but the amount was an insult. There's been no love lost between the Ushers and Dunstans. As events transpired, the case did not go to court. It came to light that the police had found a bourbon bottle in Dunstan's car. A nurse came forward who swore she'd smelled alcohol on his breath in the emergency room. Results of a blood test suddenly appeared: Wheeler Dunstan had been legally drunk at the time of the accident."

"But the bottle was planted?"

"Yes. I don't know when or how. Your father's money bought it all, Rix. Especially damaging was the revelation that Wheeler Dunstan was an alcoholic. It was a well-kept secret, but somehow your father found it out. Dunstan's advertisers began deserting him in droves. In the end, he took the offer and settled out of court. What else could he do?"

"And Dad got off with a wrist-slap?"

"A fine of a few thousand dollars, and a suspended sentence for the driver." Edwin watched the flickering flames, his shoulders hunched and his long legs stretched before him. "Up until that point, my eyes were closed. After I realized what your father had done— the *lengths* he'd gone to in order to avoid judgment—something inside me began to erode. I knew that Dunstan was working on an Usher history for years before I decided to help him. We have an agreement: I furnish him with the documents he needs, but I do not break my vow of silence. I say nothing of what I know of the Ushers. I will not discuss Walen's business affairs. I deliver the materials, leave them, and pick them up later. By the time the book is completed, Walen will be dead and Cass and I will be in Florida."

"Edwin," Rix said, "I went to see Wheeler Dunstan, to take a look at his manuscript. He wouldn't show it to me, but I traded information to him so I could find out how he was doing his research. I told him Dad's condition, and that Katt was going to take over the business. I had another reason for going there, too. Edwin, *I* should be the one writing that book. Not an outsider. I don't care what Dunstan's gone through." He heard the hard desperation in his voice; it shamed him, but he kept on talking. "I *need* to write that book. I've got to. I took the library key from you so I could go through the old documents in there. Somehow, I have to make Dunstan trust me enough to let me on the project. If nothing more, I've got to get my name on it as a co-author."

Edwin sighed deeply, and shook his white-crowned head. "My God," he whispered. "How did you and I come to this point, Rix? Are we both to be consumed by sickness and loathing?"

Rix pulled up a chair beside Edwin and touched the man's arm. "I can't let this opportunity get away from me. I've been thinking of doing my own book on the family for years! Talk to Dunstan for me. Tell him I can help him finish the book. Let *me* take him the materials he needs. But make him understand how important it is to me. Will you do that?"

Edwin didn't reply; he stared at the fire, the dim orange light painting his face with highlights and shadows.

"*Please*," Rix begged.

Edwin covered Rix's hand with his own. "I'll talk to him," he said. "Tomorrow morning. I don't know how he'll react to it, considering how he feels about all Ushers. But I'll talk to him."

"Thank you. I need a book like this, Edwin."

"Is it so important to you?"

"Yes," he replied without hesitation. "It is."

Edwin smiled, but his eyes were dark and sad. "I love you, Rix. No matter what you do, I'll always love you. You brought light into this house when you were a small boy. I remember . . . we used to have our little secrets. Things you'd tell me that you didn't want anyone else to know." His smile turned melancholy. "I suppose it's only right that we share this one last secret, isn't it?"

Rix stood up, bent over the chair, and hugged Edwin. The old man seemed to be made entirely of jutting bones and tight sinews. Edwin lifted a hand to pat Rix's shoulder, and they clung together, framed in firelight, without speaking.

24

The wind screamed across Briartop Mountain, and New Tharpe sat up in his cot, with cold droplets of sweat on his face.

He'd dreamed of the Lodge again—the massive, illuminated, majestic Lodge where figures moved slowly past the glowing windows as if in some ghostly ballroom—but this time there'd been a difference. He'd been standing on the lakeshore, staring across at the house, and suddenly a pair of upper balcony doors had come open and someone had stepped out. The figure had motioned for him to hurry across the bridge, and New had heard his name called from the distance by a familiar voice.

It was his father's voice, calling him from that glowing palace. His father was standing on the balcony, urging him to cross the bridge, to hurry to the Lodge because the celebration was in New's honor. *Come home,* his father had called. *We're all here, waitin' for you to come home.*

New had balked, though the pull of the Lodge on him was an irresistible force. In the dream he'd felt his skin ripple into goosebumps of fear and excitement. His father, an indistinct figure on the upper balcony, had waved and called, *Hurry, New! Come home with me!*

Across the long bridge, the Lodge's front doorway had opened, throwing out a wide shaft of beautiful golden light. There was a figure standing in that doorway, its arms stretched out to receive him. New couldn't make out who it was, but he thought it wore a dark coat that flapped in the wind.

The Lodge wanted him, he knew. The figure in the doorway wanted him. If New crossed that bridge and entered the Lodge, he could have everything he'd ever desired. He'd never have to lie down on a hard cot in a cold room again; he'd have fine clothes, and good food to eat, and a rug to cover the floor in his bedroom, and books to read and time to wander the green forests of Usherland and know

200

what it was like to call the Lodge his home. He stood at the entrance to the bridge, poised on the edge of a decision. He wanted to cross; he wanted to make his legs move.

But then the wind had screamed and he'd awakened, and now, as the wind shrilled past the cabin, leaking through holes in the roof and walls, he imagined it left a faint, seductive whisper in its wake:

—come home—

He lay back down, bringing the thin blanket up to his chin, and stared at the ceiling. Joe Clayton and his wife had visited the house this afternoon, to see how New was doing. Birdie had trotted along, and barked irritably outside the window. Mr. Clayton had told New and his mother that the damnedest thing had happened this morning when he'd come out to feed Birdie: he'd found the dog standing about thirty yards from the house, staring toward the woods. Birdie was frozen in a point position, his tail standing straight up and his head ducked low. The dog wouldn't respond when Mr. Clayton called him. A thrown pinecone bounced off Birdie's side, and still the dog didn't move. It was only when Mr. Clayton had gotten right next to the animal and whacked his hand on Birdie's rump that the dog whirled around in a crazy circle, snapping at its tail and yowling. Birdie had stretched for about ten minutes, and then he was so hungry he'd almost snapped the food bowl up in his mouth. That dog, Mr. Clayton told New, is old and crazy and not worth a damn—but he sure can hold a point position like you ain't never seen!

Through chinks of silence in the rushing wind, New could hear Birdie's faint barking. It was the wind spookin' him, New thought. It could put even a dog's nerves on edge.

He closed his eyes, inviting sleep.

And then he heard the roof creak above his head.

At once his eyes were open again. He stared upward.

Timbers groaned softly. Then the roof creaked in a different place, over near the corner of the room.

New struck a match from the pack on the table beside his cot, turned up the lantern's wick, and lit it. The light spread slowly, and New swung his legs out from under the blanket.

Above his head, the roof moaned like an old man in sleep. New lifted the lantern high.

His heart pounded as he saw the pine boards bending inward. He heard a long, slow scraping—a claw, testing the roof's strength. Whatever was up there moved again; New followed its progress by watching the boards bowing. Then there was a sharp *crack*! and a nail clinked to the floor beside New's foot.

The animal remained still, as if listening.

New was frozen, watching the roof strain where the animal stood. It was the same heavy nocturnal thing that had been prowling around the cabin after his pa had died; whatever it was, New thought, the thing had to weigh upwards of three hundred pounds. It stalked across the roof, creaking wood marking its trail. The roof was weak; New feared the creature's weight might bring it crashing through.

A board popped loose with a high whine. The animal stopped again. In the silence left as a rush of wind swept by, New could hear the thing's low, rumbling growl.

It was the same ominous sound he'd heard when he was trapped in the pit.

Greediguts, New thought. The black panther that ran with the Pumpkin Man, now separated from New only by a thin layer of weather-warped pinewood.

Get away from here! New commanded mentally. *Get away!*

The animal didn't move. New felt the hair at the back of his neck stir. The musky odor of a predatory cat filtered down into the room. New sensed that the creature was aware of him, or that it had seen a glimmer of light through cracks in the timbers. A claw scraped across wood; the thing was sniffing, picking up his scent.

New hurriedly put on his jeans and a heavy dark blue sweater. Then he took the lamp and went to the front room, where he lifted his pa's shotgun from its rack near the door. He broke open the breech to make sure it was loaded with two shells, then clicked it shut again. Above him, the roof groaned. The creature was following him.

In the kitchen, he took the flashlight from its place on a shelf. Armed with the shotgun and the flashlight, New was about to go outside when his mother's voice stopped him.

"Somethin's on the roof!" she whispered. "Listen to it!" She stepped into the range of the lamp that New had set aside, her face pallid and her arms wrapped around her chest. She was wearing a ragged old flannel robe; fear sparked in her eyes like ice crystals. "What is it, New? What's up there?"

"I don't know," he replied. He wasn't sure it was Greediguts; it might be something else that had wandered out of the deep woods. "I'm gonna go find out."

Myra's glance flickered toward the shotgun and the flashlight. "No!" she said urgently. "I ain't gonna let you do that!"

The roof was speaking again; boards popped and groaned as the creature moved over their heads. It was pacing back and forth. The roof was buckling badly where the thing stood; another nail popped loose and fell to the floor.

"Pa would've gone out," New said.

"You ain't your pa!" She grasped her son's arm. "It'll go away. It don't want nothin'. Just leave it be!" She suddenly cried out as nails burst free with the sound of firecrackers going off. New flicked on the flashlight and pointed it upward. The creature had moved across a particularly weak area of the roof, and several boards had cracked loose. His light probed through a hole the size of his fist.

New couldn't hear the thing moving anymore. Either it was off the roof, or it was standing very still. Wind shrilled through the hole and filled the room with a foretaste of winter. He gently pulled free from his mother's grip. "Pa would've gone out," he repeated, and she knew there was nothing more to say.

New followed the flashlight beam off the porch. He was already shivering with the cold. The wind roared around him, and dead leaves rolled through the air, snapping wildly at his cheeks as they passed. While Myra stood in the open doorway, New stepped off the porch and aimed his light up at the roof.

There was nothing up there. New played it slowly back and forth, the shotgun cradled under his right arm, his finger near the trigger. He could hear Birdie baying, and the eerie sound made his flesh crawl.

New walked around to the side of the house. The light revealed nothing.

As he started to turn, something grabbed him by the back of the neck. He could feel claws digging in, and his finger almost squeezed a shot off—but then he reached back and closed his hand around the small treebranch, still bearing a few dead leaves, that had fallen onto his neck. He flung it away in angry disgust.

"New!" his mother called. "Come on back in the house!"

He shone the light up into the trees. Most of the branches still held leaves and defeated the flashlight's beam. The treetops swayed back and forth in the wind's relentless currents.

New continued around to where his mother waited. He passed

the discarded old washing machine and stood near the pickup truck, shining the light along the roof again.

"You see anythin'?" Myra called, her voice thin and nervous.

"No, not a thing. Whatever it was is long gone by now."

"Well, come on in out of the cold, then! Hurry!"

New took a step forward—and then his blood turned icy.

He smelled Greediguts, very close to him—the musky rank scent of a hunting cat.

New stopped, aimed the light upward into the trees. The wind roared past, almost throwing him off balance. Branches bent and swayed. Dead leaves tumbled down. It was close, very close . . .

And then he heard his mother scream, "*New!*" and he whirled around toward the pickup truck.

Something was slithering out from underneath the truck; it moved so fast that New had no time to aim the shotgun. He fired wildly even as he leaped backward, and the truck's passenger door dented in as if punched by a huge fist. But then the monster—a sinewy dark shape that moved like velvet lightning—had burst out of its hiding place, and as it suddenly reared up on its hind legs, towering over New by more than a foot, it was caught for a second in the glare of the light.

The creature was a black panther from a madman's nightmare. Its massive head was misshapen and elongated, its sharp-tipped ears laid back along the skull, its chest ridged with muscle. The beast's eyes were an incandescent, hypnotic golden green, the pupils rapidly shrinking to vertical slashes in the light. As New staggered backward in shock, he saw the creature's claws extend; they were three inches long and curved into vicious hooks. Its mouth opened, exposing yellow fangs—and from the mouth came a high, bloodcurdling cry that sank to an eerie rattle. The body was covered with short jet-black hair, though on its underbelly the skin was gray and leathery.

Still balanced on its hind legs, the monster leaped forward in a blur of motion.

New was ready with the shotgun. The second shell exploded—but the panther had twisted suddenly to one side, ducking the pellets. It landed on all fours, whirled to attack New's rear, and hurtled toward him.

He had no time to protect himself. Three hundred pounds of animal fury were about to crash into him.

Through his panic, a vision in his mind shone with diamond clarity: the panther flinging itself toward a wall of rough stones that stood between them. The wall was a phantom construction of crooked blue lines and angles that pulsated in the air; through it he could see the panther, and their eyes locked.

The wall's THERE! he shouted to himself.

A guttural grunt of pain came from the beast's throat, as its leap was blocked in midair. Some of the blue phantom stones were jarred out of place—but then Greediguts was tumbling backward. It slammed into the pickup truck's side and whirled around in a mad circle, snapping at the air. New caught a glimpse of its tail, writhing wildly back and forth, and heard the menacing buzz of a snake's rattles.

The blue wall was fading quickly. Holes broke open as if through smoke. On the porch, Myra was screaming for help. Greediguts shook its head violently, blinking its eyes in dazed confusion, and sprang toward the boy again.

This time New visualized pieces of jagged glass in the wall, and made it four feet thick. He could hear his brain humming and cracking like a machine. The wall strengthened, throbbing with power.

Greediguts hit it headfirst. For an awful instant the wall shook, and New feared the beast was going to rip right through. He felt the shock as if someone had struck him hard in the forehead.

The beast howled and fell back, sprawling on its side. When it scrambled to its feet, its eyes were glazed and wary, its head lowered. Through the fading wall they faced each other. New's heart was hammering, but he stood his ground; the panther lifted its head to smell the air, and New saw a long black forked tongue dart quickly from its mouth.

The wall was as thin as silk. Threads of pain were beginning to run across New's skull. All his attention was focused on the animal; he heard his mother's frantic shouts as if from within a dark, distant well.

Greediguts lifted a foreleg and clawed at the air. The beast began to pace back and forth, darting in and then feinting back. Its gaze was fixed on him, and New felt the rage sear through to his soul. The panther's eyes flared like bursts of fire.

The wall was almost gone, wisping rapidly away.

Build it back! New told himself. The wall is *there*, strong and thick!

It began to take on definite lines once more, stone by stone. His head was pounding, and he felt the panther's stare on him; the thing was trying to hypnotize him. As their eyes met and locked again, New felt a terrible, cold power puncture his resolve. A dark whirlpool of dizziness began to spin around him.

Greediguts was motionless. Its tongue flicked out, disappeared again.

The wall between them trembled and started to fall apart. *No!* New said mentally, trying to visualize it as he had before. Build it back, strong and thick! But it was fading away, and the disrupting pain in New's head was savage.

The panther was waiting, ready to leap.

—little man—

The soft, mocking voice had curled around New's throat like a velvet whip.

—little man of the house—

It came from nowhere and everywhere, so cold it ached in his bones. The wall was full of holes, swaying like a spiderweb.

—little man of the house what are you going to do?

The panther sprang, its jaws opening wide. It ripped through the smoky wall, claws stretched toward the boy who stood frozen before it.

Less than three feet from slashing New's head off, Greediguts was hit by something in the air and lifted up over New, turning end over end. New felt a freezing wave of power strike him, flinging him to the ground as the panther's claws swiped at empty air above his head.

Greediguts was carried six feet past New, and slammed into the base of an oak tree with the sound of crunching bone. The animal roared in surprise and agony—and when it hit the ground again, it leaped into the underbrush.

New heard the thing crashing away; in another moment there was nothing but the noise of the wind in the trees. His nerves jangled, and as his mother reached him, he looked up into her stricken face and babbled, "Pa would've gone out long gone long gone Pa would've gone out . . ."

She sank down to her knees and held him in her arms as his mind continued to skip like a scratched record. When his feverish babbling stopped, he began sobbing hysterically.

Myra held him close. His heart was beating so hard she feared it was going to explode. Then she caught a movement from the corner of her eye and she looked toward the road.

A thin figure stood there, right at the edge of the forest. The wind was whipping through a long dark coat.

Then she knew she was crazy, because she blinked and whatever it was had vanished.

"Come on, now," she said gently, though her voice was shaking. She could not understand what she'd seen—the monster panther leaping at her son and being knocked down in empty air—but she knew that tonight her son's life had been saved by something she dared not question: a powerful witchcraft that lingered in the unsettled air like the acrid odor of brimstone.

The wind swirled around them, keening and pulling, coming from different directions at once. Myra helped her son to his feet, and together they walked toward the cabin. She had seen the shine of the monster's eyes as it began to crawl from under the truck; whatever kind of thing it was, it had had sense enough to wait until New's back was turned. He was in danger; she knew that now, saw it clearly. Though she might close her eyes to the Pumpkin Man and the other things that roamed Briartop's woods, there was no mistaking that the creature had lured New outside to kill him. He was all she had now, and she didn't know how to protect him.

But there was one who might.

She helped her son stagger through the door, then closed and bolted it.

At the forest's edge, the Mountain King stood like a frail sapling, watching the Tharpe house. He had not moved during New's confrontation with the panther, but now his shoulders stooped forward wearily, and he leaned on his twisted cane for support. He was cold, and his nose was running. Frost lay deep in his bones; in his shallow breathing he could hear the rattle of phlegm.

He waited, listening to the wind. It spoke to him of death and destruction, the world in a state of passage. Dead leaves whirled around him, and some snagged in his beard. He wiped his nose with the back of his hand and thought that years ago, when he still had good sense, he could've slammed Greediguts against that oak so hard the hide would've shredded right off its bones. As it was, he'd given the panther a good hard jolt—but Greediguts would find a place to hide and lick its wounds, and by first light it would be on the prowl again.

The panther wouldn't return here tonight. For now, the boy was safe.

But *who* was he? And what was his part in the battle that the Mountain King had been fighting ever since the night that comets had fallen on Briartop Mountain? Those were questions the old man couldn't answer.

He shivered and coughed repeatedly into his hand. His lungs had begun burning lately. When his spasm was over, he started the long trek home.

25

In the Gatehouse, Rix had made a disturbing discovery.

One of the books he'd brought up to his room from the library the night before was a ledger, dating from 1864, that listed the names, duties, and wages of every servant at Usherland. There were three hundred eighty-eight names, from apprentice blacksmith to master of the hounds, and everything in between.

But the volume that riveted Rix's attention was the casebook of a Dr. Jackson Baird, director of a place called the Baird Retreat, in Pennsylvania. The Baird Retreat was a private insane asylum. The casebook, old and brittle, with many missing pages, monitored the month-to-month progress of Dr. Baird's patient: Jessamyn Usher, Ludlow's first wife and the mother of Erik.

Rix sat at his desk, the casebook opened before him and light spilling over his right shoulder. For the past hour he'd been engrossed in a chilling account of madness, his reading interrupted only when an occasional ferocious blast of wind jarred his concentration. Jessamyn Usher, Dr. Baird wrote with a rigid hand, was brought to the Retreat in November 1886. Judging from a portrait Baird had seen when he'd visited the Lodge, Jessamyn Usher had once been an elegant young woman with curly ringlets of light brown hair and softly luminous gray eyes.

On November 23, 1886, a snarling madwoman in a straitjacket was locked in a padded room at the Baird Retreat. She had pulled out most of her hair, her lips and tongue were mangled from being continually bitten, and her eyes were red-rimmed, burning craters in a moon-white face. Ludlow did not accompany his wife; she'd been brought by four servants, including Luther Bodane, Edwin's grandfather. When Jessamyn was admitted to the Retreat, she was twenty-six years old, and hopelessly insane.

Rix had continued to read, fascinated by this new-found skeleton in the Usher closet. Though Jessamyn was the well-educated daughter of a millionaire New England textile manufacturer, in the seven years of her marriage to Ludlow Usher she had deteriorated into something very nearly animalistic. It was four months before Baird could even stay in the same room with her and not fear an attack. Her symptoms, Baird wrote in December 1887, included profligate violence, profanity, gnashing of teeth, garbled and meaningless prayers shouted at the top of her voice, and physical seizures "during which the unfortunate Mrs. Usher had to be bound to her bed with leather straps, her mouth stuffed with cotton, lest she bite off her tongue."

Jessamyn's condition, Baird wrote, seemed to have had its beginning with the birth of Erik, in April 1884. On several occasions, Jessamyn—whose favorite pastime had been working with her roses, dandelions, and camellias in the estate's greenhouse—had tried to murder the infant.

It took Baird until the summer of 1888 to persuade the madwoman even to talk about her son. Up until that point, the name "Erik" would send her into a tirade of cursing and praying. But during that fateful summer, the storm that raged within Jessamyn's mind began to abate—or perhaps, Rix thought, Baird had simply found the hurricane's eye. In any case, Jessamyn was lucid at times, and gave the doctor an insight into her condition.

She had to kill Erik, she informed Dr. Baird, because he'd been touched by Satan.

Erik was still an infant when it happened, she'd said. A violent thunderstorm had awakened her after midnight; she feared the thunder and lightning almost as much as Ludlow did, because she'd been taught by her puritanical father that in the voice of thunder was the booming disapproval of an angry God, and the lightning was His spear to cut down sinners. Many times, as she huddled under the sheets while a storm raged outside, she imagined she felt the entire Lodge shake—and once the windows of her magnificent bedroom had burst after a particularly loud blast of thunder.

On this night, a frenzy of rain slashed at the Lodge. As thunder boomed and echoed, she imagined she heard the walls cracking. Somewhere in the house, glass broke: a window shattering. Rising from her bed, she went down the hallway to Erik's nursery. And as she opened the door, she saw the thing, illuminated by a blue flare of lightning: a figure, standing over Erik's crib, that had the shape of a husky, broad-shouldered man—but was not a man. Its flesh was a pale gray, and appeared to have the sheen of wet leather. In the lightning's glare, Jessamyn had time to see that the creature's hand was placed on the sleeping child's forehead—and then the thing swiveled toward her with violent but graceful motion, like the spin of a ballet dancer.

For an instant she saw its face—cruel-featured but strangely handsome, its thin mouth twisted into a half-smile, half-sneer—and she almost swooned. Its eyes were like a cat's: dark golden green, hypnotically intense, the pupils wide.

And before the lightning's glow could fade, the creature had disappeared.

She screamed; the baby awakened, and began screaming too. She knew what she'd seen, and feared she was losing her mind. She could not bear to approach the baby; turning from the room, Jessamyn fled down the hallway in a panic until she fell down a flight of stairs, almost breaking her back. And there she lay until a servant found her and Ludlow was summoned from his chamber.

She'd seen the incarnation of evil touch Erik, Jessamyn told Dr. Baird. Had seen the creature place its hand on the child's head in a gentle, protective gesture. The meaning, at least for Jessamyn, was clear: Erik had Satan's work ahead of him. He would grow up with the mark of Satan on his brow. There was no end to the calamities he would bring upon the world if he was allowed to live. Erik had to be killed before his inherent evil manifested itself. To that end, Jessamyn tried to poison the infant, but was interrupted by his nanny; tried to throw him down a stairwell, but was restrained by Jenny Bodane, Luther's wife and the family's cook. After this, she was locked in her room, but got out by way of the window ledge, stole Erik from the nursery, and took him down to the roaring fireplace in the banquet hall.

Ludlow himself found her as she was about to fling Erik into the flames. As he rushed her, she picked up a poker with her free hand and slashed viciously at her husband's head. Ludlow blocked the blow with his ebony cane, but then she struck again—with all the strength of desperation in her arm—and the poker hit Ludlow squarely across the temple, knocking him to the floor, where he lay motionless, blood pooling around his head.

Then Jessamyn held the screaming child by its neck, like an unwanted puppy, and stepped toward the fire.

But in the next instant Erik was snatched away from her. Incredibly, Ludlow had staggered up from the floor, his face a grotesque mask of blood, to save his son. Jessamyn launched herself at his throat, and they grappled before the flames. Ludlow, though dazed with pain, was able to hold her back with his cane until servants could restrain her.

All through 1888 and 1889, as Rix saw in the entries, Jessamyn's condition fluctuated from calm lucidity to raving madness. At the end of October 1889, Dr. Baird decided to write to Ludlow Usher with the news that his wife's condition was hopeless.

Ludlow arrived in December, in the company of Luther Bodane and two other servants, to see Jessamyn for one last time. Less than two months later, Jessamyn Usher was found dead in her room; she'd ripped open the goosedown pillow with her teeth and swallowed feathers until they were jammed in her throat, choking herself.

"Lovely," Rix muttered when he finished the casebook. He pushed it aside as if it were covered with slime, and wondered if Ludlow would have been so eager to save Erik if he had known what lay ahead for both of them. Jessamyn's description of the creature standing over Erik's crib sounded like something from a Roger Corman horror flick. Of course, she was looking for an excuse to rationalize her hatred of Erik, maybe because she felt the child had come between her and Ludlow. Whatever the motivation, it was lost in the past.

Someone tapped quietly at Rix's door, and he tensed. It was almost two o'clock—who would be prowling around except Puddin'? Boone had left around eleven for his club and the inevitable poker game. Rix went to the door, which had a chair and suitcase stacked against it, and said, "Who's there?"

"Mrs. Reynolds. Would you open the door, please?"

Rix did as she asked. The corridor's lights were off, and Mrs. Reynolds held a silver candelabra with four burning white candles. It was the first time Rix had seen her without the surgical mask, and his initial impression of her sturdiness was emphasized by her strong, square jawline. Still, it was obvious that caring for Walen was wearing away her rocklike constitution; her face was haggard, the candlelight illuminating dark blue hollows beneath her eyes, and fine wrinkles etched around her mouth. Her gaze was vacant, unfocused—she was running on empty.

"He sent me," she said, accustomed to whispering. "He wants to see you."

"Right now?"

She nodded, and he followed her along the hallway. When Rix paused to switch on the lights, she said quickly, "No. Please don't do that. I've had the servants turn off most of the lights in the house."

"Why?"

"Your father ordered it," she explained as they walked. "He says he can't stand the sound of electricity running through the wires."

"What?"

"He says it's a high, crackling whine," Mrs. Reynolds continued. "Sometimes he can hear it more acutely, and he says it disturbs his sleep more than any other sound. I've been increasing his dosage of tranquilizers and sleeping pills, but they don't have much effect on his nervous system anymore."

They were nearing the stairs to the Quiet Room. The smell of decay—which Rix had gradually gotten used to on the other side of the house—was now so strong and sickening that he stopped at the foot of the stairs, fighting nausea. I can't go up there again! he told himself, as his stomach quaked. Jesus Christ!

Mrs. Reynolds looked back at him from a few steps ahead, the yellow candlelight throwing her long shadow across the wall. "You'll be all right," she said. "Just try to breathe through your mouth."

He followed her up, toward the white door, and put on two surgical masks and a pair of gloves; then he held the candelabra for her while she did the same. Just before Mrs. Reynolds opened the door, she took the candelabra back and blew the candles out.

The darkness enveloped him; for a terrible few seconds he felt the icy panic of being lost in the Lodge again, not knowing in which direction to move. Then she gripped his hand and led him into the Quiet Room. The door was closed noiselessly, and she guided him across the room to Walen's bed.

The oscilloscope had been turned off. Walen's low, irregular rasping was the only sound. Rix rapped his shin against a piece of furniture, but said nothing. Mrs. Reynolds released his hand, and he could feel himself being watched. Walen's breathing continued until it was finally broken by a hoarse, almost unintelligible grunt. Rix had to strain to understand his father's voice.

"Get out," Walen commanded the nurse.

Rix didn't hear her leave, but he knew she must have obeyed. Walen shifted—slowly, agonizingly—on the bed. He spoke, and once more Rix had to concentrate to understand: "Bitch'll have me in diapers next." He sighed painfully; the sound of that exhaled breath—

a precious breath, let go only with hesitation—wrenched at Rix's heart. It was such a human sound, almost gentle, as soft as smoke.

"I abhor the night," Walen whispered. "The wind comes at night. I never listened to it before. Now I hear myself as if I'm screaming in a hurricane."

"I'm sorry." Though Rix had said it as quietly as possible, he heard Walen gasp. Rix flinched, his hands gripped into fists at his sides.

"Keep your voice down, damn it! Oh God . . . my head . . ."

Rix thought he heard his father sob, but it could have been a curse instead. Rix squeezed his eyes shut, his nerve about to break.

It was a minute or two before Walen spoke again. "You haven't been up to visit in a while. What's wrong? Do you have something better to do?"

Did the old man know what he was up to? Rix wondered. No, of course not! There was no need for paranoia. "I . . . thought you needed your rest." He whispered so softly he could hardly hear himself.

This time there was no mistaking Walen's short, harsh laugh. "My rest," he repeated. "Oh, that's a good one! Yes, I must have my rest!" He stopped to catch his breath, and when he spoke again his tone was more vulnerable than Rix had ever heard it. "I'm almost ready to die, Rix. This isn't my world anymore. I'm tired . . . I'm so tired."

Rix was caught off guard. Perhaps the idea of death was finally weakening Walen, but he sounded completely different from the way he had when Rix had come in here a few days before.

"How's Margaret?" Walen asked. "Is she bearing up?"

"Pretty well."

"I can hear Boone and Puddin' arguing at night. At least it occupies my mind. And Katt? What's your judgment about her?"

Judgment? Rix thought. A strange choice of words. "She's okay."

"And you? What about you?"

"I'm all right."

"Yes." The sarcasm had returned. "I'm sure you are. Damn that wind! Listen to it scream! Can't you hear it at all?"

"No."

"Enjoy your silence while you can, then," Walen said bitterly. Wastes gurgled through the tubes under Walen's bed, and he gave a mutter of disgust.

Again, Rix's eyes were getting used to the darkness. He could see the skeletal shape lying on the bed. Across the pillow, beside Walen's head, was the dark slash of the ebony cane. Walen's thin arm was outstretched, the hand clenched around the cane as if he were about to strike out at something.

"What were you researching in the library before you got sick?" Rix asked; the question had come out before he could monitor it.

Walen was silent for a long moment. Then he said, "Sick? *Sick?* I wish I *were* sick. A sickness can be cured. Oh, you should've seen that goddamned doctor's face when he came up here the last time! He turned as white as a fish belly, and all the time he was bending over me with his little pencil flashlight, taking my pulse and temperature and all sorts of ridiculous things! He wants me to go to a hospital." He grunted hoarsely. "Can you imagine that? Reporters swarming around like maggots? Nurses and doctors bothering me at all hours of the day and night? I told him he was out of his mind."

Rix nodded. Walen had pointedly avoided the question. He decided to try another angle of attack. "I've been in the library," he said calmly. "I asked Edwin for the key, because I wanted something to read. I found a book in there. It was a book of nursery rhymes, and it was dedicated to Simms Usher." He had opened the lion's cage with the lie, and he waited for a response.

Silence from Walen.

Rix pressed on. "Today I rode over to the cemetery, with Katt. I found Simms's grave. Why have you hidden the fact that you had a younger brother?"

Still Walen didn't reply.

"What happened to him? How did he die?" He was curious as to whether Walen's story would jibe with Wheeler Dunstan's.

"What are you doing?" Walen asked finally. "Tearing the library apart?"

"No. I didn't think you'd mind if I went inside and looked around."

"I *do* mind! Edwin was a fool to let you in there without asking me first!"

"Why? Are you trying to hide something?"

"Those documents in there . . . are very fragile. I don't want them disturbed. Before I 'got sick,' as you put it, I was reading through some materials for a business project."

Rix frowned, puzzled. "What do family documents have to do with a project for Usher Armaments?"

"It's nothing that concerns you. But since you ask about Simms,

I'll tell you; I haven't hidden anything. Simms was my younger brother, yes. He was retarded. He died when he was a child. That's the end of it."

"How did he die? Natural causes?"

"Yes. No . . . wait. It had something to do with the woods. I haven't thought of Simms in a long time, and it's hard for me to recall things. Simms died in the woods. He was killed by an animal. Yes, that's it. Simms wandered into the woods, and a wild animal killed him."

"What kind of animal?"

"I don't know. That was a long time ago. What does it matter now?"

Why indeed? Rix thought, then said, "I don't suppose it does."

"Simms was retarded," Walen repeated. "He liked to chase butterflies, but he'd never catch the damned things. I remember . . . when they brought what was left of him to the Lodge. I saw the body before Father pushed me away. There were flowers clutched in his hand. Yellow dandelions. He was picking *flowers* when the animal jumped him! I remember how much Mother cried. Father locked himself in his study. Well . . . that was a long time ago."

Rix was disappointed. There was no mystery about Simms's death, after all. Walen had never mentioned Simms because it was obvious he'd never fully recognized his younger brother as a human being, just as a retarded simpleton who was picking flowers when he was killed.

"I called you up here," Walen said, "because I want to announce something to the family through you. At breakfast you will inform them that there will be no more electric lights burning in this house. All electric appliances will be cut back as much as possible. I can't control the sound of the wind, or of heartbeats or of goddamned rats scratching in the walls—but sometimes I can hear electrical current running through the wires. Twice today it happened. The sound grates on every bone in my body. Do you understand?"

"I know they won't like it."

"I don't care what they like or don't like!" he hissed. "While I'm alive, I'm still the head of this house! Do you understand?"

"Yeah," he said.

"Good. Then do it. You can go now."

Feeling like a dismissed servant, Rix started to thread his way through the darkness to the door; but then he stopped and turned toward Walen again.

215

"What is it?"

"I'll do the favor for you if you'll do one for me. I'd like to know about Boone's talent agency."

"His talent agency? What about it?"

"That's what I'm asking. You put up the money for it. What does the agency *do?*"

"It contracts and hires out talent. What do you think?"

Rix smiled thinly behind the two surgical masks. "What kind of talent? Actors? Singers? Dancers?"

"That's business between Boone and myself, and none of your concern."

Rix's senses sharpened. Walen's evasiveness told him he was walking on forbidden ground, and he was determined to find out why. "Is it something so bad you don't want anyone else knowing?" he asked. "What's brother Boone into? Pornography?"

"I said you can go now," Walen rasped irritably.

It dawned on Rix that whatever Boone was doing, Walen didn't want Katt or Margaret knowing. Maybe that was another reason Puddin' wasn't allowed to leave the estate—not only did she know too much about the Usher family, she had learned what Boone's talent agency did. "I can find out from Puddin'," he said calmly. "And I'm sure Mom would like to hear all about it." He started toward the door again.

"*Wait.*"

He paused. "Well?"

"You've always despised Boone, haven't you?" Walen whispered. "Why? Because he's got more guts than ten of *you?* You've brought me nothing but shame. Even when you were a boy, I saw how spineless you were." The cold cruelty in his father's voice stabbed Rix. His stomach tightened in his effort to inure himself to the pain of Walen's contempt. "You never fought back. You let Boone step on you like a piece of dogshit. Oh, I *watched* you. I know. Now you've got hate festering in you, and you don't know how to let it out, so you want to hurt *me.* You never were anything, and you never—"

Rix stepped forward. Anger shattered his tense self-control. His face flamed, and he almost shouted, but at the last second he clenched his teeth together. "You know, Dad," he said in a barely checked whisper, "I've always thought the Gatehouse looked great all lit up. I could probably go from room to room right now and make this house shine like a Christmas tree." Shame stabbed at him, but he

216

couldn't stop himself, nor at the moment did he want to; he had to go on, to fight back, cruelty against cruelty. "Think of all that electricity running through the wires! Wouldn't that be great? Have you taken your tranquilizers lately, Dad?"

"You wouldn't do it. You haven't got the courage."

"I'm sorry"—Rix raised his voice to a normal speaking level, and Walen convulsed—"I didn't hear that. The agency. What does it do?" There were tears of rage in his eyes, and his heart was hammering. "*Tell me!*"

"Quiet! Oh God!" Walen moaned.

Rix mouthed the words with slow exaggeration: "Tell me."

"Your . . . brother . . . contracts performers. Entertainers . . . for shows."

"What kind of shows?"

Walen suddenly lifted his head from the pillow. His body was trembling violently. "Sideshows!" he said. "Boone's agency . . . finds freaks for carnival sideshows! *Get out! Get out of my sight!*"

Rix had already found the door. He stumbled on the stairs in the darkness, and almost fell. Mrs. Reynolds was waiting in the corridor with her newly lit candelabra, and as Rix tore the masks off his face he told her she could return to the Quiet Room, that his father had finished with him.

When she was gone, Rix leaned against the wall, fighting nausea. His temples were aching violently, and he pressed the palms of his hands against them.

What he had just done repulsed him. He felt unclean, tainted by Walen's decay. It was something, he realized, that Walen himself might have done, or Erik, or any of the Usher men who'd gone before them. But he wasn't like them! Dear God, he *wasn't*!

It took a few minutes for the sickness to pass. The headache lingered longer, then slowly faded away.

Left within him was a cold, unaccustomed excitement.

It was a new-found sensation of power.

Rix breathed deeply of the reeking air, and then he moved away into the darkness.

Five

TIME
WILL TELL
THE TALE

26

Gray clouds were scudding across the sun as Raven Dunstan guided her stuttering Volkswagen up Briartop Mountain. An occasional strong gust of wind parted the trees and hit the car, and the tires slipped on a thick layer of decomposing leaves.

She'd found Clint Perry's house about an hour before, and told the man where she wanted to go. Perry—a lean, hawk-nosed man in overalls—had looked at her as if she were crazy. It was a long haul up there, he'd warned her, and the only road was so bad it had busted the bottom out of his truck when he'd gone up with Sheriff Kemp a couple of months before. Raven insisted that Perry draw her a map, and offered him twenty dollars to go with her, but he said— nervously, it seemed to Raven—that he had better things to do than to go running all over the mountain.

She'd already climbed well past the Tharpe house, passing other rundown shacks hidden in shadowy hollows. She came to the crossroads that Perry had indicated on the map, and took the road that branched off to the left. Almost at once the wheels of her car were being battered by potholes. The road reared up so steeply she was sure the car couldn't make it, but she fought the gears and was rewarded when the grade leveled off. To the left, through breaks in the forest, she could look over the side of Briartop onto Usherland. The chimneys and spires of Usher's Lodge speared through thin, low-lying clouds.

The torture to her car went on for another mile or more, and she cursed her stupidity at coming up here. Then, abruptly, she turned a wooded bend and the road stopped at a group of large boulders. A path snaked between the rocks and vanished into the forest.

Following the directions Perry had given her, Raven left her car and walked up the path. It was steep, and her leg was aching before she'd gone thirty yards. Coils of thorns curled from the woods; the vegetation on either side of the path was impenetrable. But then, at the crest of the rise, Raven caught her first glimpse of the ruined town that stood atop the mountain.

To call it a town, Raven realized, was a wild exaggeration. Perhaps it had been a small settlement of some kind more than a hundred years ago, but now all that remained were piles of stones, a jutting chimney here and there, and an occasional standing wall. A couple of stone structures were still mostly intact, but only one of those had any semblance of a roof, and the other had gaping holes in its walls. Oddly, the ruins were not overgrown with weeds, thorns, and kudzu vines; though a few straggly bushes had struggled up from the dark, bare earth, the ruins sat at the center of a clearing strewn with rocks. Even the sparse trees that had taken root around the ruins looked dead and petrified, their leafless branches frozen into weird angles. The place appeared desolate, totally deserted for many, many years.

Raven was cold; she lifted the collar of her corduroy jacket around her neck. If indeed an old man lived up here, she wondered, how in the world did he survive? Raven followed the path into the ruins. Her boots crunched on the brittle ground; she stopped, bent down, and scooped up a handful of earth.

Bits of glass glittered in her palm. She let the earth sift between her fingers, then stood up again. As she walked amid the ruins, Raven saw that most of the crumbling stones resembled lumps of coal. Sometime in the past, a fire of brutal heat had burned here. She moved aside fallen leaves with her foot, and looked down at clumps of glass in the ground.

And then she walked around to the far side of a standing wall, and stopped. On the black stones was the pale gray silhouette of a human being, arms splayed as if in impact with the wall. The body was contorted like a question mark. At the figure's feet was another shape, barely recognizable as a human being, lifting one arm as if in supplication.

A nearby jumble of loose stones caught her attention. She bent down carefully, because of the pain in her leg. One of the stones had a rusted nail driven into it. Another showed the outline of a hand and wrist.

Raven ran her fingers over the stone. She was reminded of pictures she'd seen in a book about Hiroshima. In those photos, outlines of the atomic bomb victims were left burned into walls—

222

just as these figures were. Whatever had happened here, Raven thought uneasily, the results—the silhouettes, the black stones, the ground burned to clumps of glass—were uncannily similar.

Raven rose to her feet. What kind of destruction had left its mark here? And when? Why was this town built on top of the mountain? Who were its inhabitants?

She was pondering those questions when she turned away from the rubble and found the old man standing about ten feet away, next to the scorched wall.

He was leaning on his twisted cane, his head cocked so that he could see through his good eye. His ragged clothes were filthy, and the wind buffeted the long dark coat he wore. "Find somethin' of interest?" he asked, his hard gaze drilling through her.

It was the same old man that Raven had almost hit on the road. "I . . . didn't know you were there."

He grunted. "Watched you look at that wall. Watched you bend over them stones. I been right here."

Impossible, Raven thought. If so, why hadn't she seen him when she'd walked around the wall in the first place?

"Who are you?" he asked. "What do you want here?"

"My name's Raven Dunstan. I own the *Foxton Democrat*." There was no recognition in that single staring eye. "The newspaper down in Foxton," she explained. "I've come up to find you."

"You've found me, then." He glanced in the direction from which she'd come. "You climb up the mountain in that little yaller car? Wind'll pick that thing up and toss it clear down to Usherland."

Again, Raven was puzzled. The car wasn't visible from here. How did he know it was yellow? "The road's not too good, but I made it. Do you live alone here?"

"Alone," he replied. "And not alone. What's troublin' your leg?"

"I . . . hurt it, a long time ago. In an accident."

"You were a little girl," he said, stating a fact, and touched her knee tentatively with his cane.

"Yes." She stepped away from him. A sharp spasm of pain pierced her knee.

He nodded, hawked, and spat phlegm on the ground. When he breathed deeply again, Raven could hear the rumble of fluids in his lungs. His complexion was a chalky yellow. She stared at the network of scars that covered almost all of his face; the right eye was gone. The left eye, though covered with a thin gray film, was pale green and held a gleam of crafty intelligence. He was very thin, shivering a bit in the cold, and she had no idea how old he was; he

223

could be anywhere from seventy to a hundred. One thing she was certain of: he was sick.

"Chilly out here in the open," the Mountain King said, and nodded toward the sky. "Weather's changin'. Clouds creepin' in before the wind. Be a storm directly." He lifted his cane off the ground with a trembling hand and pointed toward the shelter that still had the remnants of a roof. "That's my house. It'll be warmer inside there." Without waiting for her, he turned away and started toward it, picking his path with the cane.

Raven was appalled by the old man's living conditions, but the walls did block the wind. There were a few charred pieces of wood in the cold fireplace. Empty cans littered the floor. A mattress on the floor was covered with a tattered orange blanket, and newspapers poked out from underneath it. The place, to Raven's way of thinking, was thoroughly disgusting.

The Mountain King eased himself down to sit on the mattress. Raven heard his bones creak. He had a fit of coughing that went on for a minute or so, then he spat in an empty peach can beside the bed. His face crinkled distastefully. "I can't pee," he said in a wounded tone. "I wish I could, but I can't."

"There's a doctor at the clinic in Foxton who might be able to help you."

"A *doctor*?" the old man snapped. He snorted and spat into the can again. "Doctors are licensed killers. They put pills and needles in you. I won't go to Foxton. Too many people. I'll stay where I am."

"How long have you been sick?"

"Since the comets fell," he answered. "I don't never recall *not* bein' sick. It comes and goes. Still cold in here, ain't it?" He cocked his good eye toward the fireplace.

Raven felt the rush of heat at her back before she heard the sudden *whoosh*! of flame. Startled, she whirled toward the fireplace. The logs were burning. The old man hadn't touched them, but they were afire. "How . . . did you *do* that?" she asked.

"Do what?"

"The fire. How did you . . . light the fire?"

"Hush!" The Mountain King grasped his cane and stood up. It took him a little while longer to straighten his back, and he hissed with pain. Cans and bottles rolled around his feet as he hobbled to the door and peered out. "Somebody's comin'," he announced. "Two people. Woman and man. No. Woman and boy. Comin' up the road. Boy's drivin'. It's *him*." He paused, his cane thrust out before him like an antenna. "Yep," he said. "It's him, all right."

Raven was still staring at the burning logs; her senses were spinning, and she'd barely heard what the old man had said. She held her hands out toward the heat to test its reality.

"The woman sees that yaller car," the old man muttered. "She knows it. She wants to go back down the mountain." He glanced quickly at Raven. "She don't like you worth a tinker's damn."

"Who?" Raven rubbed the side of her head with numbed fingers. "Mrs. Tharpe?"

"Yep. She's scairt of you." He paused, then grunted with satisfaction. "The boy's got more sense. They're comin' up the trail." The Mountain King hobbled out to meet them.

Left alone, Raven backed away from the fireplace. She felt oddly off balance, trespassing in an alien world that did not conform to her laws of reality. The old man hadn't touched those logs ... yet they'd burst into flame; he'd known someone was coming from a distance of a hundred yards or more; he'd even verified that Myra Tharpe feared her. What kind of man was he, and why did he choose to live alone in these ruins? Raven looked around the disordered house. Buckets had been placed under holes in the roof to catch leaks. Dead leaves, bottles, and cans were scattered everywhere.

Her gaze came to rest on the mattress, and slowly she came to realize something that she hadn't before.

Beneath the orange blanket was the vague outline of a body.

Raven stared at it without moving. Then, slowly, she approached the mattress and pulled the blanket back.

Underneath was a hodgepodge of rags, newspaper and magazine pages. A damp, moldy smell drifted up. The figure was more apparent now, buried beneath the rags and papers. Raven allowed her hand to knock one of the rags to the floor. There were more papers beneath. She grasped the edge of a yellowed newspaper page and carefully lifted it.

She found herself looking at a frail, skeletal hand and arm.

The displacement of another clump of rags revealed part of a small ribcage.

The Mountain King, Raven realized as she stepped quickly away from the mattress, was sleeping with a skeleton in his bed.

The fire spat sparks. Raven looked over her shoulder and saw the old man standing just inside the doorway. How long he'd been there she didn't know, but he seemed uninterested in her now; he crossed the room to warm himself before the flames, and coughed several times to loosen the congestion in his lungs.

In another moment, New Tharpe came into the house; he was

bundled in a sweater and brown jacket, his face very pale except for the faint red lines where the thorn scratches were healing. He carried a paper sack. Myra Tharpe stopped in the doorway, her mouth twisting bitterly. "Well now," she said, "looky here. I seen that car of yours down there. If New hadn't talked me into stayin', we'd be long gone by now. Seems you turn up like a bad penny, don't you?"

"I do my best."

Myra entered the house, her nose wrinkling. She stood near the door, her back protected by a wall. Her small, frightened eyes darted between Raven and the Mountain King. "Give him what we brung, New."

New offered him the sack. The old man took it tentatively, looked inside, and then carried it over to a corner where he dumped the contents on the floor. More canned food rattled out.

"Didn't have no peaches," Myra said nervously as he picked through the cans. "Brung you some mixed fruit, though. And a couple cans of beef stew."

The Mountain King had selected the mixed fruit. He shook it and held it to his ear.

"It's fresh," Myra assured him. "Bought it just a few days ago, down at the market in Foxton."

He grunted, obviously satisfied. His eye was fixed on the boy. "New. Is that your name?"

"Yes sir. Newlan Tharpe." New was trembling inside, but he was determined not to show it. When he and his mother were walking up the path, the Mountain King had suddenly appeared *behind* them. Then, without a word, he'd led them up through the ruins to this desolate old place. New's mother had raised hell when she'd recognized Raven Dunstan's car, but New had soothed her; since they'd come up this far, they might as well go on. What did it matter that the newspaperwoman was up in the ruins too? Myra had said it mattered a lot, but the appearance of the Mountain King had stopped further argument.

"How old are you?"

"Fifteen, sir."

"You know how old I am?" the old man asked, with a trace of pride. "I was born in . . . let me think . . . I was born in nineteen-ought-nine. When I was fifteen, I . . . " His voice trailed off. Then he said, "I was right here. That was after the comets fell. I'm not clear in the head no more. But I recall the year I was fifteen, because that was the year Lizbeth turned eleven . . . and *he* almost snatched her."

"Lizbeth?" Raven glanced toward the mattress.

226

"My sister. It was her and me, after the comets fell. We come up here together. That was in . . . " He frowned, trying to remember, and then shook his head. "A long time past."

"Who almost snatched her?" New asked. "The Pumpkin Man?"

"New!" his mother warned.

"Him," the old man said. "The Pumpkin Man. The Briartop Stalker. The Child Snatcher. Whatever you want to call him. I know him for what he really is: an agent of the Devil himself. Lizbeth and me set us some traps for rabbits. She went out near dusk to see what we'd caught. She come out through the woods and seen him, standin' so close she could've touched him. He grabbed at her, and she took to runnin'. She could hear him right behind her, gettin' closer and closer; she said he could run like the wind, and not thorns nor vines nor nothin' slowed him down. Lizbeth run so fast she couldn't hardly get no breath. And all the time he was callin' for her to stop, to lay down and rest because she was tired, and there wasn't no use in tryin' to get away."

"He *spoke* to her?" Raven asked.

The old man tapped the side of his head. "In here. She heard him in here. She said his voice was like a cool stream on a hot day, and he made you want to lay down and rest. But she knew who he was, and that he was tryin' to trick her. So she didn't listen; every time she wanted to stop runnin', she thought of that sound the comets made when they was comin' down, and that kept her goin'. She didn't stop till she'd come back here, and she never went out without me again."

"Lizbeth saw his face? What did he look like?"

"His face . . . changed." The old man had placed one finger atop the can of mixed fruit, pressing here and there as if he were trying to poke through the tin. "First he had a face, and then he didn't. Lizbeth said she seen the white of his skin . . . and then his face was gone. There was nothin' but a hole where his face should've been." He turned his attention to the boy again, tilting his head to one side. "You've seen him, too. Ain't you?"

"Yes," New replied.

"And his black cat, Greediguts. He come a-callin' last night, didn't he?"

"Yes." New felt as helpless as a lock under a key; he could sense the Mountain King picking and probing at him, gradually springing him open.

"Your ma's afraid," the Mountain King said softly. "Powerful afraid. There's been a fear in her heart for a long time. It makes her near

227

'bout blind. But *you*—you're just beginnin' to see clear, ain't you?"

"I don't know."

"Tharpe," the old man whispered. His breathing was a low rumble of congestion. *"Tharpe.* The man who lived in that house was your pa?"

New nodded.

"And what was his name?"

"Bobby," Myra offered.

"Bobby Tharpe. I seen him, comin' and goin'. Sometimes I stood all night in the woods across the road from your house, just watchin'. I followed him to the Tongue, and saw him look down on Usherland. I knew what was in his mind, callin' and tauntin' him. I followed him many a time when he left his house and walked the woods. Oh, he never saw me—but I was there, all the same. Once he went down from Briartop to that Lodge, and he stood on the shore and he wanted to go inside so bad he could hardly stand it; but he resisted. I *helped* him resist, 'cause I knew he couldn't do it alone. Just like you couldn't get out of them thorns alone, boy. Nor could you hold back Greediguts alone."

"What?" New whispered.

"I don't know nothin' about you," the Mountain King continued, "just like I didn't know nothin' about your pa. But I *do* know the Lodge wanted him; and I know it wants you, as well. I seen you on the Tongue, too. I seen the way you stared down at that house, a-wantin' to walk its halls and run your fingers over that fine marble. Greediguts didn't come to kill you last night; it came to test you, to find out if you're stone or paper. Before your pa died, he was weakenin'. You ought to give thanks he *is* dead—'cause he was about to go into that Lodge, and what he would've come back out as . . . you wouldn't want to know."

Raven shook her head, utterly confused. To her, the old man was speaking gibberish. Was he insane, or was *she?* "No one lives in Usher's Lodge," she said. "It's empty."

"I didn't say no *person* lived in there, woman!" the Mountain King told her scornfully. His gaze flicked toward her like a whip, then back to the boy. "Ain't no person wanted your pa. Ain't no person wants *you.* That Lodge is more than halls and fine marble, boy. It's got a black heart, and a voice like a knife in the night. I *know*—'cause it's been workin' at me ever since the comets fell. Chidin', a-tauntin' and callin' me, slippin' through my dreams, tryin' to strangle me. Just like it did to your pa, and like it's doin' to you. Only I'm an old man, and pert' soon Greediguts is gonna slip up to

228

my house and I'll be too weak to hold it off. That'll be the end of me; but the Lodge wants you now. Like it wanted your pa."

The old man gripped his walking stick tightly. His eye was unflinching. "He was about to give in, boy. The stones he'd built in his soul were comin' apart at the seams. That's why . . . I had to make sure he couldn't listen no more."

Myra sucked in her breath. New hadn't moved, but now his heart was pounding.

"I killed him, boy," the Mountain King said quietly. "Surely as if I'd put a gun to his head and blowed his brains out. He come upon me on his way down the mountain, the day it happened. I knew the kind of work he did. He was weak, so it didn't take much; all he had to do was fill up a tire with air—and keep fillin' it till it blew up in his face. He never even knowed what he was doin'."

New was silent; all the blood had rushed from his face, and blue veins throbbed at his temple. It was Myra who spoke first, in an incredulous, hoarse voice: "You . . . you ain't nothin' but a crazy old man!" She came up behind her son. "You didn't even know my Bobby! Ain't nothin' special about you! You're just a crazy old liar!"

"Look at me, boy," the Mountain King commanded. He thrust his cane out and rested it beneath New's chin. "You know if I'm lyin' or not, don't you?"

New brushed the cane aside. He looked helplessly at Raven, and started to speak, but then his voice cracked and he stood there dumbfounded, his sallow face mirroring the battle of emotions within him. He forced himself to return the old man's gelid stare. "You're . . . a crazy old man," New said, with an obvious effort. "Ain't nothin' to you a-tall!" Abruptly he turned and left the house; Myra shot a poisonous glance at Raven and hurried after her son.

The Mountain King sighed deeply. His lungs rattled, and he fended off a fit of coughing. "He knows," he said when he'd recovered his breath. "He didn't want to say it before his ma, but he knows."

And you're as nutty as a Christmas fruitcake, Raven thought. The shape of the skeleton under those rags and papers sent a shiver up her spine. She'd assumed it was the old man's sister—but what if it *wasn't*? What if it was the skeleton of one of those children whose pictures were on the posters she'd had printed up? "When did your sister die?" she asked.

"I don't know the year," he said wearily, and rubbed his good eye. "She was twenty years old . . . or twenty-two. I can't recall. You seen her bones."

"Why didn't you bury her?"

"Didn't want nothin' gettin' to her. Swore I'd protect her, and that's what I did." He hobbled over to the bed, lifted the tattered blanket, and reached under a mass of rags. "Didn't want the thing that killed her to chew her bones." He withdrew a small skull that had been all but crushed; the lower jaw was missing, the nasal area smashed in. "The pant'er did this. Caught her in broad daylight, at the stream." Gently he set the skull down again and picked up the can of mixed fruit he'd set aside. "The boy knows," he muttered. "He *knows*."

"Knows what?"

The Mountain King stared at her, and smiled thinly. "That he's like *me*," he said, thrusting his forefinger through the top of the can as if it were wet cardboard. He withdrew the finger and licked fruit syrup off.

Raven had had enough. She fled the house. Behind her she could hear the old man laughing; his laughter erupted into spasmodic coughing. She ran past the figures on the wall, over the ground that had been scorched to glass, and she never looked back.

When she reached her car, she received a new shock.

The Volkswagen now faced downhill. Something had picked up the car and turned it around. She slid quickly under the steering wheel and started the car.

She was almost halfway down Briartop when she realized she'd *run* through the ruins.

Her limp was gone.

27

When Wheeler Dunstan opened the front door, Rix offered him the Baird Retreat's casebook. Dunstan paged carefully through it, taking his own sweet time, and then he motioned Rix inside without a word.

Dunstan put the casebook on a table and began filling his corn-cob pipe with tobacco. "I had a call from Mr. Bodane this mornin'," he finally said. "He verified what Raven told me about you, that you're a published writer. Called the library yesterday to see if they had any of Jonathan Strange's books over there. They didn't. So I sent one of the fellas from the *Democrat* over to the bookstore at Crockett Mall." His wheelchair whirred across the room to a bookshelf, and he showed Rix the paperback copies of *Congregation* and *Fire Fingers*. "Read a little bit out of each of them last night. They ain't too bad—but they ain't too *good*, either."

"Thank you," Rix said dryly.

"So." Dunstan turned the wheelchair around and regarded him thoughtfully through a haze of pipe smoke. "You want to help us with the book, and you figure I'll go for the idea since you're a published writer."

"Something like that."

"This is a project I've been workin' on for a long time. I suppose you could say"—his mouth curved to one side—"that it's a labor of love. Raven and I are a good team. I'm not so sure we need another member."

"Maybe you don't," Rix agreed, "but I've shown you how serious I am about this. I'm taking a hell of a risk by coming here. I had to sneak out after lunch like a thief. I can get you whatever you need from the Gatehouse library. I can help you with the writing. And most important, an Usher name on the cover will give it credibility. Have you thought about that?"

Dunstan didn't reply, but Rix saw his eyes narrow almost imperceptibly. He had scored a point, Rix thought. "I brought you the casebook. And I've told you what you wanted to know, haven't I?"

The other man grunted. "I've known about the Baird Retreat for months. I digested that material and returned the book to Mr. Bodane. Sorry, I'm still not sold. I can't figure out exactly *why* you want to help so badly." His teeth were clamped around the pipe's stem like a bulldog's. "If you think you're gonna waltz in here and get your hands on the manuscript—maybe screw it up, for all I know—you're wrong, my friend."

This was like trying to find a chink in a granite wall. "Edwin trusts me," Rix said, nettled. "Why won't you?"

"Because I'm not the trustin' type."

"Okay, fine. Then what can I do to *make* you trust me?"

Dunstan pondered the question. He rolled the chair over to the bay window and watched gray-bellied clouds scudding across the sky, then looked at Rix. "Mr. Bodane entered this deal with the stipulation that he supply documents only—no verbal information. In his own way, I guess he's still bein' loyal to Walen. I admire that. He wouldn't tell me what Walen's condition was, and that's why I

231

had to find out from you. I've got some questions that need answers: things that connect events of Usher history. And only an Usher can give me the answers."

"Try me."

Dunstan motioned toward a chair, and Rix sat down. "Okay. I want to know about the cane. The black cane with the silver lion's-head. Why's it so important to your family? Where'd it come from, and why does every patriarch carry it like some kind of royal scepter?"

"As far as I know, Hudson Usher brought it with him from Wales. Old Malcolm probably carried it, too. I think whoever possesses it is recognized by the family as the head of the estate and the business. There's no secret about that."

"Maybe not," Dunstan said, "but maybe it's more than that, too." He let smoke leak from the corner of his mouth. "The cane wasn't always in your family. It was stolen once, from Aram Usher—your great-great-grandfather—and was lost for almost twenty years. In those twenty years, your family had more than its share of bad luck: Aram was killed in a duel, his son Ludlow was almost killed several times, Ludlow's half-sister, Shann, had a career tragedy, Usherland was overrun by Union troops, and your family's steamboat, railroad, and textile businesses went bust."

This rush of information was startling to Rix. "Are you suggesting there's a connection between all that and the *cane?*"

"Nope. Just speculatin'. That was probably the most disastrous period of Usher history. The only thing that didn't suffer too much was the armaments business. That rolled in a fortune during the Civil War—especially since Usher Armaments sold rifles, bullets, and artillery pieces to both sides. Old Aram was smart. His heart might've belonged to the South, but he knew the North was gonna clean house."

"Who stole the cane?" Rix asked, intrigued by these new facts of Usher history. "A servant?"

"No. An octoroon gambler from New Orleans named Randolph Tigré. Or at least that was one of his names. I say 'stole' only figuratively. Aram's second wife, Cynthia Cordweiler Usher, gave it to him."

"Why?"

"He was blackmailin' her. She was the widow of Alexander Hamilton Cordweiler, who owned steamboat lines, a network of railroads, and a big chunk of the Chicago stockyards. Cordweiler was sixty-four when he married her; she was eighteen."

232

"Blackmailing her? What for?"

Dunstan's pipe had gone out, and he took a few seconds to relight it. "Because," he said, "Cynthia Cordweiler Usher—your great-great-grandmother—was a murderess." He smiled faintly at Rix's grim expression. "I can tell you the story, if you want to hear it. I've put together bits and pieces from various sources, and I've had to guess at some of it—from what happened later." He raised his bushy eyebrows. "Well? Got the nerve to hear it, or not?"

"Go ahead," Rix replied.

"Good. It starts in the summer of 1858. Ludlow was about four weeks old. Aram was in Washington on business. If he'd been home, things might've taken a different turn. Anyway, a gentleman caller came to the Lodge. He waited downstairs while a servant took his calling card up to Cynthia's bedroom . . . "

The smoke swirled around Wheeler Dunstan's head as he spoke. Rix listened intently, and imagined that in the blue whorls of smoke were faces—the ghosts of the past, gathering around them in the room. The smoke formed pictures; the Lodge on a sunny summer's day, light streaming through the windows and across the hardwood floors. A lovely, strong-featured woman in bed, with an infant suckling at her breast. And a card in her trembling hand that gave the name of Randolph Tigré.

◆ ◆ ◆

"Send him away," Cynthia Usher told her maid, a strapping young black woman named Righteous Jordan. "I'm occupied with my son."

"I told him you wasn't gonna see him, ma'am," she said; Righteous stood almost six feet tall and had a stomach as wide as a barrel. "Told him right to his face, but he say it don't matter, that I was to give you his card."

"You have. Now go back downstairs and tell him to—"

"Good morning, Mrs. Usher." It was a soft, silken voice that raised goosebumps on Cynthia's arms. Righteous whirled around indignantly. Randolph Tigré, wearing a natty tan suit and carrying a thin riding crop, was leaning casually in the doorway. His teeth gleamed in his handsome, coffee-and-cream-colored face.

"Lord God!" Righteous tried to block the man's view. "Don't you have no decency?"

"I don't like waiting, so I followed you up here. Mrs. Usher and I are old . . . acquaintances. You can leave us now."

Righteous's cheeks swelled at such impertinence. It was bad

enough that this man had talked his way through the front gate—
but for him to be standing there while Mrs. Usher was feeding her
little baby was downright scandalous. He was smiling like a cat, and
Righteous's first impulse was to pick him up and heave him down
the stairs. What stopped her from doing so was the fact that he was
the most handsome man she'd ever seen; the large topaz stickpin
in the center of his black cravat was the exact color of his keen,
deepset eyes, and he had a neatly trimmed mustache and beard. The
creamy hue of his flesh made Righteous appear, by contrast, to have
recently bathed in India ink. He wore tan calfskin gloves, and English
riding boots polished to a high, warm luster. To be a free man of
color was one thing, Righteous thought, but for him to flaunt himself
openly in these troubled times was begging for a beating. "Get yourself out of here while Mrs. Usher arranges herself!" Righteous snapped
protectively.

Cynthia had laid the infant down on a silk-brocaded pillow,
and now she calmly buttoned her gown to the throat.

"I'm not the coalstove stoker, Missy," Tigré said. His eyes had
flashed like warning beacons, and there was a shade of menace in
his voice. "Don't use that tone with me. Tell her, Mrs. Usher. We're
old friends, aren't we?"

"It's all right," Cynthia said. Righteous looked at her incredulously. "Mr. Tigré and I . . . know each other. You can leave us
alone now."

"Ma'am? Leave you alone up *here*? In your bedchamber?"

"Yes. But I want you to return in a quarter of an hour . . . to
escort Mr. Tigré out of the Lodge. Run on, now."

The black woman snorted and stormed out. Randolph Tigré
stepped aside as she passed, and gave a hint of a bow. Then he closed
the door and turned toward Cynthia Usher with a cool, insolent
smile. "Hello, Cindy," he said softly. "You look breathtaking."

"What the *hell* are you doing here? Are you insane?"

"Now, now, that's not proper language for a lady of leisure, is
it?" He strolled around the sumptuous bedroom, his hands exploring
the textures of blue velvet, carved mahogany, and Belgian lace. He
lifted a jade vase from her dressing table and examined the intricate
workmanship. "Exquisite," he murmured. "You're a woman of your
word, Cindy. You always vowed you'd own exquisite things someday—and now look at you, mistress of Usherland."

"My husband will be returning shortly. I advise you to—"

Tigré laughed quietly. "No, Cindy. Mr. Aram Usher left for

234

Washington by train yesterday morning. I followed his coach to the station. He's a nice-looking man. But then . . . your head was always turned by a wide pair of shoulders and a tight pair of trousers, wasn't it?" He plucked a hand-painted Japanese fan from its ceramic stand and stretched it open, admiring the colors. "You've struck it rich again, haven't you? First Alexander Cordweiler—and now Aram Usher." Tigré nodded toward the gurgling infant. "*His*, I assume?"

"You must be out of your mind to set foot on this estate!"

"In fact, I've never been more sane. Don't I look fine?" He showed her his matching topaz cufflinks, and produced a gold pocket watch studded with diamonds. "I was always lucky at cards. The gaming boats that run from New Orleans to St. Louis are packed with sheep who bleat to be sheared. I'm happy to oblige them. Of course . . . sometimes my luck needs a helping hand." He opened his waistcoat and patted the small pistol he carried in a leather holster. "Your husband produces fine guns."

"Either state your business, or get out of my house." Her voice shook and she was speared with shame.

Tigré walked over to the far side of the room, peering out the windows upon the lake. "I have a present for you," he said. He turned and flipped something—a silver coin, sparkling in the sunlight that spilled through the window—onto the bed. It landed at her side. Cynthia reached for it—but her hand froze in midair. Her fingers slowly curled into a fist.

"It's a reminder of the good old days, Cindy. I thought seeing it would please you."

She had recognized the object. How he'd gotten one of them, she didn't know, but her business-honed mind rapidly grasped the situation: the little silver coin could destroy her life.

Tigré came to the foot of the bed. She caught the odors of his pungent cologne and minty brilliantine—old, familiar aromas that, to her horror, made her heart beat faster. She pulled her knees protectively to her chest under the sheet.

"You've missed me, haven't you?" he asked. "Yes. I can tell. I could always read your eyes. That's why we were such a good team. You would entertain the customers with your stories and laughter—and then the judgment of God would fall on their heads. I never missed once with that hammer, did I? But they died happy, Cindy; you needn't fear the fires of hell."

The baby began crying. Cynthia held Ludlow close. "That was a long time ago. I'm not the same woman."

"Of course not. How many millions did you inherit from Cordweiler? Ten? Twenty? Your riverboats are comfortable, I'll say that. I play my best games of poker on the *Bayou Moon*." Slowly his smile began to fade. A thin sneer replaced it, and Tigré played his fingers over the leather riding crop. "You never answered my letters. I began to have the feeling you didn't want to see me again. After all, *I* introduced you to Cordweiler . . . or have you forgotten? Tell me something—how did you do it? Rat poison in his cake? Arsenic in his coffee?"

She stared icily at him. Ludlow strained at her bosom.

"No matter," he said, with a curt wave of his hand. "However it was done, you covered your tracks well. Which brings me to another question: When are you going to murder Aram Usher?"

"Get out," she whispered. "Get out of here before I call for the police!"

"Will you? I don't think so. We're the same, deep inside. But hammers aren't your style—yours is the slick word and the wet kiss. I'm tired of waiting for my just due, Cindy." He nodded impatiently toward the infant. "He's hungry. Why don't you take out your tit and feed him?"

She didn't respond. Tigré leaned against the bed's scrolled walnut cornerpost. "I've come to be fed, too. At the first of every month, you're to deliver ten thousand dollars in an envelope to the Andrew Jackson Suite of the Crockett Hotel in Asheville."

"You're insane! I don't have that kind of cash!"

"No?" Tigré reached into his pocket. With a flip of his hand he filled the air with shining silver coins. Cynthia flinched as they fell around her, striking her on the face, hitting the bed and the infant's crib, clattering on the floor. "I have a boxful of those. Ten thousand dollars, every month. I'll even show you how reasonable I can be; this month I'll only expect five thousand dollars. *And* that handsome cane your husband carries with him."

"That's an heirloom! He even sleeps with it! It would be impossible to—"

"Hush," Tigré said gently. "I want that cane. I admired it yesterday at the train station. Get it away from him, I don't care how. Fuck him senseless—you were always adept at that." He glared at the crying infant. "Can't you shut him up?"

"I won't be blackmailed," Cynthia vowed defiantly. "You don't know who you're talking to: I'm Cynthia Cordweiler *Usher*! My husband loves me, and I love him. He won't listen to your filth!"

Tigré leaned forward, his golden eyes bestial with barely controlled rage. "You forget—*I* know where the bodies are buried. The Chicago police might like to learn who and what you really are. Aram Usher's a smart man; he'll dump you in the gutter if he even thinks . . . Damn it to hell!" He suddenly darted around the crib and snatched the crying child from Cynthia's arms. She grasped for the baby, but Tigré laughed and quickly stepped backward. He slid his hand around Ludlow's neck.

"Little tit-sucking bastard," he breathed, his eyes wild with fury. Cynthia had seen him like this before, and she didn't dare make a sound. "If you were mine, I'd wring your neck and throw you out that damned window! Go on, scream for your mother! *Scream!*"

"Give him to me." She was desperately trying to remain calm. Her voice cracked, and her arms trembled as she reached for her child.

Tigré thrust his grinning face toward the infant's. "You'll remember me long after I'm gone, won't you? That's good. I like to leave my mark." He held the child over Cynthia's arms and dropped him like a sack of laundry. As she caught him, Tigré reached forward and ripped her gown open. Buttons flew. Both of Cynthia's breasts were exposed. She clutched the child to her, and he began to suckle.

"Mrs. Usher?" Righteous called from beyond the door. "You all right, ma'am?"

Tigré laid his riding crop against her cheek.

"Yes," she said in a whisper. Then, louder: "Yes! I'm . . . I'm fine. Mr. Tigré is just leaving."

"You remember what I said. Five thousand dollars and the cane. From then on, ten thousand a month." He traced her cheekbone with the crop. "You have a lovely complexion, Cindy. You always were a beauty. Perhaps you'll visit me at the Crockett Hotel yourself?"

"Get out!" she hissed.

"I'll be waiting for your first payment," he told her, withdrawing toward the door. He stopped to smile and bow gracefully, and then he left the room.

Quickly, Cynthia set Ludlow aside and began to gather up the coins. She stuffed them hastily into the pillowcase to dispose of later.

A week afterward, Aram's cane disappeared from the parlor. Servants scurried through the Lodge in search of it. Cynthia surmised that one of the servants had stolen and sold it. Aram spent long hours locked in his room, disconsolate, after firing half of the staff.

Cynthia stayed to herself, spending most of her time with the infant, who slept in the fur-trimmed crib beside her bed.

Less than three months later, a shriek from Cynthia in the middle of the night brought Aram running from his chamber down the corridor. He burst in to find her strangling his son; Ludlow's face was blue in the lamplight, and his small body writhed as he fought for breath. He tore her away from him, but she screamed, "He's choking!" and Aram realized something was caught in the baby's throat.

He wrenched Ludlow's mouth open and dug in with his fingers. "Help him!" Cynthia begged frantically. Aram picked the child up and held him by the heels, trying to shake the object loose. Ludlow's throat was still blocked. Cynthia grasped the bellcord and began tugging at it, summoning servants from a lower floor. The bells of alarm echoed through the halls, an eerie chorus of disaster.

Keil Bodane, old Whitt's son, reached the room first. He rushed toward Aram, took the infant in his arms, turned him upside down, and whacked him hard on the back. Whacked him again. And a third time.

A gurgling cough burst from the baby's throat. Something clinked on the floor and rolled away. Then Ludlow howled as if trying to wake the dead. Sobbing, Cynthia took him and rocked him in her arms.

"What's this?" Aram bent to the floor, picked up something, and held it to the light. Cynthia saw the glint of silver—and the breath halted in her own lungs. " 'The Willows,' " he read from the coin. " 'Room Number Four. Cindy.' " When he looked up at her, his face was already freezing into the hard mask that he would wear for the rest of his life. "Explain to me," he whispered, "how a whore-house token almost strangled my son to death."

◆ ◆ ◆

Wheeler Dunstan watched Rix carefully. "Cynthia must have missed one of the tokens when she was gathering them up. The thing had lodged somewhere in the baby's crib. Ludlow swallowed it. And so her secret was out. When she was sixteen years old, she was a working prostitute at a whorehouse in New Orleans."

"What happened? Did Aram divorce her?"

"Nope. I think he really loved her, very much. He'd been married once before, to a Chinese girl in San Francisco, and he had a daughter by her: Shann, who in 1858 was twelve years old and studying music in Paris. But he admired Cynthia's business ability and of course he adored Ludlow. A divorce would've ruined Cynthia socially, and probably financially, too."

"What about Tigré? If he had such a hold on her, he wouldn't give up so easily, would he?"

"Aram found him at the Crockett Hotel—it stood where the Crockett Mall is now—and publicly challenged him to a duel. Of course, dueling was against the law, but Aram Usher had connections in high places. Cynthia begged him not to fight, because Randolph Tigré was an expert shot, but he wouldn't listen. They met in a field not too far from here. Tigré even brought the cane. They were to fight with gold-plated Usher pistols." Dunstan smoked for a moment in silence. "It was no contest. Tigré shot him between the eyes, and Aram Usher fell dead on the spot."

"And then Tigré went after Cynthia again?"

"No," Dunstan replied. "Aram loved her; he wanted to protect both her and the boy. When Keil Bodane checked Aram's pistol, he found it was unloaded. It had *never been* loaded. In essence, Aram had committed suicide—and Randolph Tigré, a black man with a gambler's reputation, had committed murder. Tigré was forced to flee the state. In death, Aram had won. His will provided that Cynthia take over the armaments business and the estate, but it would all go to Ludlow on his eighteenth birthday."

"What about the cane?" Rix asked. "How did it get back into the family?"

"That's another question I can't answer. Ludlow retrieved it—but how, I don't know." He took the pipe from his mouth and held it between his palms. "There are a lot of questions that need answers. Sometimes I think I'll never find them. This book is important to me—damned important." Dunstan clenched his hands together, knots of muscle standing up in his forearms. "Maybe I've spent six years workin' on it, but it's been in my mind for a long time."

"Ever since the accident?" Rix ventured. "Edwin told me about it. I'm sorry."

"Fine," Dunstan said bitterly. "You're sorry about it, my wife is dead, my daughter has deep emotional and physical scars, I'm crippled—and Walen Usher sat behind a wall of lawyers who said I was drunk when we crashed. He went home to his Lodge, and I had to fight with every ounce of strength in my body just to keep my newspaper. I saw how the Usher mind worked—take what you please, when you please, and the consequences be damned. From that point on, I wanted to find out everything I could about you Ushers. I'm going to finish this book, no matter what your family throws at me—and then, by God, people will know the truth: that you Ushers have the moral sense of maggots and no conscience at all, and you'll sell your souls for the almighty dollar."

Rix started to protest, then reconsidered. His presence here, he realized, was proof of what the man had said; morally, he was betraying his family in pursuit of the money and recognition this book might bring him. Still, what choice did he have? If he wanted control of this project, he first had to control Dunstan's trust. "How can I help you?" he asked calmly.

The other man stared at him in silence, trying to make up his mind. "Okay," he said finally. "If you really want to help, I'll give you the chance. As I said, I need some questions answered: How did Ludlow get the cane back? How did Cynthia Usher die, and when? What happened to Shann?" His eyes were icy with determination. "Ludlow was a young genius with a photographic memory. I've read that he built a workshop somewhere in the Lodge's basement for his inventions. What were they? Then there's another question—a larger one, and probably the most important of all."

"What?"

Dunstan smiled slightly, with a trace of arrogance. "You find me the other answers first. Then we'll talk again."

"And you'll show me the manuscript?"

"Maybe," Dunstan said.

Rix nodded, and rose to leave. For now, he'd have to play this game Dunstan's way. "I'll be back," he promised, and went to the door.

"Rix?" Dunstan called after him. Rix paused. "You be careful," Dunstan told him. "You don't know Walen the way I do."

Rix left the house and went to his car under a sky dappled with gathering clouds.

28

Rix drove past the Gatehouse after leaving Dunstan's, heading toward the Lodge. He was in no hurry to return to the house, where masking tape had been placed over all the light switches. He would have to do his searching in the library tonight by candlelight. Walen's stench was getting stronger; it ambushed Rix from around corners, crept under doors, and permeated the clothes in his closet. At the breakfast table, when Rix had announced what Walen wanted done, Margaret had sat like a statue with her fork halfway to her mouth; she'd blinked slowly, lowered the fork, and looked across the table at him as if he'd lost his mind.

Katt had been shaken as well. "You mean we've got to live in the *dark*?"

"That's what he told me. We can use candles, of course. We've got enough silver candelabras around here to light up a cathedral."

"Not one electric light?" Margaret had asked in a soft, strained voice. The glassy sheen on her eyes worried Rix; she looked close to a nervous breakdown. "Not *one*?"

"I'm sorry. He said no electric lights or appliances of any kind, except those in the kitchen."

"Yes," she murmured. "Yes, of course. Otherwise, how would we eat?"

"I'm surprised Dad didn't call *you* in to deliver the message," Rix had told Katt. "I didn't think he trusted me that much."

Katt had showed him a twitch of a smile. "That's because he knows how much I hate the dark," she'd said nervously. "I have to sleep with the lights on. He knows that. It's stupid, I know, but . . . the dark scares me. It's like . . . death closing in around me or something."

"Come on, it won't be that bad. We'll have candles. We can all walk around like we're in a Vincent Price movie."

"Trust you to think of it that way!" Margaret had snapped at him. "We're in a dire emergency, and you make tasteless jokes! My God!" Her voice got higher and more shrill. "Your father's sick, and you make jokes! This family is in crisis, and you make jokes! Did you make a joke when you found your wife dead in the bathtub?"

By sheer willpower, Rix had stopped himself from smashing his breakfast plate against the wall. He'd forced his food down and gotten out of the room as soon as he could.

He saw the Lodge's chimneys and lightning rods through the thinning trees, and he involuntarily slowed the Thunderbird. When he reached the bridge, he braked the car and sat with the engine idling. Before him, the bridge's paving stones showed the wear and tear of a hundred years of hooves, carriage wheels, and automobile tires. Black lake water was ruffled by the wind, and ducks fed on reeds in the rocky shallows.

The mountainous Lodge, with its bricked-up windows, stood

like the silent centerpiece of Usherland. What secrets had it watched over? Rix wondered. What secrets did it still contain?

He heard the high whine of the Jetcopter approaching, and looked up as it roared over the Lodge and veered toward the Gatehouse helipad. Frightened birds rose from the trees and fled. Who was coming in this time? The two men he'd seen a few days before? If Walen permitted them to use the Jetcopter at a time when he couldn't stand noise, then they were obviously important to him. Walen was working on his last project—what was it? What had he been researching in the old books?

A movement near the Lodge caught his attention. There was a palomino horse tied up under the stone porte-cochere that guarded the Lodge's main entrance. Spooked by the helicopter's noise, it was pulling at its tether. The reins held fast, though, and after a minute or so the beautiful animal settled down.

Someone was inside the Lodge, Rix thought. Boone? Katt? What were they doing in there, prowling around in the dark?

Rix's hands tightened around the wheel. He guided the Thunderbird forward a few feet, onto the bridge, and stopped again. Then a few more feet—at a crawl, as if he feared the stones might collapse beneath him. At the bridge's midpoint, Rix felt sweat trickling down under his arms. The Lodge seemed to fill up the horizon. When he reached the far end of the bridge, he saw that the face of the Lodge was covered with minute cracks. In some places, chunks of stone and marble had toppled to the ground. The decaying carcasses of birds lay around the bases of the walls, their feathers caught like snowflakes in the untrimmed hedges and flowerbeds. Ornamental statues of fauns, centaurs, Gorgons, and other mythological creatures stood around the island, guarding marble fountains, meandering pathways, and overgrown gardens. Rix peered up through the windshield at the array of gargoyles and statues that decorated the upper ledges of the house. From the rooftop more than a hundred feet above, the stone lions watched him approach.

The Lodge was clearly in need of attention. Vines were snaking up the walls, probing into cracks and crevices. Black stains indicated water seepage. The driveway was pitted with holes, and the island's expensive grass had eroded away to show the rough, rocky soil beneath.

Rix stopped the car. He hadn't been this close to the Lodge since he was a little boy; he was amazed to find his feeling of irrational fear slowly changing to a sense of awe. No matter what he'd thought of the Lodge, he knew it had once been a stunning master-piece. The craftsmanship that had gone into the gargoyles, finials, arches, balconies, foliations, and turrets was truly majestic; much of the work probably couldn't be duplicated today at any price. How much would a house like the Lodge be worth? Rix wondered. Thirty million dollars? At least that much, without one stick of furniture. He guided the car beneath the porte-cochere. The palomino was tied to one of several iron hitching posts near the sweeping stone stairway that led to the massive oak front door. Rix cut the engine, but did not leave the car. The front door was wide open. Above it was a green-and-black marble representation of the Usher crest: three rear-ing lions separated by bendlets.

Rix didn't have long to wait. In less than ten minutes, Boone, carrying a bull's-eye lantern, came through the doorway. He stopped abruptly when he saw the Thunderbird; then he recovered, pulled the door shut and descended the stairs.

Rix rolled his window down. "What's going on?" His voice quavered; in the presence of the Lodge he was a jittery fool.

Boone kicked away dead leaves that had been blown onto the steps. "What're you doin', Rixy?" he asked without looking at his brother. "Spyin' on me?"

"No. Are you doing something worth spying on?"

"Don't be cute," Boone said sharply. "I thought you stayed away from the Lodge."

"I do. I saw your horse from the shore."

"And so you drove across the bridge to have a look, huh?" Boone smiled slyly. "Or did you want to have a closer look at the Lodge?"

"Maybe both. What were you doing inside there?"

"Nothin'. I come over here sometimes, to walk and look around. No harm in that, is there?"

"Aren't you afraid of getting lost?"

"I ain't afraid of *nothin'*. Besides," he said, "I know my way around the first floor. It's simple when you figure out how the cor-ridors run."

"Does Dad know you come over here and walk around?"

Boone smiled coldly. "No. Why should he?"

"Just curious."

"Curiosity killed the cat, Rixy. You know, I'm surprised at you. You must have more nerve than I thought. After what happened to you inside there, I never thought you'd get even this close to the Lodge. How's it feel, Rixy? Can't you remember gettin' lost in there?

243

The way the dark closed in on you? The way you screamed, and nobody could hear you?" He leaned against the car, snapping the lantern on and off in Rix's face. "I've got a light. How's about you and me goin' in the Lodge again, together? I'll give you the grand tour. Okay? How about it?"

"No, thanks."

Boone snorted. "I didn't think so. Long as you're in that car, you figure you're safe, huh? Bad ol' Lodge can't get you in that car. See, you ought to be like one of the heroes in those books of yours—they've got the guts to go into dark places, don't they?"

It was time to strike. Rix said, "Dad told me. I know about the freaks."

Boone's thin little smile was jarred. It began to fade; a wildness surfaced in Boone's eyes, the look of an animal trapped in a corner. Then he got himself under control and said easily, "So he told you, so what? I run a good business. Place talent with carnivals and sideshows all over the Southeast! Hell, I made a half-million bucks last year, after taxes!"

"Why the charade? Because you didn't want Mom and Katt knowing what sort of 'talent' you really promote?"

"They wouldn't understand. They'd figure it was beneath an Usher. But they'd be wrong, Rixy! There's a demand for freaks. Armless, legless, midgets, alligator-skinned boys, Siamese twins, deformed babies and animals—people pay to see 'em! Somebody's got to make a profit off it. And somebody's got to find the freaks, too. Which ain't as easy a job as you might think."

"It sounds like a real heartfelt career," Rix said. He could imagine his brother driving out to some dusty old farm where a deformed animal pulled at its chain in the barn, or haggling with a lowlife abortionist who kept "extra-special" fetuses floating in jars of formaldehyde.

"What now? You gonna tell everybody within shoutin' distance?"

"If you're not ashamed of what you do, I wouldn't think you'd mind."

Boone put the lantern down on the hood of the Thunderbird. He crossed his arms and looked at Rix through hard, dead eyes. "Let me spell out how things are, Rixy. After Dad signs over the business and the estate to me, I can either put you on an allowance or cut you off clean."

Rix laughed; his hand was resting on the knob to roll up the window if Boone reached for him. "Dad's passing everything to Katt! Don't you understand that yet?"

"Sure. And I'm the man in the fuckin' moon! A woman can't handle the business! I've got *ideas*, Rixy. Big ideas, for both the business and the estate." When Rix was silent, Boone plowed ahead. "There's a town in Florida, near Tampa, where only freaks live. That's all the town is, just freaks. 'Course, they don't allow no tourists. But what if *I* was to build a town between here and Foxton, and fill it full of freaks myself? Then folks could come in, pay one price, and poke around all they pleased! It'd be a freakshow that went on twenty-four hours a day, three hundred sixty-five days a year!" Boone's eyes had begun to gleam with excitement. "Hell, the damned thing could be like Disney World, with rides and everything! And if you'd mind your manners, I'd see that you got a cut of the gate."

Disgust had blocked Rix's throat. Boone was grinning, his face slightly flushed. When Rix found his voice, the words came out strangled. "Are you out of your damned mind? That's about the most repulsive idea I've ever heard!"

Boone's grin cracked. In his brother's gaze was a flash of hurt that Rix had never seen before, and he realized Boone had shared a dream with him—a twisted dream, perhaps, but a dream all the same. For an instant Rix thought Boone would react with characteristic anger, but instead he drew himself up straight and proud. "I knew you wouldn't understand," he said. "You wouldn't know a good idea if it bit you on the ass." He took his lantern and walked to his horse, untied the reins from the hitching post, and swung himself into the saddle. "I'm a reasonable man." He forced a chilly smile. "I'm perfectly willin' to give both you and Katt an allowance, provided neither of you lives within five hundred miles of Usherland."

"I'm sure Katt'll have something to say about that."

"She'll leave me alone, if she knows what's good for her."

"What's that supposed to mean?"

"It means I know some things about our little sister that might spin your head around, Rixy. Dad will never give her Usherland. It's gonna be mine. You'll see. *Giddap.*" He kicked his heels into the horse's flanks and galloped away toward the bridge.

Bastard! Rix thought. He watched Boone ride into the distance, and then he started the engine. He was about to follow Boone when he glanced at the Lodge's door.

It was standing wide open.

He'd seen Boone close it. A flurry of dead leaves spun across the steps and was sucked into the Lodge's throat.

He sat staring numbly at the open doorway. An invitation, he thought suddenly. It *wants* me to come closer. He laughed nervously, but he didn't take his eyes away from the entrance.

Then he forced himself to get out of the car. He took the first and second steps with no problem; on the third step his knees turned to putty.

The darkness beyond the doorway wasn't total. He could make out the shapes of furniture in the gray twilight, and a violet-and-gold carpet across a leaf-littered floor. Figures were standing in the gloom, seemingly watching him.

See, Boone had said mockingly, *you ought to be like one of the heroes in those books of yours.*

He climbed the last four steps. His stomach was doing slow flipflops as he stood on the threshold of the Lodge for the first time in more than twenty years.

In his nightmares he had seen the Lodge as a dusty, horribly grim, haunted palace. What he saw now amazed him.

Before him was a beautiful, elegant foyer that was perhaps twice as large as the Gatehouse's living room. From white marble walls protruded a dozen life-sized brass hands, offered to receive hats and coats. He realized that the watching figures were statues of fauns and cherubs that gazed toward the door, their eyes made of rubies, emeralds, and sapphires. Suspended from the vaulted ceiling, an immense chandelier of polished crystal spheres glistened. Beyond the foyer, a few steps led downward to a reception area floored with alternating black and white marble tiles. At its center stood a fountain, empty now, where bronze sea creatures reclined on rocks. The rest of the house was shrouded in darkness.

Rix had forgotten how magnificent the interior was. The statues in the foyer alone must be priceless. The workmanship of the marble, the ceiling, the brass hands on the walls—all of it staggered his senses.

He imagined how the Lodge must have looked during one of Erik's parties, ablaze with festive lights. The fountain might be spouting champagne, and guests would dip their goblets in over the side. Aromas from the past found him: the scent of roses, fine Kentucky bourbon, Havana cigars, and starched linen. From deep within the Lodge he seemed to hear the echoes of otherworldly voices: faint notes of a woman's laughter, a chorus of men singing a bawdy song in drunken glee, a business conversation in hushed, stiff tones, a man's booming voice calling for more champagne. All of it overlapped, changed, became a silken, seductive whisper that said

—*Rix*—

He felt the voice in his bones. Wind swirled around him, caressing his face like cold fingers.

—*Rix*—

Leaves danced on the foyer's floor. The wind strengthened, and there was a suction that tried to pull him across the threshold. The eyes of the statues were fixed on him, the brass hands reaching toward him.

—*Rix*—

"No," he heard himself say, as if speaking underwater. He grasped the door's oversized bronze handle and started to swing it shut. But the door was heavy and seemed to resist him. As he pushed against it, he thought he saw something move in the deep gloom near the marble fountain. It was a slow, sinuous movement, like an animal stretching. Then his eye lost it, and the door slammed shut with a dull *boom*.

He abruptly turned away and descended the stairs, then slid behind the wheel of the Thunderbird. He was trembling, his stomach knotted with tension. Whom had he spoken to? he asked himself. What was in there, trying to lure him beyond the safety of the doorway? If the Lodge did have a voice, he decided, it was born of his own imagination and the moan of the wind roaming the long corridors and cavernous rooms.

He started the engine, and couldn't resist looking toward the Lodge again.

The front door was wide open.

He put the car into gear and sped along the driveway and back across the bridge.

29

Rix entered the Gatehouse living room and went to the decanters to pour himself a stiff drink. As he splashed bourbon into a glass, he heard his mother say, "Where have you been?"

He turned toward her voice. She was sitting in her chair before the fireplace, wearing a white gown and a diamond necklace. Rix poured his drink and took a long swallow of it.

"Where have you been?" she asked again. "Off the estate?"

"I was driving around."

"Driving around *where*?"

"Here and there. Who are Dad's visitors?"

"General McVair and Mr. Meredith, from the plant. Don't change the subject. I don't think I like your sudden disappearances very much."

"Okay," he shrugged, trying to think of an excuse to pacify her. "I went to Asheville, to see a friend of mine from college. Then I drove by the Lodge." His hand was shaking as he lifted the glass to his mouth again. What had happened at the Lodge only a short while ago now seemed as vague and strange as an unsettling, half-remembered dream. He felt jittery and irritable, and all he could see in his mind was that open doorway, and beyond it the magnificence of the Lodge. "Where's Katt?" He'd noted that her pink Maserati was missing from the garage.

"She's driven into Asheville, too. Sometimes she has lunch with friends."

"So it's all right for her to leave, but *I* can't. Right?"

"I can't understand your comings and goings," she said, watching him carefully. "You say you drove by the Lodge? Why?"

"Jesus! What is this, an inquisition? Yes, I drove by the Lodge. No special reason. I saw Boone over there, too. He was prowling around inside with a flashlight."

Margaret turned her attention to the small flames that flickered in the hearth. "He loves the Lodge," she told him. "He's said so a hundred times. He goes inside to walk the hallways. But I've warned him about the Lodge, Rix. I've told him . . . not to trust the Lodge *too* much."

Rix finished his drink and put the glass aside. "Not to trust it? What do you mean?"

"I meant what I said," she replied evenly. "I've warned him that someday . . . someday the Lodge is not going to let him come out again."

"The Lodge isn't alive," Rix said—but he recalled the imagined aromas and sounds, the faint whisper of his own name like someone beckoning him in, the dark form that had moved near the marble fountain. What would have happened, he wondered, if he had continued into the Lodge? Would that door have swung shut behind him? Would the rooms have lengthened and twisted crazily out of shape, as they had when he was a child?

She sat for a moment as if she hadn't heard. Then she said softly, "I loved the Lodge, too. Walen and I lived there during Erik's last days. That was a terrible time, but still . . . I thought the Lodge was the most beautiful house on earth. Walen warned me not to go off alone in the Lodge, but I was a stupid, headstrong girl. I decided to explore it by myself. I went from one exquisite room to the next. I followed corridors that seemed to go on for miles. I took stairways that I'd never seen before—and never saw again." She looked up from the fire at him. "I was lost for ten hours, and I've never been so frightened in my life. It must have been awful for you, wandering in the dark. If Edwin hadn't found you . . . God only knows what might've happened."

"It's a miracle I didn't break my neck on a staircase," Rix said.

"Not only that. No . . . not only that." She paused, as if trying to decide whether to continue or not. When she spoke again, her voice was pitched very low. "Erik was always building onto the Lodge. The work stopped not because the job was finished—but because the workmen wouldn't complete it."

"Why? Wasn't he paying them enough?"

"Oh, he was paying them, all right," she said. "Paying them triple wages. But Walen told me they stopped because they were afraid. One day before Walen and I were married, thirty workmen went into the Lodge. Twenty-eight came back out. The other two . . . well, the other two did not. And never did. I've always thought that, somehow, the Lodge would not let them go."

Rix had never heard his mother talk this way about Usher's Lodge. It both unnerved and fascinated him. "Why did you and Dad decide to leave the Lodge after Erik died?"

"Because it's just too big. And I never got over that feeling of being lost in there, almost . . . as if I were at the Lodge's mercy. Besides, the Lodge is unsteady. I've felt the floors shake under my feet there. At the center of the house, the walls are cracking." She was nervously fingering the rings on her hands. "We didn't brick in the windows because of the birds, Rix; we bricked them in because they kept shattering. Over the years, every window in the Lodge has exploded outward. Why that is, I don't know. I just know . . . I dreaded thunderstorms when we lived there. Thunderstorms, particularly violent ones, when thunder shook the house, scared me to death. It was during those that most of the windows blew out."

Thunderstorms, Rix thought. He remembered Ludlow's fear of them from Nora's diary, and Nora's perception of the Lodge trembling around her. Erik had said the Lodge was built in an area that was prone to earthquakes. Could severe thunderstorms, Rix wondered, actually be *triggering* quakes?

"I think Boone's love of the Lodge is a dangerous infatuation," Margaret said. "He's been after me lately to have the electricity turned on again in there. It wouldn't surprise me if he actually wanted to move into the Lodge." She hesitated, and Rix saw dismay pass over her face. "I've always thought that for some reason the Lodge was meant to *attract* thunder and lightning, with all those rods and tall spires on the roof. When a storm comes over the mountains, it seems to be drawn right to that house." She said it with a hint of revulsion. "If the thunder is loud enough, it almost shakes the Gatehouse to pieces."

"There was an earthquake around here in 1892 or 1893, wasn't there? Didn't it damage the Lodge?"

She looked at him questioningly, as if she wondered where he got his information, but then she said, "I don't know, but I wouldn't be surprised. I was sitting right in this room four years ago, when most of the windows on the north side of the house exploded. One of the servants had to be taken to a hospital. Cass was cut on the arm. And I've been in the dining room several times when the plates trembled on the table. So perhaps we do have tremors from time to time—though it's nothing like living in the Lodge at the height of a thunderstorm."

"The windows on the north side?" Rix walked across the room to the north-facing picture window and pulled aside the curtain. He was facing Briartop Mountain and the Lodge. "I never heard about that."

"After it happened, we never discussed it among ourselves. Walen said it was a freak thing—something to do with air pressure, or a jet breaking the sound barrier or something. The rain got in and made an awful mess, I remember."

Rix turned toward her. "Did that happen during a thunderstorm, too?"

"Yes, it did. There was glass all over the rug, and I'm lucky it didn't put my eyes out when the window blew in."

"The windows blew *inward*?" he asked, and she nodded. Earthquakes, thunderstorms, and the Lodge, he mused—was there a connection between them? She'd said that the Lodge's windows exploded *outward.* That seemed to suggest a disturbance in the air, rather than a quake—maybe a shockwave, he thought. But a shockwave from *what?*

"I'm going to tell you something I've never told a living soul," Margaret said. She peered into the fire, avoiding his gaze. "With all my heart, I despise Usherland."

It was spoken with such conviction that Rix couldn't reply. All his life, he'd assumed that his mother gloried in the grandeur of Usherland, that she'd rather live nowhere else on earth. "At first," she continued, "I thought Usherland was the most beautiful place in the world. Perhaps it is. I loved Walen when I married him. I still do. Oh, he's always been a loner; he doesn't really need anyone, and I understand that. But before Erik passed his scepter to Walen, your father was a carefree, happy young man. I saw him the afternoon he came down from Erik's Quiet Room with that cane clenched in his hand. I swear to you, he looked as if he'd aged ten years. He locked himself in his study for three days and nights, and on the fourth morning he came out, because Erik had died in the night." She lifted her chin, and her glassy eyes met Rix's. "From that time on, Walen was different. He didn't smile anymore. He turned his entire life into his work." She shrugged. "But I hung on. What else could I do? Having you children gave me something to occupy my time."

"And you blame Usherland for changing Dad?"

"Before that scepter was passed, your father and I took vacations. We went to Paris, to the French Riviera, to Madrid and Rio de Janeiro. But after Walen became the master of Usherland, he refused to leave it. There was always the business to answer to. Usherland had seized both of us, made us into prisoners. These"— she motioned wanly at the walls—"are our gilded bars. The time is coming," she said, "when that scepter will be passed again. I pity the one who accepts it. You others will be free, to lead your lives as you please. I hope both of you live them very far away from Usherland." She sighed deeply and without strength, as if released from a great burden. Rix came over to stand beside her. She looked frail and tired, an old woman with a strained, overly made-up face. Rix felt she wouldn't live very long after Walen's death. Everything she was, her total identity, was enmeshed in Usherland. Katt would of course insist that she stay here, but Margaret's life had been lived as a decoration in the house of Walen Usher.

He felt an overwhelming surge of pity for her. How could it be,

251

he wondered, that one's own parents were often the most distant strangers? He leaned over to kiss her cheek.

She shifted uncomfortably, and turned her face away. "Don't. You smell like bourbon."

Rix stopped, and straightened up until his back was rigid.

Their silence was interrupted by a light tapping on the door. "What is it?" Rix said curtly.

The doors slid open. A maid peered tentatively in. "Mrs. Usher? The gentlemen would like to speak with you, ma'am."

"Send them in," Margaret told her, and Rix saw a transformation come over his mother as suddenly as if a switch had been thrown in her head. She rose from her chair and turned to greet her visitors with the smooth, gliding motion of a practiced hostess, her eyes bright and her smile turned to full incandescence.

The uniformed man that Margaret had identified as General McVair—heavyset, craggy-featured, with close-cropped gray sideburns and small eyes as powerful as pale blue laser beams—came into the living room. He was followed by Meredith, from the armaments plant. Meredith wore a dark blue vested suit, and had short blond hair flecked with gray. Aviator-style sunglasses obscured his eyes. Handcuffed to his left wrist was a black briefcase.

" 'Scuse us, please," General McVair said, with a deep-fried Southern accent that sounded, to Rix's ear, highly exaggerated. "Miz Usher, I wanted you to know we were on our way. Thank you for your hospitality."

"You're ever so welcome, General. I know Walen appreciates your visits."

"Well, I'm sorry to intrude at a time like this, but I'm afraid business is business." His eyes moved from her to Rix.

"Oh, pardon me. I don't think you've met our youngest son. Rix, this is General McVair—I'm sorry, but I don't know your Christian name." She fluttered her hands helplessly.

"Call me Bert. All my friends do." He shook Rix's hand with a grip that threatened to grind Rix's knuckles together. Rix squeezed back just as hard, and a look passed between them like two wary animals sizing each other up. "I expect you know Mr. Meredith?"

"We've never met." Meredith's voice was soft and reserved, and his mouth twisted like a gray worm when he spoke. He didn't offer his hand.

McVair seemed to examine Rix's face right down to the pores on his skin. "You favor your father," he decided. "Got the same

252

nose and hair. Your dad and I go back a long way. Saved my skin during Korea, when he sold us about ten thousand incendiary devices that were jim-dandies. Of course, anything your dad's business cooks up is worth its weight in gold." He smiled broadly, showing large, even teeth. "Make that *platinum*, times bein' what they are."

Rix nodded toward the briefcase Meredith held. "Working on something new?"

"The company is, yes," Meredith replied.

"Mind if I ask what it is?"

"I'm sorry. It's classified."

Walen's final project? Rix wondered. Pendulum? He smiled at the general. "Can't even give me a hint?"

"Not without you signin' a lot of papers and goin' through a big long security check, young fella." McVair returned the smile. "Some folks we'd rather not mention sure would like to get a look at it."

Meredith glanced at his wristwatch. "General, we've got to be getting back to the plant now. Mrs. Usher, it was good seeing you again. A pleasure to meet you, Mr. Usher."

Rix let them get to the door, then he tried a shot in the dark. "What's Pendulum going to do for you, General?"

Both men stopped as if they'd run into a glass wall. McVair turned, still smiling, though his eyes were cold and wary. Meredith's face was impassive. "What say, son?" McVair asked.

"Pendulum," Rix replied. "That's the name of my father's last project, isn't it? I'm curious to know exactly what it is, and how the Pentagon's going to use it." He suddenly realized that he'd seen a face very similar to McVair's before: the overfed, florid face of the cop who'd called him a "fuckin' hippie" before the baton had cracked down against Rix's skull. They were the same breed of animal. "Pendulum," he repeated, as McVair stared at him. "Now that's a name to conjure with, isn't it?" He smiled tightly, his cheek muscles aching. He had a dizzying sensation of being out of control, but he didn't give a damn. These two men represented everything he detested about being an Usher. "Let's see now, what can it be? A nuclear missile that homes in on an infant's heartbeat? Time-release capsules of plague virus?"

"Rix!" Margaret hissed, her face contorted.

"Nerve gas, that's it!" Rix said. "Or something that melts a person's bones like jelly. Am I getting warm, General!"

253

McVair's smile hung by a lip. Meredith urged softly, "I believe we should go now."

"Oh, not yet!" Rix said, determined to push it to the limit. He took two steps forward. "We're just beginning to understand each other, aren't we?"

Meredith grasped the general's arm, but the other man quickly shrugged him off. "I've heard a lot about you, boy," McVair said calmly. "You're the one who got his noggin busted at that so-called peace rally and had your face spread all over the newspapers. Well, let me tell *you* something. Your dad is a patriot, and if it wasn't for men like him, we'd be down on our knees beggin' the Russians not to lop off our heads! It takes more brains to build military deterrents than it does to go marchin' in hippie parades! You may have cut your hair, but it must've grown clear through your brain!" He glanced at Margaret. "I regret this outburst, ma'am. Good afternoon to you." He touched the brim of his cap and quickly followed Meredith out of the room.

Rix started to go after them, ready to continue the argument. Margaret said, "Don't you dare!" and he stopped at the door.

She came toward him like a thundercloud. "I hope you're proud!" she rasped, her eyes wide. "Oh, I hope you're feeling like the king of the world! Have you lost your mind?"

"I was expressing my opinion."

"God save us from your opinions, then! I thought I taught you good manners!"

Rix couldn't hold back a short, sharp laugh. "Manners?" he said incredulously. "Jesus Christ! Where's your soul? Is it covered over with white silk and diamond necklaces? That bastard was walking out of here with another killing machine that *my* father dreamed up!"

Margaret said stiffly, "I think you'd better go to your room, young man."

A strangled scream caught in his throat. Couldn't she understand? Couldn't *anyone* understand but him? No amount of fine clothes or furniture or food or expensive cars could alter the simple, terrible fact that the Ushers *fed* on death! "Better still," he said, "I'll get the hell out of here!" He whirled away from her and stalked out of the room with her shouts flung at his back.

Halfway up the stairs, he knew he'd let himself go too far. Pain rippled up the back of his neck and hammered at his temples. Colors and sounds began to sharpen. He staggered, had to stop to grip the

254

banister. It was going to be a bad one, he knew—and where could he hide? His heartbeat was beginning to deafen him. Jagged images tumbled through his mind: his emaciated father, dying in the Quiet Room; the Lodge's open door, leading into darkness; a shining silver circle with the face of a roaring lion; a skeleton with bloody eyeholes, swinging slowly in a doorway; Boone's distorted face saying "Peed your pants, didn't ya?; Sandra's hair floating in the bloody water . . .

His bones ached as if they were being pulled from the sockets. He stumbled up the stairs, heading toward Katt's Quiet Room. The skin on his palms sizzled on the banister.

In Katt's bedroom, Rix pulled open the closet door. The closet was large, with clothes hung from metal racks and a hundred pairs of shoes on wall shelves. He pushed the clothes away from the rear wall, as the pain increased and his eyes were almost blinded by the frenzy of colors. He felt wildly along the wall, sweat oozing down his face.

His fingers closed around a small knob, and he turned it frantically, praying that it wouldn't be locked.

It came open. Rix squeezed himself into a space as small as a coffin. The walls and floor were covered with thick foam rubber. When Rix pushed the door shut, all sounds—water thundering through pipes, the hiss and moan of the wind outside, the artillery-boom of a ticking clock—were dramatically softened. Still, the noise of his own heartbeat and breathing was inescapable. He moaned, clamped his hands over his ears, and curled into a tight ball on the floor.

The attack was worsening. Under his clothes, his flesh stung and sweated.

And, to Rix's horror, a sliver of light was entering beneath the door. Normal vision would have been unable to see it, but to Rix it pulsated like a white-hot ray of neon. The light's heat scorched his face; it became the blade of a sword that lengthened across the floor, quickly becoming sharper and brighter.

Rix turned his face away—and into the fierce red glare of what felt like a heat lamp. The light was reflecting off an object on a shelf just above his head. He put his hand up there—felt earplugs, a velvet mask with an elastic band, and a small metal box. Light was hitting the corner of the box, exploding like a nova. Rix slipped the mask over his eyes and waited, trembling, for the attack to fade or strengthen.

Over the booming of his heartbeat came a nightmarish, garbled sound that at first he didn't recognize. It steadily grew louder, and at last he knew what it was, and from where it came.

255

The Quiet Room.

It was his father's mirthless laughter.

Rix's spine bowed under the full weight of the attack, and when he cried out, his head almost blew apart.

30

—*New*—

The voice was as smooth as black velvet. It reached him in his sleep, probing delicately into his mind.

—*come home*—

He turned restlessly on his cot, entwined in the thin blanket.

—*come home*—

The Lodge oozed light that shimmered in gilded streaks on the lake's surface. The night was warm, scented with roses from the gardens. New was standing on the lakeshore, at the entrance to the bridge, and he watched the figures moving back and forth past the glowing windows. On the night breeze came a whisper of music—a full orchestra, playing, of all things, the kind of jumpy hoedown tune his pa had liked to listen to on the Asheville radio station.

—*come home*—

New cocked his head to one side. The music faded in and out. The Lodge was calling him. The beautiful, magical, fantastic Lodge wanted him, *needed* him. He blinked, trying to remember what his ma said about Usher's Lodge. Something bad, but now he couldn't remember exactly what it was, and the thought drifted off like the notes of music and the lights on the water.

Hooves clattered on stone. A coach led by four white horses was coming across the bridge. Its driver wore a long black coat and a top hat, and he flicked a whip over the horses to keep their pace crisp. When the coach drew closer to New, the driver smiled.

"Good evening," the man said. He wore white gloves, and there was a feather in the band of his hat. "You're expected, Master Newlan."

"I'm . . . expected . . . ?" He was asleep, he knew, in the cabin on Briartop Mountain. But everything looked so real; he touched the bridge's stone and felt its roughness beneath his fingers. The coachman was watching him like an old friend. New realized he was still wearing what he'd gone to bed in: his long woolen underwear and one of his pa's flannel shirts.

The coachman said patiently, "The landlord expects you, Master Newlan. He wants to welcome you home personally."

New shook his head. "I . . . don't understand."

"Climb in," the coachman said. "We're celebrating your homecoming—at long last."

"But . . . the Lodge isn't my home. I . . . live on Briartop Mountain. In a cabin, with my ma. I'm the man of the house."

"We know all that. It isn't important." He motioned with the handle of his whip toward the Lodge. "That can be your new home, if you like. You don't have to live on the mountain anymore. The landlord wants you to be comfortable, and to have everything you desire."

"The . . . landlord? Who's that?"

"The *landlord*," he repeated. His smile never faltered. "Oh, you know who the landlord is, Master Newlan. Come on now, he's waiting. Won't you join us?" The coach's door clicked open. Within were red satin seats and padding.

New approached the coach and ran his fingers over the ebony-painted wood. A sheen of dew came off. I'm asleep! he thought. This is only a dream! He looked back at the dark mass of Briartop, then at the glowing Lodge.

"Would you like to drive?" the coachman asked. "Come on, then. I'll help you up. The horses are easily handled."

He hesitated. Something evil lived alone in the Lodge, his ma had said. Something all alone, waiting in the dark. He remembered the Mountain King, and the old man's warning to stay away from the Lodge. But the Lodge wasn't dark now, and this was a dream. He was asleep in his bed, and safe. The coachman stretched out his hand. "Let me help you up."

What was inside that massive house? New wondered. Wouldn't it be all right to enter it in his dream? Just to see what it looked like inside?

The orchestral music swelled and faded. "That's right," the coachman said, though New didn't remember speaking.

New slowly reached up and grasped the man's hand. The coachman smoothly pulled him up, slid over, and gave him the reins. "The landlord's going to be pleased, Master Newlan. You'll see."

"Giddap," New said, and flicked the reins. The horses trotted

forward and maneuvered to turn the coach around. They started
. over the bridge, their hooves clopping on the stones. The coachman
put a gentle hand on his shoulder.

Before New, the bridge began to telescope outward, to lengthen
so that the Lodge receded in the distance. They had a long way to
travel, maybe a couple of miles or more, before they would reach
the front door. But that was all right, New decided. This was a dream,
and he was safe on Briartop Mountain. The coachman's hand was
reassuring on his shoulder. The Lodge isn't evil, New thought. It's
a beautiful palace, full of light and life. His mother had probably
lied to him about the Lodge, and that crazy old man on top of the
mountain didn't have a lick of sense in his head. How could the
Lodge be evil? he asked himself. It's a beautiful, magical place, and
if I want to, I can live there—

"Forever," the coachman said, and smiled.

The horses' hooves made a rhythmic, soothing cadence on the
stones. The long, long bridge continued to telescope, and at the end
of it was the brilliantly lighted Lodge, waiting for him, needing him.

"Faster," the coachman urged.

The horses picked up speed. New grinned, the wind whistling
past his ears.

And as if from a great distance, he heard someone shout, *No!*

New blinked. A freezing chill had suddenly passed over him.

The coachman's whip snapped. "Faster," he said. "*Faster!*"

New was listening. Something was wrong; he was trembling,
and something was wrong. The horses were going too fast, the coachman's hand was gripped hard into the meat of his shoulder, and then
a voice ripped through his mind with a power so intense it seemed
to strike him square in the forehead—

NO!

New was jolted hard, his head snapping backward. The horses
reared, straining against their traces—and then they distorted, changed,
whirled away like smoke. Beside him, the coachman fragmented
into pieces like dark wasps that snapped around his head before
they, too, vanished into threads of mist. The coach itself altered
shape—and in the next instant New was sitting inside the pickup
truck, with his hands on the wheel. The engine was running, and
the lights were on. New, wearing only what he'd gone to bed in,
was totally disoriented; when he looked over his shoulder he saw
that he'd driven the truck about fifty yards from the house.

The Mountain King, his single eye like a blazing emerald, hob-

258

bled into the range of the lights. He thrust his cane forward like a sword, and though the old man's mouth didn't move, New could hear the voice in his mind: *No! You won't go! I won't let you go down there!*

The engine was racing. New realized his foot was still pressed to the accelerator, yet the truck wasn't moving. He took his foot off; the truck shivered violently, and the engine rattled dead.

"New?" It was his mother, calling from the house. Then, her voice panic-stricken: "New, come back!" She began running toward the truck, fighting against a blast of cold wind.

The Mountain King stood firm, his coat billowing. The veins were standing out in his thin neck, and his eye was fixed on New with fierce determination.

Oh, Lord, New thought, I would've kept on driving, right down the mountain to the Lodge. It wasn't a dream . . . wasn't a dream at all . . .

He opened the door and started to get out of the truck.

And a black, huge shape leaped into the light, attacking the Mountain King from his blind side.

New shouted, "Look out!" But he was too late. The old man sensed movement and tried to whirl around, but the black panther was on him, clawing into his shoulders and slamming him to the ground. The cane spun past New and landed in the dirt. Greediguts bit into the back of the Mountain King's neck, the monster's eyes shining like moons in the headlights.

New leaped out of the truck. The old man was screaming as Greediguts flayed the flesh off his back. Rubies of blood sprayed up into the air. New looked for a weapon—a stick, a rock, anything!— and saw the gnarled cane lying a few feet away. He picked it up, and as his hand closed around it, an electric tingle coursed up his forearm. He ran toward the panther. It released the Mountain King and started to rise on its hind legs, the rattles on its serpentine tail chirring a warning.

New feinted. Greediguts swiped at him, missed. New leaped to one side and struck Greediguts across the triangular skull with all his strength.

There was a *crack*! that made his eardrums pop, and blue flame burst from the tip of the walking stick. New was knocked flat. The stench of charred hide reached him. Greediguts was spinning in a circle, snapping and clawing at empty air. Where the cane had struck, the animal's skin was burned raw red.

The stick had scorched New's hands. Flickers of blue flame danced up and down its length. Before New could recover and strike at the panther again, Greediguts leaped into the foliage. New heard it crashing away—and then it was gone.

As Myra reached her son, New was bending over the Mountain King. The old man's back and shoulders were mangled, the flesh peeled away to the bone. Deep tooth marks scored the back of his neck, and were bleeding profusely. "God Almighty!" Myra cried out when she saw the wounds.

The old man moaned. Myra couldn't believe that anything so torn up could still be alive. "Ma," New said urgently, "we've got to help him! He'll die if we don't!"

"Nothin' we can do. He's finished. Listen to him, he cain't hardly breathe!" She was looking around, terrified of the panther's return, and backing away from the old man.

"There's a clinic in Foxton," New said. "The doctors can do somethin' for him!"

She shook her head. "He's through. Ain't nobody can live, tore up like that."

New rose to his full height. "Help me put him in the back of the truck."

"No! I ain't touchin' him!"

"Ma," he said firmly. He wanted her to stop moving away, before she broke and ran. "*Stop.*" He'd said it so sharply he flinched at the sound of his own voice.

Myra obeyed. She stood motionlessly, her mouth half open, her eyes beginning to glaze over. She looked like a statue, only her brown hair moving, blowing around her shoulders.

"You're gonna help me put him in the back of the truck." New unhinged the tailgate and let it drop open. "Pick up his arms, and I'll get his legs."

Still she hesitated.

"*Do it,*" he said, and again he heard—and felt—the icy force in his voice.

Myra lifted the Mountain King's upper body as New held his legs. He weighed about as much as a good-sized fireplace log. Together they got him in the back of the truck. Myra, who seemed to be lost in some kind of a trance, stared at the blood on her hands.

"We need some blankets for him, Ma. Would you get a couple from the house?"

260

She blinked, wiped her hands on her thighs, and shook her head. "No . . . blankets. Not gonna . . . get my good blankets all . . . bloody."

"Go get 'em," New told her. "Hurry!" His green eyes were fierce. Myra started to speak again—but the words froze in her throat. Blankets, she thought. Blankets got to get blankets. It suddenly seemed to her that fetching blankets from the cabin to cover the old man was the reason for her entire life. She could think of nothing but the blankets; nothing mattered in the world but bringing them from the house.

"*Run*," New told her.

She ran.

New rubbed a throbbing spot at his left temple, just above the ear. His entire body felt bruised and stretched. He had formed in his mind an image of his mother doing what he'd told her, just as he'd formed the glowing blue wall of stones that had protected him from Greediguts. She had obeyed his mental commands with just a quicksilver flicker of hesitation. This was a different element of the magic that had begun with the knife in the thorns, New realized. He had commanded her with his mind, and it had been *easy*—as easy as shouting *boo!* at a squirrel and knowing it would flee.

Whatever the magic was inside him—witchcraft, black or white—it was getting stronger.

The panther might've torn the old man's head off if he hadn't attacked with the stick, New thought. He held the stick up, examining it. There was the smell of brimstone about it. What kind of walking stick was it that looked like an old dead limb by the side of the road, but could spit fire?

Magic. There was magic in him, and in the Mountain King, too. There was magic of a different nature in Greediguts and the Pumpkin Man—and yes, in the Lodge as well. His dream had been so real; if it had been uninterrupted, might he have driven the pickup truck—like a black coach crossing a long bridge—right down to the Lodge?

The Mountain King stirred. "New," he whispered hoarsely. He struggled to form words, his gashed face lying in a pool of blood. "Don't . . . let it win . . . " His voice trailed weakly off, and his single eye stared vacantly.

Myra was coming, running with three thin blankets in her arms.

The silken voice crept into his mind, from nowhere and everywhere, and it sounded stronger than ever before, more confident, more darkly eager:

—come home—

Something in the Lodge, he knew, was trying to command him—just as he had so easily made his mother go for the blankets.

—come home—

He took them from her and quickly spread them across the old man's body. Her task done, she was breaking free again; she stepped back dazedly, as New slipped the stick in beside the old man and slammed the tailgate shut.

"Get in the truck, Ma. I'll drive us down."

"He's . . . finished, New. Ain't no . . . reason to . . ."

"Get in the truck."

Wordlessly, she did as he told her. As New slid under the wheel, Myra stared fixedly ahead, her arms wrapped around herself for warmth. New started the engine and put the truck in gear.

—New—

The voice shimmered and echoed through his head. He didn't know how much longer he could withstand its seductive pull. But one thing he did know: he was uncovering within himself layers of power, each stronger than the one before. Now, lifting the knife seemed like child's play to him. He was finding out that he could do things he'd never dreamed of before—and he liked the feeling. He liked it very, very much.

As they drove down Briartop, New glanced at his mother and thought very hard of making her fold her hands in her lap, just to see if she would. Her arms twitched.

When he looked at her again, she'd done what he wanted.

Except that her hands were folded as if in prayer. Her face was a blank mask but for her eyes—glittering, sunken, and very scared.

31

By the amber glow of a few dozen candles stuck in candelabras around the library, Rix was methodically going through the Usher documents. Books, letters, ledgers, and photo albums lay in stacks around the desk. He opened a mildewed volume under the light and saw that it was an account book, the figures and notations entered in strong, clear handwriting. It listed dates—from 1851 and 1852—and amounts of money paid to various creditors. The Brewston Gunpowder Works in Pittsburgh had received twelve thousand dollars. Uriah Hynd and Company of Chicago had been paid fifteen thousand dollars. The Hopewell Lead Casing Foundry had gotten ten thousand dollars of Hudson Usher's money. The closely spaced entries went on, page after page.

Rix felt off balance, his vision blurring. "Damn!" he said softly, and leaned against the desk with his head bowed until the dizziness passed. He was still weak from the attack, and had been in bed for most of the afternoon and evening. His outburst had been forgotten, or at least forgiven, by his mother: she'd had Cass serve him his dinner in bed.

But it wasn't only the lingering effects of the attack that gripped him with deep depression. It was what he'd found in Katt's Quiet Room, the object that was now hidden beneath his bed. Sick to death, he'd wanted to stay in his room during dinner to avoid looking into his sister's face.

What had *happened* to this family? Rix asked himself. What further depths of evil and self-destruction could there be? Boone's plans for an amusement park of freaks on Usher property had been repulsive enough, but somehow that was in character for Boone. What Katt was doing, though, was totally unexpected. Christ! Rix thought. Surely Walen didn't know about it! If he did find out, God help Katt!

Rix returned to his work. Searching through the remnants of past lives now seemed the only thing that could take his mind off the present. Rix followed the entries, noting which ones got most of the money. The gunpowder works was listed several times, for varying amounts. Not happy with Hopewell, Hudson had tried seven different lead-casing foundries. Even the servants' salaries were written down, right to the penny.

But Rix paused at the sixth notation for Uriah Hynd and Company. The amount listed was always fifteen thousand dollars—quite a sum, and even more than Hudson was paying for gunpowder. What did the company sell to him? Rix wondered. There was no indication as to what sort of business Uriah Hynd and Company was.

He came to the end of the account book. During 1851 and 1852, Uriah Hynd and Company had been paid fifteen thousand dollars on a total of nine separate occasions. It was the only company listed so many times. Whatever it had sold to Hudson was lost in the past. Rix put the book aside and began to dig to the bottom of another box.

He uncovered a newspaper, old and brittle, falling to pieces

263

even as he gently lifted it out. It was a copy of the *St. Louis Journal*, dated the tenth of October, 1871. The bold black headline blared, HUNDREDS DIE IN CHICAGO BLAZE; and below that, in smaller type: GREAT FIRE DECIMATES FRONTIER CITY; INTERVIEWS WITH SURVIVORS, PARTIAL LISTING OF DESTROYED BUILDINGS AND BUSINESSES.

Beneath the layers of headlines was an artist's rendering of the city in flames, as seen from the shore of Lake Michigan. The picture showed hundreds of people fleeing the conflagration. The *Journal* had compiled interviews with about twenty survivors found in a field hospital, and among them Rix recognized a familiar name: Righteous Jordan.

Rix spread the paper carefully out atop the desk, and sat down to read the woman's story. In an emotion-charged, often hysterical voice, Righteous Jordan told the writer what had happened on October 8, 1871. It was the same date, Rix remembered, as that on Cynthia Cordweiler Usher's tombstone.

As Rix read, several of the candles around him sparked and hissed. He could imagine the great city in flames, buildings exploding, whole rooftops lifting off in the hurricane of fire, the earth shuddering as tons of bricks slammed into the streets. Righteous Jordan was speaking from the dead, and as Rix listened he could hear the din of screams, cries to God, clatter of hooves on cobblestones, and alarm bells ringing. Chicago was burning. Righteous Jordan, along with Cynthia and thirteen-year-old Ludlow Usher, were fleeing before the flames in a careening coach driven by elderly Keil Bodane.

◆◆◆

"Lord God!" Righteous shrieked. "We gon' turn over!"

"Hush!" Cynthia commanded. A gust of hot wind had hit the coach broadside, making it pitch crazily. Keil was using his whip to keep the Arabians from rearing. "Keil's a good driver. He'll get us out of this."

A bedlam of bells rang out. Clybourne Street was snarled with other coaches, carriages, and wagons of all sizes. People were running, dragging sacks filled with belongings from Clybourne Row mansions. Ashes and cinders spun thickly through the air. The night had brightened like an eerie orange noon to the west, where the fire had started. Fireballs as big as steam engines hurtled across the sky, smashing into buildings and spreading the blaze faster than a man could run. Sitting beside his mother, with Righteous Jordan filling the seat before him, young Ludlow flinched at the reverberating explosions. Their force shook the ground, as if the entire city were trembling in its death agonies.

They had left everything behind but the clothes they wore. As the flames had neared the Chicago River, Cynthia had ordered her servants to bury in the yard the jewels, silver, and fine art collected in the white mansion she'd inherited from Alexander Hamilton Cordweiler. When the fireballs had started jumping the river, setting ablaze everything they touched, Cynthia told the servants to take the other coaches, carry whatever they pleased, and run. It was all too clear that the fire would not be sated with the Irish shanties and cowbarns—it was reaching out to engulf Clybourne Row with equal greed.

"I saw that fire comin' through the winders!" Righteous said. "I *knew* it wasn't gon' be stopped! Little ol' river wouldn't stop a fire like that, no sir!"

"Keil will get us safely to the harbor." Cynthia planned on boarding her private steam yacht and sailing out on Lake Michigan until the danger was over. "As soon as we break free of this traffic, Keil should be able to find a faster route."

"We're more than a mile from the lake," Ludlow said quietly. He looked at neither of them, instead peering out the window at the approaching wall of flames. His face glowed bright orange with reflected light, but his eyes were dark. "It's moving quickly, Mother. The wind's blowing too hard."

She squeezed his hand and managed a brave smile. "We're going to be fine, Ludlow. Stop that whimpering and squirming about, Righteous! You'll throw the coach over!"

Over the noise of confusion outside, they heard the crack of Keil's whip. "Go on, damn you!" he yelled. "Move out of the way!"

"We'll get there," Cynthia said, but uncertainty strained her voice. Something exploded perhaps a block or two away, and Ludlow gripped her hand so tightly the knuckles ground together.

The coach lurched ahead, stopped, and lurched violently again, moving amid a melee of other vehicles and struggling humanity. Where the streets intersected, crashed carriages were being hauled out of the way, people swarming frantically over the wreckage. Maddened horses bucked and kicked as cinders scorched their backs. The acrid, lung-burning smoke was getting thicker, and the fireballs roared overhead like cannon shots.

Finally breaking free of the crush, Keil Bodane turned the coach off Clybourne and onto Halsted Street, heading toward the waterfront. The Arabians responded with speed, their flanks singed by cinders. The streets were littered with burning debris. Bars had been broken into, and whiskey flowed in the gutters from staved-in barrels. Crazed people stopped to drink their fill until the whiskey caught fire and exploded in their faces. Other people ran at the coach, trying to grab hold, but Keil whipped the horses for more speed. A pistol was fired, the bullet shearing off a splinter of wood inches from Keil's knee.

And as Keil veered the coach around the corner of Halsted onto Grand Street, he was met by a wagon full of burning haybales, its team running wild and a charred corpse at the reins.

The Arabians hit the other horses with a force that snapped bones and threw Keil Bodane like a stone from a slingshot. The entire coach, still moving at breakneck speed, then crashed into both teams of horses and turned on its side, its gilded wheels shattering.

"God have mercy!" Righteous screamed—and then her face hit Ludlow's knee as the boy was wrenched from his seat. Cynthia was thrown violently to one side, her head crunching against the coach's intricate scrolled woodwork. As the coach slammed to the ground, it was dragged thirty more yards by the crippled Arabians. The burning haywagon careened onward, its team injured but still trying to escape the fire.

After the crash, as cinders pattered down on the cobblestones and the pall of smoke darkened, a few desperate men stole the three Arabians that could still stand. The fourth lay in the street, two legs broken. Near it was the body of Keil Bodane, whose skull had been crushed against a lamppost.

"Get out!" Cynthia ordered a sobbing Righteous Jordan. "Hurry! Climb up through the door!" Righteous, her front teeth knocked loose by Ludlow's knee and her face covered with blood, hauled herself through the coach door above her head, then leaned in again to help Cynthia up. Ludlow pulled himself out, a long gash across his forehead and his nose broken. His eyes were pewter pools of shock.

"Miz Usher! Miz Usher!" Righteous grasped the other woman's shoulders. The entire left side of Cynthia's face was turning purple and swelling rapidly. Blood leaked from both ears onto her black velvet jacket.

"I'm . . . all right." Her voice was slurred. "We've . . . got to get to the lake. Help me . . . get Ludlow to the lake."

266

"Mr. Bodane!" Righteous called—and then she saw his body lying in the street. His head had cracked open like a clay jug.

"Righteous." Cynthia gripped her maid's thick wrist. Her bloodshot left eye, Righteous saw with horror, was beginning to bulge from her face. "You . . . take care . . . of Ludlow," she said with an effort. "Get him to the lake. Luther . . . will know . . . what to do. Luther won't . . . let him die."

Righteous knew she was babbling about Luther Bodane, Keil's son, who'd stayed behind, this trip, to watch over Usherland. "We're all gon' get to the water," she said firmly, and helped Cynthia to the ground. Ludlow clambered off the coach; he stood staring numbly at Keil's corpse as other people hurried past, some of them stepping on the body.

Righteous asked Cynthia if she could walk, and Cynthia nodded. The injured eye wouldn't focus, the flesh around it blackening. Cinders hissed down on them, and Righteous crushed them out with her fingers when they sparked in her mistress's hair. "We got to go!" she called to the boy. "Got to get to the lake!"

His forehead bleeding badly, Ludlow followed as Righteous Jordan began to help Cynthia down the middle of Grand Street.

They joined the throngs who hobbled, staggered, stumbled, and ran toward Lake Michigan. A thunderous roar shook the street beneath them, and windows shattered like shotgun blasts as buildings collapsed only a block behind. Red-and-purple fireballs shrieked overhead. The crowds had gone mad; people were breaking into stores, looting whatever they could carry, from topcoats to violins. A woman on fire was dancing a crazy jig on the curbside, caught under the weight of seven or eight mink coats she'd just stolen. Someone threw her into the gutter, where she fell into a stream of running whiskey and was instantly incinerated. A naked man yelled, "Destruction! God's wrath on Chicago!"

Righteous's flesh was blistering. She spat out two teeth and kept right on going, pushing through the crowd, taking Ludlow's hand so he wouldn't be swept away. Over the noise of screaming and shouting, there was a sound like a thousand locomotives with their boilers about to blow. As Righteous looked back, huge sheets of flame leapt into the sky, the glare almost blinding her. Rooftops lifted into the air, spinning away out of sight. The earth trembled under the impact of crashing tons of brick. Ludlow was transfixed, staring at the conflagration behind them, tears running down his cheeks. She jerked him back to his senses and kept moving.

Cynthia Usher slipped off Righteous's shoulder, almost falling before Righteous could catch her.

"Mother!" Ludlow wailed through blistered lips. He clutched her waist, trying to keep her from falling, as bodies roughly shoved past them.

Ludlow looked up into his mother's distorted, hideously swollen face. She was smiling at him.

"My angel," she whispered, and touched his hair.

And then blood exploded from her nostrils and around the staring orb of her left eye. Ludlow was splattered. Righteous almost swooned, but held herself steady; she'd felt the life leave Cynthia Usher in a single sigh. She eased the corpse to the ground, pushing away people who staggered too close. "She gone," Righteous told the boy. "We got to go on ourselves."

Ludlow screamed, "No!" and threw himself across the body. When Righteous tried to pull him away, he attacked her savagely. She reared back her right fist and struck him squarely in the jaw, then caught him in her arms as he fell.

Carrying the moaning boy, Righteous fought toward the lake. By the time they'd reached the shore, their clothes were little more than smoking rags. People by the hundreds were immersed in the oily water. Boats were darting here and there, picking up swimmers. Most of the yachts had already been stolen from their slips, and those that remained were afire. Righteous went into the lake up to her neck, then wet Ludlow's face and hair to keep the cinders from burning him.

It was almost an hour before she lifted the boy into the hands of soldiers aboard a ferryboat, then climbed up herself. Ludlow, his clothing tattered and his face puffed with burns, stood at the railing, watching Chicago's destruction. When Righteous touched his arm, he pulled quickly away.

Lord God! she thought. She had realized, as she would tell a reporter in another few hours, the truth of the matter: with both his mother and father gone, Ludlow Usher at thirteen was in control of everything—the estate, the family business, all the other businesses that had belonged to Mr. Cordweiler. He was, Righteous knew, the wealthiest thirteen-year-old boy in the world.

She watched him, waiting for him to cry, but he never did. He held his spine as stiff as an iron bar, his attention riveted to the fire on shore.

The soldiers were helping a man and woman aboard from a

rowboat. Both were well dressed, the man in a dark suit with a diamond stickpin, the woman in the dirty remnants of a red ballroom gown. The man regarded Righteous and Ludlow and turned to one of the soldiers. "Sir," he inquired, "must we share this vessel with niggers and tramps?"

◆ ◆ ◆

Rix came to the end of Righteous Jordan's story. He glanced over the other articles. Chicago had burned for twenty-four hours, and the fire had destroyed more than seventeen thousand buildings. One hundred thousand people were left homeless. The flames had been helped along by at least nine firebugs. The firemen had been slow to react that night because they were so tired; during the week before the Great Fire, they'd answered more than forty alarms.

He looked up at the portrait of the brooding Ludlow Usher. Thirteen years old and one foot in hell, Rix thought. How had he kept his sanity?

Rix had found the answer to Dunstan's question about the death of Cynthia Usher. Tomorrow he would take this newspaper to him. But the cane—how and when had Ludlow gotten the cane back from Randolph Tigré?

Printed in small type in several columns on the next page was a listing of businesses that had been destroyed. They were not in alphabetical order, and Rix had to read patiently before he found what he was looking for.

Uriah Hynd and Company, Grocers.

A *grocery* store? Rix thought. Hudson Usher was spending fifteen thousand dollars a whack on groceries from Chicago? Why didn't he simply buy his groceries in Asheville?

Rix carefully folded the paper and rose from his chair. For now, the questions would have to wait. He blew out all the candles except those in one candelabra, and used it to light his way upstairs.

And when he opened the door to his room, the golden light illuminated Puddin' Usher—lying languidly in his bed, waiting for him.

She smiled sleepily, yawned, and stretched. Her breasts peeked over the top of the sheet. "You been a long time," she said huskily. "Thought you'd never come to bed."

He closed the door, alarmed that someone might hear. "You'd better get out. Boone will—"

269

"Boone ain't here." Her eyes challenged him. "Ol' Boonie's long gone to his club. You ain't gonna turn me down this time, are you?"

"Puddin'," Rix said as he put the folded paper on his dresser, "I thought you understood what I told you. I can't—"

She sat up and let the sheet drop away. Her breasts were fully exposed, and she wet her lips with her tongue. "See how much I need you?" she asked. "Now don't tell me you don't want some of it."

The candlelight flattered her, made her look less harsh and more vulnerable. Rix's body was responding. She stretched like a cat. "You're not *afraid* of Boone, are you?" she asked teasingly.

He shook his head. He couldn't take his eyes off her.

"Boone says you can't keep a woman," she said. "He says you're a half-step short of bein' queer."

Rix set the candelabra down.

"Come on," she insisted. "Let's see what you can do."

He started to tell her to get out; he wanted to say it, but suddenly he couldn't make himself. A thin smile had begun to play around the edges of his mouth. Why not? he thought. It would be wrong, yes—but hadn't it been wrong for Boone to treat him like dirt all these years, to crow and caper and plot all kinds of nasty little tricks? This was the chance to pay him back that Rix had been waiting for. He brushed away the small voice inside him that urged him not to.

"Why not?" he said, and his voice sounded like that of someone he didn't know.

"Good." She kicked off the sheets, her body wantonly exposed to him. "Blow out them candles, then, and let's get to it."

32

Boone was drunk on Chivas Regal, and he'd lost seven thousand dollars in two fleeting hours at the country club poker table. It was dawning on him that his old buddies were conspiring to cheat him. As they laughed and clapped him on the back and lit his Dunhill cigars for him, Boone silently mulled over how he would destroy them.

He took his red Ferrari through the quiet streets of Foxton at almost ninety, whipping past an old battered pickup truck coming from the opposite direction. For spite, Boone rammed his hand down on the horn; it blared several notes of "Dixie." As the car roared out of Foxton, Boone sank his foot to the floor and the Ferrari leaped forward like a rocket.

He would buy the Asheville Heights Country Club, he'd decided. For whatever price. Maybe the board members would put up a statue of him in the foyer. The least they could do was to name the club after him. In a few days he was going to be one of the richest men in the world. Dad can't hold on much longer, he thought—but he had mixed emotions, because he loved the old man. Walen had taught him how to be tough; he'd taught him that no one could be trusted, that everybody was out to make a killing. They'd had long talks, when Boone was younger, about how money was what made a man a success. Money is power, Walen had told him many times; without it, the world will run over you like a steamroller. He'd pointed to Rix as an example of what Boone should avoid: Rix, Walen said, was a dreamy, unrealistic coward who would never amount to his weight in shit. It had pleased Walen for Boone to beat on his younger brother.

Still, there was something about Rix that scared Boone. Something deep, something hidden away from everyone. He'd seen it spark in Rix's eyes several times in the last few days: a hatred and bitterness so twisted it could commit murder. And Rix had tried to stab him in the dining room. Boone regretted not having smashed his teeth out right in front of everyone. Rix would've gone crying to his room.

Boone slid the Ferrari around curves, barely tapping the brakes, grinning at the thrill of speed. Katt thought she was going to get everything, he knew—but she was dead wrong. He had Puddin' to thank for Katt's downfall: the last time Katt had jaunted off to New York for a weekend, Puddin' had rummaged through her closet for a dress to wear and had discovered the entrance to her Quiet Room. Puddin' had shown him what she'd found in there, and Boone had taken it straight to Walen, who at that time hadn't yet sealed himself in his own Quiet Room. Boone would never forget the old man's expression of shock and disgust. Prob'ly buyin' the shit in Asheville, Boone had said. Prob'ly spendin' a damned fortune on it, too.

Walen had told him to put it back where it had been, and that he would take care of Katt in his own way.

Boone knew what that meant. Dad might be stringing her along now, but she'd been cut out of the inheritance.

Rain began to patter on the windshield. Boone quickly slowed down. He wasn't so drunk he wanted to end up as a bloody smear on the road. As he rounded the bend and drove toward Usherland's gates, he hit the switch under the dashboard and the gates opened smoothly for him, then closed again when he'd passed through.

He couldn't bear to return to that room where Puddin' lay sleeping. She thinks she's got me by the balls! he snorted. Well, after he got his hands on all those billions, he could have his choice of beautiful women. Puddin' wasn't as pretty as she used to be. The beauty-queen gilt had rubbed off, and underneath was pure country cardboard. He drove slowly past the dark Gatehouse and followed the road toward the Lodge.

What a showplace the Lodge was going to be when he moved in! He was going to throw out all those damned dusty antiques and suits of armor and shit, put some nice new furniture in. There would be a whole floor full of video games, and in the basement he'd have grottoes of fake rock, where colored lights played on steamy water. He'd have a master bedroom with red walls and a huge bed draped in black fur, and there would be a mirrored ceiling. There would be no end to the parties, and if he wanted to, he'd ride his horses right up and down the corridors.

Boone often went to the Lodge to walk in it, visualizing how it would look once he lived there. Sometimes he told Puddin' and his mother that he was going to the stables, but instead he'd go to the Lodge. It was the most beautiful place in the world, he thought. Its majesty and immensity sometimes almost made him cry; and in the silence of the Lodge he could sit in an overstuffed chair and know that soon—very soon—all of it would belong to *him*.

He'd never feared the Lodge. The Lodge loved him, too, and wanted him as its master. In the dreams he'd been having for the past few months, he'd seen the Lodge aflame with lights, and figures drifting past the windows as they would at the party Boone planned to give as soon as he moved in. Lately the dreams had been coming almost every night, and in some of them he'd heard his name called by a soft, beckoning voice that had brought him up from sleep in eager exhilaration.

The Lodge wanted him. The Lodge was waiting to embrace him, and he would love it all the days of his life.

Boone drove across the bridge and parked under the porte-cochere.

Then he got out in the misty rain, stumbled around to the trunk, unlocked it, and retrieved his bull's-eye lantern and a map he'd made of the first floor. He clicked the lantern on and shone it up the steps.

The Lodge's front entrance was open. Several times he'd come out here before and found the door wide open. He'd mentioned it to Edwin, who'd promised to keep an eye on the place. There was little danger of someone breaking into the Lodge, Boone knew. Not with all those stories about black panthers and the Pumpkin Man roaming near the estate. Boone's guess was that the Lodge was shifting, and the door wouldn't shut properly anymore. From the looks of the deep cracks in the walls, the house was under a lot of internal pressure. Reinforcing the Lodge would have top priority when Boone took over.

He followed the beam of his lantern into the Lodge. At once he felt giddy with pleasure; he was back in his favorite world again, and he almost shouted with joy. He moved through the foyer, past the massive fountain with its carved statues, and into a cavernous reception area with royal blue sofas and chairs, mahogany tables, and flags from every country in the world hanging from the ceiling. The silence in the Lodge was complete as Boone continued through a series of huge rooms. Entering a winding corridor, Boone followed it for perhaps forty yards and then opened a large sliding door. Beyond it was the main study, and Boone's flashlight picked out familiar sights: several black leather chairs arranged around a low rosewood coffee table, a dark slab of a desk with lion's heads carved into it, a rug made from the hides of polar bears, and shelves filled with a variety of decanters and glasses. A short stairway led down to a door that Boone had found was securely locked. He crossed the room to the fireplace of black marble; the charred remnants of the last fire he'd lit in here still cluttered the hearth. Beside it was a brass barrel of wood left over from Erik's day, and some newspapers Boone had recently brought in. He spent a few minutes getting new pieces of wood arranged in the hearth—banged his head against the marble and cursed drunkenly—and then stuffed paper under it, touched his cigar lighter's flame to it, and stepped back as the fire quickly grew. The old, dried-out wood burned fiercely. The room took on a festive glow. Boone put his lantern aside and went to the shelves.

He'd finished off some damned fine whiskey the last time he was here at night. He sniffed at several decanters before the delicious aroma of cognac filled his nostrils; with a satisfied grunt, he poured himself a glassful and then sat down behind the desk. Going down, the stuff was as mellow as melted gold. He might sleep here tonight, he thought. Just pull up a chair in front of the fire, to help cut the chill, and he'd be fine. He thought of old Erik sitting at this desk, signing important papers. He and Erik would've gotten along just dandy, he was sure. They would've respected each other.

Boone drank his cognac and listened to the fire burn. He felt at peace here, safe and secure. He smelled woodsmoke instead of his father's decay. How much longer he could stand living in the Gatehouse, he didn't know. Sipping the last of the fragrant cognac in his glass, Boone paused. He put the glass down and cocked his head to one side.

Lying on the coffee table, next to a large cigar box, was something that hadn't been there this afternoon.

It was a bulky book, trimmed in gold. Boone stood up and went over to it, playing his fingers across the fine leather. He took it nearer the fireplace and opened it.

Inside were old photographs glued to the pages. Boone knew Erik had loved pictures; walls of the Lodge's first floor were covered with photographs from Erik's time. But what *kind* of photographs these were quickly became apparent. Boone's stomach clenched involuntarily.

They were pictures of corpses.

Soldiers, Boone realized. Frozen in every position of death. They were pictures taken on the battlefield, in field hospitals and morgues, closeups of soldiers tangled in barbed wire or blown apart at the bottom of muddy trenches, bodies almost denuded of flesh, ripped to pieces by land mines or grenades, crushed into the earth by trucks or tanks. As far as Boone could tell from the uniforms and the backgrounds, they were of World War I vintage. Another series of pictures showed decapitated bodies, followed by heads on slabs. Boone stared at death in all its grisly forms, and though the fire was strong and warm, he felt his skin crawling.

The book held several hundred pictures. Some of them, separated from the glue, drifted down around Boone's feet. Erik had loved pictures, Boone thought. And maybe these were the kind of pictures he loved the best.

Something slammed elsewhere in the Lodge, making Boone jump. A door, he thought, his mental processes sluggish. Did somebody slam a door?

And then it came to him with chilling, sobering clarity: the front door had slammed shut.

274

Boone stood very still, listening. Mutilated corpses with the faces of young boys stared up at him. Boone dropped the book on the floor and stepped away from it, wiping his hands on his pants. Then he took his lantern and went out into the corridor.

It seemed much colder now in the Lodge; he could see the faint plume of his breath, curling from his mouth. He retraced his steps along the corridor.

Then, abruptly, he stopped.

"No," he whispered, and his voice echoed around him *no no no no . . .*

His light had fallen upon a wall of rough stones, where no wall had been when he'd come through the corridor before. He approached it, touched it; the stones were cold, and very real. Stunned, he retreated and tried to think how he'd gotten turned around. Careful, Boonie old boy, he told himself. There's no problem. Just get back to Erik's study, right?

He walked to the study's open doors and stopped on the threshold. His light shone into the interior of the Lodge's elevator. The study was gone.

He looked into the room across the corridor, and found that it was a music room with a white grand piano, a pump organ, and a harpsichord. On the ceiling was a painted blue sky with fleecy clouds. In all the times Boone had come into the Lodge and strode down this corridor, he'd never before seen this chamber. The next arched doorway led into a large parlor decorated with feminine frills and painted pale pink. His map, which shook as he held it close to the light, showed no such room on the first floor. Shaken, Boone stood outside the elevator where the study had been a few minutes before. Okay, he said mentally, I've just gotten a little bit fucked-up here. No problem. I'll keep walkin' until I find a room that looks familiar, and then I'll figure my way out.

The corridor led him on, twisting and turning, branching off to each side, passing staircases that vanished beyond the range of the light. Boone saw no room he recognized through any of the dozens of doorways. His palms were sweating, his face frozen into a crooked, disbelieving grin. He was dizzy and disoriented. What had happened to Rix could happen to him, too, he realized. Oh Jesus Christ! he thought. I've got to find the way out!

And with a final twist to the left, the corridor ended at a wide staircase that ascended into darkness.

Boone examined the map. He'd found ten staircases in his explorations of the Lodge's first floor, but he'd never seen this one before. If he didn't know where he was, the map was useless. I'll go back, he decided. I'll sit my ass down in front of that elevator and wait for somebody to see my car out front. No problem.

Boone had taken only a few steps when his legs locked. He gave a soft, scared whimper.

His path was blocked by another wall, adorned with old framed pictures of the Lodge.

He laughed nervously, a strangled sound that echoed faintly around him. That wall hadn't been there before. The corridor had sealed itself behind his back. But the pictures indicated the wall might have been there for fifty years.

The air was turning bitterly cold, and Boone could see his breath whirling before him. He guided the light over the wall. Atop the picture frames was a thin layer of dust. He hammered at the bricks with his fist, but, like the rest of the Lodge, the wall had been built to endure for generations.

Now he had no choice but to climb the stairs. Except, when he returned to the staircase, he found it had changed directions, and now *descended* into the Lodge's depths.

He gripped the banister and squeezed his eyes shut. When he opened them again, the stairs still led downward. Lost! he thought, tottering on the edge of panic. Lost like a rat in a maze! But the maze was being changed as he went along, Boone realized. Was this what it had been like for Rix, a long time ago? The corridors blocking themselves, staircases changing direction, rooms shifting from one minute to the next?

Fear flared in his belly. I've got to get out! he screamed inwardly. The only way open to him was the staircase, and he started down it.

Boone's teeth chattered from the cold. The stairway curved into the darkness, and Boone gripped the banister tightly to keep from slipping as the angle of the steps steepened. At the bottom, his lantern illuminated walls and floor of rough granite, an archway into a corridor that angled off beyond the light's range. Dead electric bulbs were fixed to the walls; above them were smears of soot where torches had once been the sole source of light.

Boone knew he was on one of the uppermost basement levels. It was colder down here than at the top of the stairs—a bone-aching, fierce cold, unlike anything Boone had ever experienced. He couldn't stand it, and he decided he'd be better off upstairs; he started climbing up again, shaking with the cold.

After seven steps, his head suddenly bumped the ceiling. The staircase had come to an end.

"Oh Jesus," Boone croaked. Trapped! he thought wildly. The Lodge had sealed him up and he was trapped! "Help!" he shouted, and his voice cracked.

The Lodge's silence mocked him.

He slammed his fist against the ceiling. It isn't there! he thought. The damned thing can't be there! Tears stung his eyes, and as he stood trying to understand what was happening to him, he could sense the immense weight of the Lodge above him, like a huge, merciless beast.

"I love you," he whispered to the dark. Tears slipped down his cheeks, and froze on the point of his chin.

At the bottom of the stairs, Boone faced the corridor that led toward—what? he wondered. More stairs, hallways, and rooms that would shift and solidify behind his back? I can wait here until somebody finds me, he told himself. Sooner or later, somebody will get me out of here!

But he was freezing, and he knew he had to keep moving. Already his joints were stiffening, the breath rasping in his lungs. He had no choice but to enter the corridor, his light probing the darkness before him.

He'd gone perhaps twenty yards when he thought he could hear a faint throbbing—a distant rhythm, like the pulse of machinery. But there was no electricity—how could a machine be working? Farther along the winding corridor, Boone felt vibrations—slow and steady, like the beating of a massive heart—through the soles of his shoes. Whatever was working lay beneath him, on the level below.

His light fell on another archway, cut into the wall on his right. He was afraid to look over his shoulder, afraid that the way he'd come had closed itself behind him. And if that had happened, he would lose his mind. The Lodge was guiding him, he realized. Pushing him, manipulating him. Had it done the same to Rix?

He remembered why he and Rix had come into the Lodge: to play hide-and-seek with the Devil. He'd said it to scare his brother—but now something in the Lodge was playing hide-and-seek with *him*, and he knew that this game had turned deadly.

He went through the archway, and into an enormous chamber filled with beasts.

The light reflected off the eyes of lions, tigers, bears, cheetahs, pumas, panthers, zebras, antelopes. The room was full of them, frozen in postures of attack, packed closely together in an eerie menagerie. Their silent snarls seemed to be directed at Boone, who had realized after an initial shock that this was a storeroom filled with Erik's stuffed hunting trophies.

The room held hundreds of animals, their shadows scrawled on the walls by Boone's lantern. He backed away from them, and turned to get out.

But the archway was gone, blocked by stones, as if it had never been there at all.

Boone's knees almost buckled.

And from behind him came the rumble of something breathing.

He twisted around, stabbing in all directions with the light. Among the stuffed beasts, nothing moved.

"I'm Boone Usher!" he shouted, and the echoes *Usher Usher Usher* swirled around him in the frigid air.

A crouched tiger suddenly pitched forward and fell, its snarl rigid, its limbs still stiff. Behind it, something black caught the light before it darted away.

Boone began to sob. "I'm Boone Usher," he whispered. "Damn you, listen to me—" The tears froze beneath his eyes. He backed against the wall and slid down, crying softly, his nerves shattered. Another animal toppled over, followed by a third. Wetness spread at Boone's crotch; he huddled into a protective ball, shining the lantern straight ahead.

The noise of something breathing grew closer, coming from all directions at once.

And then a foul, icy breath touched Boone's cheek.

He twisted to one side, aiming the light.

A monstrous black panther with luminous golden-green eyes stood motionless, not five feet away. For an instant Boone thought it was another sawdust-stuffed trophy—but then its mouth slowly, slowly opened and a black forked tongue emerged to quiver in the air.

The panther was watching him. Across its skull was a raw red streak that looked like a burn.

Boone tried to scream, but no sound would squeeze out. He pressed his back against the stones, his face contorting with terror.

The panther settled on its haunches, its eyes never leaving his. There was a high rattling sound as its tail slowly moved back and forth.

Freezing tears gummed Boone's eyelids together. He began to laugh and wail alternately, as his terror split open and madness oozed out.

Silently the panther leaped.

It fastened its jaws around Boone's face and then clamped them together. The wall was splattered with his brains and blood, the lantern falling from Boone's hand to the floor. The panther dug its claws into Boone's shoulders, holding the writhing body down, and began to peel the flesh from Boone's head. Then it bit into Boone's throat, cutting off his voice in mid-squeal. It crunched into the ribcage, its fangs bursting through tissue and bone, until its snout found the beating heart. With a quick twist of its massive head, the panther wrenched Boone's heart from the chest cavity and devoured it with one shuddering gulp.

Steam rose from the corpse. The panther greedily lapped from a widening puddle of gore, then began ripping Boone's body into pieces and gnawing on the bones. Its eyes rolled back in its head with pleasure.

When it had consumed its fill, the monster turned away and, its belly distended with what had been Boone Usher, left the store-room through the archway less than three feet distant.

Six

---◆◆◆---

VALLEY
OF THE
SHADOW

33

Logan Bodane followed the beam of his flashlight, deep into the Usher woods.

It had been raining for the past half hour, but now only a fitful mist swirled past the light. The forest held a thick, wet, earthy odor. Raindrops pattered from overhead branches, and the wind stirred restlessly through the treetops.

Logan walked noiselessly along the riding trail, slowly sweeping his light from one side to the other. Soon he was amid the crumpled cages of the ruined zoo, and he continued to the place where the animal carcasses were hung. Most of them had been stripped to the bone by flies and ants, but three new ones—a fox and two squirrels—had been added recently. Beneath them, the blood from their slit throats had formed crusted pools.

The hardest part of it had been climbing the trees to tie the wires around branches so the carcasses would dangle well above the path. Ever since he was a little boy, Logan had been a good hunter. If there was anything in the world that set him apart from other folks, he thought wryly, it was his ability to track animals—in his own very special way.

Logan retreated a few yards off the path and sat down with his back against a boulder. He switched off his light and sat motionless in the dark, listening to the roving wind.

Last night he thought he'd heard the thing, coming through the brush toward the hanging bait. Then, less than twenty feet from him, it had suddenly stopped. Logan's senses had sharpened, and he'd caught the distinct smell of a predatory cat. But when nothing had moved again for more than thirty minutes, he'd turned on his light and seen that whatever it was had silently gone.

Maybe it had been Greediguts, maybe not, Logan told himself. If there really *was* such a thing. But if a monster panther did hunt the forests of Usherland, sooner or later it would be drawn here by the smell of blood and meat. Logan had come to this spot every night to wait for several hours, and had seen bobcat and fox tracks in the dirt, but never pawprints of anything as big as the panther was supposed to be.

Greediguts was the main reason Logan had decided to take this job. He'd been wanting to try his skill at finding the panther for a long time, and being invited to live at Usherland put him right in what was supposed to be the monster's territory. His only weapon was a knife with a serrated blade, which he kept in a leather sheath on his right ankle. If there was such a creature as Greediguts, and the panther did come this way, Logan knew he'd have to be fast, faster than ever before. But it was more of a challenge this way, and he had faith in his own very special talents.

It was time now. He began breathing slowly and rhythmically, pressing his back against the boulder. Through his flannel shirt he could feel the ridges and hollows of the rock, and he mentally commanded himself to become part of it, to merge flesh with stone. Slowly his pulse rate began to drop. He shivered once as his body temperature lowered, then he overcame that lack of concentration and willed himself to stay perfectly still. His breathing slowed until it was almost imperceptible. In his motionless face, Logan's pupils had dilated to the size of dimes. His heartbeat had all but stopped.

If anything roamed near, Logan might appear to be an irregular outcrop of rock. He could remain in his frozen posture for hours, if necessary, but could also leap to his feet within seconds if he desired.

A few days before, he'd stood in the garden watching Kattrina Usher walk from the Gatehouse to the garage. He liked the promise of her tight, sleek body, her rear moving suggestively in her pink jumpsuit. She was the best-looking woman he'd ever seen, worlds away from the Taylorville girls he'd sometimes gone out with. As she passed him, he'd said hello, but she'd looked at him distastefully, and for an instant Logan had felt like something that slithered from under a rock. Then she was gone, on along the garden path. Logan knew that look: she thought she was too good even to speak to him. He'd watched her go to the garage, and desire had burned like coals under his ribs. She was like Granddad Robert's dog Mutt, Logan thought in the silence of his trance; it had bothered him how Mutt used to avoid him, once even snapping at his offered hand. So it was a challenge to practice his talents on Mutt, to make the animal come to him wagging its tail and fawning before he'd bashed it in the head with a ball-peen hammer.

Logan had figured out which window was Kattrina's, and sometimes he stood beneath it, peering up. Edwin had caught him doing that yesterday afternoon, and had told him he was supposed to be working in the laundry. Edwin watched him all the time, and Logan knew Cass didn't like him worth shit. Edwin had said he was abusing their "relationship of trust"—whatever the fuck *that* meant—and not showing up for the various jobs he was supposed to do on the estate. Logan didn't care; he wasn't planning on staying around Usherland very much longer. This chief-of-staff shit was stifling his freedom; all he wanted was enough money to buy a new car and head off to California.

But maybe, Logan mused, before he left he might have to try his talents out on a person. Like Kattrina. He remembered that look, and it twisted his insides. He'd make her come to him, fawning and begging and wagging her tail. Or maybe he'd try them out on that Rix bastard. Make that arrogant son of a bitch put a pistol barrel between his teeth and pull the trigger, or cut his wrists open in the shower. That'd be worth looking forward to, as long as he didn't have to clean up the mess.

Animals like domestic dogs and cats were the easiest. Wild animals took more control. Once, at the Asheville zoo, he'd stood in front of a cage where a wolf bitch was suckling her young. The wolf had stared coldly at him, and he at her. He'd suddenly known what he wanted her to do, and he'd carefully formed the picture in his mind of the bitch doing it. Beside him, a little kid had called excitedly for his mother, and that had jarred Logan's concentration so he'd had to start all over again. He'd repeated the picture again in his head, fixed it in his mind, and made it move. The she-wolf was strong, and for a while she'd resisted him.

But after a few minutes she'd picked up the pups and, one by one, crushed them in her jaws.

The little kid beside Logan had burst into tears. As Logan left, the wolf was nudging her pups, trying to make them feed again.

He'd tried it only once with a person: Mr. Holly, his geometry teacher in high school. Mr. Holly was a gangly old geezer who wore bow ties and suspenders, and was going to flunk him. One morning in class, Logan had stared at Mr. Holly when the old man was rattling on about areas of triangles, and had caught his gaze. Logan had formed the mental image of Mr. Holly in his rustbucket Ford, with his foot pressed down hard on the accelerator. Mr. Holly's mouth had stopped spewing formulas. Logan had added details to the picture: the car was racing along the county road between the high school and Taylorville, and ahead was the Pearl Creek Bridge. Inside the Ford, Mr. Holly was sitting with a zipper across his mouth, the same kind of smug look on his face as when he told Logan he was in danger of summer school. *Twist the wheel*, Logan had commanded mentally, and pictured the old man spinning the steering wheel violently to the right, sending the Ford crashing into the bridge's concrete railing so hard that Mr. Holly was ejected halfway through the windshield before the steering column pierced his guts. When Logan had let the vision fade out like a movie, Mr. Holly said he felt sick and needed to be excused. The whole class had heard him puking in the hall.

But he was back the next day. For more than a week, Logan played the same movie in his head. At the very least, it interrupted the old man's boring lectures. Soon, Logan tired of the game and began thinking up ways to cheat on the final exam.

A month later, the *Foxton Democrat* said that Mr. Paul Holly of Taylorville, aged fifty-eight and a geometry teacher for more than seventeen years, had died when his Ford hit the Pearl Creek Bridge. The scuttlebutt around the school, which Logan had heard with a stunned sense of satisfaction, was that crazy old Holly had left a suicide note to his wife that had *Twist the wheel* written on it a hundred times.

But the teacher who'd taken Holly's place in May had flunked Logan anyway.

Logan had always kept his talents to himself. He didn't understand where they'd come from, or why he had them, but he knew his control was getting better. He didn't want his mom and dad knowing—what would they say if they found out what he'd done to Holly? Logan regretted having cut Mutt open; that had been damned stupid, but Granddad hadn't called Edwin about it, so he figured he'd gotten away with his little experiment.

The almost imperceptible cracking of a twig brought Logan out of his trance. Within a minute his pulse had returned to normal, as had his body temperature. His senses quested in the darkness. He could smell a cat, prowling close by.

Brush stirred near the path. Careful, Logan warned himself. If the bastard jumps at me, I'd better be ready. He was hoping to stun it with the light before it had a chance to attack him. He waited a moment longer, listening, then aimed the light toward the path.

He switched it on.

The beam exploded onto a skinny bobcat with tattered ears, its tongue licking hungrily at the crusted blood beneath the newly hung carcasses.

Its eyes flared in the light, and Logan saw its hind legs tense for a leap into the underbrush. He quickly decided that he wanted to add it to the collection, and summoned the image of the bobcat frozen on the path, sending that image like a cold spear that left his mind and linked him with the animal. The bobcat tried to leap, but its will was sapped. It scrambled in a circle, snapping at its tail.

Logan concentrated on the image, strengthening it, slowing the animal until it stood panting and confused on the path, its legs stiff and its mouth open in a snarl. Its eyes had begun to frost over.

Logan could feel it trying to tear itself loose, and he kept the image firmly in his mind as he approached. Except for the movement of its sides as it breathed, the bobcat might have been a stuffed hunting trophy. Logan bent down a few feet from the animal, looking at the pink tongue and the gleaming, exposed teeth. He unsnapped the knife from its sheath at his ankle, then extended his arm and jabbed the bobcat's side.

The animal's mouth opened wider, but its legs didn't move.

It always amused him to see them like this—helpless, waiting for the killing stroke. He had an animal snare in his mind, and he could trap or release them as he chose. Of all the animals he'd caught, killed, and hung from the wires, the squirrels had been the toughest because they moved so fast. It was harder to stop them when they were on the run.

Logan traced the bobcat's ribs with the point of his knife. The animal shivered suddenly, then was motionless again. He put the blade to the soft flesh of the bobcat's throat and jabbed inward, then slashed with a skill born of much practice.

Blood jetted over his arm before he could get out of the way. The bobcat shuddered, a high hissing noise coming from its mouth.

It was hard to hold them when they felt that pain, and Logan moved backward in case the link snapped. In another few seconds it did, and the bobcat shrieked, clawing wildly at empty air, its body out of control and writhing in agony. With cold, clinical interest, Logan watched it die. Finally the bobcat lay on its side in its own blood, and its breathing stopped.

Logan wiped his blade on the animal's fur, then snapped it back into its sheath.

And when he stood up, the flesh at the back of his neck crawled. He sensed at once that he was being watched by something very close.

He spun around, probing with the light. He saw nothing but trees, rusted cages, hanging vines, and rough-edged boulders. Still, his flesh tingled; something was there, very near, but what it was he couldn't tell. Greediguts? he thought, and felt a shiver of panic. No, no—it wasn't an animal. There was no animal scent in the air. He swept his light back and forth across the path. Whatever watched him was as good as he at merging with its surroundings.

His legs were stiffening, turning freezing cold. Move! he told himself. Get back to the house!

He tried to move his feet, and whimpered softly when he found that his knees were tightly locked. The cold was rapidly spreading through his body, weighting his limbs.

His fingers involuntarily opened; the flashlight fell to the ground.

Run! he screamed mentally. His legs wouldn't move. His brain was going numb with the cold, and he realized that he was being invaded, just as he'd invaded the bobcat a few minutes before. His heart was pounding, but his thought impulses continued to slow, like the frozen gears of a machine.

Spraying out across the ground, the light touched the shoes of a figure standing before him on the path, barely ten feet away.

Logan tried to cry out, but the muscles of his face were frozen and he couldn't open his mouth. His teeth ground together as he fought against a power that held him, but he knew that against this overwhelming force he hadn't a chance to break free.

The veins in his neck stood out; his eyes glistened with terror.

Pump . . . kin . . . Man, Logan thought before his mind shut down like an icehouse.

The figure stood motionless before him for a moment longer, then silently approached and stretched out a hand to touch Logan's face.

34

Twelve miles from Usherland, the telephone was ringing insistently in the Dunstan house.

Raven came out of her bedroom to answer it, switching on the hallway light. It was after three o'clock, and Raven had been reading since eleven, when she found sleep impossible. She picked up the phone. "Hello?"

"Miz Dunstan?" It was Sheriff Kemp's drawl. "Sorry to wake you up so early. I'm over here at the Foxton Clinic, and . . . well, a couple of hours ago the Tharpe woman and her boy brought in the old man who calls hisself the Mountain King. He's tore up pretty bad—"

"What happened?"

"Animal got him. The Tharpes won't talk to me, but it looks like they know what went on up there. The emergency nurse called me as soon as she saw how bad off the old man was."

"An animal? What kind of animal?"

"The Tharpes won't say. The doc here tells me they've done everything they can for the old man, but it don't look like he's gonna pull through. I'm callin' because the boy says he wants to see you. He says he'll talk to you, but not to nobody else."

"All right. Give me fifteen minutes." She hung up and dressed hurriedly in jeans and a dark blue pullover sweater, then put on a pair of warm socks and her battered but reliable hiking boots. She ran her hands through her black curls and shrugged into her brown tweed jacket. The books she'd checked out of the Foxton library that afternoon were on the table beside her bed. The librarian had looked at her as if she had two heads when Raven had told her what she needed.

After she'd driven down from Briartop Mountain, she'd sat shaking in her car on the side of the road. The things she'd seen the Mountain King do were beyond rational explanation. Her knee had been healed by one touch of his cane. The Volkswagen had been turned around by a superhuman force.

What Sheriff Kemp had said in his office had come back to her:

Then there's the stories about the witches, too . . . Supposed to be that Briartop used to be crawlin' with 'em . . .

The book she'd been reading when the telephone rang was called *Dark Angels*, a history of witchcraft and black magic. It lay open on the table to one of its weird, phantasmagoric illustrations: a seventeenth-century Welsh woodcut showing a figure in black standing atop a mountain, arms upraised, summoning an army of reptilian demons. Crouched at its feet was a shape that resembled a huge dog—or a panther, Raven thought. In the book Raven had read about the power of the Evil Eye to command men and animals, about spells and magic wands passed down through generations of both "black" and "white" witches, and about the witch's familiar—a beast created by satanic power to protect and help its master.

The other two books—one by Bill Creekmore entitled *No Fear: The World Beyond*, the second called *The Unfathomed Mind*—dealt respectively with life after death and extraordinary mental abilities. Raven had paged through a fourth book as well, and found that it included many elements of the witchcraft lore from the history volume: Rix Usher's *Congregation*, which she'd picked up from the shelf where her father had left it. She wondered what his reaction would be if he knew how close to the bone his fiction had carved.

Wheeler had rolled his chair into the hallway as she left her bedroom. She told him who'd called, and why, and said she'd be back before dawn.

As she drove toward Foxton, a scatter of hard rain hit the windshield. Dead leaves whirled before the headlights, and she tightened her grip on the wheel.

The question of the ruins themselves continued to nag at her. What had happened up there to burn the outlines of human beings on stone walls? She'd asked her father about the ruins today, but he didn't know who had lived up there, or how old the ruins were. The town that had stood at the peak of Briartop Mountain was not listed in any historical volume in the Foxton library, and a call to the Asheville library turned up nothing, either. There was no record of the people who'd lived there, where they'd come from, or—most importantly—what had happened to them.

The Foxton Clinic, a small red-brick building, stood a block away from the Broadleaf Cafe. A couple of doctors and nurses comprised the staff of the place, which saw more cases of flu and cold sores than anything serious. At night, Raven knew, one nurse ran the clinic and a doctor was on call.

But tonight the sheriff's car was parked in front, beside the Tharpes' pickup truck and two other cars. Raven guided the Volkswagen into a space and hurried inside.

Sheriff Kemp was sitting in the waiting room, paging through a copy of *Field & Stream*. Across the small room sat Myra Tharpe and her son. As Kemp stood up to greet her, Raven glanced at Myra Tharpe and saw that her shoulders were slumped, her vacant gaze fixed to the floor. Beside her, Newlan—wearing a flannel shirt and a baggy pair of trousers that were obviously not his—rose quickly to his feet when he saw Raven.

"We got us a mess here," Kemp said. His face was slack and unshaven, his eyes red from lack of sleep. "The old man's tore up like you wouldn't believe. Whatever it was jumped him from behind. Broke his ribs and collarbone, smashed his nose and jaw, too. Thing must've had godawful teeth, judgin' from the wound on the back of his neck."

"New" Raven asked. "What attacked him?"

He glanced uncertainly from Raven to the sheriff, then said to her, "The panther. It was Greediguts, Miz Dunstan."

Kemp snorted. "Ain't no such thing! It's a story you mountain people made up!"

"Like we made up the Pumpkin Man?" His voice was calm and steady, but the power in it made Kemp's thin smile slip right off his face.

"Lord God . . . " Myra Tharpe whispered, clenching her hands tightly in her lap.

"You saw it?" Raven persisted.

"I was standin' as close as I'm standing to you right now when the panther jumped the old man from behind. I . . . guess he was too concerned about me to know it was creepin' up on him. The Mountain King was outside our house. If it wasn't for him, I might've gone down to . . . " He let his voice trail off, and then he picked up the gnarled walking stick from where it leaned against his chair. "I hit Greediguts with this," he said, "and ran it off."

"A *stick?*" Kemp scoffed. "You're tellin' us you ran a black panther off with an old stick?"

"It's . . . more than that." He ran his hand along the wood. "I don't rightly understand *what* it is, but it burned Greediguts across the head. Knocked me flat on my back, too." New handled it care-

291

fully, with great respect; though he couldn't sense the power in it anymore, he felt as if he were holding a loaded shotgun.

That stick, Raven thought, had put her shattered knee back together. Spells and magic wands. Witches on Briartop—

"Miz Tharpe, you look faint," Kemp said. "Can I get you some water?"

She shook her head. "I'm all right, thank you."

Kemp returned his attention to the boy, and narrowed his eyes. "You been dippin' into the moonshine keg? Maybe a cat did jump the old man, but there ain't no such thing as Greediguts! I say a good-sized bobcat—"

"Is a bobcat black, Sheriff?" New moved forward a few steps. "Can it rear up on its hind legs and stand six feet tall? Does it have a tail that rattles like a snake's? You saw the Mountain King. You don't really believe a bobcat did that to him, do you?"

"I've had enough of this!" Myra Tharpe suddenly shrieked, and shot up from her chair. Her eyes blazed at Raven. "It's you who started all this . . . this *evil*! You, with your damned questions and nosin' about! The panther would've let us be if it hadn't been for you! Damn you to hell, woman! I should've shot you the first time I seen you!"

"You gone crazy?" Kemp asked. "What's Miz Dunstan got to do with this?"

"She stirred up things!" Myra pointed at Raven, her skinny hand trembling. "Comin' up the mountain, goin' up to the ruins, askin' fool questions about the Pumpkin Man and things that are best left alone! Oh, you couldn't take no for an answer, could you? You had to keep on a-stirrin' and a-stirrin' until you drew the very Devil hisself out of the cauldron!"

Calmly, Raven met the other woman's fierce stare. "You never wanted Nathan to be found, did you? You knew those men wouldn't find him and you didn't *want* them to. Why was that? Why did you refuse to talk about the Pumpkin Man, or to let your son tell me what he'd seen?"

Myra's face splotched with rage. "Because," she said with an effort, "if outsiders go up on Briartop lookin' for the Pumpkin Man, there'll be death and destruction for everybody in this valley! My ma knew it, and her ma before her! The Pumpkin Man is left alone! If anybody tries to stop him from takin' what he wants, he'll cause the earth to split open and take us all down to hell!"

292

Kemp was wide-eyed. "What in the name of Holy Jesus are you jabberin' about?"

"An earthquake!" Myra screeched. "He'll send an earthquake to destroy us all, like he did that autumn of 1893! Oh, the outsiders went up into the woods with their guns and bloodhounds and they started prowlin' over every inch of Briartop! They kept the Pumpkin Man from takin' what he wanted, and he cracked the earth open! Houses disappeared, boulders smashed people flat, the whole mountain shook like it was gonna split in two! My ma knew it, and her ma, and back a hundred years! Everybody on Briartop knows it, and they know not to talk about the Pumpkin Man to outsiders or let outsiders 'help' us! The Pumpkin Man takes what he pleases! If he's denied, it's destruction for us all!"

"You mean . . . the Briartop people believe the Pumpkin Man *sent* the earthquake of 1893?" Raven asked. She'd read an account of it in one of the old *Democrats*: on a sunny November morning, the tremors had begun, and within minutes every window in Foxton had shattered. The most violent activity had been centered on Briartop Mountain, where severe rockslides destroyed many backwoods cabins and killed twenty-two people. Even Asheville suffered broken windows from the aftershocks.

"We don't believe it!" Myra said sharply. "We *know* it! The law came up to Briartop with their bloodhounds. They searched the mountain all through the autumn, and staked the trails out after the sun went down. They denied the Pumpkin Man what he wanted— and he struck back. There's not been another earthquake since then, because we don't deny him . . . and we make sure no outsiders do, neither!"

The only year that the number of disappearances had declined was 1893, Raven remembered. "You mean . . . you people give up your children *deliberately*? Why don't you just leave the mountain? Go somewhere else?"

"Where?" she sneered. "Our families have always lived on the mountain! We don't know any other home but Briartop! Most of us couldn't live in the outside world!"

"You do know that the Ushers own Briartop Mountain?"

"We know it. The Ushers leave us be. We don't pay no rent. If a child goes out alone in the dark, or strays too far from home, then . . . maybe that child's *meant* for the Pumpkin Man."

"Like Nathan was?" Raven asked coldly.

Myra's dark eyes damned the other woman. "Yes," she answered. "Most all the families on Briartop got more mouths than they can feed. The Pumpkin Man takes three, four, sometimes five a season. We know that, and we harden our hearts to it. That's a fact of life."

There was a moment of tense silence. "New," Myra whispered, and held her hand out for her son. He didn't accept it. "Don't look at me like that," she begged. "I've done all I could do! If it hadn't been Nathan, it would've been somebody else's child. The Pumpkin Man cain't be denied, New! Don't you understand that?" A tear trickled down her cheek. New's stare scorched her.

"The . . . Pumpkin Man ain't real," Sheriff Kemp said weakly, glancing back and forth from New to Raven. "Everybody knows . . . it's just a *story*. Ain't no such thing as—"

"Sheriff?" A nurse had come into the waiting room. "He's regained consciousness. He wants to see the young man."

"Is he going to live?" New asked her.

"His condition is critical. Dr. Robinson doesn't think he could survive the trip to Asheville, so we're doing what we can for him. Other than that, I can't say."

"Go on, then," Kemp said to New as he eased himself into a chair. "Jesus Christ, I can't make heads or tails of this mess!"

"New?" Raven stepped forward as he followed the nurse. "I'd like to see him, too. All right?"

He nodded. Myra gave a soft sob and crumpled into a chair.

In one of the clinic's small rooms, a white-smocked doctor with sharp features and thinning gray hair turned toward New and Raven as the nurse showed them in. The room smelled strongly of antiseptic. On a bed, the Mountain King lay facedown, his back covered with a sheet. He was hooked up to two IV bottles, one containing whole blood and the other a yellow liquid that Raven assumed was glucose. The Mountain King's head was turned so his eye faced the door, and he was so pallid that the network of veins at his left temple stood out in royal blue relief. Mottled black bruises were scattered across his face, and stitches had been taken in a long, jagged gash across his forehead. A bandage covered the bridge of his nose. Under its pale film, his eye was dark green and unblinking. Raven could hear his slow, labored breathing.

Dr. Robinson's expression told Raven all she needed to know about the old man's prospects of survival. He left the room and closed the door behind him.

New approached the bed, clutching the walking stick with both

294

hands. But for the faint rising and falling of the sheets as he breathed, the Mountain King was motionless. Then his mouth twitched, and he said in a raspy, garbled voice, "It's . . . time. Come closer, boy, so . . . I can see you."

New stood at his bedside. "I'm here."

"Somebody's . . . with you. Who is it?"

"The newspaper lady, from the *Democrat*."

"The lady with the yaller car," the Mountain King remembered. "She had a hurt knee. Tell her . . . to come closer. I want her to hear it, too."

New motioned her over. The Mountain King's eye was fixed directly ahead, looking at neither of them. "It's time," he repeated. "I've got . . . to pass it on."

"Pass what on?" New asked.

"The tale. It's time to tell the tale." One thin, bruised hand emerged from beneath the sheet, and groped for New. "Take it," he commanded, and New did. The old man squeezed his hand so hard that New thought his knuckles were going to break. "You've . . . got the wand. That's good. You keep it. Oh, I've got a hurtin' in my ribs . . . "

New sucked in his breath. A ripple of fiery pain had shot across his own ribcage. The old man's hand wouldn't let him go. "You . . . listen to me," he rasped. "Both of you. I want to . . . tell you about the ruins . . . up on Briartop. I'll tell it . . . like my pa told me . . . before the comets fell." For a moment he was silent, breathing harshly. "Greediguts tried to get me . . . before I could pass it on," he said. "Them ruins used to be a whole town, full of people. But they . . . wasn't ordinary people. My pa . . . said they'd sailed from England . . . back when this country was just bein' settled. They . . . come down from the north . . . and they built a town of their own. Up on Briartop, where they could live in secret." The Mountain King's eyelid sagged and fluttered. Still, his grip on New's hand didn't weaken.

"A coven," he whispered. "It was . . . a town of warlocks and witches."

Raven looked at New, saw the boy's eyes narrow—and she knew he realized it was true, just as she did. She leaned closer to the old man. "What happened to that town?"

"Destroyed . . . by fire and wrath," he answered, and drew a pained, rattling breath. "One of their own . . . done it." Raven was silent, waiting for him to continue. "One of their own," he said

295

softly. "One who'd done . . . what to the Devil is . . . the worst blasphemy of all."

"What?" Raven prompted.

The Mountain King's gray lips curled into a smile. "He . . . fell in love. With a girl from another town. A . . . *Christian* girl. He wanted to give up what he was . . . and marry her. But the others knew . . . knew they had to stop him. He was one of the strongest . . . warlocks of 'em all." He had to pause, gathering strength to speak again. "He must've gone through the fires of hell itself . . . in decidin' which path to take. 'Cause once the Devil leeches into you . . . he's like a drug . . . that beats you down and beats you down and keeps you needin' more." His eye fluttered again, then closed; but his grip was so strong it was grinding New's fingers together. "But . . . he loved her more . . . than he needed evil," the Mountain King whispered. His eye opened. "He made up his mind, and he went down . . . to the town in the valley. It's . . . called Foxton now."

As the old man spoke, his hand clutching the boy's, scenes began to form in New's mind—ghostly, faded images of people in dark clothes with white, stiff collars, a town's narrow dirt streets bordered by picket fences, horses and wagons stirring up a shimmering haze of dust, men in deerskin jackets and floppy hats, farmers plowing fields in the distance. One man in a three-cornered hat and a long dark cloak dismounted his horse in front of a small white house—then stopped, because on the door was a wreath of black ribbons.

Carrying a bouquet of wild flowers he'd brought from the forest, he was admitted by a tall, sad-eyed older man in dark clothes. The sad-eyed man told him what had happened: she had gone up to the attic room yesterday morning, and there she'd tied a rope around a rafter and hanged herself. There was no reason for it! Who could understand why such a lovely girl had done it? Her mother, the older man said, had found her, and was now confined to bed.

The man in the three-cornered hat slowly bowed his head. The flowers scattered to the floor. At his sides, his hands curled into fists. Who saw her last? he asked softly.

Her mother and me, came the answer. There was no sense in it! She went to bed and rose happy as a lark! Oh . . . she'd been troubled over a little traveling man selling knives and brushes who'd stopped for a cup of water. She'd spoken with him for a while, and after he was gone she said she wished wanderers such as he could find the love and happiness of a family. But why did she kill herself? *Why?*

296

On the floor, the flowers were turning brown. They were dead when the man in the three-cornered hat turned and stalked out of the house.

"The coven . . . had killed her," the Mountain King said. "He knew it. They'd . . . sent one of their own . . . to plant the seed of hangin' herself . . . in her mind. He went back up the mountain . . . and he summoned all the power of death and destruction from his soul . . . "

Blinding, white-hot flames filled New's head. The intensity of it scared him, but when he tried to pull away, the Mountain King held him fast. He realized he was seeing scenes of the past from the Mountain King's mind. New could do nothing but hang on, as a firestorm of awesome proportions blazed behind his eyes. He saw stone cabins blasted to pieces, burning bodies hurled against walls, charred corpses melting into the scorched and glassy earth. A wall exploded in blue fire, and the stones tumbled straight for him with terrible speed . . .

"They fought him hard. But they . . . wasn't strong enough to match him. Most of 'em died . . . some ran. He'd figured out the truth . . . that evil existed . . . to destroy love. When he was through . . . he built himself a cabin on the mountain. He . . . took it on hisself to watch over them ruins . . . to make up for his sinnin'. That man," the Mountain King said, "was my great-great-grandfather."

"But . . . if he gave up what he was, how did he keep the magic?"

The Mountain King scowled. "He gave up evil . . . not what was *born* in him. The Devil didn't teach him magic . . . just used it. Magic's an iron chain . . . that links gen'ration to gen'ration. The man don't find Satan. Satan finds the man." He paused, breathing harshly. His voice was quieter, almost gentle, when he continued: "Boy. What I want to know is—why are you like *me*?"

"I'm not," New said quickly.

"You are. The magic's in you somethin' fierce. Satan . . . finds the man. He's callin' you, like he called your pa . . . and like he called me, all these years. He wants the power that's in you . . . wants to twist it . . . wants to have you. *Tell me.* Are you descended . . . from one of those who ran from that coven?"

"No. I . . . " He stopped abruptly. His father had been like him. Who *was* his father? Bobby Tharpe had been raised in an orphanage near Asheville, but had chosen to live on Briartop. Who had his parents been? "My . . . pa was brought up in a state home," he said. "I don't know anythin' about his family. My ma . . . "

"A state home?" The Mountain King sounded choked. "How . . . old . . . was your pa when he died?"

"He wasn't sure what year he was born. But he said he was fifty-two."

The Mountain King released a soft, exhausted whisper. "Lord God . . . he was born in 1931. I've . . . killed my own son."

His grip weakened, and New wrenched his hand away.

35

Rix was jarred awake by Puddin's snoring. Her body was sprawled across him, and she smelled like an animal. She'd attacked him feverishly when he'd come to bed, clawing at his back and biting his shoulders. She was used to roughness, and Rix had tried unsuccessfully to calm her down. Her thrusting was so hard it had bruised his pelvis. After the race to orgasm was over, Puddin' had clutched to him, alternately sobbing and asking him in baby talk if she wasn't the best piece he'd ever had.

My God! Rix thought, as a snake pit of guilt opened in his stomach. What's *wrong* with me? I just made love to Boone's wife! She lay heavily on him, a fleshy burden. He felt tainted and dirty, and knew he'd only used Puddin' for revenge. Still, she'd asked for it, hadn't she? She was the one who crawled into my bed! Rix told himself. I didn't go looking for her!

He tried to ease out from under her; Puddin's snoring stopped, and she mumbled something in the slurred voice of a little girl.

There was a quick, furtive movement in the room. Rix sensed it rather than saw it directly. He looked toward the chest of drawers, could see the vague shape of someone standing there.

Boone, he thought. His heart kicked. He could envision Boone coming at them drunkenly with a candelabra to bash in both their skulls.

But the figure didn't move again for perhaps twenty seconds. Then, very slowly, began inching toward the door.

"I can see you," Rix said. "You don't have to creep."

Puddin' shifted position. "Huh? Whazzat?"

Rix reached for a box of matches on the bedside table. As soon as he moved, the figure bolted toward the door and darted into the darkness of the corridor. Rix pushed Puddin' aside—she cursed, turned over and started snoring again—and lit a match, touching the wicks of the candelabra he'd brought up from the library. In the amber glow he saw that several drawers had been left open; his closet door was still ajar. He got out of bed, put on his jeans, and walked out into the hallway.

Nothing moved in the range of the flickering light. The Gatehouse was quiet. He walked slowly to the end of the long corridor, and stopped at the stairs that led to Walen's Quiet Room. His father's decay seemed to hang in the air in dense layers. Rix's stomach lurched, and he quickly retraced his path. He stopped before his mother's door and listened; there was no sound beyond. Next was Katt's room. He stood outside it, listening for any telltale noises, and then touched the doorknob.

It was damp.

Rix looked at his palm. His hand was slick with sweat. Slowly he turned the knob and cracked the door open.

The candlelight slipped inside and illuminated Katt's pink-canopied bed. She was asleep, her head on the pillow, her face turned away from him.

Rix closed the door. Walen's reek seemed suddenly, sickeningly worse. He crinkled his nose with revulsion and looked back along the corridor.

And the candlelight fell upon a walking corpse whose gray flesh had tightened and fissured, oozing yellow fluid, the eyes about to burst from the skull, the lower jaw hanging and exposing blackened gums.

Rix cried out in horror, almost dropping the candelabra.

The thing staggered backward on spindly legs, a shrill shriek escaping the ruin of a mouth. It grasped the rotted nubs of its ears—and Rix saw that it held the ebony cane.

It was his father.

By candlelight, Walen Usher was a hideous, contorted figure wearing a shroud of white silk. As his face stretched in a scream and his eyes glinted wetly, the flesh ripped alongside his misshapen nose, fluids dripping down onto the gown.

"*What is it?*" Margaret shouted, about to emerge from her room.

"Get back!" Rix commanded. "Don't open your door!" The

sound of his voice stopped her. Walen went mad, flailing with his cane, knocking over vases and fresh flowers.

"Oh God oh God—" Katt keened from her doorway.

Walen turned, hands clasped to his ears, stumbling toward the stairs to the Quiet Room. Before he'd taken three steps, he lost his balance and pitched forward on his face; his body lay twitching violently.

Mrs. Reynolds, wearing her mask and gloves, emerged from the corridor's gloom. "Help me!" she ordered Rix as she bent beside Walen. "Hurry!"

Rix realized that she wanted him to help her pick Walen up, and his flesh crawled.

"Hurry, damn it!" she snapped.

He put the candelabra on a table and forced himself to grasp his father's arms. The flesh was spongy and soft, like wet cotton. As they lifted Walen, the cane dropped from his hand to the floor. "Help me get him upstairs," Mrs. Reynolds said. They carried him back to the Quiet Room, and in the dark—where Rix held his breath and clamped a scream behind his teeth—returned Walen to bed. The old man instantly contorted into a fetal position, moaning softly.

Outside the Quiet Room, Mrs. Reynolds closed the door and snapped on her pencil flashlight, shining it into Rix's ashen face. "Are you all right? I can give you a sedative, if you'd—"

"What was he doing out of that room?" Rix asked angrily. "I thought he couldn't leave his bed!"

"Whisper!" she hissed. "Come on." She led him down the stairs. Katt and Margaret had both come out of their rooms and were huddled together. Down the hallway, Puddin' was shouting to know what was going on.

"Shut your mouth, you tramp!" Margaret yelled at her, and she was quiet.

"I'm sorry." Above her mask, Mrs. Reynolds's eyes were bloodshot. "I dozed off. I have to sleep whenever I can. Last night I woke up and found him out of bed. It must've taken every bit of his strength to get down here." She nodded toward the candles. "He must've panicked because of the light. The screaming didn't help, either." She took her mask off and wadded it in her fist.

"What'd he expect? Jesus Christ, I've never seen anything like that in my—" He was almost overcome by a surge of dizziness and

300

nausea, and he had to lean against the wall to catch his breath. His pulse thundered.

"You're supposed to watch him every minute!" Margaret said stridently. Her face was coated with white cream, a plastic bag over her still-sprayed hairstyle. "You're not supposed to let him out of that room!"

"I'm sorry," she repeated, "but I have to sleep, too. One person can't watch him all the time. I've already suggested that you hire someone else to—"

"You're being paid what *three* nurses would charge!" Margaret told her. "And when you took this job, you understood you'd be working alone!"

"Mrs. Usher, I've got to rest. If I can only get a few hours sleep, I'll be all right. Can't someone else sit for him for a while?"

"Certainly not! You're the trained professional!"

"Edwin," Rix said, as his head began to clear. "Somebody call Edwin. He could sit with Dad."

"That's not his job!" Margaret snapped.

"*Call him, damn it!*" Rix shouted, and his mother flinched. "Or would *you* like to go up there and sit in the dark with . . . that *thing*?"

Her eyes bright with anger, Margaret marched forward. Before Rix could ward off the blow, Margaret had lifted her hand and slapped him hard across the face. "Don't you dare speak about your father like that," she seethed. "He's still a human being!"

Rix rubbed his cheek. "Barely," he replied. "Just thank God you didn't see him, Mother. I'll ask you again—do *you* want to go up and sit with him?"

She started to reply harshly but then hesitated, scowling at Rix and Mrs. Reynolds. She strode to the telephone down the corridor and dialed the Bodane house.

"Thank you," Mrs. Reynolds said. "I had no idea your father was strong enough to make it down those stairs."

"Where did he think he was going? Out for a walk?" Rix saw the ebony cane lying on the floor, and bent to retrieve it. As his hand closed around it, a powerful jolt darted up his spine. He straightened, examining the fine silverwork of the lion's face; it reminded him of the silver circle that flashed in his nightmares of the Lodge, but it wasn't quite the same; this lion wasn't roaring.

It was a beautiful cane. Here and there were nicks in the ebony, and exposed was a dark, glossy wood. It was lighter than he'd imagined it would be, and balanced so perfectly that he could probably hold it on the tip of his forefinger.

His hand had begun tingling; the sensation was creeping up his arm.

Ten billion dollars, he thought as he stared at the cane. My God, what a fortune!

An image formed in his mind, slowly strengthening: himself— older, with gray hair and a handsome, time-etched face—sitting at the head of a long boardroom table, the cane in his hand as subordinates displayed production graphs and charts; himself at the Pentagon, pounding a table with his fist and watching with satisfaction as grandfatherly men in military uniforms shrank from him; himself at a magnificent party, surrounded by beautiful women and fawning men; himself striding like a king down the long concrete corridors of the armaments factory as machines pulsed behind the walls like metallic heartbeats.

Katt's hand flashed out. She gripped the cane, and Rix's visions fragmented, faded away. They held the cane between them for an instant. Katt's eyes were fierce, her forehead beaded with tiny drops of sweat. Startled, Rix released his grip, and Katt clutched the cane to her with both hands. What was I thinking? he asked himself, as his stomach twisted with self-disgust. That I actually *wanted* Usher Armaments? The defiance slipped from Katt's face. She was his sister again, not the stranger she'd been a few seconds before.

"Edwin will be here in a few minutes," Margaret announced, returning from the phone. "Of course you realize, Mrs. Reynolds, that I will speak to Dr. Francis about this."

"Do what you please. You know as well as I do that Mr. Usher insisted on one nurse only. And I *earn* my salary, Mrs. Usher. If you don't think so, I'll pack my bag and leave right now."

Margaret's face tightened, but she didn't reply.

Mrs. Reynolds glanced at Katt. "He'll want his cane back. He hasn't been without it since I got here."

Katt hesitated. Margaret said, "Give it to her, Kattrina."

With what seemed to Rix like great reluctance, Katt handed the cane to Mrs. Reynolds. The nurse turned away and went back to the Quiet Room without a word.

Rix's hand was still tingling, and he rubbed it with the other. When he looked up, he caught Katt's gaze again—and he knew she'd been in his room, and why.

She said, "I'm going back to bed." Her voice was pitched slightly higher than usual.

"Lord, what a start that was! I'm going downstairs for a cup of coffee to steady my nerves, if either of you cares to join me." When neither of them answered, Margaret took the candelabra and walked along the corridor toward the staircase, flinging a scathing glance at Puddin', who stood wrapped in a sheet outside Rix's door. She stopped in her tracks, realizing at once what must have been going on. "My God," she said. "One of my sons isn't enough for you, is it?"

Puddin' answered by flashing the sheet open. Margaret muttered, "*Filth!*" and hurried to the stairs.

In the dark, Rix said quietly, "I have what you're looking for, Katt."

She paused in her doorway, framed against the faint blue dawn light that was beginning to creep through the bedroom windows. "I knew you must," she replied calmly. "I've already searched Boone's room. Where is it?"

"Under my bed."

"Get it for me, Rix. I need it."

"How long?" he asked.

"Does it matter?"

"Yes. How long?"

"Two years." The words fell like hammerblows across Rix's skull. "Get it for me."

"What if I don't? What if I flush it down the toilet where it belongs?"

"Don't be stupid. It's easy to get more."

After his attack had passed in Katt's Quiet Room, Rix had taken off the blindfold and returned it to the shelf behind his head. The metal box up there had drawn his curiosity, and he'd taken it out into the bedroom to open it. Inside were two hypodermic syringes, a half-burned candle, several thick rubber bands, a scorched spoon, and a small packet of white powder. "Why?" he said. "That's all I want to know."

"Come in and close the door," she said, a hard edge in her voice. Rix followed her inside and did as she asked. Katt struck a match and lit several candles around the room. The sweat sparkled on her perfect face like tiny diamonds, but her eyes were dark and deeply sunken, like the eyeholes of a skull.

"Why heroin?" Rix whispered. "Jesus Christ! Are you trying to kill yourself?"

"I'm not an addict." She blew the match out. "Why did you steal it? Were you going to show it to Dad? Or have you already?"

"No. I haven't, and I didn't plan to."

"Sure." She smiled tightly. "Tell me another one. You were going to show it to Dad, weren't you? You were going to go up there and tell him all about Katt the junkie, weren't you?"

He shook his head. "I swear to you, I—"

"Don't *lie*, damn it!" Her smile faded, replaced by a twisted, angry sneer. "Why else would you have stolen it if you weren't going to blackmail me with it? I saw the way you held Dad's cane! You know as well as I do what having that cane means! You want it just as much as I do!"

"You're wrong," Rix said, stunned at how little he really knew about his sister. "I don't want anything, Katt. For Christ's sake, why heroin? You've got everything anybody could want! Why are you trying to destroy yourself?"

She turned away from him and went to the window, staring out across Usherland with her arms crossed over her chest, hugging herself. The sky was plated with dense, low-lying clouds, shot through with purple and scarlet. The wind keened sharply, and a scatter of red leaves swirled against the window. "Don't pretend you care," Katt said hollowly. "It doesn't suit you."

"I do care! I thought you were off drugs! After what happened in Japan—"

"That was nothing. Just bad publicity, because I'm Walen Usher's daughter. What were you doing in my Quiet Room? No one ever goes in there but me."

"I had an attack. I didn't rummage through your room, if that's what you mean."

"What now?" She shivered, and looked at Rix. "Are you going to Dad?"

"I said I wasn't. But you've got to get help, Katt! Heroin's a damned serious—"

She laughed. It was a silky laugh, but the sound grated on Rix's nerves. "Right. Pack me off to a sanitarium. Is that the idea? Then you and Boone can fight over the estate without little Katt getting in the way. Same old Rix, so goddamned predictable. You and Boone were always at each other's throats, and both of you were so intent on killing each other that you pushed little Katt aside. Little Katt was pushed and shoved so much that she went into her shell—and she stayed there for a long, long time."

Katt smiled, the sweat sparkling on her cheeks and forehead. "Well," she whispered, "little Katt's grown up now. And it's my turn to shove. I've always wanted the business, Rix. I got into modeling because it was easy, and because Mom encouraged me. But I wanted to prove the point that I can handle responsibility—and I know what to do with money."

"Nobody ever doubted you were intelligent. And God knows you've made more money than Boone and me put together!"

"So," Katt said, staring intently at him, "why couldn't you love me?"

"*What?* I do love you! I don't understand why—"

"I let them find the pot, that time in Tokyo," Katt continued. "When I called home, I asked for you to come and help me. I didn't want Dad or Boone or the lawyers. But you didn't come. You never even called to see if I was okay."

"I knew Dad and Boone would bring you home! Besides, there wasn't a hell of a lot *I* could've done to help you!"

"You never cared enough to try," she said softly. "I admired you so much when we were children. I didn't care about Boone. It was you I loved, most of all. But you never made time for me. You were too busy hating Dad and Boone for the things you thought they'd done to you, and later—when we were teenagers—you were too busy brooding over the business."

"I've always had time for you!" Rix protested, but even as he said it he knew he was lying. When had he really listened to his sister? Even when they'd gone out riding together, he'd manipulated her into going over to the cemetery. He'd always used her as a pawn in his struggles against Boone and Walen, used her to spy on Margaret for him, all without regard for her feelings.

"You lucked out when we were kids. At least you had Cass and Edwin. Mom bought me dolls and dresses and told me to go play in my room. Dad set me on his knee once in a while and checked my teeth and fingernails. Well . . . that was a long time ago, wasn't it?"

"Maybe I wasn't the best brother in the world," Rix said, "but that doesn't have a damned thing to do with you shooting heroin!"

She shrugged. "The drugs came along when I had the agency. I started with tranquilizers, because I didn't want to have an attack on a location shoot. Then for fun I tried LSD, PCP, coke—whatever was handy. The heroin started for a different reason."

"What?" Rix prompted.

"Then . . . I wanted to see what the junk would do to me." She

305

ran her fingers over her flawless cheekbones. "What do you see when you look at me, Rix?"

"A beautiful woman, whom I feel very sorry and scared for right now."

She took a step closer to him. "I've seen other beautiful women who got hooked on drugs. Within a couple of years, they were wrecked. Look at me; *really* look." She traced a finger under her eyes. "Do you see any wrinkles, Rix? Any sign of sagging? Can you see anything that might tell you I was thirty-one, instead of ten years younger?"

"No. Which is why I can't understand the heroin. For someone who takes such meticulous care of—"

"You're not listening to me!" she said fiercely. "I don't take care of myself, Rix! I never have! I just *don't* age!"

"Thank God for your good genes, then! Don't try to kill yourself!"

She sighed and shook her head. "You're still not listening, are you! I'm saying that the heroin should have had a physical effect on me. Why hasn't it? Why doesn't my face ever *change*, Rix?"

"Do you know how many women would kill to look like you? Come on! If you expect me to give you back that junk so you can continue some kind of stupid experiment on yourself, you're crazy!"

"I'll get more. All I have to do is drive to Asheville."

"You're committing slow suicide," Rix said grimly. "I'm not going to stand by and watch it."

"Oh no?" She raised her eyebrows, her smile mocking him. "My suicide would suit your purpose, wouldn't it? You want the estate and business for yourself. I saw it on your face when you held that cane. Why else would you have come home? Not for Dad. Not for Mother. And certainly not for Boone and me. You've pretended not to be interested; maybe, all those years, you were pretending to turn your back on the business so you could find out how Boone and I felt. I see the real *you* now, Rix. I see you very, very clearly."

"You're wrong." Rix was stung by Katt's accusation, but he saw she'd made up her mind about him and there wasn't much he could say or do.

"Am I?" She stepped forward until she was only a foot or so away. "Then you look at me and tell me you can walk away from ten billion dollars."

Rix started to tell her he could, but the images of power he'd felt when he held the cane whirled through his mind. Ten billion dollars, he thought—and felt something deep inside him, something that had hidden and festered far from the light of his convictions, writhe with desire. Ten billion dollars. There was nothing he couldn't do with that much money. Hell, he could buy his own publishing company! Katt had been right, he realized with sickening clarity. If Usher Armaments didn't build the bombs, missiles, and guns, somebody else would. There would always be wars and weapons. His days of marching in peace parades suddenly seemed ludicrous; had he ever believed a few dissident voices could make a difference? The radical heroes of that era were now Wall Street businessmen, establishment politicians, and greedy merchandisers. Nothing had been changed, not really. The system had won, had proven itself unbeatable.

Had he come to Usherland, he asked himself, because he wanted a share of the inheritance? Had he been waiting all these years, hiding his true personality, in order to seize some of the Usher power?

The skeleton swung slowly through his mind.

Like a pendulum, he thought—and shunted the image aside.

"It's blood money," he said, and heard the weakness in his voice. "Every cent of it."

Katt was silent. Behind her the sky was turbulent, a gray and scarlet sweep of ugly stormclouds advancing over the mountains. The sun's rays probed through for an instant like an orange spotlight, and then the clouds closed again. The grim dawn grew darker.

"When Dad signs everything over to me," Katt said quietly, "I'm going to give you and Boone a yearly allowance of a million dollars. Mom will get five million a year. She can stay in the Gatehouse if she likes. So can Boone. I'm planning on living in New York. I wanted to tell you what I intend to do, because I'm not cutting anyone out. You can write pretty damned comfortably on a million a year."

"Yes," he replied tonelessly. "I guess I can."

"Bring the stuff to me, Rix. I need it."

Why not? he thought. Why not cook it for her and jam the needle in her vein? If she wanted to kill herself, why not help her? But he shook his head. "No. I'm sorry. I won't do it."

"I don't know what you're trying to prove—but you're not proving it."

"I don't know, either," he said, and left the room so her tormented, desperate stare wouldn't drive him insane.

In his bedroom, he ordered Puddin' out. She whined to stay, then cursed him when he shut the door in her face. He took the metal box from beneath the bed and flushed the heroin down the toilet.

He looked at himself, by candlelight, in the bathroom mirror. Since he'd returned to Usherland, the lines around his mouth and in the corners of his eyes had faded dramatically. His eyes were clearer than they'd been in years. There was color in his cheeks. His premature aging had seemed to reverse itself in the space of only a few days. Even his hair shone with new vitality.

But his face unsettled him. It was like looking at another face that had gathered around the bones—the face of someone who'd been lurking within his flesh and was finally emerging into the light.

It was the composite, he realized, of the faces in the library's oil paintings. Hudson, Aram, Ludlow, Erik—they had merged within him like a dark stranger in his soul. They lived inside him, and no matter how hard he fought against their influence, he could never really banish them. Didn't he deserve some of that ten billion dollars just for being born an Usher?

He didn't want Katt's handouts, he told himself. There was no way she could handle the pressure of Usher Armaments—not with a drug problem and a death wish! She was trying to buy his silence and cooperation. But maybe she could be persuaded that she needed an advisor?

My God! he thought, shocked at the turns his mind was taking. No! I'm my own man! I don't need any blood money!

Ten billion dollars. All the money in the world. Someone would always make the weapons. And, as Edwin had said, the Usher name was a deterrent to war.

Rix took off his jeans and stepped into the shower. When he'd finished, he dressed in a pair of dark blue pants and a white shirt from his closet. He chose a gray cardigan sweater—one of the new items that Margaret had provided for him—and put it on. The buttons were burnished silver, and were stamped with the Usher coat of arms.

He went downstairs to continue his research in the library. His mind was still confused, torn between the opposite poles of idealism and reality. The past seemed the only safe place to hide.

It was the future that he dreaded.

308

36

I've killed my own son, the Mountain King had said.

New Tharpe sat in the clinic's waiting room with the old man's cane across his knees. On the other side of the room, Raven was using the pay phone, and Myra Tharpe sat in a corner and hadn't moved for almost an hour.

New stared at his mother. Conflicting emotions raged inside him. She hadn't wanted Nathan to be found. The men who'd gone out searching hadn't really wanted to find him, either. Nathan had been a sacrifice to the Pumpkin Man, like all the other children who'd disappeared over the years. But *could* the Pumpkin Man send an earthquake to destroy Briartop if he was denied? Was there a way to destroy him, or would he have the run of the mountain forever? His mother was afraid. He could smell her fear, as sour as buttermilk. *Stretch*, he ordered her mentally, and pictured it in his mind.

She hesitated for a couple of seconds, then stretched like a marionette on a string. When she was through, she sat exactly as before. Her lank hair hung down and obscured half of her face.

New turned his attention to Raven Dunstan. *Scratch your head*, he commanded.

She glanced at him, but was engrossed in her conversation. Her left hand casually came up and scratched the back of her scalp.

Was there any limit to the magic? he wondered. He thought of the knife rising from the tangle of thorns; of the lamp lifting from the mantel; of the blue wall of stones that had protected him from Greediguts; of his mother, sitting with her hands clasped in the truck on the ride down to Foxton. If this magic had been in him from birth, as the Mountain King seemed to believe, then New thought it might have been unlocked by his rage in the thorn pit. There had never been a reason for him to need the magic before that day—and now he realized that if the Pumpkin Man had not taken Nathan, he might never have been aware of what lay dormant in his mind.

And if what the Mountain King had told him was true, then

New was descended from a line of warlocks and witches that stretched back hundreds of years.

The old man, dying now in a room down the corridor, was his grandfather.

The comets had fallen on the Fourth of July, when he was ten years old, the Mountain King had told him and Raven. Lizbeth had been six, and the year was 1919. The comets had shrieked down from the sky, their blasts shaking the cabin. Shocked from sleep, he'd run out to the front porch and seen the surrounding forest on fire. His father was shouting that they had to gather up what they could and flee. A red streak flashed overhead, and when the explosion tore trees from the ground, the boy who would later be called the Mountain King knew the end of the world had come.

His mother put Lizbeth in his arms and told him to get away, then ran back in to help her husband. Holding his sister tightly, the boy ran from the house through the flaming woods as Lizbeth cried in terror. There was a high, piercing wail that grew deafeningly loud. He looked back and saw the figures of his mother and father coming out of the cabin.

And then there was a blinding flash of fire and the cabin exploded, timbers spinning through the air. Something hit him in the face, knocking him on his back as the hot shockwave swept past. His next memory was of Lizbeth's hair and night clothes on fire, and himself trying to put out the flames with his hands. His hands were covered with blood, and when his sister saw his face, she screamed.

He couldn't remember how they'd gotten to the ruins. It might have been hours or days later that they huddled together in the stone structure that would become their home. His father had brought him up here and told him the story of his family's past, and the boy remembered how quiet it was, how desolate, how no one else would come up here because it was thought to be a haunted place.

Lizbeth was badly burned. Her mind had slipped away, and most of the time she sat crouched in a corner, rocking herself and crying. He was half blind, tormented by pain, fearful of every noise in the woods. But later—and how much later he didn't know—he left Lizbeth and went down the mountain to where their home had stood. Only a pile of rubble remained. He went through the ashes, found a few scraps of clothes that he and Lizbeth could wear, a pair of his father's boots, a few cans of food that had survived—and his father's charred corpse. The only thing recognizable about it was the

310

gold tooth at the front of his father's skull. Clutched in one hand was the crooked walking stick that had been carved from a piece of hickory by his great-great-grandfather. The stick, though badly scorched, had withstood the fire. It had been passed from generation to generation, his father had told him, and contained within it was both his ancestor's rage and the love he'd felt for the girl in the valley. It was an awesome thing that had to be handled carefully, for it held depths of power that were as yet unfathomed.

He worked the stick loose from the corpse's grasp, and returned to the ruins. Soon afterward, his injured eye hardened and rolled out of his head like a gray pebble. His wounds puckered and scarred. He returned one day from gathering firewood to find Lizbeth playing with the stick. Her trance had broken, but the only thing she recalled was the shriek of the falling comets.

As the years passed, blurring and merging with each other, they rarely left the ruins. They grew closer; their love changed from that of a brother and sister, though the Mountain King couldn't say when or how it had happened.

In May of 1931, Lizbeth delivered a baby boy—her only infant that hadn't been born dead or miscarried. She was eighteen, and the Mountain King was twenty-two. In the autumn of that year, Lizbeth was seen with her baby at a creek near the ruins. Before a week was out, the sheriff came up the mountain and found them.

New could imagine how they'd appeared: an emaciated, filthy man and girl in rags, the infant playing on the littered floor. The sheriff had called the county seat to find out what to do, and some people came to take the child to a state home.

The Mountain King had said he almost killed them; he could have, he said. It would have been easy. But deep in his heart, he knew the baby would be better off. The state people tried to coax them down from the mountain, but neither would leave. They took the child away in a brown Ford after promising to bring them food and clothes, but as far as the Mountain King knew, those people never set foot on Briartop again.

But, New wondered, why had his father chosen to settle on the mountain after growing up in the state home? Had the place of his birth been rooted somehow in his subconscious? Had he been drawn back to it because he sensed the same evil that the Mountain King now said held sway over Usherland? New remembered what his mother had told him about his father's nightmares: he saw the end of the world in his mind. Was it some kind of dim ancestral memory

311

of the coven's destruction? He'd never know for sure; but whatever had been calling his father was now beckoning to him, from Usher's Lodge. What lay in wait for him, inside that house? And what would happen to him if he dared face it?

"New," Raven said, breaking the boy's chain of thought. She stood next to his chair, her notepad in hand. "My father verified the old man's story. On the Fourth of July, 1919, Erik Usher fired cannons at Briartop Mountain; the falling shells were what the Mountain King called comets. The fire destroyed a dozen cabins and killed at least seventeen people." She consulted the notes she'd written down. "There was a list of the dead and missing in the July tenth issue of the *Democrat*. A couple named Ben and Orchid Hartley were killed—but their children, named Elizabeth and Oren, were never found."

"Oren Hartley," New said. "That's his name, isn't it?"

"I think so. There's no way to verify his story of the baby, though, unless we talk to someone at the state orphanage. The sheriff's records may show something—though I doubt it."

"Do you believe him?"

Raven nodded. "Yes, I do. Why would he invent it? I think Oren Hartley is your grandfather. The rest of the story . . . I don't know. I've seen those figures burned into the walls up at the ruins. I've seen what the Mountain King can do. But . . . I still can't make my mind to accept it, New. I've always thought of witches, warlocks, and magic wands as superstitious folklore." She frowned, looking at the stick across the boy's knees. "He said . . . you were like him. What did he mean?"

New took a deep breath, held it for a second, and then let it leak out. He put his hands around the stick and looked across the room at the pay phone.

Raven saw the boy's green eyes brighten vividly. A vein pulsed rhythmically at his right temple. He was immobile, shutting out everything except what he was concentrating upon.

Raven heard something clicking behind her, and she turned toward the sound.

The pay phone's dial was spinning. There was a metallic snap, and a few quarters tumbled out of the coin-return slot, jingling to the floor.

New directed his attention somewhere else. A white ceramic ashtray on a table near the door leaped up and clattered down. Magazines jumped, their pages flapping. A trashcan whirled like a top, balanced on its rim. The chairs in the room started hopping, leap-frogging over each other. The telekinetic display went on for more than a minute before the objects were still again. Then New looked up calmly at Raven.

Her face was ashen. "Oh," she said softly.

"It's been inside me all this time," New told her, "but I never needed it until I fell into the thorns. Maybe it was in Nathan, too. I don't know." His composed expression suddenly cracked, and Raven had a glimpse of the scared little boy underneath. "I feel like my insides are on fire," he said. "I think . . . I can do anything I want to do. *Anything.* I could make you dance if I wanted to. I could crack the walls of this place wide open. I'm scared, because . . . I'm not sure I know how to control it. All I have to do . . . is want something to happen. If I want it hard enough, it does."

Her first impulse was to draw away from him, but his expression of appeal held her firmly. "I don't know what to tell you," she said. "I guess . . . you have to do what you feel is right."

"If what the Mountain King says is true, then . . . my ancestor worshiped Satan before he destroyed that coven. There was evil in him, or the Devil wouldn't have called him. How do I know . . . there's not evil down deep in *me*, too?"

"Why do you think that?"

"Because I *like* the magic," New confessed. "I like the feelin' it gives me. I can do anything I please. And . . . Lord help me, but I want to answer what's callin' me from the Lodge." He lowered his chin, his fingers caressing the stick's rough wood. "One half of me . . . wants things to be like they were, before I fell in them thorns. The other half is *glad* it happened. I'm afraid of that part of me, Miz Dunstan." She watched his fingers tighten around the stick. "I don't want to lose . . . who I used to be."

Raven reached out hesitantly, touching his arm. She felt his bones under the shirt. Ordinary bones, she thought, the same as anyone else's. "You won't," she said, but she knew how little she understood of what this boy had been going through. In the short span of a week, his life had changed—as had her own. Her search for the Pumpkin Man had led her into a dark maze of witchcraft, the past, and strange family ties. What lay at the maze's center? she wondered. What was leading her through the blind alleys and twisted corridors between the past and the future?

She knew: Usher's Lodge. She'd known ever since that day she'd spoken to Myra Tharpe in the Broadleaf Cafe, and Myra had mentioned "something dark" that lived alone in the Lodge. At first, Raven had thought that perhaps someone *did* live in it, as much of a hermit as the Mountain King—someone who came out at night to roam the forests, able to snatch children away without leaving a trace behind. Rix Usher had said the Lodge was kept unlocked; it would be a perfect shelter for a madman who wanted to enact the legends of the Pumpkin Man.

She'd known that somehow she would have to get into that house herself, to search through its darkness for traces of the child-killer she thought might be hiding there. But after listening to New tell her how he felt—and *heard*—the Lodge calling him, as it had beckoned his father and the Mountain King as well, Raven realized the Lodge might be hiding much more than the Pumpkin Man.

Satan finds the man, the Mountain King had said to New. *He's callin' you, like he called your pa and like he called me, all these years . . . He wants the power that's in you . . .*

If some insidious force of evil dwelt at Usherland, Raven thought, might it be trying to draw New back to the web his ancestor had escaped?

Dr. Robinson came around the corner into the waiting room. Both New and Raven turned their attention toward him. Myra Tharpe still sat slumped over, all her energy gone, her spirit defeated.

"How is he?" Raven asked.

The doctor shook his head grimly. "He's fading. I'll tell you, though, he's one strong old bird. We've done all we could, but . . . his system's taken a jolt. Did either of you know he's had pneumonia for quite some time? And he's so anemic his blood's as thin as dishwater. By all rights, he should've been bedridden over a year ago." He glanced at New. "I understand that you told the nurse he has no next of kin. No one to notify . . . to arrange things, I mean."

"I'll pay the bill," Raven said. "I told the nurse that."

"That's not what I mean. The old man's dying. I hate to be so blunt, but . . . who's going to make arrangements for the body? Sheriff Kemp?"

"No sir." New rose from his chair. He looked at his mother, who hadn't moved, and then back to Dr. Robinson. "I was wrong, sir. He does have next of kin. He's my grandfather, and I'll take care of him."

"*New*," Myra rasped, but he paid no heed.

314

"Oh. I see." It was clear that Dr. Robinson *didn't* see, though he was seemingly satisfied. "Well . . . in that case, you've got some mighty strong blood in your veins, son. Your grandfather's a fighter."

"Yes sir," New said. "Can I see him?"

"I doubt if he'll know you're there, but go ahead if you like."

"Do you want me to go with you?" Raven asked, but New shook his head and left the waiting room.

When he was gone, Dr. Robinson said quietly to Raven, "The old man's hanging on by his fingernails. I don't know why, but he won't let go."

New stood in the Mountain King's room, listening to his faint breathing. Dim gray light filtered through the blinds at the single window. The lamp over the old man's bed had been turned off. The Mountain King didn't move. New stood where he was for a while longer, then turned to leave.

"Boy," the old man whispered weakly. "Don't . . . go yet."

New moved closer to the bed. "Are you hurtin'?" he asked tentatively.

"No. Not no more. He got me, didn't he?" The Mountain King chuckled hoarsely. "Old sumbitch . . . got me when my back was turned. Few years ago . . . I would've torn the hide right off his bones."

"Miz Dunstan found a story in an old newspaper," New told him. "It was about . . . the comets that fell. Your name is Oren Hartley."

"Oren . . . Hartley," he repeated. "That sounds . . . like a sissy preacher's name. That ain't me, boy. I'm the Mountain King." He said it with defiant pride. "Did . . . that story have my folks' names, too?"

"Your father's name was Ben. Your mother's was Orchid."

"Oh. Those are . . . right nice names, I reckon. They kinda ring a bell, but . . . it's been so long. Take my hand, boy. Hold it tight."

New grasped it. The Mountain King's hand was cold. "What I did to your pa," he whispered, "I did . . . because I was afraid. He was weakenin'. He . . . didn't know who or what he was . . . and he was about to answer what was callin' him."

"What would have happened to him if he'd gone down to the Lodge?"

"The Lodge," the Mountain King hissed bitterly. "It ain't . . . just a house, boy. It's the Devil's sanctuary. It's . . . a church to worship evil. If your pa had gone there . . . what lives in that house would've snared him. There's . . . a power in the Lodge that calls you, and promises . . . everything in the world to you. But all it wants . . . is to *use* you. To catch and hold you . . . like them thorns on the mountain." He gave a soft, weary sigh. "You don't much like your life, do you? Sometimes . . . you wish you could live at Usherland, and not have to . . . go back to that cabin. Ain't that right?"

"Yes."

"Where you live ain't important," he said. "It's what . . . lives in *you*. Them Ushers have got money . . . but they live in a cage, without knowin' it. Once in a while they bump their heads on the bars. All their money can't buy 'em the key. You be . . . proud of who you are, boy. The rest'll take care of itself. And your ma . . . she's just scared for you, 'cause she loves you. Don't begrudge her that."

"She didn't want the men to find Nathan," he replied coldly. "She didn't *want* Nathan to come home!"

"Yes, she did. If she . . . pretended not to, it was to keep herself goin' on. You're all she's got now. I reckon . . . I had a part in that." He squeezed New's hand. "Do you forgive me, boy? For what I done to your pa?"

"I miss him. I miss him a lot."

"I know that. But . . . it had to be done. Do you see that?"

"Yes," New said.

"At least . . . he died as the man you knew. Not . . . as what he would've been, if he'd gone down to the Lodge."

"What happened to Nathan?" There was steel in his voice. "Where did the Pumpkin Man take my brother?"

"I don't know. All I know is . . . the Pumpkin Man is part of it. Part of what's callin' you from Usherland. I don't know what the Pumpkin Man is, or why he takes those young'uns."

"And what would happen to me," New asked, "if I went down to the Lodge?"

The old man was silent. In the distance, New heard the throaty rumble of thunder. "Then . . . you'll be walkin' right into the snare," the Mountain King said. "Like a dumb animal . . . about to have its throat cut."

"I'm going to go to the Lodge," New told him. "I decided when I was sitting out there, waiting. I'm going to find out what's inside. You know that, don't you?"

"I . . . feared it. Boy . . . if I could stop you, I would. I'd do anything to stop you. But . . . I'm all used up. I'm tired. I've passed the wand to you, and told the tale. The rest is . . . on your shoulders."

New could feel his grip weakening. The old man whispered, "Lizbeth . . . who's to take care . . . of Lizbeth now?"

He was slipping away. The core of ice inside New suddenly cracked. What would the words hurt? he asked himself. And then he said softly, "I forgive you."

The Mountain King's hand strengthened again, for just a second or two. "I'm . . . gonna turn loose now." His voice was barely audible. "I want you to go out . . . and tell 'em the Mountain King wants to rest."

"Yes sir."

The old man opened his hand—and his arm slithered down, hanging off the bedside.

New thought he could still hear him breathing, but he wasn't sure. Thunder vibrated over the valley, shaking the windowglass. New backed away from the bed, and quietly left the room.

"I want to go somewhere to be alone," New told Raven in the waiting room. "I need to do some thinking."

"The *Democrat* office is just down the street. There won't be anyone there this early. Do you want me to take you?"

He nodded, and then went over to his mother. "Ma?"

She flinched, her hands folded prayerfully in her lap.

New gently touched her cheek, and when she looked up at him, there were tears in her eyes. "I want you to take the truck and go home," he said. "Will you do that?"

"Not without you. I'm not goin' anywhere without—"

"I'm the man of the house now, Ma. You told me that a hundred times. If you want me to be the man, I've got to act like one. I've got to make my own decisions. There's a storm comin'. I want you to take the truck and go home." He could easily make her do it, he knew. It would take no more than a mental shove. He almost did it—*almost*—but then he said, "Please."

She started to object; then she saw the man in her boy's eyes, and stopped. "All right," Myra said. "All right. I'll go home. But how will you—"

"I'll make out."

Myra stood up, looked from her son to Raven Dunstan and then back to New again. "You will . . . come home too, won't you?"

"Yes ma'am. I'll come home."

She took the keys from him and went out of the clinic under a sky that churned with stormclouds.

New stood at the door until she'd driven away. "What's on your mind?" Raven asked him.

"Huntin'," he answered calmly. "I've got to figure out how to make a snare of my own."

37

Rix heard the rumble of distant thunder as he sat in the library, examining by candlelight one of the first items he'd found: the small, moldy black book with its mathematical formulas, obscure ink sketches, and bars of music. The formulas were much too dense for Rix to follow, though he'd always been pretty good at math. They resembled some sort of advanced physics project, with notations for weight and velocity. What the hell were they for? he wondered.

The musical notations were particularly puzzling. They were extremely intricate, with dozens of sharps and flats. Whose composition were they, and what was their connection with the math formulas? He turned a few brittle pages and looked at the sketches of the long rods with half-moon, round, and triangular shapes at their bottoms. He felt he should know what those were; the symbols were familiar, but he couldn't quite place them.

A quiet tapping at the library's door startled him. He closed the book, paused for a few seconds, and then got up, went to the door, and cracked it open.

Edwin, immaculate in his Usher uniform and cap, stood outside. "I thought you might be in there," he said.

Rix opened the door wider to let Edwin in, and closed it again after he had entered. "I was doing some reading. How's Dad?"

"Sleeping. Mrs. Reynolds is back on duty now." Edwin appeared pale and haggard from his time spent with Walen in the Quiet Room. The skin seemed to have shrunken over Edwin's facial bones, and Rix could smell Walen on his clothes. "You didn't have breakfast this morning," Edwin said. "Cass is worried about you."

Rix glanced at his wristwatch and saw that it was almost nine o'clock. "I'm all right. I just didn't feel very much like eating this morning."

"You need to keep your strength up." He looked at the black book that Rix held. "Did you find something of interest?"

"I think so. Look at this." He went over to the desk and opened the book under the candlelight, turning to the mathematical formulas. "Do you have any idea what this technical stuff might be?" he asked. "It looks to me like a physics problem."

"Physics?" Edwin frowned. "I wouldn't know. My best subject in school was English." He examined the figures for a moment before he shook his head. "Sorry. I can't tell where it begins or ends."

He showed Edwin the bars of music and the drawings. Edwin said one of the sketches reminded him of horseshoes, but he couldn't fathom the rest of them.

Rix closed the book. "Do you know anything about Dad's new project?" he asked. "Katt's told me it's called Pendulum, but that's all she knows."

"Your father's never trusted anyone with his business projects. Least of all, me. I've seen the military men coming in and out, of course, but that's none of my concern."

"Haven't you ever wondered what goes on at Usher Armaments?"

"Yes, I've wondered. Often." Edwin crossed the room and regarded the portrait of Hudson Usher. "Strong features," he said in a reverent tone. "That was a man of great willpower and determination. You have his eyes, Rix."

"I think you're avoiding my question."

"Perhaps . . . I've made certain I *have* avoided it, all these years." He turned to face Rix. In the soft golden light he was a figure of great poise and dignity, from the crown of his cap to the toes of his spit-shined shoes. The candlelight glinted off the silver buttons of his blazer. "I told you before. I abhor war, but someone will always wage it, Rix. That is a fact of our miserable existence. You have to believe that your family's weapons help deter war. That outlook has taken me through many a cold night. It would be better for you if you could share it."

"How do you mean?"

"Your peace of mind." Edwin took off his cap and ran a hand through his thin white hair. "I know the pressure you've been under these last few years. With Sandra's death, and your career difficulties—and now your father's condition. You were always a sensitive boy. I know living in the world out there has been very hard on you. Hasn't it?"

"Yes," Rix said.

Edwin nodded. "When you called me that day from New York, I could hear the desperation in your voice. I heard it again when you

319

were telling me about that family history you want to write. The world can be a treacherous place, Rix. It can destroy sensitive people."

"I have been under pressure," Rix admitted. "A lot of it. I think . . . it must've started when Sandra died. I loved her so much, Edwin. After she died . . . it was as if part of me had died, too—like a light being turned off. Now I just feel dark inside." He paused, but sensed that Edwin was waiting for him to continue. "And . . . I've been having nightmares. Actually, flashes of things that I can't really get a grip on. Boone hung a plastic skeleton in the door of the De Peyser's Quiet Room, so it would swing right in my face. I keep seeing that damned thing in my mind, Edwin—only it gets bloodier every time I see it. And—this sounds crazy, I know—I keep seeing something that scares the hell out of me: it looks like a doorknob, with the face of a roaring lion on it. It's made of silver, and it just floats there, in the dark. Can you think of a door like that, some- where in the Lodge?"

"There might be," Edwin answered. "But there are *thousands* of doors in the Lodge, Rix. I can't say I've paid much attention to their knobs. Why? What does the Lodge have to do with it?"

"I'm not sure, I just think . . . I must've seen a door like that, when I was wandering in the Lodge. And that trick skeleton was plastic, but now . . . it seems so *real*."

Edwin said softly, "That was a terrible experience for you. Alone in the darkness for hours. I thank God I found you when I did. But that was a long time ago, Rix. You have to let your fears of the Lodge go. I'll admit, though, the Lodge turned me around often enough. Several times I was so lost I had to call for help. Which brings me to why I was looking for you. Have you seen Logan this morning?"

"Logan? No. Why?"

"I think he's run away. We had a disagreement the other day. Logan seems to think his work hours are too demanding. He was gone from his room this morning, when I went in to wake him up."

"Good riddance," Rix said curtly. "Logan could never take your place. You should realize that by now."

"I honestly thought Logan had the potential to do something with his life. Cass told me I was being foolish; maybe she was right." He scowled, an expression Rix was unused to seeing on Edwin's placid features. "Logan has no discipline. I should've known that, after Robert told me about all the scrapes he's been in. Well . . . I wanted to give him a chance, because he's a Bodane. Was that so wrong?"

320

"Not wrong. Maybe just too trusting."

"That's exactly what Cass says. I'm not going to call Robert yet; I'll give Logan the rest of the day. But if Logan can't do it, who's going to take my place?" He massaged the knuckles of one hand. "The boy needs a good whipping to straighten him out."

"He's long past that," Rix said.

Edwin grunted. "I haven't gone over to the Lodge yet. If Logan went in there alone after I told him not to, he's as stupid as he is disobedient. Well, I won't bother you with Logan. Unfortunately, he's *my* problem." He started across the library to the door.

"Edwin?" Rix said, and the other man stopped. Rix motioned toward the cardboard boxes. "I've been going through those to find out how Ludlow Usher got the ebony cane back into the family. I know it was stolen away by the man who killed Aram Usher in a duel, and it was gone for at least thirteen years. Obviously the cane is very important. Do you have any idea how Ludlow might've retrieved it? Any stories you might've heard from your father or mother?"

"No," Edwin replied—but he'd said it too quickly, and at once Rix's interest perked up. "I'd better see if I can track down—"

Rix planted himself between Edwin and the door. "If you know anything at all, I want you to tell me. Who's it going to hurt? Not Mom, and certainly not Dad. Not you or Cass, either." He saw the indecision on Edwin's face. "Come on. Please, I need to hear what you know."

"Rix, I don't—"

"It's important to me. I have to know."

Outside the library, thunder echoed like a bass kettledrum. Edwin said in a resigned voice, "All right. I do know how Ludlow found the cane. When I was about Logan's age, I was just like him; I hated to work. I found a good hiding place—the library in the Lodge's basement." He smiled vaguely. "I used to steal cigars from the drawing room and smoke them down there. It's a wonder I didn't set fire to the house, with all those books and journals around. Naturally, I read a great deal, too."

"And you found something about Ludlow and the cane?" Rix prompted.

"Among other things. It was in a volume of old newspaper clippings. Of course, that was a long time ago. I'm not sure my memory is very reliable anymore."

"Tell me what you remember. Anything."

Edwin still looked uncertain. He started to protest again, but then he sighed and slowly eased himself into a chair. "All right," he said finally, watching a candelabra burn on a table near him. "I know that Luther Bodane, my grandfather, went with Ludlow to New Orleans in the summer of 1882. Ludlow wanted to see his half sister, Shann. She was in a convent outside the city, and had been there for more than eight years."

"Shann was a nun?" Rix asked. "I thought she was a concert pianist. Didn't she study music in Paris?"

"She did. Obviously she was a musical prodigy, because she was composing when she was ten years old. As I understand it, Shann was in Paris when her father was killed. His death must have been a terrible shock to her; she was a shy, gentle girl who idolized Aram Usher. But she finished her education. Her final examination at the academy was an original concerto, which she played for the head-mistress." Edwin's eyes seemed to darken as he saw beyond Rix and into the past. "The concerto was written in honor of her father. Shann graduated with high marks. When she returned to America, she immediately started a concert tour."

"So how did she become a nun?"

"The academy's headmistress hanged herself after Shann left," Edwin continued, as if he hadn't heard Rix's question. "On her tour, Shann played what came to be known as the Usher Concerto. There are dozens of clippings in the Lodge's library praising her performances. The tour continued for more than four months, and everywhere Shann played she was a phenomenal success. Then the suicides began."

"Suicides? I don't understand."

"Neither did anyone else, at first. A dozen people in New York City, ten in Boston, eight in Philadelphia, another dozen in Charleston. And all of them had heard the Usher Concerto."

Rix recoiled inwardly. He remembered the faded photograph of the little girl sitting happily at her white grand piano. "You mean . . . the *music* had something to do with their suicides?"

"Evidently so." Edwin's voice had taken on a grim tone. "The music was so . . . beautifully strange that it worked on the imagination long after it was heard. The press began to put everything together. When Shann stepped off the train in New Orleans with her entourage, the newspapermen were waiting for her like a pack of hounds. There was a mob outside the station; they called her a murderess, shouted that she was a witch who'd discovered some sort of satanic symphony. The stress was too much for Shann, and she collapsed in the terminal. For the next several years, she lived

322

in a New Orleans sanitarium. She joined the convent after she was released."

"And she never came back to Usherland? Isn't she buried in the cemetery?"

"No. The monument was erected to her memory, but Shann was buried in New Orleans. It's unclear exactly why Ludlow went to see her; possibly he was trying to bring her back home. In any case, she wouldn't leave the convent." Edwin hesitated, arranging his thoughts. His shadow was scrawled on the wall behind him. "There'd been heavy thunderstorms and flooding in New Orleans, and the trains had been canceled," he continued quietly. "Ludlow and Luther booked passage on one of the last of the old Cordweiler steamboats, the *Bayou Moon*. According to the newspaper accounts, the boat was in decrepit condition. Anyway, somehow Ludlow let himself be lured into a backroom poker game—and that's the beginning of how he retrieved the family scepter . . . "

As Edwin spoke, the muffled boom of approaching thunder rang out over Usherland. In his imagination, Rix saw the once proud *Bayou Moon*, now an unsightly patchwork of cheap timbers, plowing northward along the swollen Mississippi. A high-stakes card game was in progress in a lamplit room, and twenty-four-year-old Ludlow Usher sat down at the round table for what was to become much more than a game.

◆ ◆ ◆

Mr. Tyson—the top-hatted older gentleman who had struck up a conversation with Ludlow at the bar—introduced him to the other three players. Ludlow had given his name as "Tom Wyatt," aware that the older gentleman was probably looking for a sheep to fleece. The Usher name might be known to him, and this was a precaution Ludlow often took with strangers.

Ludlow nodded toward each of them in turn: a heavyset, bald-headed man who wore flashy diamond rings and gave his name as "Nicholls, with two *l*'s"; a coffee-colored man named Chance, who wore a gray goatee and had a brown velvet eyepatch over his right eye that matched the color and cloth of his suit; and a lean Negro who called himself Brethren and wore a ruby stickpin through one flared nostril. A glass of whiskey was poured for Ludlow, a fine Havana cigar was offered to him, and the game of five-card draw was under way.

The *Bayou Moon* rocked and heaved over rough water, its timbers groaning as if about to split apart. Fifty- and hundred-dollar bills littered the card table, and the oil lamps arranged around the room glowed through shifting layers of blue cigar smoke. Ludlow expected to lose his money quickly and return to the bar for the rest of the long trip to St. Louis—and so he was surprised when, less than an hour later, he'd won almost five thousand dollars.

Tyson poured him another whiskey and complimented him on his shrewd handling of the cards. Ludlow had done nothing particularly shrewd; in fact, most of his winnings had come when the other players folded. Nicholls, with the practiced delivery of an ex-thespian, suddenly offered the suggestion that all bets should be doubled. "It's doom on my own fool head, I know," he said with a thin smile, "but perhaps this young man's luck will change."

"I'm not so sure, Mr. Nicholls," Tyson replied. "Our Mr. Wyatt has a canny look about him. What say, Mr. Wyatt? Are you agreeable?"

Ludlow knew he should take the money and run. All eyes were on him. There was a moment of strained silence. Ludlow decided to play it out. "I'm agreeable," he said.

To his amusement, he continued to win with no apparent effort. Ludlow's quick, retentive mind was calculating the odds on each hand; it took no genius to realize he was being primed for disaster. It began slowly, as Brethren won a thousand-dollar pot that was mostly Ludlow's money. Then Ludlow was only winning one hand out of four, and his stack of chips was dwindling fast. Still, just when it appeared that Ludlow might fold and rise from the table, he was allowed to win a substantial pot. They were toying with him, he knew, and had to be all in it together for such clockwork precision. Perhaps Tyson had chosen him as a mark because of his well-cut clothing, or his diamond stickpin, or the wad of cash with which he'd paid his bar bill. Though their faces were innocently concerned with their own cards, the men seemed to know exactly what Ludlow held, and bet accordingly. Ludlow was puzzled; how were they doing it?

He stopped drinking the whiskeys that Tyson pressed on him, and concentrated with a vengeance on the cards. Ludlow was down to his last thousand dollars of winnings when his fingers touched three tiny raised dots in the lower left corner of the king of spades. The other cards he held also had a combination of dots in the same place; they would not be perceived, Ludlow realized, by a drunken man who was convinced the tide of luck would again return in his favor. The cards were marked in what seemed to be random patterns of faint dots—an intricate code that told the dealer exactly what

324

cards each man held. Ludlow smiled inwardly at the double challenge that faced him: to decipher that code, and to gain control of the deck.

"Well," he said, adding a slur to his voice as he lost another four hundred dollars, "I think that'll be all for me, gentlemen." He started to rise.

Tyson clasped his arm. "One more hand, Mr. Wyatt. I sense you're a very lucky man today."

Ludlow won the next hand, and the one after that as well. Then his losing streak started in earnest. His winnings were gone, and he was playing with Usher money. Control of the deck circulated around the table, with Chance's chips on the rise.

For the next hour, as the *Bayou Moon* fought the river currents and rain thrashed down in torrents, the mind behind Ludlow's mask worked like a machine. He calculated odds like a master mathematician, his fingers playing over the series of dots, entering each combination and the card it signified into memory. He began to fold more regularly, to conserve his money, and subsequently—with a quick glance from Chance to Tyson that Ludlow caught from the corner of his eye—his "luck" returned with a heavy pot, encouraging him to bet recklessly the next round.

As long as he could deal, Ludlow knew, he would stand a better chance of beating them at their own game. But they had more experience than he, and he would still have to play the bewildered fool—until the time was right to destroy them. He focused all his concentration on the cards he dealt, letting the marked corner slide against his finger, but he was clumsy at it and only recognized half of the cards.

He had to wait six more hands before he got the deal again. This time, he did it more slowly, deliberately. Though he lost to Brethren, Ludlow's percentage of correct calls went up considerably. When he dealt the next time, Ludlow was down seven thousand dollars of his own money. There was blood in the eyes of the other men; they smelled fresh meat, and were pressing forward for the kill.

And now it was time. "Gentlemen," Ludlow said, as he cut and shuffled the deck, "I feel lucky. What say we up the ante?"

A slick smile spread over Tyson's face. "Another thousand dollars apiece, Mr. Wyatt?"

"No sir," Ludlow replied. "Another *ten* thousand dollars apiece. In cash." In the sudden silence he put the deck carefully down in front of him and peeled off the bills from the roll in his coat. He laid the money out in the middle of the table.

"That's . . . a hell of a sum of money," Nicholls said, his eyes dancing around at the other men.

"What's wrong?" Ludlow feigned stupid surprise. "Aren't you gentlemen up to it?"

"Ten thousand dollars as ante for *one* hand?" Brethren took the cigar from his mouth, his black eyes slitting. "What's the limit?"

"The sky," Ludlow said. "Is anyone willing to play?"

The silence stretched. Tyson cleared his throat nervously and slugged down a shot of whiskey. Across the table from Ludlow, Chance stared fixedly at him, smiling coldly. "I'll play," Chance said. He brought a wad of bills from his own brown velvet jacket, counted out ten thousand dollars and tossed the money to cover Ludlow's. Brethren said, "I'm out, men." Nicholls sputtered with indecision, then added his money to the pot. Tyson paused; his eyes had turned reptilian, and studied Ludlow's face. Then he grunted softly and came up with ten thousand dollars.

Now Ludlow had to be both careful and precise. He dealt slowly, sliding the dots against his finger, identifying each card before he dealt the next. When the cards were out and the draw had been dealt, Ludlow had a pair of tens, the queen of hearts, the five of diamonds, and the five of hearts. By his calculations, Tyson had two aces, Nicholls a mixed hand, and Chance held two pair, jacks and nines.

"Bets?" Ludlow asked softly.

Tyson opened with a thousand dollars. Nicholls met it, and so did Chance.

"I'll see your thousand," Ludlow told them, "and raise you another ten thousand." He peeled the bills off and flung them to the table.

A soft cough of cheroot smoke left Nicholls's mouth. Tyson's face had begun to take on a yellowish cast; he picked up his cards and stared at them as if trying to read the future. Ludlow met Chance's gaze across the table, their faces revealing nothing. "Well?" Ludlow asked silkily.

"A gambler who runs away," Tyson said as he laid his cards on the table, "will live to win another day. Sorry, gents."

Nicholls had a bead of sweat on his nose. With a resigned moan, he pushed away his worthless hand.

"You think you've got me, don't you?" Chance's single eye was the color of a murky topaz. "No sir, I don't believe you do." He

326

began to count off the bills—but after eight thousand three hundred dollars, his luck had run out.

"You're short, sir," Ludlow said. "I think that finishes you." He started to rake the money toward him.

But Chance's hand shot forward, the fingers clamping around Ludlow's wrist. The gambler's eye was blazing, a bitter twist to his mouth. "I have something," Chance said tersely, "that I think may make up the difference." He reached down to the floor beside his chair—and placed upon the table an object that bleached the blood from Ludlow's face.

It was the lion-headed Usher scepter.

"A beauty, isn't it?" Chance asked. "It used to belong to a rich man. Look at the workmanship in that silver lion's-head. Look at the ebony, as smooth as glass. It was given to me by that rich man's wife. She and I were, shall we say, well acquainted?"

Ludlow looked into Chance's face and realized he'd been playing cards with the man who'd killed his father. His heart had begun pounding, the blood rushing into his face again. "What . . . makes you believe that stick is worth seventeen hundred dollars, sir?"

"Because it's *magic*," Chance said, leaning toward Ludlow with a conspiratorial smile. "You see this patch, Mr. Wyatt? I was shot in the face in Atlanta six years ago. Point-blank, with a derringer. I lost my eye, but I lived because I had that cane in my hand. Two years ago, a man on a train stabbed me in the stomach. The knife went deep . . . but the wound was healed in a week. A woman cut me in the neck with a broken bottle in Kansas City. The doctor said I should've bled to death, but I didn't. I had that cane in my hand. It's magic, and that's why it's worth seventeen hundred dollars and a lot more."

Ludlow picked the cane up and examined the lion's-head. His hands were shaking.

"It's full of luck," Chance told him. "Look at me. I'm walking proof."

And Ludlow said in a choked voice, "Your luck . . . has just run its course, Mr. Tigré."

Chance—Randolph Tigré—looked as stunned as if he'd been kicked in the head by a horse.

"My name is Ludlow Usher. You murdered my father, Aram Usher. I think the police would like to—"

And then Tigré leaped violently to his feet with a shouted curse, throwing the table over onto Ludlow. Cards, money, and chips flew through the air. Nicholls squalled like a scalded cat, and Tyson fell over in his chair. As Ludlow toppled backward with the cane in his grasp, Tigré was already drawing an Usher "Gentlemen's Defender" revolver from a holster under his coat. "No!" Brethren shouted, grabbing for the other man's arm. The gun went off, blasting one of the lamps to smithereens. Burning oil splattered across the floor and wall. The second shot blew the side of Tyson's head off as he was staggering to his feet. Then Tigré shoved Brethren aside and fired twice through the upturned table. One bullet snagged Ludlow's sleeve, and the second caught the edge of his left ear like a burning whip. "Murder!" Nicholls shouted. "Help!"

Tigré fled for the door, burst through it and into the narrow passageway. Ludlow went after him, revenge fiery in his veins. As he came through the door and onto the promenade deck, he found Tigré standing at the rail six feet away. With an animalish growl, Tigré brought the pistol up to fire into Ludlow's face.

But Ludlow was faster with the cane. He struck the other man's arm, upsetting his aim, and the bullet blazed over his shoulder. Then Ludlow barreled headlong into him; they smashed together and there was a sharp cracking sound as the rail broke. Clinging to each other, Ludlow and Tigré fell over the side into the churning river.

Underwater, Tigré hammered at Ludlow with the pistol. They turned over and over, blinded by mud, wrenched by tremendous currents. Ludlow's back slammed against something hard. A pounding, roaring noise filled his head—and he realized they'd been pulled underneath the *Bayou Moon*. The boat's hull was over their heads, the grinding paddlewheel dangerously close.

His flailing fist struck Tigré's body. He grasped the man's coat, but a booted foot kicked him in the stomach and precious air exploded from Ludlow's mouth. Tigré wrenched free, desperately swimming away. A fierce downward current caught Ludlow, and in the next instant he was caught in the branches of an underwater tree less than ten feet below the surface. He struggled to free himself, the last of his air burning in his lungs.

Tigré was caught in a current that hurled him toward the surface. His head slammed against wood, and then he gasped for breath. His relief turned rapidly to terror. The river boiled around him, and he was being lifted out of the water by his neck. His head was caught between the spokes of the paddlewheel. As it brought him up from the river, Tigré screamed with the pressure on his head and neck. His scream became strangled, and the knot of people who watched in horror saw Randolph Tigré's body writhe as his neck snapped. As

328

if on a hideous revolving gallows, Tigré was borne up by the paddlewheel and then down into the water—and up again, lifeless and covered with mud.

And in the paddlewheel's wake, a tree that had been weighted down with mud rose suddenly from the bottom of the river. From its upper branches dangled Ludlow Usher, half-drowned and battered—but clutching in his hand his father's cane.

◆◆◆

Rix was staring up at the brooding portrait of Ludlow. "Randolph Tigré believed the cane protected him from death?" he asked softly.

"At least that's the story Nicholls gave the reporter. Of course, he might've said anything to get off the hook."

"I remember . . . Mom said something a couple of days ago about Dad being thrown from a horse and falling on his head." Rix turned toward Edwin. "She said he got up and brushed himself off, and he was just fine. As far as I know, Dad's never really been seriously injured."

Edwin raised his eyebrows. "Are you saying the *cane* had something to do with that?"

"I don't know. But if Tigré could survive all those injuries while he was in possession of the cane—"

"You're thinking like a fiction writer," Edwin said. "It's just a cane, not a magic wand. I repeated the story as I recalled it from a newspaper article—and I think it goes without saying that the newspapers in those days exaggerated wildly."

Rix stared for a silent moment at Edwin. "What if it *is* magic?" he asked. "A good-luck charm or something? That's why it protected Tigré until Ludlow got it back. And that's why every Usher has kept it so close to him. Look at those portraits." He motioned with a sweep of his hand. "The cane's within reach in every picture."

Edwin nodded. "I know that. But the cane's a symbol of power, too. It would naturally be in all the pictures, and naturally the Usher patriarch would always have it close at hand." The thunder sounded nearer, and Edwin flinched slightly. "The storm's building. I expect we'll have a downpour before long." He rose from his seat. "I was reluctant to tell you that story because of what I knew about Shann and the Usher Concerto. That's not something that would reflect very well on your family."

Rix walked beneath the portraits, noting where the cane was positioned in each one. "There's something more to that cane than a symbol of authority, Edwin," he said firmly. He recalled the almost overwhelming sense of power he'd felt course through him when he held it. Had the men in those portraits experienced the same feeling? Looking at Aram's picture, he was struck by a new thought. Had Aram realized he was going to die on the day of that duel because he no longer had the cane? And had he used that realization against Tigré by simply failing to load his pistol?

"Well, I've got to find Logan. If you see him, please tell him to report to Cass or me." Edwin paused at the door. "And make sure you eat lunch, Rix. There's no sense in weakening yourself."

"I will," Rix said, and Edwin left the library.

Now he had the information that Wheeler Dunstan wanted. Perhaps, also, Dunstan could shed some light on the notebook containing the sketches and math formulas.

Carrying the notebook, Rix went out of the library. He was crossing the smoking room when a violent clap of thunder crashed over Usherland. The delicate mechanism of the ornate grandfather clock, which no longer chimed the hours due to Walen's condition, let out a soft, musical tinkle. Rix glanced at the brass pendulum— and stopped immediately. Realization clicked into place in his mind like the tumblers of a lock.

He opened the book to the sketches and compared them with the long pendulum rod, with its half-moon decoration at the bottom.

The sketches were of *pendulums* with varying shapes of pendulum bobs.

Pendulum, he thought. Walen's secret project. But this book obviously predated Walen. Whose was it? And what did it mean?

As he stood looking from the book to the grandfather clock, he imagined he felt the floor shiver—for just a fleeting second—under his feet. A wall groaned softly, and then was silent.

He waited, his heartbeat picking up, for another vibration, but none followed.

He had a lot of questions to ask Wheeler Dunstan, and he hurried up to his room to get the newspaper account of Cynthia Usher's death.

And this time, Rix vowed, he intended to see the manuscript of *Time Will Tell the Tale*—one way or another.

Seven

THE
LODGE

38

Raven and New were alone in the *Democrat* office. It was a cluttered place with a few desks and typewriters, a row of filing cabinets, and metal shelves that held dictionaries, encyclopedias, and recent copies of the paper. At her desk, Raven sat drinking a cup of strong black coffee from the Mr. Coffee machine, and trying to compose her thoughts. On her blotter was a scatter of paper clips she'd straightened out. The IN compartment of the wire-mesh organizer on her desk held stories from the gardening editor and the features editor, color negatives of the fall foliage, and pictures of several young ladies who were getting married the following week—all items from a world that suddenly seemed very remote.

New stood across the room, clutching the Mountain King's stick and staring at the poster with the four children's photographs on it that Raven had taped to a wall. Beyond the *Democrat*'s plate-glass window, the morning had become a strange purple-tinged twi-light. The thunder continued, still at a distance, but there had been neither lightning nor rain. The wind was rising, swirling grit along the sidewalk.

The boy had been silent since they'd arrived here from the clinic. After his demonstration in the waiting room, Raven avoided catching his gaze. She was afraid of him, of what might be lurking inside him, trying to break loose. It was like being around a muscle-bound brute with a short temper, though Raven didn't think the boy would intentionally hurt anyone. Still, she sensed his tension; there was a fuse burning within him, and she didn't know what the spark might set off when it reached the end.

He moved away from the poster and looked at the encyclope-dias. "You read all these books?" he asked.

"Not all of them, but a little in each one."

"You must be smart. To write stories and all, I mean."

"Not necessarily. It's just a job, like any other."

New nodded thoughtfully. He selected the *B* volume and paged through it. "I don't go to school much anymore," he said. "Ma keeps me home to help around the house. The teacher came once to find out why I wasn't in school, but Ma said there were more important things for me to be doin'."

"She's wrong. You should be in school. Your mother can make out without you."

"I'm the man of the house now," he told her, as if that made all the difference. "Ma says I need to be findin' a job pretty soon."

"That'll be hard, without a good education."

"I guess so," he agreed. "It's just . . ." He looked up at her with a pained expression. "I don't want to stay on Briartop Mountain all my life. I don't know what I want to do; I don't know what I *can* do yet. I feel like . . . I'm in a cage or somethin'. Maybe that's why . . . I dream about the Lodge so much. It seems like goin' down to that Lodge is the only way I can ever get off the mountain. Usherland is so beautiful from up high. Briartop is all thorns and rocks. Nathan and I . . . used to talk about what we were gonna be." A fragile smile played quickly across his mouth. "Nathan wanted to fly planes. We could stand and watch 'em pass over, headin' to Asheville, I guess. They looked like they were a thousand miles away."

"And what did you say you wanted to be?"

"You . . . promise you won't laugh?"

"I promise."

"Before he died," New said, "Pa used to read me stories from old magazines. Stories about detectives and cowboys and spies. I guess when I was a kid I wanted to be a detective, and carry a badge and all. After Pa died, I started . . . makin' up my own stories, in my head. I never wrote any of 'em down or anything, 'cause Ma would've thought I was actin' like a kid. I know you have to be real smart and all, but . . . I sure would like to be able to write down what was in my head. I'd like for other people to see the pictures in my mind. Does that make sense?"

"You mean you'd like to be a writer?"

He shrugged, but Raven saw a hint of color in his cheeks. "I don't know. I don't have the education for it, I guess. I mean . . . it's pretty hard to do, right?"

"It takes patience and practice. But that doesn't mean you can't do it."

He returned the book to its place on the shelf and walked over to the window, where he stood facing the street. Briartop Mountain was a massive gray shape whose peak vanished in the low-hanging clouds. His hand tightened around the stick. "I should've been able to help Nathan," he said softly. "I should've been able to do *somethin'*!"

"What happened to Nathan wasn't your fault. It wasn't your mother's, either. She's afraid of the outside world, New. That's why she doesn't want you to go to school—because she's afraid you'll leave her alone on the mountain. She doesn't want you to outgrow Briartop."

"I don't want to stay there all my life. I want to—"

He stopped speaking, and Raven saw his spine stiffen. He took two steps away from the window, his head cocked to one side as if listening.

"New?" Raven tensed. "What is it?"

He didn't answer. A dull throb of thunder made the window shake. He thought he'd heard his name called in a soft, seductive voice that was neither masculine nor feminine but something more elemental, as if the wind and the thunder itself could speak. He listened carefully, expecting and dreading the voice.

It came—faint, urging, meant for him alone:

—*New*—

Answer, he told himself. He said mentally, *I'm here.*

—*come home come home come home*—

The voice was stronger now, and eager. New felt it battering at his mind, trying to sink deeply. "The Lodge wants me," he told Raven. "I can feel it, even from here." As the voice continued to pull at him, he turned toward Raven. His face was strained, his eyes dark green and full of purpose. "I'm going to it," he said. "I'm going to find out what's in that house, and why it wants me."

"A storm's coming. There's no way for you to get into Usherland, anyway. The gates are—"

"Won't go through the gates," he said. "There are trails going down from Briartop to Usherland, through the woods." But how could he protect himself from whatever waited in the Lodge? He had the cane, though he didn't fully understand how it would help him. No, he needed something else: a snare, something he could trigger and control when and if he needed it. He looked around the

335

office, and his gaze settled on a tape dispenser atop a nearby desk. He picked it up and peeled off some tape. "Do you have any tape stronger than this?" he asked.

Raven opened a desk drawer and brought out a roll of filament tape that she used to seal packages for mailing. He took it from her, examined it, and then put it in his pocket. "That'll do." He looked sharply at her. "Will you drive me to the cabin? I can take the truck down to Usherland from there."

"Are you sure you want to do this? I can call Sheriff Kemp, and—"

"And what?" he challenged her. "The sheriff can't help me. Nobody can. Whatever's in the Lodge wants *me*. I have to find out why."

Raven slowly untwisted another paper clip. The boy's eyes pierced her, and she knew nothing could stop him. She took her keys from her purse and unlocked the lower drawer of her desk, bringing from it a camera case with a thirty-five-millimeter Canon and a flash attachment. "All right," she said. "I've always wanted to see what the Lodge looked like inside."

"No." His voice snapped through the air. "I don't know what's in there. I won't take you with me."

Raven's stomach was knotted at the prospect of entering the Lodge; under any other circumstances, she would have leaped at the opportunity to penetrate the Usher world. Now, the unknown both terrified and tantalized her. "I *know* what's in the Lodge," she replied. "Answers. To your questions, and to mine. If you want a ride up Briartop, you'll have to take me the rest of the way, too."

I could make her do as I please, New thought. I can keep her out of the Lodge, if I want to.

"I deserve to know," she said firmly, distracting him from his thoughts. "If you want to go in, we'd better get ourselves some good lights from the hardware store, a couple of those big lanterns that won't go out if they're dropped. And waterproof, too, from the look of those clouds." She stood up and put the strap of the camera case around her shoulder. "Well?" she asked.

New decided he'd let her think he'd take her in, and then he'd send her back to Foxton once they got up the mountain. He could not take the responsibility of protecting her from whatever waited in the Lodge.

"How about it?" Raven prompted.

He nodded, sliding his hand into his pocket to touch the tape. "All right. Let's go."

39

A jagged spear of lightning flashed over the mountains as Rix pulled the Thunderbird up in front of Wheeler Dunstan's house. In the air was the chlorine odor of ozone, and dust whirled up from a distant field.

Rix walked up the front steps and pressed the door buzzer. He carried the notebook and the newspaper account of Cynthia Usher's death under his arm. As he waited, Rix glanced uneasily down Dunstan's gravel driveway. He'd passed a brown van that was pulled off the road, about twenty yards from the entrance to the driveway, and he recalled seeing the same van a few days before. Was Dunstan's house being watched? he wondered, scanning the woods. If so, whoever it was had seem him in a highly visible Usher vehicle. Another concern nagged at him as well. When he'd gone out to the garage, he'd seen that Katt's car was missing. Had she gone to Asheville to score more heroin? Boone's Ferrari had been gone, too, but Rix figured he was sleeping off a bad night at the country club. He pressed the buzzer again, then turned to watch the woods at his back. Anyone spying certainly had a clear view of him.

"Who is it?" Dunstan asked from the other side of the door.

"Rix Usher."

Locks clicked open. Dunstan, the corncob pipe clamped firmly between his teeth, guided his chair backward to allow Rix entry. Rix stepped in and closed the door behind him.

"Lock it," Dunstan said, and Rix did. "Sorry it took me so long to get up here. I been workin' since way before daylight." He looked strained, with dark circles beneath his eyes. He glanced at the items Rix held. "What've you got?"

"First this." Rix handed him the fragile newspaper pages. "It's an account of Cynthia's death in Chicago."

Dunstan took his chair into the parlor, where the light was better, and Rix followed. The last red embers of a fire glowed brightly in the hearth. "Okay," he said when he'd finished reading, "this clears up one question. What about the scepter?"

Rix sat down and told him the story that Edwin had related. Dunstan listened intently, blue whorls of smoke curling above his

337

head. When Rix had finished, Dunstan's flinty stare was impassive. "I need documents to prove all that," he said.

"Edwin says the clippings are in the Lodge's library."

"Don't do me much good there. Can you get 'em for me?"

"Edwin might be able to. I'll ask him." He offered Dunstan the black notebook. "I wanted you to look at this, too."

He opened it and slowly paged through it, his brow furrowing. "This come from the Lodge's library? What's all this figurin' mean?"

"I hoped you'd be able to tell me."

"Nope. Sorry. What're these drawin's here?" He tapped the page of sketches.

"I think they're clock pendulums. But why they're in that book, and what they mean, I don't know."

"Ludlow was always interested in clocks," Dunstan mused. "Kept 'em around him all the time. Could be this is one of his notebooks, but I can't make any sense out of this arithmetic or the music notes." He placed the book on his lap and looked up at Rix. "You know that Ludlow was an inventor. Supposedly he was always workin' on somethin' down in that workshop of his in the Lodge. Could be this is one of his projects."

"You mean a weapon of some kind?"

"Who can say? I've heard that visitors to Usherland sometimes saw sparks jumpin' off those lightnin' rods on the roof. Ludlow locked himself in his workshop for days at a time. There's no tellin' what he was up to, but more than likely it had somethin' to do with the business."

Rix took the notebook back from Dunstan and examined the sketches again.

"If it's a weapon," Dunstan said, "what would *music* have to do with it?"

"I don't know," Rix replied—but he was already forming a theory. Shann had been a musical prodigy. The Usher Concerto had affected people in a way that drove them to suicide like lemmings. When Ludlow had gone to visit her in New Orleans, had he been trying to tap into Shann's musical ability for the Pendulum project? Was that why he'd wanted her to renounce the convent and return to Usherland? There was no way to find out unless he learned what Pendulum was. "Yesterday," Rix said, "you mentioned another question you have about my family. You said it was an important question. I'd like to hear it."

Dunstan rolled his chair to the hearth and used a poker to probe at the remaining bits of charred wood. Then he returned the poker to its stand with the other fireplace tools and paused thoughtfully before answering. He swung the chair around to face Rix. "I saw Walen before your grandfather died. He was handsome, full of energy. Looked like he could take on the world with one hand tied behind his back." He struck a match and relit his pipe. "A month after Erik died, Walen's limo had a flat tire a block away from the *Democrat* office. I moseyed out to take a look, while Edwin Bodane used a pay phone to call for another car. I got one glimpse of Walen before he pulled the curtain across his window." He looked long and hard at Rix. "It wasn't the same man."

Rix frowned. "What do you mean? It wasn't Walen?"

"Oh, it was Walen, all right. But an old, broken-down Walen. I'll never forget his eyes—he looked like he'd had a visit from the Devil himself. He had that cane in his hand; I remember that, too. But I've never seen such a change in a man in so short a time."

"I suppose Erik's death affected him."

"Why should it? From what I understand, Walen wasn't a doting son. Now listen to this: Erik had a nervous breakdown on the night of Ludlow's death. It was during one of Erik's fancy parties. Ludlow called him up to the Quiet Room. A couple of hours later, some of the guests heard hell breakin' loose in Erik's study. They got in and found Erik havin' a fit—smashin' furniture, throwin' things against the walls. It took four or five men to hold him down till somebody could call a doctor. Then Erik locked himself away for a month." Dunstan lifted his eyebrows quizzically. "Why?" he asked. "Erik hated Ludlow. Why would Ludlow's death drive him crazy?"

"It shouldn't have," Rix said. "If anything, I'd think Erik would've danced with joy."

"Right. Erik did everything he could to hurry along his father's death. And Walen was no better a son; he wouldn't have lifted a finger to help Erik. Why, then, did both of them react the way they did?"

"I don't know."

"Neither do I. Nor does anybody else. But I'll tell you what *I* think." Dunstan leaned forward, his eyes bright blue and intense. "Somethin' passed from father to son at the last minute. Maybe some kind of information, or some responsibility that neither Erik nor Walen figured on. I think Ludlow told Erik somethin' in that Quiet Room, right before he died, that almost drove Erik insane."

"And Erik passed whatever it was to Walen before *he* died?"

"Yes. Which is why Walen's health broke right after his father died. Both Erik and Walen were okay again, with the passage of time. Maybe the shock of it wore off, or they just went on because they had no choice. My question is, what's passed from father to son, just before the patriarch dies?"

"The cane," Rix said. It seemed an obvious answer.

"No, it's more than that. The cane's no surprise. I think this is somethin' that's hidden until the last minute—some responsibility that needs to be carried on from one generation to the next. I've asked Edwin about it, but of course he won't say. He just brings the documents, leaves 'em, and then picks 'em up again when I'm through." He folded his hands before him. "The answer may be in the Lodge's library. I need to find it."

"I can't go into the Lodge, not after what happened to me when I was a boy."

"But you could go in with Edwin, couldn't you? He could take you down to that library."

Rix shrugged. The idea of entering the Lodge, even with Edwin, made his stomach ache with dread. "I don't know. But what would I be looking for?"

"Business records. Property titles. Anything on Hudson Usher. Maybe something about the ancestors in Wales. Aram's marriage to Shann's mother, in San Francisco. He met her when he went there to find his Aunt Madeline, against Hudson's strict orders. Maybe documents on the Pennsylvania estate, and Roderick's death. It's supposed to be an Usher museum down there, and if there's an answer to the question in any written form—that's most likely where it'll be."

Rix ran his hand over the notebook's moldy cover. From outside, the boom of thunder sounded nearer. If he did find the courage to enter the Lodge again, he told himself, it would have to be for a damned good reason. "I want to see your manuscript now," he said.

"Not yet. I'll show it to you when you bring me what I want to see."

Rix looked up into the other man's stern, set expression. He realized suddenly, with a twist of anger in his guts, that Wheeler Dunstan was playing with him, using him as an errand boy with no intention of letting him share in the book. "*Now*," Rix demanded. "I've already risked enough for you. I could search through that library for a year and never find what you're looking for! If my father finds out what I'm doing, he'll—"

"Disinherit you?" Dunstan asked slyly. "I thought you had no interest in the business."

Rix winced inwardly at the sarcasm in Dunstan's voice, and now he damned himself for ever getting involved with the man. Even if he did hope, deep in his soul, that he might get a sizable chunk of the Usher fortune, he'd be finished if the house was being watched. He had to salvage something out of the wreckage! "Now you listen to me," he said coldly. "I've proven to you that I can help you write this book. I think I deserve to read the manuscript."

"No. I'm not letting anyone see it until it's finished."

"You don't know what I've put on the line by being here, damn it!" Rix rose angrily from his chair. "I'm not working for *you*! If you want me to go in the Lodge and do your dirty work for you, you're going to have to show me what you've written already! I won't risk anything more until I see the manuscript for myself!"

Dunstan opened his mouth to speak again—and then his face seemed to freeze, his eyes glazing over as if he were staring right through Rix. One hand slowly came up and took the pipe from between his teeth. And in a strange, eerily emotionless voice, Dunstan said, "I won't show my book to anyone."

"There won't be a book worth publishing if you don't let me help you!" Rix snapped. "Who's going to bring you documents after Edwin leaves?"

Dunstan's face remained masklike. "I won't show my book to anyone," he repeated.

Rix was angry enough to strike him, but the man seemed to be in some kind of trance. What the hell's wrong with him? Rix thought. Raven had never seen the manuscript, either. Why not? What was Dunstan trying to conceal? Rix glanced at Dunstan's shirt pocket, where he kept his office key with the little typewriter charm on it. Rix walked purposefully toward the man, who seemed not to even acknowledge his presence, then stepped quickly behind the chair and thrust his hand into Dunstan's pocket. His fingers closed around the typewriter charm—but as he brought his hand out, Dunstan suddenly gripped it with a strength that almost crushed Rix's knuckles. Rix's hand opened, and the key ring hit the armrest and fell to the floor. Before Dunstan could swivel his chair around, Rix retrieved the key ring. "All right, damn you!" Rix said fiercely. "Now I'll see it for myself!" He strode toward the corridor and the door to the basement.

Thunder crashed near the house. Rix heard the clang of metal against metal, and twisted around.

Dunstan was coming at him in the wheelchair, the fireplace poker raised in his hand. Still, Dunstan's face was remote, expressionless. He was moving like a machine on wheels.

"Come on!" Rix said incredulously. "What the hell do you think you're—"

The poker flashed downward in a vicious arc. Rix reacted too slowly, and was struck hard on the shoulder. Pain coursed through his arm, and he staggered backward.

Dunstan swung again. Rix ducked to one side, and the poker narrowly missed his skull.

"Stop it!" Rix shouted. The old man had lost his mind! Before Dunstan could lift the poker again, Rix grasped the chair's armrests to shove him across the floor—but Dunstan's free hand clamped around his wrist like an iron manacle.

The dead eyes stared up into Rix's face. "I won't show my book to anyone," he repeated, in a hoarse and strangled voice. He brought the poker up for another blow. Rix grabbed at it, throwing his weight against the side of the chair. It tipped over, spilling Wheeler Dunstan onto the floor. Lifting himself on his powerful forearms, Dunstan began to drag himself after Rix.

Stunned, Rix retreated before him. Dunstan pulled himself forward, his face still set and glistening with sweat. Rix backed away, into the corridor. The door to the basement was only a few feet away. He went through it and down the ramp as Dunstan gave a guttural cry.

In the clutter of Dunstan's office, Rix realized the original manuscript could be hidden anywhere. There was no way to find it without tearing the place apart—but the word processor was still on, and displayed on the green-glowing screen was what Dunstan had been writing before Rix had interrupted him.

Rix approached the desk, shoving aside a stack of papers to get a good look.

What he saw brought a dazed half-laugh, half-moan from his throat.

There was one paragraph: *Time will tell the tale. There will always be war, and someone will always make the weapons. Time will tell the tale. The Usher name is a deterrent to war. Time will tell the tale.*

The paragraph was repeated over and over, in various combinations of sentences. With a trembling hand, Rix pressed the terminal's key that scrolled the screen down. It obeyed, and Rix read the essence of the Usher family history that Dunstan had been writing for six years.

The Usher name is a deterrent to war. Time will tell the tale. There will always be war, and someone will always make the weapons. Time will tell the tale.

It went on and on, page after page.

"Oh Jesus," Rix whispered.

There was no book. There had never been a book. Wheeler Dunstan was insane. Had he come down here, day after day for six years, and thought he was writing a complete manuscript?

There will always be war, and someone will always make the weapons. Time will tell the tale—

Rix ran from the basement and up the ramp, his heart hammering so loudly he could hardly think. In the parlor, the wheelchair still lay on its side, but the man had crawled away. The poker was on the floor, near the notebook Rix had dropped. He picked the book up. Outside, thunder crashed and rain began to slam against the roof. Within seconds, a downpour started that was so dense he couldn't see his car through the bay windows.

As Rix neared the front door, he saw Dunstan lying on his face on the floor, his arms curled beneath his body. To leave the house, Rix would have to pass him. Dunstan's body suddenly trembled, and then he slowly turned his face toward Rix.

Dunstan's eyes had rolled back in his head, showing only the bloodshot whites. Sweat gleamed on his pallid cheeks and forehead. His mouth gasped for air, then formed barely intelligible words: "I won't . . . show my book . . . to anyone."

He brought his right hand up from under his body. In it was an Usher .357 Commando.

Rix leaped to one side as the gun went off. A fist-sized hole spouted shards of wood from the parlor wall.

Rix crouched on the floor behind the meager protection of a chair, the fireplace at his back. The Commando held five more bullets. Over the drumming of the rain, Rix heard Dunstan dragging himself across the floor. He tensed to run for the corridor, but the fallen wheelchair was in the way. If he tripped over it, Dunstan could put a shot right through his back. He looked wildly around for something with which to protect himself. The fireplace shovel leaned against the hearth. Rix glanced at the red embers, then took the shovel and scooped up ashes and fragments of smoking wood.

Rix waited, listening to the slow slide of Dunstan's body. He

343

would get only one chance; if he didn't calculate it exactly, Dunstan would blow him away.

His pores leaked cold sweat; still he waited, trying to visualize how and where Dunstan would be lying. He heard the man shove aside a piece of furniture; a lamp clattered to the floor.

Wait, he told himself. Lightning flashed outside the windows, followed almost at once by a roll of thunder that shook the house.

The sound of Dunstan's dragging body stopped.

And Rix thought: *Now!*

With a burst of adrenaline, he shoved the chair forward with his shoulder. Across the room, Dunstan fired; the bullet tore through the fabric inches from Rix's face, spraying him with smoking cotton. Before Dunstan could readjust his aim, Rix rose up and flung the embers.

The other man got off a third wild shot as the embers scattered across his face and the front of his shirt. The bullet whined past Rix's head, smashing one of the bay windows. Rain and wind swept into the room. Then Dunstan was writhing on the floor, the embers sizzling on his cheeks and scorching through his shirt.

Rix grasped his wrist and tried to shake the Commando loose. Dunstan's other hand came up, grabbing at Rix's sweater. Rix brought his fist down on the man's elbow—once, twice, and again, as hard as he could strike. Dunstan's fingers opened, and the Commando fell to the floor. Rix picked it up and scrambled away from the man.

"All right," he said huskily. "It's over."

Dunstan stared blankly up at him, red welts across his cheeks and forehead. Then his face collapsed and he began sobbing like a child. Rix couldn't bear to look at him; he emptied the three remaining cartridges from the Commando into his pocket, then put the gun out of Dunstan's reach, atop the mantel.

At the rear of the house, Rix found a telephone and dialed the operator, asking for the sheriff's office. The line crackled and hissed with static. When the telephone was answered, Rix said there had been an accident at the Dunstan house near Taylorville, and hung up as the woman asked his name.

There was nothing more he could do. He thought of calling Raven, but what could he say to her? Sorry, but her father was insane and had tried to kill him, and there had never been a book? His nerves were jangling as he returned to the parlor. Dunstan lay on his side, breathing shallowly, his stare fixed and vacant.

Rix stood over the man, as wind and rain slashed at him through

344

the shattered window. Rage stirred within him, gathered and coiled. He had cooperated with Dunstan for nothing, had risked whatever inheritance he might receive for an Usher history that had never existed.

Dunstan gave a soft, tormented moan. One arm was flung out at his side, the fist tightly closed.

He made a fool of me, Rix seethed. Because of him, I risked everything!

The brown van. If Dunstan's house was being watched by some-one that Walen sent, then . . .

Rix's hands clenched at his sides, his nails digging crescent moons into the skin of his palms. And from deep within him, from that dark stranger in himself that he did not know and had denied existed inside his skin, came the urge to kill.

He looked at the gun on the mantel. One shot would do it. The barrel pressed against Dunstan's skull, the man's blood and brains running with the raindrops on the wall. One shot.

—*do it now*—

Rix looked into his hand. He'd brought the three bullets out of his pocket.

—*do it now*—

Lightning streaked, hit the earth somewhere close. Thunder filled the house.

Rix held the Commando. He started to slide a bullet into the chamber.

—*do it now*—

He clicked the cylinder shut. Sweat and rain streamed down his face. The gun felt good in his hand; it felt like power—absolute, unyielding power.

He turned toward Wheeler Dunstan, walked to him, and aimed the gun downward at his head. One shot. Do it now.

His hand was shaking. A cold rage had taken control of him, yet he seemed detached, as though watching himself from a distance. The dark stranger in his soul whispered urgently for him to squeeze the trigger. This was no longer Raven's father lying on the floor; this was Walen Usher's bitterest enemy, and because of him Rix had put all his faith in a nonexistent book. He had risked everything to help Dunstan—and now he would be cut off from the Usher fortune without a dime. His finger tightened on the trigger.

Dunstan moaned, and his fist began to open.

In the palm was a silver button. It was one of the buttons from

Rix's sweater, and he realized Dunstan had yanked it off when Rix fought for the gun.

A silver button, Rix thought. He tried to think past the whisper that urged him to kill Raven's father. A silver button. Where had he seen—

His head pounded fiercely, and the voice within him shrieked *DO IT NOW!*

His finger convulsed on the trigger, and at the same time Rix heard his own desperate cry.

The Commando fired, gouging wood from the floor six inches from Dunstan's skull.

Rix turned and, with a shout of anger and revulsion, flung the gun through the broken window.

He picked up the silver button and ran from the house, through the sheets of rain to his car. At the end of the driveway, he saw that the brown van was gone. He sank his foot to the floor, causing the Thunderbird to fishtail dangerously. His hands gripped the wheel hard, and his shame at being so close to murder brought bitter tears to his eyes.

He had almost done something that—for the first time in his life—would have made his father very, very proud.

40

The drive to and from Asheville had been a route through hell. At the wheel of her Maserati, as the rain slashed in gray sheets across the road, Katt's concentration had narrowed down to a burning candle, a spoonful of bubbling heroin, and a hypodermic syringe.

The windshield wipers didn't help much. She trembled for need of the junk; her skin felt raw, peeled open. Her nerves sputtered in little panics. Even the palms of her hands in her lambskin driving gloves felt flame-blistered. A flash of lightning startled her, and for the first time in a long while she feared an attack.

Taped beneath her seat was a packet containing a quarter-ounce of heroin, purchased an hour before from an Asheville investment banker that Katt knew as "Mr. Candy Garden." Margaret had introduced them at a party several years before, and later had confided

346

to Katt that she hoped her daughter found him attractive; after all, he was one of the most eligible bachelors in North Carolina.

She guided the Maserati through Usherland's gates and swept past the Gatehouse toward the garage. She pressed the button under the dashboard that raised the door to the Maserati's stall, then drove into the cool darkness.

The garage lights hadn't come on, Katt noted, and assumed that the storm might have blown a circuit or something. She'd have it looked at. She cut the purring engine, deposited her keys in her purse, and took the precious packet from its hiding place. The anticipation of quiet, restful dreams soothed her. In them she was always a little girl whose main preoccupation was tagging after her older brother, or riding horses along the gentle Usherland trails, or watching the clouds make pictures as they formed and broke over the mountains. Her dreams were always of summer, and in them she wore bright little-girl dresses. Sometimes her father visited her dreams, and he always smiled and said how pretty he thought she was.

Katt got out of the car. Suddenly, with a muted growl of gears and chains, the garage door began to descend.

Startled, she turned to watch the door sink to the concrete floor. There was a master control panel elsewhere in the garage that opened and closed all the stall doors, but it was way over near the limo. The murky gray light was cut to a sliver, then disappeared as the garage door met concrete.

Katt stood in total darkness. The rain beat a maniacal tattoo against the garage roof, and Katt felt as if she were drowning in black water. Her fear of the dark had immobilized her. She had made sure that even her Quiet Room allowed a chink of light; she preferred the pain of light to the horror of the dark.

"Where are the lights?" she said aloud to quell her rising panic. "There should be lights on in here!"

Headlights! she thought. She fumbled for the keys in her purse, then her fingers closed around the furry rabbit's foot on her keychain. She leaned into the Maserati, slid the key in, and switched on the ignition. When she turned on the headlights—their beams directed at shelves holding cans of oil, transmission fluid, fan belts, and various automotive tools hanging from wall hooks—she almost sobbed with relief. She reached beneath the dashboard to open the stall door again.

A cold, muscular arm slid around her throat from behind, pulling her out of the car. Her scream was canceled as it began by a hand clamped to her mouth.

Katt struggled wildly to break free. She could smell a man's body odor. His unshaven cheek scratched her ear. "Don't fight," he whispered. "There's no use fighting."

She continued to thrash, but she was weakening. *Don't fight,* the voice repeated in her mind, sapping her willpower. *There's no use fighting.* The command kept echoing inside her head, steadily gaining power as if it were being shouted by someone who was coming closer and closer. Hopelessness invaded her, and as her struggling stopped she heard, as if in a nightmare from which she couldn't awaken, the man's satisfied grunt.

"I'm going to let you go," he said. "You're not going to scream. You don't have a voice anymore. I'm going to let you go, and you're going to stand right where you are."

Not going to scream, she thought. No use fighting. Not going to scream. Stand right where you are.

He released her.

She wanted to scream; her throat vibrated, the muscles straining to pull a scream up through her mouth. Not going to scream. You don't have a voice anymore. No use fighting.

Her arms and legs were icy. She tried to move them, found she couldn't even unlock her elbows. Stand right where you are. The more she strained to move and scream, the harder and more hopeless moving and screaming became. No use fighting. Not going to scream.

The man walked in front of her, and in the wash of the Maserati's headlights, Katt recognized Logan Bodane.

She'd seen him a few times, hanging around the Gatehouse. His face was different now; his eyes glittered dangerously in the slack, gray-tinged flesh. His mouth was twisted in a sick grin. The gray Usher blazer he wore was dusty, but not wet. Neither was his tangled mass of coppery red hair. The part of Katt's mind that could still form coherent thoughts judged that Logan had been in the garage before the rain started. Waiting for her, for this moment?

Logan's gaze played slowly over Katt's body. Then he looked directly into her face, and his eyes seemed to flame like baleful blue lamps.

—smile—

His silent, mental command slid into Katt's mind like the point of an icepick. It sank deeply, with a prick of pain.

348

Katt felt her mouth twitch. The corners slowly arched upward in a grotesque rictus, while tears of terror rolled down her cheeks.

"That's nice," Logan said aloud. With one quick, violent motion he tore open the front of her pink jumpsuit. She gasped for breath; the smile stayed fixed on her face, and still she was unable to move. In her mind his voice—*smile no use fighting smile not going to scream stand right where you are*—continued to batter back and forth.

Logan retreated a pace to admire her body. "It's comin' for you," he whispered, his eyes dancing back and forth from Katt's face to her body. "Yeah, it's comin' right now. The executioner, I mean. It'll be here soon. I've seen it." He grinned, well pleased with himself. "I don't mean to let you go to waste before it gets here." He advanced on her.

Katt trembled violently, but could not break loose from whatever hold Logan had on her. As he grasped roughly at her breasts, his mouth on her throat, Katt couldn't even close her eyes. An inner scream wailed, but she had no voice. She ground her teeth in anguish.

Logan grabbed her hair and forced her head back. "Thought you were better than me, didn't you?" he asked her, his eyes narrowed into slits. "Well, I'm going to show you how wrong you were, lady." He kissed her on the mouth, jabbing his tongue in while his hand began to slide down her stomach.

Her teeth, Katt realized. She could still use her teeth.

Logan made a guttural, bestial sound and clutched at her breasts. His tongue probed deeply into her mouth.

And Katt caught it between her teeth.

Before Logan could jerk his head away, Katt bit down with all the fury and strength she could summon.

When Logan screamed, the mental chains that had held Katt fast broke apart. They scattered like dead leaves in a high wind. Feeling rushed back into her limbs with a pins-and-needles tingling. But still she continued to bite down on his tongue, as he screamed and fought to shove her away.

She felt his tongue rip. Blood filled her mouth.

Logan staggered backward, blood streaming from between his lips, and fell to his knees on the floor. He struggled to rise, his mangled roar spewing more blood.

Katt spat flesh out of her mouth. She started to run, but Logan seized her ankle and almost threw her down. She flailed, trying to break free—and then she saw the tire-iron, hanging from one of the wall hooks, within reach. She grasped it, and turned toward Logan as he heaved himself off the floor. His frenzied *NO!* exploded in her mind, but her arm was already on its descent. The tire-iron crunched down on Logan's skull.

He fell to his hands and knees, his head lolling. She stood over him and struck him again, across the right shoulder blade. There was a noise like a broomstick cracking. Logan pitched on his side, his eyes blazing wildly in his blood-smeared face.

Behind Katt, the cans and tools on the shelves suddenly came alive. They leaped in all directions, a can of antifreeze hitting Katt in the side, a pair of jumper-cables snapping through her hair, a wrench flashing past her cheek. The Maserati's windshield shattered. Freezing currents of Logan's misdirected power smashed back and forth across the garage, breaking more windshields, upsetting more cans and tools. A shockwave struck Katt, throwing her against the hood so hard that she lost her breath. Then she reached into her car and found the garage door switch, pressing it frantically. The garage door began to slide open, letting in gray light and blowing rain.

She ran, ducking under the door and into the storm. The rain almost beat her down, but she kept going, up through the gardens toward the Gatehouse. She slipped on a mossy stone and fell, gashing her knee. Around her the trees were in tumultuous motion, dead leaves whirling past her in miniature tornadoes. She looked back over her shoulder—and panic flared anew.

A massive, dark, and unrecognizable shape was coming after her, leaping the ornamental hedges and drowned flowerbeds.

"Help me!" Katt shouted toward the house, but her voice was shredded by the storm. In the next flash of lightning the Gatehouse was briefly illuminated—and Katt thought she saw a figure standing at a window, looking calmly out at the gardens.

She struggled to her feet and ran again. After another few strides, she felt the hair on the back of her neck stand up, and she knew with a terrible certainty that she would not make the Gatehouse.

As she twisted around, the monster behind her tensed and leaped through the rain like an ebony battering ram. Katt screamed, but the black panther's jaws closed around her throat and snapped her neck as she was falling backward to the stone path. She had a sensation of breathlessness, a hot crushing pain on her throat—and then she tumbled headlong into the dark.

She was dead a few seconds after her body hit the ground.

The panther gripped her by the neck and quickly dragged her off into the underbrush. Nearby, a marble faun played its silent pipes in the downpour.

Within minutes, the rain had washed away all traces of Kattrina Usher from the garden stones.

41

"It's raining harder," Raven said as New returned from his room in the Briartop cabin. He'd put on a pair of jeans and wore a patched brown corduroy jacket over his flannel shirt. "The roads are going to be flooded."

"Maybe," he said distractedly. He glanced at his mother, who sat silently in a chair, with the picture of Bobby in her lap. Rain dripped from a dozen leaks in the ceiling, tinkling and plopping into a variety of bowls, cups, and metal pots. Raven and New had reached the cabin when the storm broke, its thunder shaking the flimsy walls.

"You're not goin' down there." Myra didn't look at her son; her fingers ran repeatedly over Bobby's picture. "You're just a boy. You don't know your own mind."

"I'm the man of the house." New tugged at the sleeves of his jacket. "It's time I acted like it."

"How? By gettin' yourself killed? Or worse?" Her watery, unfocused gaze found Raven, who stood across the room, peering out the window at the storm. Raven's black hair was soaked, and matted into tight curls. "Miz Dunstan," Myra said, with heartfelt pleading in her voice, "don't let my boy go down there alone. Please . . . I'm beggin' you."

"We're going together," Raven said, "as soon as the storm lets up."

"No." New zipped his jacket up. "We're not goin' together." He looked defiantly at Raven. "I'm goin' by myself, Miz Dunstan. You're stayin' right here. And I'm not waitin' for the storm to play out, either."

"I meant what I said at the office. God knows, I wish there was another way, but there isn't. I'm going with you."

"The Lodge wants me, not you. I can't stand here and say I can protect you, 'cause it'd be a lie."

"I can take care of myself," Raven said firmly. "I have, for a long time."

New stared at her, probing for a weak spot. She was a stubborn woman, and he sensed that she wasn't easily moved, once she'd made up her mind. His ma was water, but Raven Dunstan was mountain rock.

Thunder cracked and boomed. The windows rattled in their frames.

—New—

The summons was stronger now, pulling him urgently toward Usherland and the Lodge.

—come home—

It faded in and out, drifted away in a silken hiss that became the noise of rain on the roof.

"Don't go." Myra's voice cracked. "Oh Lord, don't go, don't go, don't go . . ."

"I have to find out what happened to Nathan," he told her. "I won't sit on this mountain for another harvest season while the Pumpkin Man takes his pick. And I'm gonna face whatever it is in the Lodge, Ma."

Raven touched New's shoulder, and as he turned his attention to her, intending to command her to stay in the cabin until the storm had passed, he saw the fierce strength in her eyes, the need to know for herself what lay inside the Lodge's walls. He remembered the poster of the children's faces. Maybe she did deserve to find the answer she sought, but he was still afraid for her. How could he protect her against something as strong as the power that called him from Usherland? He almost delivered the command—almost— but then he said, "I'm ready to go now. Are you?"

"I'm ready."

"Lord God," Myra breathed, and caught back a sob.

New retrieved the stick from where he'd propped it near the door. "Ma?" he said, and when she looked up at him from the picture, tears spilled down her face. "I'm gonna come back," he vowed. "But this is somethin' I have to do. Can you understand that?"

"Your pa wouldn't have—"

"I'm not him. I'm nobody but me. I love you, Ma, but I've got to go down to that house."

She gazed at him for a long moment, and then she whispered, "God help you, then. The both of you."

New bent over her and kissed her cheek. Her tears dropped softly to his father's picture.

"I love you," she said, as New and Raven started to leave—and the sound of those words gave New a resolve he'd never known before.

The rain thrashed down as New guided the pickup truck away from the cabin. Only the windshield wiper on his side worked, but it kept the glass clear enough to see through. The two plastic bull's-eye lanterns that Raven had bought at the hardware store sat between them, and Raven wore her camera case around her neck.

"The tape," Raven said. "What did you use it for?"

"My snare," he replied, and offered no more.

The summons was in his mind, throbbing through his bones, eagerly calling to him from Usherland. The first narrow road that New followed was blocked by a fallen tree. He backed up and found another. It, too, was obstructed by deep craters of water and thorns. The third was too steep for the truck to negotiate. As New drove the truck down a fourth trail that twisted precariously through the woods, the tires slipped on loose rocks. The trail narrowed, the fenders barely scraping between tree trunks. Raven rolled down her window to help guide him, the rain flailing into her face.

"We can't make it!" Raven told him. "We'll have to turn back!"

He didn't answer. The beckoning voice of the Lodge was stronger, almost joyful with triumph, an eerie merging of the wind, rain, and thunder. Inching along the trail, the truck steadily penetrated deeper into Usherland.

And abruptly, as the truck rounded a sharp curve, the summons stopped.

New put his foot on the brake. The truck slid forward ten feet before the wheels locked.

Directly in front of them, the trail ended at what appeared to be a dense thicket of dark green vegetation. The truck's headlights couldn't penetrate it. On both sides of the trail, black thorns grew in vicious whorls, like barbed wire.

"There's no way to get through there," Raven said. "You'd need a damned tank!"

But New was staring into the underbrush ahead. This trail had been used recently, and used often; the ruts were too deep, too fresh. He guided the truck forward, and saw something metal glint in the midst of the thicket. He let the truck slide down to where the trail ended before he braked again, and at this distance it was clear what lay just ahead.

353

It was some kind of square structure, covered over with green netting that effectively served as forest camouflage. A large hole had been cut through the netting at ground level, the rest of it securely staked down.

Raven's first thought was that it might be a squatter's cabin— but what squatter would live on Usherland? The camouflage netting disturbed her. Whatever the structure was, it was meant to be hidden.

"Let's take a look," New said, and picked up one of the lanterns. He grasped the stick and got out of the truck. Raven followed him through the driving rain, carrying the second lantern.

As New ducked through the hole, he switched on his light. It was a green-painted clapboard structure, larger inside than it had first appeared. Their lanterns reflected off corroded metal.

"A garage," Raven said softly. "What's a garage doing out here?"

It held three vehicles: a battered old tan Ford, a dark green pickup truck, and a black Rambler pitted with rust holes. None of them had license plates, but shoved back in a cobwebby corner was a cardboard box that gave up a few old North Carolina plates to Raven's light. Most of their numerals were obscured beneath dried mud.

New shone his light into the Ford. A black canvas bag lay in the rear floorboard.

It was large enough, he thought grimly, to hold a child's body.

On the front seat of the pickup truck was a scatter of peppermint candies, still in their wrappers.

Raven looked into the black Rambler. On the floorboard was a map, and she opened the door to examine it. As she picked it up, a large gray rat squeaked and scurried from beneath it, under the protection of the seat.

"Jesus," she said quietly, but she opened the map and saw that it depicted the immediate area around Usherland. There were red checkmarks—dozens of them—near the thin lines of backcountry roads. Raven's stomach had begun to clench, and she heard New say in a taut voice, "Over here."

He was standing at the rear of the garage, pointing his light downward. When Raven reached him, she felt cold air on her face. A thick, damp smell wafted up. She aimed her own lantern toward the ground.

The floor was made of hardpacked dirt. But their lights disappeared down a narrow set of stone steps cut into the earth.

New took a deep breath and descended them, probing his way with the stick. There were eight steps, and at the bottom a tunnel formed of rough, damp stones stretched on beyond the range of New's light.

But his lantern picked out an object lying on the tunnel floor perhaps ten feet away. His heart hammering, New bent to grasp it, and his hand closed around the object.

"What is it?" Raven asked as he came out. "What did you find?"

"A tunnel. I think I know where it goes." His voice was hollow, and above the light, New's eyes were rimmed with darkness. "And I know why it's here." He opened his hand to show her what lay in it.

It was a child's toy, Raven saw. A blue yo-yo.

"Nathan's," New said. "The Pumpkin Man took Nathan along that tunnel. I think . . . this was left here for me to find."

"Then the tunnel—"

"Leads to the Lodge. Maybe it goes right under the lake." He slipped Nathan's toy into his jeans pocket. "Are you still sure you want to go with me?"

"We need a weapon," she said. "We should've brought a gun, or—"

"That wouldn't do any good. Whatever it is would be expectin' a gun. But maybe I know somethin' it might not expect."

"What?"

"I *am* a weapon," he said. "You can go back, if you like. I'll give you the keys, and you can take the truck."

"No," she replied. "I have to see for myself."

New searched her steady gaze. "All right. Then I'll go through first. Stay close to me."

He didn't have to tell her a second time. They started into the tunnel, and within a moment or two the noise of the storm faded away. Water began leaking from the ceiling, and when Raven caught some of it in her hand and held it to the light, she saw the black stain of peat. They were underneath the lake.

As Raven followed the mountain boy, her nerve threatened to snap. Hairline cracks in the ceiling streamed with water. The tunnel had been here for a long time. Who had built it? Hudson Usher, when he first constructed the Lodge? If the Ushers and the Pumpkin Man were somehow connected, why was it that the Pumpkin Man hadn't appeared until 1872? The Ushers had been here since the 1840s. What *was* the Pumpkin Man, and how had he been able to roam freely for more than a hundred years? What had happened to the missing children? Her answers, she felt, lay before her in the darkness at the other end of this tunnel.

Distant thunder echoed along the tunnel. It must have been a huge crash, she thought, for them to be able to hear it down here.

New stopped. "Listen," he whispered.

Coming from the tunnel beyond was a low bass rumble, the growl of an awakening beast. But it wasn't an animal's noise; it sounded like a combination of off-key notes, the bass vibration of some kind of machine. Raven felt the sound in her bones, and even her teeth ached. New touched the walls of the tunnel. The stones were trembling. They could feel the vibration in the floor. Stressed mortar cracked and popped all around them.

Then, as suddenly as they had begun, the strange notes died away.

An earth tremor? Raven wondered. My God, she thought; if a quake split the tunnel ceiling open, the lake would pour in over their heads. But what had caused that rumbling noise? Raven's teeth were still throbbing.

"Okay?" New asked, his voice echoing *okay? . . . okay?*

"Yeah," she said shakily. "I'm still with you."

But as she followed New, trying to concentrate solely on the circle of light before her, Raven became increasingly aware of soft scraping noises from the darkness at her back.

She turned and shone her light in the direction from which they'd come.

"What is it?" New asked.

"I don't know." Raven brushed her damp curls back from her forehead. The light showed nothing but tunnel stones and trickles of water.

But from the darkness beyond came a faint *chirrrrr* that sounded like the warning of a rattlesnake.

And then New realized why the hole had been cut into the camouflage netting. The panther had entered the tunnel behind them, and blocked the way out. "Let's keep goin'," he told her. "I want you to watch behind us. If you see anythin' move, let out a holler."

"Damn straight," she breathed.

They continued. Raven heard quick, furtive scrapings—like the sound of claws on stone—but whatever was following them stayed far enough behind to avoid the light.

New's beam illuminated another set of steps, leading up to an open doorway. They had come to the end of the tunnel. Above them

356

sprawled the massive Lodge, he suspected, and within it the answers to questions that would change him forever. He paused, a chill of indecision and fear sweeping through him.

Satan finds the man, the Mountain King had said.

His ancestor had been a man who worshiped the lord of darkness. Was there a spark of that same kind of evil in *him*? Had he been beckoned and lured by a force that could fan that spark into a flame again?

He remembered how he'd made his mother act like a mindless puppet on strings. But the worst part, the very worst, was that he'd *liked* the power. It had first broken free from his rage in the thorn pit, but now he knew that the act of controlling the magic knife, or making his mother do what he wanted just by thinking about it, was child's play. There were other things he could do, other powers that lay deep inside him, steaming and pulsing to be set loose from the furnace of his soul. He wanted to set them free, wanted to explore the limits—if there were any—of the powers he commanded. He felt like a greedy flame that could burn his old life, as a boy trapped by the confines of Briartop Mountain, into ashes.

And suddenly he feared himself—what lived in him, in the darkest basement of his soul—most of all.

Raven let out a quick, hoarse gasp. "Oh . . . my God," she whispered.

New turned.

Greediguts' eyes were golden-green lamps in the dark. Slowly the monster emerged into Raven's light—first its blood-smeared maw, then its black skull with the lightning-streak burn across it—and began to slink toward them. Its muscular body blocked the tunnel, and its leathery, scaled tail rose up and snapped brutally in the air.

42

Rix drove the Thunderbird into its garage stall and, closing his eyes, sank his head forward against the wheel.

So close, he thought. I came so close to putting a bullet through Dunstan's skull! Dear God, I wanted to kill him! I *wanted* him to die!

He flinched at the memory of the Commando going off. He was still sick to his stomach, and had been forced to pull off the road outside Foxton to throw up. A moment or so afterward, a brown van had slowly passed him and disappeared into the rain.

He was beyond caring now. If he was under surveillance, there wasn't a thing he could do about it. The Usher history had vanished in lunatic smoke. He could start the book himself, but it would take years to finish. *Years.* He had counted on sharing the work that Dunstan had already done, but now that was impossible. What would he do while he was compiling the research? Another horror novel? The failure of *Bedlam* still hung like an ax over his head.

He had almost killed Wheeler Dunstan, he realized with sickening clarity. He couldn't finish the book on his own. He didn't have the strength to finish such an enormous, exhausting task; he was all the things Walen had called him that he'd lashed back at so vehemently. Walen knew him better than he knew himself—but he thanked God that he'd moved that gun just before it went off.

He'd seen that the door to the Maserati's stall was open. The lights weren't working, and the interior of the garage was gray and gloomy. He thought bitterly that Katt must have been in a hurry to shoot herself up.

Ten billion dollars, he thought. Why should he have to kiss Katt's hand and settle for an allowance from a junkie? How could she run Usher Armaments? And Boone would drive the business right into the ground!

"Oh God," Rix whispered. What's *happening* to me? All I really need is a little money to get by on, just enough to keep me going! And it's blood money, he thought. All of it's blood money.

But somebody would always make the weapons. There would always be wars. The Usher name was a deterrent to war, wasn't it? What was wrong with claiming his share of the business and estate?

What do I believe in? he asked himself desperately. He felt lost and frantic. Had his beliefs been like Dunstan's book—nothing but hollow, meaningless jabbering? Had he ever really been opposed to Usher Armaments? Or was he striking out at his father in the only way he knew, by cursing and denying the business that was the cornerstone of the Usher family?

Behind his closed eyes, the skeleton swung slowly from side to side.

Sandra's hair floated in bloody water.

A small hand reached toward a silver circle with the face of a roaring lion—but this time, as the hand stretched upward, the door-knob began to shrink. It became tiny, and the hand covered it.

Rix opened his eyes as thunder pealed over the garage. The doorknob. It was something he should remember. Something important. Trying to remember exactly what it was, and where he'd seen it, made his head ache fiercely. He tucked the notebook under his sweater and left the garage, hurrying through the gardens to the Gatehouse.

He was drenched when he entered the house. As he walked past the living room, he heard his mother call, "Rix!"

She came out into the hallway after him. Though she was dressed immaculately in a dark blue gown with a necklace of sapphires and pearls, and her makeup was perfect, her eyes were wide with panic. "Where have you been?" she demanded shrilly. Her lipstick was bright red, like the edges of a wound.

"Out."

"You're dripping wet! Look at the water you've tracked in!"

"I'm sorry. I couldn't—"

"Where's Boone?" Her voice shook. "Boone's not home, and neither is Katt! The storm's getting worse! The radio says there might be flooding!"

"Katt's car is in the garage." She'd undoubtedly sneaked in, he thought, to shoot up in her Quiet Room.

"Well, she's not here! And Edwin called Boone's club! He left there after midnight!"

"Calm down," he told her. Right now he didn't give a damn where Boone was, but he saw that Margaret was about to fall to pieces. "They can take care of themselves. Boone'll find a place to wait until the storm's over."

"I'm worried, Rix! Maybe you should call the sheriff, or the highway patrol."

"We'll hear if anything happens. There's no use in begging trouble."

Margaret's frightened eyes searched his face. "You look sick. What's wrong with you?"

"I'm okay." His head was still hurting like hell, and he was shivering and had to get out of his wet clothes.

"Lord, look at the mess you've tracked in on my floor!" she wailed. "And your sweater's ruined! You've pulled a button off! Can't you take care of anything?"

"It's nothing that can't be cleaned up." He reached into his pocket and brought out the small silver button. "And see, I've got the—" He stopped, staring at it cradled in his palm. It glinted orange, catching the light from a nearby candelabra.

The skeleton swung through his mind, blood oozing from its eye sockets.

Boone's plastic skeleton. The skeleton earring the cabdriver wore.

Something jarred inside Rix; the memory was close, very close, but still he couldn't grasp it. The spark of candlelight that jumped off the silver button in his palm pierced like a knife point into his mind.

Sandra's hair, floating in the bloody water.

"What is it?" Margaret asked. "What are you looking at?"

Bloody water, Rix thought. Hair floating in bloody water. A bathtub. A metal tub. What was it? What should he remember? His temples began to pound, and the images in his mind—ghostly, fragile shapes and shadows—started to fracture. He saw Dunstan lying on his side with the button in his hand, his eyes staring blindly. Except that Dunstan's face shifted and changed, melted and re-formed. The face became younger: a little boy's face, a little boy with sandy brown hair, the pewter-colored eyes mirroring shock.

Himself, Rix realized. He was seeing himself.

He held the silver button up, could see his face reflected over the Usher coat of arms. A button, he thought. Not a silver doorknob, but a silver *button!* But whose? Where had he seen one embossed with the face of a roaring lion? And what did remembering it mean?

Pain shot across his skull, vibrated at his temples. He grasped the button tightly in his hand. Not supposed to remember, he thought. It's something I'm not supposed to remember . . .

"Rix?" She recoiled from him. "My God, are you going to have an attack?"

He hardly heard her. He had thought, suddenly and clearly, of his childhood treasure box, where he kept his collection of coins, marbles, and stones. The pain pulsated behind his eyes, as if the pressure were about to blow them out of their sockets. The treasure box, he thought. There's something I put into the treasure box, a long time ago . . .

Rix passed his mother and ran upstairs, afraid that an attack was close but knowing also that he was close to remembering something important—something about the dangling skeleton, the hair

360

in the bloody water, the silver button. Something important—and terrible.

In his room, he grasped the box with shaking hands and spilled its contents out across the top of the chest of drawers. There were Indian-head pennies, buffalo nickels, a couple of old silver dollars, smooth gray stones from the Usher woods, rough black pebbles found near the lakeshore, topaz cat's-eye marbles, one that looked like a brilliant exploding star, another that held in its depths a dozen shades of cool blue. His collection had remained intact, part of the shrine his mother had kept for him, but what he was looking for wasn't here. He couldn't remember when he'd put it here, or how he'd gotten it, but what he searched for was gone.

A silver button with the face of a roaring lion. Remembering it brought a pain that bowed his back and broke a cold sweat out on his face. An attack! he thought. Oh Jesus, I'm going to have an—

"Rix?"

With an effort, he turned toward the voice. His face was chalky, his eyes rimmed with red.

Edwin stood in the doorway. He glanced from Rix to the scatter of objects across the chest, then to Rix again. "Are you all right?" he asked, a sharp note of concern in his voice.

"Yeah. I will be. I just need to—"

At once, Edwin was at his side. Edwin's comforting hands kneaded the back of his neck. "Breathe deeply and slowly. Relax, relax. Clear your mind, just drift. Relax."

Rix's muscles responded. He followed Edwin's calmly spoken instructions, and the pain began to leave him. Something dropped from his hand to the floor—what was it? He didn't care. All he cared about was the soothing power of Edwin's hands.

"You came close that time, didn't you?" Edwin asked. "But you feel better now, don't you?"

Rix nodded. The pain was almost gone. His head was clearing. What had he been thinking about? It was indistinct now, and very far away. Dunstan, he remembered. Dunstan was insane, and there was no Usher history.

But before Rix could say anything, Edwin said quietly, "He wants to see you. He said I was to bring you to the Quiet Room as soon as you came home."

"Dad?"

"He's fading. We've called Dr. Francis, but I don't think he can get here in this storm. Come on, I'll take you to him."

Rix paused, looking at the contents of the treasure box. What had been there? What was he looking for? He couldn't remember. Part of his mind seemed to have been blanked out. He frowned, trying to think.

"Rix?" Edwin urged. "You'd better go up and see him."

"Yeah. Right. I'd better go up and see him."

Edwin walked with him along the candlelit corridor to the foot of the stairs to the Quiet Room. Rix ascended the steps alone and, still dazed, put on a surgical mask to ward off the stench.

In the Quiet Room, the storm's fury was muted to a distant bass rumble. Rix stood near the door after he'd closed it, letting his eyes get used to the darkness. A few feet away from him was the vague form of Mrs. Reynolds, sitting motionless in her chair. Sleeping? he wondered. She didn't rise to greet him. He could hear his father's hoarse breathing, and followed it across the room.

"*You,*" Walen hissed.

Rix flinched. It was cold in the room, but hanging around his father's bed was the fever of decay, like a stifling preview of hell.

"Where . . . have you been . . . this morning?" Walen's whisper was so mangled, so far removed from a human voice, that Rix could hardly understand it.

"I drove to Foxton."

"Why?"

"I needed to go for a drive. To think." He saw his father's shape, curled like a reptile on the bed. The ebony cane lay beside him.

"You think . . . I'm an utter fool, don't you?"

"What?"

With the cane, Walen reached painfully out to the control panel beside the bed. A switch clicked. One of the television screens came on. Though the contrast and brightness were adjusted very low, the picture was unmistakable. It was a shot of Wheeler Dunstan's house on a sunny day. At the bottom of the screen were white numerals that gave the date and time, the seconds ticking past. Rix caught his breath; it was the first afternoon he'd gone with Raven to her house. The remote-control camera must have been hidden twenty feet or so up a tree, because there was a downward angle to the picture.

The yellow Volkswagen entered the frame and stopped in front of the house. As the two figures got out and started up the porch steps, Dunstan emerged in his wheelchair. The camera lens zoomed in. The frame froze, showing Rix, Raven, and her father standing together, linked in complicity.

362

The brown van. Usher Security.

"Mr. Meredith . . . brought that videotape to me. Look at me, damn you!" Walen commanded.

Rix forced himself to look fully at his father, and almost choked with terror. Since Rix had seen him in the hallway early this morning, Walen had deteriorated at a horrifying speed. His head was misshapen, the forehead and temples swollen by some hideous internal pressure. The gray flesh of his face was splitting open, like ill-fitting pieces of a jigsaw puzzle. Yellow fluids had leaked out, gleaming in the screen's faint glow like the mucous tracks of garden snails. Walen's eyes were deep black holes, registering no light or life.

"You've been followed . . . ever since you came here. I knew you'd show your true colors, eventually. *Traitor*," he whispered. "You miserable goddamned traitor! You're unfit to carry the Usher name, and I . . . swear I'll see you driven off Usherland . . . like a dog! There won't be a dime for you, not one! Go back to Atlanta and find some other weak little slut . . . to support you until you drive *her* to suicide, too!"

Rix had started backing away from his father's verbal onslaught, but the reference to Sandra stopped him. His face contorted; memories of a hundred unsettled scores from his youth flooded unbidden into his mind. The rage swelled within him, twisted and bitter. Rix slowly approached the bed again. "Let me tell you something, old man," he said. His voice was at a normal register this time, and Walen cringed. "I'm going to write that family history. *Me*. No matter how long it takes, I'm going to keep at it until it's finished. It'll be a good book, Dad, I promise you. People are going to want to read it."

"You . . . little fool . . ." Walen gasped, his hands clasped to his ears.

"I've found out so many enlightening details from those documents downstairs," Rix continued. "Like how Cynthia Usher murdered her first husband. And how Shann Usher lost her mind after she wrote music that made people kill themselves. Ludlow was insane before he died, locked up in his Quiet Room, raving about thunderstorms. And let's not forget about Erik, Dad. The Caligula of the Usher line. I'll be sure to write about the Fourth of July when Erik shot up Briartop Mountain, and about the deal he made to buy Nora St. Clair like breeding stock. How about that, Dad? Want me to dedicate the book to you?"

Suddenly, with a moan that made the hair stir at the back of

Rix's neck, Walen heaved himself up in bed. In the ghostly light of the television screen, his face was a rictus of hate, the yellow and crooked teeth glittering in his mouth. His arm flashed out with the ebony cane. It struck Rix sharply on the collarbone. The next blow hit Rix's shoulder, near the bruise where Wheeler Dunstan had struck him with the poker, and he cried out. When Walen flailed with the cane a third time, Rix caught it and wrenched it from his hand. A cold jolt of power shot up Rix's arm.

His hand tightened around the cane until he was holding it defiantly in his clenched fist. He held it up toward his face, saw light spark off the lion's head. Ten billion dollars, he thought. All the money in the world. Someone would always make the weapons. The Usher name was a deterrent to war. Ten billion dollars . . .

"The scepter!" Walen rasped. "Give it . . . back to me!"

Rix stepped away from the bed as Walen reached for him. Behind him, Mrs. Reynolds remained motionless in her chair.

Walen's hand stretched for the cane. Tubes tore out of his arm. "Give it back!" he commanded. "It's mine, damn you!"

Thunder shook the Gatehouse. The scepter seemed to burn into Rix's hand as if he had thrust his fingers into fire. Magic, he thought. There was magic in the cane, something powerful and protective. Someone would always make the weapons. All the money in the world . . .

A terrible, greedy laugh strained to escape from behind his clenched teeth. And from the dark stranger in his soul came the shout *I want it I want it all*!

Walen screamed. In the screen's glow, Rix saw the flesh ripple over his father's face. The bones were moving. There was a sharp cracking noise, as of twigs being snapped by a brutal hand. The fissures in Walen's face split wider.

Walen began babbling in a mad, keening whine: "Boone . . . where's Boone . . . Kattrina . . . oh God oh God I heard her scream . . . traitor you traitor . . . Edwin . . . in the Lodge Pendulum in the Lodge . . ." His body thrashed in agony. His entire head was swelling, the fissures gaping open. A steaming grayish green substance began oozing through the cracks.

Rix was paralyzed with revulsion and terror. Then he turned toward Mrs. Reynolds in nightmarish slow motion. "Help him!" he heard himself shout, but Mrs. Reynolds didn't move.

"It's . . . *you*," Walen whispered in disbelief. His head was slowly bursting apart. "Oh my God. You're . . . the next one."

There was a brittle, sickening crunch. Two tears rolled down

364

from the darkness of Walen Usher's eyes. "God . . . forgive . . ." he managed to say—and then his entire face burst open, a ragged seam running from forehead to chin. The grayish green matter, like mold that had grown too long in a hidden and evil place, bubbled out of the rip.

With a soft, relieved sigh, the body slithered to the bed and lay still. The oozing stuff that had broken through his head formed a foul halo on the sheet.

Rix stood staring at his father's corpse as shock enveloped him like a freezing shroud.

"It's done." A strong hand gripped his shoulder. "The scepter's been passed."

When Rix didn't respond, Edwin stepped around in front of him and removed Rix's surgical mask. He lifted Rix's chin with a forefinger and examined the dilated, unfocused eyes. "Can you hear me, Rix?"

He was a little boy again, lost and trembling in the Lodge's cold darkness. Edwin's voice was distant—Can you hear me, Rix?— but he followed it through the winding corridors. Edwin was there. Edwin was his friend. Edwin would protect him, and take care of him forever.

Rix flinched. The skeleton with bloody eye sockets swung through his mind. Hair floated in a bloody metal tub. Edwin's face, daubed with orange and black by firelight and shadows, emerged from the darkness. It was a younger face, and in it the blue-gray eyes held a steely glint. As Edwin's arms folded little Rix against him, the child saw orange light dance on one of Edwin's blazer buttons.

It was made of silver, and bore the embossed face of a roaring lion.

The child stared at it, mesmerized, his eyes swollen and unblinking. It was a pretty button, he thought. His hand rose up and slowly covered the button. It was round and shining and would look fine in his treasure box.

Edwin stroked the child's hair. "Rix!" His voice was as soft as black velvet. "I want you to forget what you've seen in this room. You were never here. I want you to forget. Can you hear me, Rix?"

All his attention was focused on the silver button. Nothing else mattered—not the thing behind him that dangled from a hook in the ceiling, not the bloody washtub with the hair in it—nothing but the silver button.

And the little boy who had grown up to be a man with a terrible memory locked behind the image of a silver blazer button said, "Yes sir."

The adult Rix blinked as the visions from the past whirled through his mind like a storm. Pumpkin Man's in the woods, he thought crazily. And then: No, no.

The Pumpkin Man was standing before him, wearing the face of a man he loved.

Edwin looked toward the bed, at the corpse of Walen Usher, then returned his attention to Rix. "The old passes away," he said, "and the new takes its place. Cass and I love you very much, Rix. You were always our favorite. You're the one *we* chose, a long time ago. We hoped the landlord would choose you, too."

"Land . . . lord?" Rix asked huskily, hearing himself speak as if from the bottom of a well.

"The landlord of Usherland. The *real* landlord. You have the wand now, Rix. The landlord's chosen you, and discarded Boone and Katt. You're going to make us proud, Rix; and you're going to make the landlord proud."

"I . . . don't . . ."

"I want to answer your questions," Edwin said. "I want to help you understand. But to do that we have to go into the Lodge. There's someone else the landlord wants—someone who can help you after Cass and I have fulfilled our duties."

"Logan . . . ?"

"No." Edwin shook his head. "I was wrong about Logan. I chose him to follow me, but he's too weak, too undisciplined. The landlord's chosen someone stronger. We have to go now, and we have to hurry. I want you to wait at the front of the house until I bring the limousine around. Do you understand that?"

Rix couldn't think beyond the sound of Edwin's voice. Edwin was here. Edwin would protect him and take care of him. "Yes," he answered.

Edwin led him out of the Quiet Room. Rix moved like a sleep-walker, but kept the cane gripped tightly in his hand.

◆ ◆ ◆

Ten minutes after they'd gone, Mrs. Reynolds awakened from a terrible dream. She'd been sitting here in the dark, she recalled, but then she'd drifted into a netherworld of eerie disembodied voices, angry shouts, and screams of agony. Her body had been leaden, and she'd had no voice. The last thing she remembered with anything approaching clarity was Mr. Bodane coming up to ask how Mr. Usher was feeling today. She rubbed her eyes; they were raw, as if she hadn't blinked and all the moisture had dried up.

She noticed the dim glow of the television screen, rose from her chair, and went over to Mr. Usher's bed.

Nothing in her years of training as a nurse could have prevented the scream that followed.

43

Greediguts stalked along the tunnel after New and Raven. It approached to within ten feet, then remained crouched on its muscular hind legs. Beneath the lambent eyes and bloody snout, its forked tongue flicked out and quivered in the air.

It was all Raven could do to hold back the cry of terror that was locked behind her teeth, but she stared at the beast with a stunned sense of awe as well. She knew what it was: the mythic monster that roamed Briartop Mountain and Usherland. The Pumpkin Man's familiar. The panther's eyes were fixed on New with deadly intent, its head slung low and the muscles bunched along its flanks. Though in a posture of attack, Greediguts stood like a thing of black stone, blocking the tunnel.

New saw the scorched streak across its triangular skull where the gnarled stick had struck. Greediguts was respectful of that stick, he thought—and maybe of him, too. "Up the steps," he told Raven, not daring to avert his attention from the panther. "Go ahead."

She went up, and New followed. Greediguts watched them, but remained motionless. They entered the doorway and stood in a cold, rock-floored chamber on the lowest level of the house. Their lights revealed thick granite pillars supporting the ceiling, which soared at least twenty feet above their heads. The pillars, many of which were cracked and had been repaired with mortar, were supplemented by dozens of iron pilings that sank through the floor.

Near the doorway, Raven's light found a stone staircase that ascended to the next level. As they started up, they again heard a massive crash of thunder, muffled by the walls but still carrying awesome power. The sound faded, and silence returned.

But, in another moment, New, who was several steps ahead of Raven, suddenly stopped. In the air was a faint, bass moan that seemed to pass right through New's bones. The tone began rising in volume and power, enveloping New and Raven, coming from no distinct direction but rather from all directions at once. As the bass tone strengthened—becoming the same eerie, inhuman sound jthey'd heard in the tunnel—pain stabbed their eardrums. Rock dust fell from above, and beneath their feet the staircase trembled like a rope bridge. Still the tone's force increased, making their bones throb and ache as if twisted by powerful hands. Raven's knees weakened and she tried to cover her ears, but the sound was hammering inside her with a force that she feared would crack her bones like dried clay. She was barely able to hear herself cry out in pain.

The tone began to ebb, and as it faded away, the vibrations beneath their feet stopped. When the sound was gone, New and Raven were left with a sensation of having been inside a gigantic tolling bell. Raven swallowed until her eardrums popped. She was weak and disoriented, and her muscles felt deeply bruised.

Dust swirled through the beam from New's lantern. His head pounded fiercely, and he dragged in a lungful of cold air that suddenly seemed heavy and clinging around him. "What was that?" he asked, his hearing still distorted. "An earthquake?"

She shook her head. "I don't know. It sounded like the same noise we heard in the tunnel, but I've never felt anything like that before. I thought my skull was going to split open." She swept the light around her—and froze with fear.

The panther was crouched behind her on the steps, about six feet away, its eyes blazing in the beam of light. Its tongue darted out, questing toward her.

"Don't move," New warned her. "I don't think it means to hurt us. If it was gonna attack, I think it would have by now. Just come up real slow, and walk in front of me."

Raven did as he said. The monster advanced two steps, then waited for them to start ascending again. Herdin' us, New thought. The bastard is herdin' us like sheep.

At the top of the stairs was a long corridor. The lights revealed a series of vaulted openings that led into dark, cavernous chambers. Farther along the corridor were several closed doors, sealed with brass bolts. As New and Raven searched for another staircase to the next level, New heard the scrape of the panther's claws on the stones.

He whirled around, ready to defend himself and Raven with the wand.

But Greediguts had wheeled away, and was loping down the corridor in the opposite direction. The beast vanished beyond the range of New's light. Who—or what—was it going after? New wondered grimly.

"Look at the walls," Raven said. As their lights played over the stones, New and Raven saw that the walls were covered with hairline fractures from ceiling to floor. At their feet, some of the stones had shattered like ice cubes. A frost of rock dust lay around them, and rose in wraiths before the lights. This section of the Lodge, Raven thought, was under tremendous stress; on the level directly below, the granite pillars and iron pilings supported the entire, immense weight of the house.

New, looking for a way out, probed his light through one of the openings in the corridor. He found something he couldn't make heads or tails of. "Miz Dunstan," he said, and Raven came across the corridor to see.

It was a chamber at least fifty feet wide and forty or fifty feet high, its stone walls and floor split by deep cracks. Rock dust and grit filmed what appeared to be old electrical apparatus—weird iron machines with exposed tubes and intricate networks of wiring. On a long oak worktable were bundles of cables, dusty pieces of machines, and various dials and gauges. Cables ran along the walls and snaked across the floor.

But the chamber's strange centerpiece was a discolored brass pendulum about thirty feet long that descended from an arrangement of cables, pulleys, and wooden gears at the ceiling and hung five feet from the floor. Placed on iron pedestals in an exact circle beneath the three-foot-wide, half-moon-shaped pendulum bob were eight tuning forks of varying sizes, the smallest the size of a child's fist, the largest about a foot tall.

"What the hell *is* it?" Raven wondered aloud as she approached the pendulum. She shone her light up and down the mottled gray shaft. It looked to her like the interior mechanism of a huge grandfather clock. She stepped nearer, and reached up to touch the pendulum bob with her fingers.

"Don't do that, Miss Dunstan."

They turned toward the voice. In the chamber's entrance stood Edwin Bodane, holding a flashlight. Droplets of rain glistened on his cap and his long black raincoat. His light moved from Raven to New, and he smiled faintly, the hollows deep and dark beneath his eyes and jutting cheekbones. "Welcome to the Lodge, Master Newlan."

"You're . . . the man I saw in my dream!" New realized. "The coachman!"

"If you'd come to the Lodge then—and *alone*—you could've kept Miss Dunstan out of this. It's between you and the landlord, not—" He frowned as his light picked out the gnarled stick that New held at his side. "That's *his*, isn't it? Did he give it to you?"

New nodded.

A savage grin suddenly rippled across Edwin's face. His eyes danced with joy, and Raven shuddered inwardly. She'd never seen such rampant, hungry evil on a man's face. "Good," he said excitedly. "That's good. Then . . . the old man's dead, isn't he? He must be dead, to have given up his wand."

"He's dead," New replied.

"And he gave the wand to you. Oh, that's grand!"

He's afraid of it, New thought. He's pretending not to be, but the stick scares him. Why? he wondered. Because it could do to him what it had done to Greediguts?

There was a deep boom of thunder that seemed to penetrate the walls like a mocking laugh. Edwin shone his light upward at the gears of the pendulum. "Ah, that one shook the house," he said, with clinical interest. "Miss Dunstan, you wanted to know what the machine does. You're about to learn. I'd step away from it, if I were you."

Above her head, the gears began to click and groan.

Raven stepped back, her heart pounding with dread, as the pendulum slowly began to move.

It swung back and forth, its arc widening as the clicking of the gears increased. Raven heard the air whistling around its bob as it passed directly over the circle of tuning forks.

"Listen to it sing!" Edwin said.

From the tuning forks came a cacophony of low, bone-jarring notes that merged to become the deep tone they'd heard in the tunnel and on the stairway. As the noise steadily strengthened, it became a physical force that shoved Raven backward, twisted her bones, and drove her to her knees. Behind her, she heard New cry out in pain as the tone invaded him as well. The entire floor was vibrating, and the stones in the walls grated together. Dust swirled through the air, the grit flying into Raven's eyes and momentarily blinding her. She fought for breath in what had suddenly become a chamber of horror.

370

The pendulum's arc began to slow. The moan of the tuning forks quieted. The floor and walls stopped vibrating, and as the pendulum came to a halt, the dust began to settle again.

"Thunder sometimes sets it off," Edwin said cheerfully, aiming his light through the gray dust at the machine. Raven was on her knees, gasping for breath, and New slowly shook his head from side to side to clear away the black motes that danced in front of his vision. Edwin seemed to have enjoyed the demonstration, but dust clung to his cap and raincoat and he busied himself in brushing it off. "Or rather," he amended himself, "the vibration of thunder through the walls. The pendulum's balanced so perfectly that the slightest vibration of the Lodge can set it in motion. I know its moods and caprices," he said proudly. "Isn't it beautiful?"

Whatever its purpose was, Raven had never felt such excruciating pain before, not even in the accident that had crushed her knee. She looked up toward Edwin, saw the dark holes of his eyes above the light. His grin was cold and malignant. Whatever evil force lurked here in the Lodge, Edwin Bodane was a part of it. "I thought you were helping my father!" she said. "I thought you wanted to help him write his book!"

"I offered my services, yes. But only to get close enough to him to control the project. There's no manuscript, Miss Dunstan. Oh, there was at first. Your father had already written some of it by the time I got to him. He believes he goes down into that study of his and writes a little more every day; he believes he can see it being written on the screen, and he also believes that the most important thing is to keep anyone else from seeing it. But there's no book, because I and the landlord don't want there to be one."

"The landlord? You mean . . . Walen Usher?"

"Walen Usher." He repeated the name with utter contempt. "No. I mean the true landlord. The one who summoned Hudson Usher to this place, a long time ago. Walen Usher was only a caretaker, and a poor one at that. He lacked imagination. You can see for yourselves how he let the Lodge deteriorate. But that's in the past now." Edwin reached out beside him in the chamber's entrance and drew Rix Usher closer. "Walen Usher has passed away. Long live his heir."

"Rix!" She saw that his eyes were dead, his mouth slack, the flesh of his face ashen. Clutched in his right hand was the ebony cane. He didn't respond to Raven's voice, and Edwin guided him into the chamber like a sleepwalker. Behind them, the black panther stood guard in the entrance.

"What have you done to him?" Raven asked, rising painfully to her feet.

"I've removed him. But he's fine. Or, rather, he *will* be fine. Oh, he can hear what we're saying and he knows where we are, but it doesn't matter. Nothing matters but that I'm here, and he knows I'll protect him. Isn't that right, Rix?"

Rix's mouth stretched open; a soft, terrible hissing came from his throat.

"Speak," Edwin commanded.

Rix replied, in a voice that sounded like a little boy's, "Yes sir."

New recognized the blank stare on the man's face; he'd seen it worn by his mother, when he'd made her help him lift the Mountain King into the pickup truck, when he'd forced her on a whim to fold her hands in her lap, when he'd sealed her mouth shut in the Foxton clinic. The tall, gaunt man who'd appeared as a coachman in his dream was the same as him, the same as the Mountain King. All three of them were linked by magic. "You're . . . like me, aren't you?" he asked.

"Yes. The Bodane family has served the landlord for generations. Long before the Ushers settled here, we were part of a colony that lived on Briartop Mountain."

"And when it was destroyed," New said, "the Bodanes got away."

"Ah." Edwin nodded, impressed. "You know as much about my family as I know about yours. But yours *was* part of mine once, when we shared the same coven. The landlord's been watching you, just as he watched your father and your grandfather. The landlord created the beast in his image, to be his eyes and ears."

New glanced at the panther. Greediguts was watching him balefully, standing completely motionless in the chamber's opening.

"The Mountain King resisted us to the end, didn't he?" Edwin's eyes flickered to the stick that New held. "Your father didn't have the strength of will to be useful to the landlord. But *you*, Master Newlan—you've answered us and come home, haven't you?"

"Come home?"

"The landlord only wants to love you," Edwin said gently, but his stare was dark and dangerous. "He wants to forgive you for turning away. He would've forgiven your father. He even would've forgiven the old man, if he'd come to the Lodge seeking forgiveness. All you have to do is use your magic for him—and he'll give you everything."

—give you everything—

New could feel his mind being picked at like a rusty lock. He couldn't force himself to look away from the man's electric stare. Everything, he thought, and saw the great panorama of Usherland spread out like a feast before him—the rolling hills, the verdant forests, the beautiful world of horses and fine cars and wealth beyond New's imagining. He would never have to go back to the cabin on Briartop, where wind whistled through holes in the window frames and rain leaked from the roof. He could have everything Usherland offered, if he only used his magic.

"Consider it," Edwin whispered, and turned his attention to Raven.

In his eyes glittered the cold, dark power of a warlock, a force that almost pressed her to her knees. She knew he would never allow her to leave the Lodge alive.

"Pendulum," Edwin said with a faint smile. He kept his light aimed directly at her, pinning her like a moth. "Ludlow Usher built it when he was a young man. His experience in the Chicago Fire left him with a deep respect for the power of sound; the explosions, the shrieking of fireballs, the shaking of the earth as a building fell— all of that was burned into his mind. Ludlow tested Pendulum only once—in November of 1893."

"The earthquake on Briartop Mountain," Raven said. "This thing—"

"Created vibrations that simulated an earthquake, yes," Edwin continued, like a proud father. "During the test, electrical amplifiers were placed on the Lodge's roof. They directed the vibrations toward the mountain. After it was over, Ludlow was terrified by the results. He wanted to dismantle it, but my grandfather persuaded him otherwise. Its potential as a military device, Miss Dunstan, surpasses that of the atomic bomb."

"A . . . military device?" Raven asked, stunned. "Ludlow built it for Usher Armaments?"

"The landlord recognized its usefulness. The landlord has a hand in most of the weapons the business produces. The plans are communicated to me, and I pass them along to the Ushers." Edwin shone his light on the circle of tuning forks. "Pendulum is a sonic weapon, Miss Dunstan. It's a complicated physics theory, but actually the principle is simple: the pendulum's motion creates a disturbance in the air that affects the tuning forks; in turn, they combine to form a tone that—depending on the length and intensity of the vibrations—can cause intense physical pain, smash glass, crack stone, and simulate earthquakes. What you experienced a few minutes ago was the least of Pendulum's power; if Ludlow Usher hadn't stopped the mechanism when he did during that first test in 1893, Briartop Mountain would have been leveled." He aimed the light toward the far corner, where a heavy chain dangled down from the gears and pulleys. "That controls the counterweights. As I say, sometimes thunder sets it in motion. Ludlow Usher lived in terror of thunderstorms his last years, because he knew Pendulum's potential. You can see how it's affected the walls and floor over the years. Sometimes, Pendulum's tone smashes the glass from the Gatehouse windows, and makes the entire house shake. Unfortunately, that can't be helped."

"What's it going to do? Create earthquakes for the highest bidder?" Her voice trembled, but Raven stared defiantly back at Edwin Bodane.

"This is a prototype," he said. "Just one of Ludlow's many experiments with sound. He tried to get his sister to help him develop the combination of notes that would produce a sonic weapon, but she wouldn't leave her nunnery, so he did it himself. This is a curiosity, an antique. Right now, Usher Armaments is working on miniaturizing Pendulum. Imagine it the size of a cigar box, or a transistor radio. It could be hidden near enemy nuclear plants and triggered by remote control. It could easily be smuggled across borders and hidden in unfriendly cities. The longer the tone continues, the stronger it becomes—and the stronger its vibrations." He smiled like a death's-head. "Entire cities could be reduced to rubble, without the radiation of atomic weapons. Trigger Pendulum near a fault line—and who knows what would happen? Ludlow theorized that if Pendulum's vibrations were allowed to double and redouble, the entire earth itself could be split open."

If Pendulum could do what the man claimed—and there was no reason to doubt it—then Usher Armaments would have created the most fearsome weapon in history. "If it's just a curiosity," she said, "why don't you disconnect it?"

"Oh, I can't do that, Miss Dunstan," he replied politely. "If the outsiders ever brought their bloodhounds up to Briartop Mountain again, they might find the garage and tunnel I use. They might need another earthquake to teach them a lesson in respect all over again, wouldn't they?"

"You . . . use?" Raven whispered.

"We have another destination," Edwin told her. "It's just a bit farther along the corridor. Both of you will join us, won't you?" He motioned with his light.

New had heard Edwin speaking only distantly, and could not understand most of what was said. His dreams were still fixed on Usherland, and in his mind he walked through the magnificent rooms of the Lodge, and everything he saw was his. Everything. He could live in the Lodge, if he liked. All he would have to do is use the magic.

He was needed here at Usherland. They wanted him to be the man of the house.

"Master Newlan?" Edwin said quietly. "You can leave the old man's wand here, if you like. You won't need it anymore."

New's fingers began to loosen. The stick started to slip to the floor.

—give you everything—

Edwin's voice was soft and soothing. "Leave it here, won't you?"

No! New thought. Don't give it up! He remembered what his mother and the Mountain King had said about the Lodge. It was insidious, tricky. It would destroy him. But suddenly it seemed to him that they were wrong, that both of them were afraid and wanted to keep him up on Briartop Mountain. His senses reeled—what was wrong, and what was right? He was needed here, and he could have everything. Edwin Bodane's soft voice and smile promised him everything. All he had to do was use his magic. Don't let go of the wand! an inner voice shouted. But Edwin Bodane's eyes were fixed firmly on him, and New felt the iron authority of his power—a cold power, as cold as midnight frost, as cold as the wind on Briartop. It swept his will away, and his hand opened.

The wand fell to the chamber floor.

The snare, New thought weakly. I've still got the snare, and I have to keep it.

Edwin stared at him, his head cocked to one side, a slight frown disturbing his features. He shone his light down at the wand, then into New's face again.

New realized he could not—must not—think about the snare. If the man in the cap knew . . .

He let himself be taken by the images of Usherland and the Lodge that played through his mind. Everything. Usherland would be his home . . .

"We'll go now," Edwin said, watching New's face through careful eyes.

In the corridor, Raven whirled to run. The black panther blocked her escape.

"No," Edwin whispered. The desire to flee drained out of her like water from a punctured bucket. "Come on, now, don't be naughty." She dropped her lantern to the floor. Edwin touched her hand with freezing fingers; she flinched, but let him guide her effortlessly along the corridor.

Edwin stopped before the closed slab of a door and aimed his light into Rix's face. Rix's pupils contracted, but his face remained gray and slack. "We're going through that door now. You've been through it once before, when you were lost and wandered down here. The landlord was testing you then, Rix. Trying to find out how strong you were, how much you could take without breaking. Boone and Katt broke, in their own ways. They were unfit, and had to be disposed of. But you survived." Edwin rubbed Rix's shoulder. "We're going in now. Can you hear me?"

"Yes sir," Rix said. He was a little boy, and he was having a bad dream of panthers and pendulums and loud noises that hurt his bones. But Edwin was here. Edwin would love him and take care of him.

Edwin put his hand on the knob—an ordinary one of brass, worn and discolored by many hands—and opened the door.

44

Sobbing and terrified, the little boy had seen a crack of light at the end of a long, black tunnel. He ran toward it, his knees bruised from falling down a stone staircase. There was a gash across the bridge of his nose, and his eyes were swollen almost shut from crying. He reached the light, which edged beneath a door with a rough, splintery surface. His hand searched for the knob, found and twisted it.

He burst into a cold room with walls and floor of uneven gray stones. Two torches guttered on opposite walls, casting a dim orange light with long, overlapping shadows. Somebody was here! he thought. Somebody would find him at last! He tried to cry out, but his voice was a hoarse rasp. He had screamed his throat raw during the eternity that the Lodge had sealed its corridors and redirected its staircases behind his back.

But there was no one in the chamber. Someone had been here, though. They'd lighted the torches and then gone to look for him. He could wait right here, and somebody would be back to find him.

He was exhausted from running into walls, struggling with doors that refused to open, feeling his way along corridors that had taken him deeper into a world of cold and silence. He could see the gray mist of his breath before him in the chamber, and he shivered, wrapping his arms around himself for extra warmth.

And in the torchlight, knives of different shapes glittered on wall hooks over a long, dark-stained table.

On one side of the room was what looked like a metal bathtub on wheels. Above it, dangling on a chain that hung from a rafter, was something shrouded with a long black cloth. Big hooks with sharpened points hung at the ends of similar chains. In a corner of the room was a large, rectangular metal box with a hand-crank on it.

The little boy walked toward the collection of knives. There were ten, ranging in size from one as thin as an icepick to one with a curved, sawtoothed blade. Next to the table was a grinding wheel to sharpen them with. The knives looked very sharp and well cared for. The little boy thought that the display belonged in a butcher shop. The tabletop was smeared with thick, encrusted scarlet clots. On it was a roll of brown wrapping paper and a ball of twine.

He approached the metal bathtub. The liquid in it was dark red. It was the color of one of his mother's favorite gowns. The liquid smelled like the old Indian-head pennies in his treasure box.

But in the liquid floated hanks of hair. Somebody got a haircut, he thought. Somebody got scalped.

He looked up at the black-shrouded object that hung directly over the tub. The shroud's edge was only inches above his head. He raised his arm, touching the cloth. It felt damp and slightly greasy. He pulled at it gently, but it wouldn't give. The motion of his arm made the object creak back and forth on its chain. Something dripped down into the metal tub.

Shouldn't touch, he thought. Shouldn't.

But he put both hands on the shroud's edge and yanked sharply downward.

It ripped and fell away.

"I knew you were beginning to remember," Edwin said softly, standing behind Rix in the doorway. Rix stared blankly into the darkened chamber, but a pulse had begun beating harder at his temples. "When you told me the plot of *Bedlam* over the telephone, I knew it was coming back to you. Something must've triggered a memory—I don't know what. But when you mentioned the skeletons hanging in the basement of your fictitious building, I knew you were remembering what you'd found in this room, when you were a little boy. Yesterday, I was certain when you told me about the skeleton you kept seeing in your mind—and what you thought was a silver doorknob . . ."

Rix released a quiet, agonized gasp.

He remembered the black shroud ripping, falling away to the floor.

The skeleton swung like a pendulum over Rix's head. There were still bits of flesh and muscle clinging to the bones, and its eyes were red holes of crusted blood and tissue. A hook had been driven through its back, and its mouth gaped open. The skeleton was about Rix's size.

He had backed away and slowly collapsed to his knees as the grim visage of death continued to swing back and forth, the chain rattling. Then he had fallen on his side, curling his knees to his chest, his eyes sunken and staring.

"I found you in here," Edwin said. "I told you to stand up, and I held you in my arms. I made you forget what you'd seen, and I took you out of the Lodge. I didn't want you to find it, Rix. I was trying to find you first, but it was the body of a boy I'd taken the same day you and Boone came into the Lodge. I hadn't had time to prepare it properly."

Rix's bones had become a cage of ice. He knew where he was, and who was with him, but he couldn't concentrate beyond Edwin's soft, soothing voice. Images streaked through his mind like meteors: the Rastafarian cabdriver's skeleton earring, the plastic skeleton that Boone had hung in the Quiet Room's doorway, Sandra's hair floating in the bloody bathtub. He remembered what had happened here, he remembered Edwin being with him, he remembered the small hand reaching out to cover the silver button embossed with the face of a roaring lion . . .

"It was later," Edwin continued, "that I realized I'd lost a button from my blazer. I found it in your treasure box, the day I returned the furniture to your room from the Lodge. You must've twisted it off that day, and I think your mind fixed on it to block out what you'd seen. You were looking for it today, weren't you? I think that stupid trick Boone arranged for you at the De Peyser Hotel helped trigger your memory even more." He grasped Rix's arm and led him into the chamber. New followed dazedly, and the panther's advance forced Raven in.

A match flared. Edwin began to light a series of oil-dampened torches set in the walls. His shadow grew larger. Orange light jumped and capered, flashed on the ends of the hooks that hung on chains from the ceiling, gleamed off the collection of knives over the blood-stained table, illuminated the metal bathtub and the rectangular box in the corner. As the light strengthened, Raven looked at New's face; his eyes were bright green, and he was staring straight ahead. She feared that he was already lost.

There was a pile of clothes against the wall a few feet away. Raven stood looking numbly at the little sneakers, faded jeans, sweaters and shirts, socks and underwear.

"This is where I bring them." Edwin's voice curled silkily across the room, echoing off the stones. "Most of them I can find on Briartop Mountain. Sometimes I take one of the old cars from the garage you and Master Newlan found, Miss Dunstan, and I drive a safe distance, where no one's ever heard of the Pumpkin Man. It's no different from hunting small game. Except I'm slowing down now, and sometimes they get away." He looked at Raven, a thin smile spreading across his mouth. "When I was a young man, I could freeze them at thirty yards. Stop them dead in their tracks. I could catch them within shouting distance of their houses. The landlord helped me refine the power I was born with, Miss Dunstan. I can even blind the people who come out to search for their lost children. They may look right at a footprint, and never see it. I can stand in a shadow, close enough to touch them, and they'll never know I'm there."

"You . . . bring the children here . . . and kill them."

"*Prepare* them," he corrected. "It's part of what the Bodanes do for the Ushers." He crossed the room and stood with his hand on Rix's shoulder. "Can you hear me, Rix?"

"Yes sir." Pumpkin Man's in the woods, he thought crazily.

"Something else has to be passed," Edwin said, his face close to Rix's. "First the wand that was created for Hudson Usher's great-great-grandfather. Then the responsibility of Usher Armaments. Then the knowledge. For centuries, your ancestors have worshiped the landlord. The *true* landlord of this world, not only of Usherland. The wand was a gift, a symbol of trust given from the landlord. It will protect your life, Rix, but to fulfill that trust you must do as the landlord pleases. You're his hands, Rix. I'm his voice. He's given

Usher Armaments to you, because of Walen's three children you're the one most suited to carry out what the landlord wants done."

Sandra's hair floated in the bloody water. Pumpkin Man's in the woods. Edwin was there to protect him, and he had always loved Edwin very much.

"You can use the anger that's bottled up inside you for the landlord," Edwin whispered smoothly. "I watched that rage grow over the years. I *know* what you're capable of, and I think you're just understanding it yourself. There's a cold fire inside you, and you can use it for Usher Armaments. I've been helping you, all along . . ."

"Helping . . .?" Rix rattled.

"Sandra," Edwin said. "She wasn't good for you, Rix. She was teaching you to use your anger in those books of yours. You were wasting a valuable resource that should be channeled through Usher Armaments. We talked over the phone, and I told her what I wanted her to do. I knew it would disrupt your writing. Do you understand that I did it for you?"

A tear slid down Rix's cheek. "I . . . loved . . ."

"That wasn't love. It was waste. What you're going to do for the landlord, for me, and for Usher Armaments . . . that's love."

Something twisted within New's soul. From a terrible distance, what the Mountain King had said to him started to come back: Evil . . . evil exists . . . evil exists to destroy love.

There was a long, sliding sound in the corner beside the rectangular metal box, the bone-crushing machine that Edwin had been operating when Boone blundered into the Lodge early that morning. Edwin turned—and a bloody shape with a battered face rose up from the shadows. Logan's head twitched, and one arm dangled uselessly. His eyes were bright with madness. When he opened his mouth to make a pitiful, garbled noise, blood leaked from the corners.

Edwin had brought him here from the woods two nights before, when he'd found Logan waiting for Greediguts near the ruins of the zoo. He'd decided to give the boy a demonstration of the powers he used as the Pumpkin Man—abilities that Logan had as well, but that were still raw and unrefined in him. Here in this room, Logan had acted like a kid in a candy shop as Edwin let him examine the knives. Edwin had told him everything, and Logan had been stunned to realize that he could spend the rest of his life using those knives, and that even his own father and mother and his grandparents, too, had already given their approval.

Edwin had sent him to the garage with strict instructions: he was to hold Kattrina there for the panther, but he was not to touch her. Logan's abilities were still apt to be affected by his passions, and Edwin had always liked Miss Kattrina; there was no need to defile her before the landlord's judgment was carried out.

From the Gatehouse, Cass had watched Kattrina die. When Logan hadn't returned, Edwin had gone to the garage and found blood on the concrete. A tire-iron lay nearby; one end of it was bloody, with clumps of hair and scalp on it. The hair was not the color of Kattrina's. Edwin knew something had gone wrong, probably due to Logan's refusal to obey orders.

Now, as Edwin stared coldly at the young man, he saw how much damage Kattrina had done with the tire-iron. Logan was a ruined masterpiece, and Edwin shook his head with disgust. "So," he said, "you dragged yourself back down here, did you?"

Logan, grinning witlessly with blood dripping from his chin, shambled forward.

"I was wrong about you," Edwin continued. "You don't have the discipline that's needed. I thought I could shape you . . . because I was just like you as a boy. But I was wrong, wasn't I?" He glanced quickly at the panther.

Greediguts rose from its haunches and ran across the room toward Logan. With a blurred leap, it drove the young man to the floor. Logan's legs kicked, his mangled mouth making an awful choking noise. Raven put her hands to her ears and backed away until she met a wall. Around her feet were the children's clothes. The panther's jaws began to crunch bone, and Logan was silent.

"I . . . loved . . . her," Rix whispered. Cold beads of sweat were surfacing across his face.

Edwin watched the demonic panther feed on Logan's body.

Then, satisfied, he turned toward Raven. "You'll be its next meal, Miss Dunstan. It's always hungry."

"New!" she whispered weakly. "Please . . . help me . . ."

"Master Newlan has come home, where he belongs. He'll be the next Pumpkin Man. The landlord and I will teach him very well. You see, the Usher diet is very important. If they don't eat properly, the Malady ages them before their time. Hudson Usher and his brother, Roderick, and their father, Malcolm, were trapped in a caved-in coal mine in Wales. It was weeks before they were found. But Hudson and Roderick survived by . . . sharing their father between them. The Ushers are cannibals, Miss Dunstan. For years they got their meat from a butcher shop in Chicago. Uriah Hynd also served the landlord. But, alas, the Chicago Fire destroyed his business— and the man himself."

"They . . . eat . . ."

"The children, yes. My wife makes a wonderful Welsh pie."

Her knees buckled. Before the Chicago Fire, she realized, there'd been no need for a Pumpkin Man. It was only after the fire, when the Ushers couldn't buy more human flesh, that the Pumpkin Man had come to Briartop Mountain.

New's clenched fist felt an object in his pocket. Nathan's toy. This man had brought Nathan here, and carved the meat off his bones.

His soul was shriveling. Everything, he thought. Every-thing . . . and all I have to do is use the magic. Evil exists to destroy love. Everything. All I have to do is . . .

Satan finds the man, the Mountain King had said. It's not where you live, but what lives in you . . .

Everything . . . use the magic . . .

"Master Newlan?" Edwin offered his hand. "Come to me."

He tried to resist, tried to make his feet root to the stones.

"Come to me. Take my hand."

New was pulled forward. His green eyes glowed like lamps, his face chalky and strained.

"Come home," Edwin whispered. "Let the landlord love you."

Step by step, New approached him. He was powerless to turn away. Edwin's face hung in the orange light like a misshapen moon.

Everything, he thought. Use the magic.

Their fingers met. Edwin's hand clamped solidly around New's, and the older man smiled.

New felt himself being dragged down, down into a volcanic pit; and in that steaming pit were images of hell: cities collapsing through tremendous fissures, blocks of stone crushing people running in the streets, exploding fireballs and mushroom clouds and charred bodies lying in tangled heaps, a scarlet sky full of missiles and rising screams that became the laughter of the thing that lived behind Edwin Bo-dane's face: a dark, leathery beast with yellow, catlike eyes and a forked tongue that darted out to taste the sulfurous air.

"Come home," Edwin urged.

New's mind was about to crack: Evil . . . evil exists . . . evil ex-ists to destroy love . . . God help me . . . give you everything . . . use the magic . . . it's what lives in you . . . God help me . . .

USE THE MAGIC!

The snare! he realized. The smiling monster that was the Pumpkin Man had just put his arm into the snare!

USE THE MAGIC! New shouted inwardly. He thought of Nathan being slaughtered here in this chamber, of the hundreds of children who had died in this room to be served on fine silver plates on the Usher dining table. *USE THE MAGIC!* Rage boiled in his blood, steamed through his pores, swept away the illusions of the rich life at Usherland like pieces of rotten tapestry. New's head cleared; he tightened his hand around Edwin's, felt the man's knuckles grind together.

Edwin's smile froze. In his eyes was a quick red glint of fear. He started to wrench his arm away.

USE THE MAGIC! New's hair danced with blue sparks.

And from the jacket sleeve of his outstretched arm, the magic knife ripped loose of the tape that had held it to the inside of his forearm. It tore along his wrist like a projectile, leaving a path of scorched flesh.

Before Edwin could deflect it, the magic knife drove itself to the hilt beneath his arm. It corkscrewed violently, powered by the sheer force of New Tharpe's rage, and as Edwin screamed and staggered backward, the knife disappeared into his body like a drill, spewing bone and tissue. Edwin gurgled and danced as the knife continued to drive through his body; it exited from his back in a gush of blood and hit the stone wall so hard its blade snapped off.

Edwin collapsed, but his body continued to writhe. His eyes were open, his mouth gray and gasping. Cold shockwaves of power crashed back and forth between the walls. The hooks swung violently on their chains. The knives left their wallhooks and ricocheted viciously from wall to floor to ceiling. One snagged Raven's jacket, another flashed past her face. The metal tub reared up from the floor and tumbled toward New, narrowly missing him as he leaped aside.

A blade grazed Rix's cheek with a noise like a hornet. A trickle of warm blood ran down, and the pain cracked the ice that had closed around him. As he stared at the swinging hooks, reality flooded back into him. Edwin was the Pumpkin Man. Edwin had caused Sandra's suicide. Cannibalism kept the Ushers young, warding off the Malady as long as possible. The Ushers worshiped evil, and had built Usher Armaments as an altar to the force that lived within the Lodge—the great malengine that had gathered around him and shaped him to be fuel for the furnace of destruction.

383

Edwin contorted on the floor in a spreading pool of blood. When a spasm jolted him, the shockwaves shook the walls. Like an animal snapping madly in its death throes, he was striking in all directions with his awesome, evil magic. The chamber's door blew off its hinges. The freezing crosscurrents of energy whipped back and forth, staggering Raven to the floor and throwing Rix against a wall as if he were caught in a hurricane.

New heard Raven's warning cry, and as he whirled around the black panther leaped for him, its claws extended.

He dodged aside, at the same time directing a burst of his own magic like a sledgehammer blow that struck Greediguts in the ribs and sent the beast hurtling against a wall. The panther scrabbled to its feet and attacked again, its eyes blazing with bloodlust.

New stood his ground until the panther was almost upon him, and then summoned a burst of energy like an iron spike driving itself into Greediguts' skull. The panther howled in pain and was thrown backward, crashing into the metal tub. Again it leaped up, its muscles shivering.

As the panther tensed for a third attack, New brought the table flying end over end and smashed it across Greediguts' back. The table was heavy, and New realized that much of his coiled strength had gone into driving the magic knife through Edwin Bodane. He was rapidly weakening.

Greediguts rolled on the floor, snapping at its reptilian tail— and then jumped for New with a burst of speed he hadn't expected.

He tried to aim another blow, but was drained like an overheated engine. As he flung himself to one side, talons ripped through his jacket and dug into his ribs. He cried out and fell to his knees, blood streaming down his side. Greediguts spun to face him, its tongue flicking out, and New saw the red flash of triumph in its eyes. The monster knew he was almost used up, knew his mind was now clouded with pain.

Greediguts went back on its haunches to propel itself forward, and as its jaws opened wide to smash his skull, New smelled its breath of blood and brimstone.

New glanced up. The hooks! he thought. If he could find enough strength . . .

Greediguts suddenly rose on its hind legs and hurtled toward the mountain boy.

New strained with every fiber of his body to summon and direct enough power; pain hammered through his head, and as he cried

384

out he felt a bolt of energy ripple through him, blasting from the same molten core of rage that his long-ago ancestor had possessed. It tore through his bones like a fireball, and for a terrible instant New thought that he had exploded into flames.

New's last surge of magic met Greediguts in midair. It threw the panther toward the ceiling—then, as the beast fell, it was brought violently down upon one of the swinging hooks.

The spike pierced its underbelly. As the panther shrieked and struggled, the hook plunged deeper. The weight of its body stretched the chain and bent the rafter to which it was secured. And then Greediguts began to slide along the hook toward the floor, its stomach split open, spilling coal-black organs from the gaping wound. The rafter cracked like a gunshot.

New was exhausted, unable to rise from the floor. He clasped his bleeding side, as the panther snarled and thrashed to free itself.

Cold waves of energy continued to shake the chamber as Edwin refused to die. And from the corridor, Raven heard a chilling bass moan, gaining volume and strength.

Pendulum! she thought in horror. The warlock's death throes had set the sensitive machine in motion!

Rix, fighting for balance on the trembling floor, reached Raven and helped her up. His face was gaunt and gray, except for the line of scarlet that crept down his cheek. He blinked heavily, still leaden with shock.

"We've got to get out!" she shouted at him. Across the chamber, knives that were scattered on the floor whirled up like a deadly storm and stabbed against the walls. "Can you find the way?"

He shook his head. He didn't remember how Edwin had brought him here, and he feared the Lodge would seal them in.

They'd have to go back through the tunnel, Raven realized. The rafter that Greediguts hung from was tearing loose. She pulled New to his feet and said, "Come on! Hurry!"

At the doorway, as the bass moan continued to rise, and the currents of black magic from Edwin's contorting body began to crack the walls, Rix stopped to look back at the elderly man he'd loved.

He saw only the Pumpkin Man.

Then he turned away and ran after New and Raven.

The entire corridor was shaking, chunks of stone falling from the ceiling, rock dust churning through the air and almost blinding them. "The wand!" New told Raven. "I have to get it back!"

In Ludlow's workshop, the pendulum was swinging steadily.

The tuning forks were vibrating blurs, and the bass tone had passed the pain threshold. Raven, her bones twisting as the sound pierced her, retrieved her lantern. The walls and floor shivered violently, cracks snaking across New's path as he picked up the Mountain King's wand. A piece of rock the size of an anvil fell from above, crashing only a few feet away. Rubble rained down, striking him on the head and back. The pendulum was swinging faster, and New felt a terrible pressure building in his head. There was no way to stop it, he realized. The thing was out of control, and God only knew what it was going to do. They had to get out of the Lodge as fast as they could.

The chamber's floor buckled, almost throwing New to his knees. The bass tone had become a low, demonic bellow.

Guided by their light, they ran through the pitching corridor to the staircase that had brought New and Raven from the lower level. In another moment, Pendulum's moan had reached a pitch of pure agony. Rix's eardrums were about to explode, and as he struggled down the stairs, his equilibrium dangerously unbalanced by the noise, blood burst from his nostrils.

On the lower level, the granite pillars were shivering. The iron pilings were making high whining sounds, like the strings of a harp being plucked by a madman's hand. One of the pillars cracked and collapsed, followed by a second and a third. Stones tumbled from the ceiling.

"The foundation!" Raven shouted, barely able to hear herself. "It's destroying the foundation!"

The tunnel stretched before them. Around them the stones grated and shifted. Black water poured through cracks above their heads.

Still the moan of Pendulum pursued them. Raven faltered, but Rix supported her and took the lantern before she dropped it. Water swirled around their ankles.

And then the hair stirred at the back of New's neck, and he turned toward the Lodge. Several paces ahead, Rix looked over his shoulder, then aimed the light in the direction from which they'd come. He froze with terror. The beam illuminated the panther racing after them along the tunnel, coming like a massive black machine of destruction. It dragged chain and entrails after it, the hook still buried deeply in its belly.

As the monster hurtled toward them, New tightened his grip around the wand. He had no power of his own left; he was weak, worn out, and would have to trust in the power that had been passed from generation to generation, contained within a gnarled stick that wouldn't bring two dollars at a flea market.

"Come on, you bastard!" New shouted in defiance.

Greediguts leaped, gory steam bursting from its nostrils.

New swung the stick like a baseball bat.

A blinding ball of blue flame shot from it as it met the panther's head. The monster shrieked—and for an instant both New and Greediguts were connected by the fiery wand. Then Greediguts' body was thrown backward as if it had hit a stone wall, and New fell into the water that surged around his knees, his nerves on fire.

The panther's body, its mangled head hanging on strings of tough tissue, slowly began to rise to its feet again. Its jaws snapped together, tearing at the air.

And over the wail of Ludlow Usher's machine came the sharp cracking of tunnel stones, like sticks broken in powerful hands. A section of the tunnel between them and the Lodge caved in. Black mud, water, and weeds collapsed into the tunnel. A torrent of water swept toward Greediguts, New, Rix, and Raven. Rix had time only to put his arm around Raven's waist before the water hit them with a force that knocked them backward and off their feet. He was blinded. New's body collided with him, then was tossed away.

Rix was lifted up in the thrashing water; as his head emerged into a space of air in the darkness, he heard the tunnel stones above him cracking, splitting open. Water from the lake was hammering down into the tunnel. Rix gasped for air and shouted to Raven, "Hold on!"

Raven's hand found his shoulder and gripped hard. The entire tunnel was flooding, and again the water surged over Rix's head.

They tumbled before the wild currents. Rix was thrown violently upward, his back scraping across tunnel stones that had not yet collapsed. Air burst from his nostrils and Raven was almost wrenched away, but Rix held on to her with all his strength.

His lungs burned for air. Currents swirled in all directions, pushing and pulling at the same time. A cold sweep of water threw him upward again, and he braced for another collision with the tunnel's ceiling.

But then he was tangled in weeds and mud, and he realized the current had shoved him out of the tunnel, onto the lakebed. Now the water was sucking him down again, and his body fought wildly against it. Raven was kicking too, trying to escape its suction.

They were drawn downward, halfway into the tunnel—and then another surge of water boiled beneath them, and they were thrust upward through the black water and the weeds.

Rix's head emerged into a gray curtain of rain. Beside him, Raven coughed and gasped for air. Rix's arm had been almost dislocated from the effort of holding on to her. Waves rolled over them, propelling them toward the rocky shallows. As they lay on the rough stones with the rain and the waves beating around them, Rix looked back toward the island.

The Lodge was trembling like a massive tuning fork. The glass cupola shattered, the marble lions rocked and plummeted from their positions on the roof.

Pendulum's moan pulsated in the turbulent air. It changed, became a hoarse, maddened scream that pounded into Rix's mind:

—*traitorrrrrr*—

The Lodge was falling to pieces like a house of cards. It heaved and shook, its towers and chimneys swaying, then collapsing. The roofs caved in. Lakewater battered the house, black spray shooting fifty feet into the air. The west wing shuddered and fell, the contents of rooms spilling out like jewels from a huge treasure box.

—*all for you*—

The voice of the Lodge was weakening.

With its next vibration, the entire front of the house cracked and fell away in an avalanche of marble and masonry. Revealed was an intricate warren of rooms, corridors, and staircases that slowly collapsed, one after another, and disappeared into the water. The lake had become a churning cauldron filled with beautiful trash that boiled up and then was drawn into the depths.

Suddenly the remainder of the Lodge was split by a massive seam that worked its way up from the foundation, branching off into a dozen more cracks, a hundred more, crawling inexorably across the stones.

—*traitor all for you*—

The Lodge sagged, crumbling away in what looked like a gigantic, slow-motion explosion, tons of marble plunging into the lake.

The walls fell. From the ruin of the Lodge came a shockwave that crushed Rix and Raven together, a cold fury that carried the scream *traitorrrrr* across the lake and over Usherland, echoing from Briartop Mountain in the crash of a thousand falling trees.

The voice of the Lodge and the roar of Pendulum were silenced.

Waterspouts danced like tops across the lake. Chairs, desks,

388

stuffed trophies, curio cases, beds, tables, and pianos had surged toward shore. Around the lake, the trees had been sheared off at their trunks, and much of the forest up the south side of Briartop had been leveled.

The Lodge was rubble, utterly destroyed by Ludlow Usher's sonic weapon.

When they could move again, Rix and Raven slogged through the shallows. Near the shattered remnants of the bridge, another figure lay on its side in the mud.

Rix helped Raven to the ground, and turned toward the ruins. Blood dripped from his nose, he was bruised in a dozen places, and his right arm dangled uselessly. He knew Pendulum hadn't reached its full potential; the weight of the Lodge, he thought, must have crushed the machine before it could destroy the mountain and everything else for miles around.

The front of the maroon limousine suddenly rose up from the depths. It was covered with mud, and its grille looked like a grinning, warped mouth. Then it slid slowly back into the water.

It was only then that Rix realized he still held the ebony cane in his hand. The silver lion's head had been washed almost clean of mud.

He was holding it so tightly that his knuckles ached.

Eight

THE
DECISION

45

USHER PATRIARCH DIES; LODGE DESTROYED,
FOXTON ROCKED BY TREMORS

by Raven Dunstan
Editor and Publisher, *Foxton Democrat*

Walen Erik Usher, patriarch of the powerful Usher clan
and owner-chairman of the Usher Armaments Company,
died Wednesday, October 31, at Usherland, the family's
estate seven miles east of Foxton.

Usher had been ill for several months, and was confined
to bed. The cause of death, according to Dr. John Howard
Francis of Boston, was massive cerebral hemorrhage. On
November 2, private funeral services were held at the estate,
attended by many government and armed forces officials.

Survivors include his wife, Margaret Usher; a daughter,
Kattrina Usher; and two sons, Boone and Rix Usher.

Rix Usher has been named successor to the family business. Through a spokesperson, Boone and Kattrina Usher
have announced extended travel plans.

Within hours of Usher's passing, a violent series of earth
tremors, localized in the Briartop Mountain area, leveled
Usher's Lodge, the 143-year-old landmark constructed by
Hudson Usher. According to Rix Usher, there are no plans
to rebuild.

The tremors, which were felt as far away as Asheville,
shattered windows in Foxton, Taylorville, and Rainbow City.
Taken to the Foxton clinic for treatment of injuries caused

by flying glass were Neville S. Winston, Betty Chesley, Elton Weir, and Johnny Faber, all of Foxton.

Geologists at the University of North Carolina are puzzled by the tremors, and are currently beginning a study of the area in hopes of finding their origin.

The Briartop Mountain–Foxton area suffered an earthquake in the autumn of 1893 that caused severe property damage and left more than twenty mountain residents dead.

The staff and management of the *Foxton Democrat* wish to offer their condolences to the family of Walen Usher.

It was the middle of January, and a cold wind was blowing as Raven stopped her Volkswagen before the closed gates of Usherland. She lifted the collar of her coat up around her neck and then rolled her window down. Within reach was a small speaker. She pressed the mechanism's button and waited.

"Yes?" the voice asked.

"Raven Dunstan. Mr. Usher's expecting me."

The gates clicked open to admit her. After her car had passed through, the gates locked themselves again.

She was met at the front door of the Gatehouse by a young maid who took her coat, then escorted her not to the living room— where she'd been several times since that horrible day—but upstairs, along a corridor where the only sound was that of a softly ticking grandfather clock. Raven was led to a staircase that ascended to a white door with a silver knob.

"Mr. Usher's waitin' for you," the maid said. She glanced nervously up the stairs.

"Thank you." Raven climbed up to the door, then paused. There was the faintest hint of an unpleasant odor in the air. It smelled like meat that was going bad. She knocked at the door. The silence of the house unnerved her. When Rix didn't answer, she opened the door and peered inside.

He was sitting on the edge of a large bed with a bare mattress. There were no lights in the room, and no windows, and he squinted as he looked toward the door. "Raven?" he asked. "Come in. You can leave the door open, if you like."

She entered, and approached him. The smell was stronger in here. The walls, she saw, were coated with rubber, and she knew this was the Quiet Room that Rix had told her about—the room where Walen Usher had died.

394

Rix was wearing an expensive gray suit and a blue-striped tie. In the tie was a small diamond stickpin. His face was wan and tired, as if he'd gone without sleep for a long time; there were dark circles beneath his eyes. He looked at her with a troubled gaze, and Raven saw that he held the ebony scepter across his knees.

"I came as soon as I could get away from the office," she said. "Are you all right?"

He smiled faintly. "I'm not sure. I'm not sure of anything anymore."

"Neither am I," she told him. It was cold in here, and she hugged her arms around herself for warmth. "Dad's getting better," she offered. "The doctor says he's making real progress. He knew who I was the last time I visited."

"Good. I'm glad." He ran his hand over the smooth ebony. "My mother's found a condominium, at last. She says I ought to come out to Hawaii sometime for a vacation."

"Does she . . . know about Boone and Kattrina yet?"

"I think she really wants to believe that Katt is in Italy and Boone is on a tour of Europe. Of course, she knows something's wrong. If she lets herself realize that they're dead, she'll go to pieces. She'll have to know sometime, I guess, but I'll cross that bridge when I come to it. I'm . . . really grateful for that story you wrote, Raven. I still don't understand why you didn't blow the lid off everything, but I want you to know how much I appreciate it."

She had had the chance of a lifetime, she knew, but she'd let it go. What was the point? The Pumpkin Man was dead—the chain of Pumpkin Men broken—and there would be no more children vanishing without a trace. There was still so much she couldn't comprehend about what she'd been through; sometimes it seemed like only a particularly nasty dream. Except that her limp had never returned, her father was in a sanitarium, and Usher's Lodge lay in ruins. Down deep, though, she was repelled by the thought of writing a story that would tell the mountain people exactly where their children had been going over the years. Her perception of evil had been sharpened dramatically, and when she saw a report of missing children in another newspaper, her flesh broke out in cold goosebumps. The *Democrat's* circulation continued to climb, and New Tharpe was working out just fine as a copyboy. Pretty soon, she intended to let him write his first story for the paper—but for the time being, he was going to school like any other normal kid.

"I got a letter yesterday," Rix said. "It was from Puddin' Usher. She's in New York City now, and she wrote to tell me that she'd just signed a contract with a publisher."

"What?"

Rix nodded, a grim smile stitched across his mouth. "They're going to pay her a hundred thousand dollars to write an account of her life as an Usher. She's going to do talk shows and newspaper interviews. Isn't that a kick in the ass?"

"Can she *do* that?"

"I don't know. My lawyer's looking into it right now. Jesus," he said softly. "Listen to me. I think I sound more and more like my father, every day. I look in the mirror and see his face staring out."

"What have you decided to do? About your condition, I mean?"

"No more Welsh pies," he said, and she winced. "Sorry. I didn't mean to say that. Dr. Francis called me. He still wants to run the tests I told you about. I'd have to go to Boston and stay in the hospital for a couple of weeks."

"Are you going?"

"I want to, but . . . what if there's no cure for the Malady, Raven? What if it's so deep in the Usher genes that there's no way to root it out? I watched my father die, right on this bed. What I saw I wouldn't have wished on anyone. Not even him." He looked up at her pleadingly, and whispered, "I'm . . . so afraid."

"But you have a chance," Raven said. "All the other Ushers had that chance and turned away from it. But you've got the best chance of all; with modern medical technology, there's a real possibility the Malady can be controlled, Rix. Isn't that what you said Dr. Francis told you?"

"He said they'd give it their best shot. But what if it isn't good enough? What if I have to die in this room, just as my father did?"

She shook her head. "You're not your father, Rix. You see things your own way. You don't have to live the same kind of life. But it's up to you to make the effort to change things. If you don't . . . who will?"

"I can still smell him in here," Rix said, and closed his eyes. His fingers caressed the scepter. "He's inside me. All of them— Hudson, Aram, Ludlow, Erik, Walen—they're all inside me. I can't escape from them, no matter how hard I try."

"No," she agreed, "you can't. But you can be the Usher who makes the difference for all the Ushers to come."

"I'm the last of the line, Raven. It dies with me. I wouldn't bring a child into the Usher world."

"I see. Then you've decided to turn your back on life? Are you going to lock yourself in up here and swallow the key? Damn it, Rix, you have *everything* and you can't see it! And I'm not talking about the money—you'd probably be happier if you started using it instead of letting it sit in banks. Think of the schools you could build with it! The hospitals! Think of the people who need homes and food, and there are plenty of those right in this area! You have the *chance*, Rix! You can be a thousand times the man any other Usher ever was!"

She was right, Rix knew. The first thing he could do was to build some decent houses for the people on Briartop Mountain—some brick houses, far better than the cabins that leaked rainwater like sieves. There were people who needed food and shelter, and kids like New Tharpe who wanted the opportunity of education, to stretch their boundaries far beyond the limits of their present lives. One-tenth of the Usher fortune could create a university complex that would be unsurpassed anywhere.

"Will you go to Boston with me?" he asked.

She paused, trying to read his eyes. There was light in them now. "I'd like that," she replied. "Yes. I'd like that very much."

"I . . . asked you here because I need your help in a decision I've been trying to make. I don't know if I can make it alone, but it's a very important one."

"What is it?"

"Usher Armaments," he said. "It's got to be shut down. The weapons have got to stop rolling off those assembly lines, Raven."

"If that's your decision," she told him firmly, "the *Democrat* will stand behind you."

Rix rose from the bed. He began pressing buttons on the control console, and the television screens flickered on, showing scenes of the Usher world. In the glow, Rix's face was heavily lined. "I want to shut it down, but my sister was right. Someone will always make the weapons. Does that mean there'll always be wars? Are we so hopeless that we can see no end to the destruction? My God . . . I've thought about this day after day, and I still can't decide. If I shut down Usher Armaments, more than six thousand people will lose their jobs. If I don't, there'll be no end to the weapons; they'll get more insidious, more deadly, year by year."

He held the scepter up before her. His hand was shaking. "I

know what this means now, and what it meant to all the Ushers—power. Why can't I throw this away? Why can't I snap it over my knee? God, I've tried! But something inside me doesn't want to give up the power!"

Rix's face was tormented with doubts. "Do I shut down Usher Armaments, and lose whatever influence I might have over this madness? Or do I let the factories churn out the bombs and missiles, and join the madness? What do I decide?"

"Excuse me, Mr. Usher?"

Rix looked toward the door, where the maid stood. "Yes? What is it?"

"You have some visitors, sir. A General McVair and a General Berger. Mr. Meredith's with them, and they're askin' permission to come through the front gates."

Rix sighed deeply and let the air trickle from his nostrils. "All right, Mary," he said finally. "Let them come in." He ran a hand across his face. "I knew I couldn't keep them away for long," he told Raven. "They're going to be carrying their briefcases and their plans. They're going to smile and tell me how good I look, considering Walen's tragic death. Then it'll start, Raven. What do I tell them?"

"Whatever you decide," she said, "I'll help you. I'll stand with you. Use your chance. Be the Usher who makes a difference."

Rix stared at her, and suddenly he knew what decision he would make when he faced those smiling generals in his father's house. He prayed to God that it would be the right one.

He took Raven's hand, and they went down to face the future.

46

Cold wind blew off the black lake and into New Tharpe's face.

He stood on the frigid shore, wearing the heavy fleece-lined coat that Mr. Usher had sent him while he was still in the Asheville hospital. He would always carry on his side a pattern of jagged scars, a reminder of his battle with Greediguts.

The sky was a pale, featureless gray. There was snow in those clouds, he thought. But the cold wouldn't be so bad this year, since

Mr. Usher had had the Tharpe cabin insulated. He'd offered central heating, but Myra Tharpe had said she didn't want everybody on the mountain coming to her house.

Across the lake, the ruins of Usher's Lodge jutted up from the island like broken teeth. The bridge had not been repaired, and there was no way to reach the island except by boat.

Which was fine with New. He wouldn't set foot over there for a million dollars.

He walked along the lake's edge, the water whispering at his feet. The tip of the gnarled cane he carried poked holes in the black mud where the water licked up.

When the tunnel's ceiling had collapsed, New had held on to the Mountain King's wand as he was battered back and forth between the walls. He'd been able to grip his fingers in a hole where several stones had dislodged from the ceiling, and he'd hung there like a flag as the water churned around him. He'd fought upward, the currents shoving him forward and pulling him back, and then he was spat out of the tunnel by the force of conflicting currents and pushed to the surface. Rough waves had slammed him to shore, and he'd lain stunned and gasping, with two broken ribs, until Raven and Mr. Usher had found him.

He'd come down here from the mountain several times before, to see what the lake had belched out. Once there were hundreds of silver knives, forks, and spoons stuck in the mud; once two whole suits of armor had washed up. But the strangest thing he'd found was a muddy stuffed horse that looked as if it were still running a race. On its flanks were deep gashes that appeared to have been made by spurs.

New stopped to pick up the rags of a silk shirt with the wand; then he let it fall back into the water. After it was over and he'd come out of the hospital, he'd found that his rage was gone. Nathan had been avenged, and the Pumpkin Man was dead. Greediguts was buried somewhere in the mud and debris. He hoped the Mountain King was finally at rest. He was the man of the house, and he had to go on. He was working hard at making his peace with his mother, and she collected and read the *Democrat* now that it carried his name on the masthead as copyboy.

At first she'd balked at what he'd wanted done when he got home from the hospital, but finally she agreed.

Behind the house, they'd buried the Mountain King and the bones of his sister on either side of Pa's grave.

He stopped to watch a flock of blackbirds fly across the lake. Now there was no Lodge to crash into. The birds and ducks were coming back.

He stared at the island, and ran his fingers over the wand. There was still power in the wand that he didn't understand. Sometimes he thought he should have drowned in that tunnel, but the wand had somehow given him strength enough to pull himself out.

It was often hard to keep himself under control, but he was working on that, too. One day he'd flipped Bully Boy Vickers for knocking down another, weaker boy at school. Bully Boy never knew what hit him. But for the most part, New minded his manners. Sometimes it was more fun to work for what you wanted, anyway. Like his job at the *Democrat*. Raven said his English was coming along so well that he might be able to write a story soon.

The magic was still there, though. It would always be there. He would just have to figure out when and where to use it.

He looked down at a beautiful green plate, half buried in the mud. He bent to pick it up—and exposed the black slugs that squirmed beneath it. New skimmed the green plate over the lake, and it sank in the water.

The chill reddened his cheeks. He watched the island, and listened.

Sometimes, when the wind was just right and the birds were silent, he imagined he heard a soft whisper that came from the ruins. He was never sure, though; it was just something that came and went when he wasn't listening for it.

He started to walk on—and then stopped in his tracks.

Floating amid brown weeds five feet from shore was a gray cap, splattered with mud.

New waited for the cap to wash to shore, but it was hung in the weeds. He advanced a few feet into the chilly water, then reached out with the wand and started to lift the cap out.

And as he picked it up, the thing rose up from underneath it— a muddy, decayed, and skeletal corpse, wearing a gray coat with silver buttons in the shape of roaring lion's faces.

New screamed and tried to back away, but the mud closed around his boots and locked him.

The thing—what was left of the Pumpkin Man—knocked the wand aside, reached out its long, dripping arms, and clutched New's throat in bony hands, squeezing with demonic strength ... squeezing ... squeezing ...

New gasped for breath and sat up in bed.

It was still dark outside. There was sweat on his face, and he sat until his fit of shivering had passed.

The same dream! he thought. It was the same dream again!

His mother was sleeping, and he didn't want to wake her, but he rose from the bed and took the wand from where it leaned in the corner. He went out to the front room. The last embers of the fire glowed. Outside the cabin, a restless wind moved across Briartop Mountain like the sound of something dark and lonely, searching.

The same dream. Why do I keep having the same dream? he thought.

New stood at the window, listening to the high shriek of the wind. The insulation that Mr. Usher had put in kept the house warm. He had a busy day at school tomorrow and he had to be rested, but still—he paused, listening, his face mirroring unspoken concerns.

Was it over? he wondered. Would it ever really be over? Or would the evil just take some other form and come back stronger— maybe looking for *him*?

If so, he had to be ready.

His hands tightened around the wand.

The wind changed direction and tone. It dropped to a low moan, and beat against the cabin with a strange, steady rhythm.

New listened.

And imagined he heard the sound of a pendulum out there in the dark, swinging back and forth . . . back and forth . . .

He hoped he imagined it.

Oh God, he *hoped*.